# THE FALLBROOK CHRONICLES

## THE AWAKENING

### ELLIOT STONE

ISBN: 978-1-967558-01-8 (Paperback)
ISBN: 978-1-967558-00-1 (eBook)

Library of Congress Control Number: TBD



Book design and cover image by Randy Miramontez.
Randy Miramontez Publishing
Fallbrook, CA

To my children—Randy, Brian, Marc, Bianca, Liam, and AidAn—you are my greatest adventure, my proudest achievement, and my endless inspiration. And to Brian, though you are no longer here, your light continues to guide me in ways I never imagined.

A special thanks to every person who has been a part of my journey. Every experience, every challenge, and every connection—big or small—has led me to this moment. Without you, I may not have made this journey. This book exists because of all of you.

# CONTENTS

# CHAPTER 1

# THE FIND

In the heart of Fallbrook, California—a town affectionately known as The Friendly Village—time seems to move at its own unhurried pace. The Bailey family's Victorian farmhouse rises from the morning mist like a relic of another era. Its wraparound porch, adorned with intricate gingerbread trim, embracing the home like an old friend. Despite its history, modern touches like solar panels on the southern roof mark the changing times. Nearly a mile away, Main Avenue is just beginning to wake up, as antique shops and cozy cafes flicker to life, their vintage signs swaying gently in the cool morning breeze. The scent of fresh coffee and warm pastries drifts through the air.

Bailey Family Vineyards stretches across rolling hills, a legacy passed down through generations. At its heart stands a mighty oak tree, its sprawling branches sheltering a circular bench surrounding the tree where countless family stories have unfolded. The dew clings to rows of meticulously tended grapevines, their leaves still curled against the dawn chill.

Cathy Bailey moves through her kitchen with the fluid grace of a lifelong runner, her five foot nine frame lean and powerful from years of training. At forty three, she wears her endurance like a badge, her copper-red hair catching fire in the soft dawn light streaming through the bay windows. Already dressed in her running gear, she steals glances at her phone, watching for Pokémon Go notifications—a passion that's outlasted countless other mobile gaming trends. The app has turned their old oak tree into a coveted gym location, much to her daily delight.

Ancient floorboards creak their usual greeting as Logan, her nineteen-year-old son, shuffles into the kitchen. Standing six feet tall, his dirty blonde hair falls slightly over his round glasses. His eyes bleary, but his scientist's mind is already cataloging the day's tasks as he makes a beeline for the coffeemaker. The aroma of fresh brew fills the air, mixing with the scent of bacon and herbs from Cathy's window garden.

Joe follows, his work boots in hand. At six foot one and forty five years old, he carries an air of quiet strength as silver threads catch the light in his dark hair. He settles at the kitchen table, his broad shoulders easing into the chair, and his presence brings a sense of steady comfort to the morning chaos, his warm smile reassuring everyone around him. The wall behind him chronicles their family history in photographs: grape harvests, wine bottling, picnics under the old oak tree—moments frozen in time yet somehow still alive as the sun brightens the wall. His weathered fingers absentmindedly found the worry stone in his pocket, a ritual as familiar as his first cup of coffee. The smooth river rock had always helped him maintain his patience during the spirited family exchanges that punctuate most mornings.

The last to appear is Zoe, sixteen, and at five foot nine her features are a mirror image of Cathy's, though there's a softness in her expression that belies her striking resemblance. Her fingers fumble with the delicate locket her grandmother gave her on her twelfth birthday, the silver chain slipping through her grasp as she tries to fasten it around her neck. Today, something about her energy is different—muted, as if her usual spark had been dimmed. She moved slowly, hesitantly, and when she reached the counter, she stood there for a moment, almost uncertain, before settling in.

In the kitchen, life continues with its familiar rhythm—Logan, ever the mischievous one, making yet another attempt to steal bacon from the frying pan; Cathy, her eyes lighting up in victory as she celebrates another Pokémon caught; and Joe, as always, observing the familiar chaos with quiet amusement, a silent witness to the morning's dance.

"Logan, if you don't stop stealing my bacon, I swear—" Cathy's threat dissolves into a laugh as her phone buzzes. "Yes! Finally caught that shiny Ditto! I had no idea they were in the wild."

"Cathy, hon, your eggs are burning," Joe comments from the worn kitchen table, wrestling with his vineyard-stained work boots.

"They're not burning, they're developing character," she said, rescuing them any-way. Her phone chimes again. "Oh! There's a raid starting at our gym in twenty minutes!"

The kitchen's sunlight streams through windows framed by Cathy's thriving herb garden, catching dust motes and coffee steam in its golden beams. At the center, the massive butcher block island bears proud battle scars from countless family meals, while overhead, copper pots gleam alongside Zoe's artistic creation—dried grapevines from last years harvest woven into an intricate tapestry.

Zoe sits quietly at the counter, her scrambled eggs untouched. "Dad," she said, her voice carrying a note of uncertainty, "I feel... weird. Like something's humming, but I can't hear it. Does that make sense?"

"Oh, here we go," Logan smirks, his hand sneaking toward her plate. "What's wrong this time, Butt Nugget? Alien beings? Ghosts in the night?"

"Logan," Joe warns, though amusement softens the edges of his voice.

The farmhouse responds with its own morning symphony—creaking timbers, set-tling foundations, the subtle whisper of warming wood. Rows of meticulously planted grapevines stretched toward the horizon beyond the dining room's south window. A crystal prism catches the light, painting Zoe's concerned face with rainbow patterns as she frowns at her brother.

"I'm serious," she insisted, tucking an errant copper curl behind her ear. "It's like... like when your foot falls asleep, but in my head."

"That's called thinking, sis. Must be new for you."

"Children," Cathy intervenes, finally setting down her phone. "Logan, finish your breakfast. Zoe, honey, if you're not feeling well—"

"No, I need to work on my reading assignment." Zoe straightens, though her eyes betray her unease. "I'm fine, really."

Beyond the kitchen windows, the vineyard beckons. Five acres of Petite Sirah and Grenache vines spread across the gentle slope, each row revealing Joe's engineering precision. The fog lifted slowly, unveiling the irrigation system Logan helped install. Black tubes threading between grapevines like patient guardians, drawing from a spring that Zoe had inexplicably discovered beneath the property, one of many mysteries that seems to follow in her wake.

The family disperses with practiced ease: Cathy toward her beloved Pokémon gym beneath the oak tree, Logan to the western slope where early bud break demands attention, and Joe to the south corner's ongoing gopher battle. Zoe lingers on the porch, her hand pressed against an ancient wooden post, sensing the pressure of generations who'd stood in this same spot. The humming in her head intensifies, pulling her like a compass needle toward her father's receding figure. Without conscious decision, her feet carry her down the familiar path between the grapevines.

Behind them, the Victorian farmhouse keeps its silent watch, shadows stretching across dew-kissed grass. Wine bottle wind chimes create their crystalline melody, while a red-tailed hawk's cry echoes across the valley—nature's own greeting to another morning at Bailey Family Vineyards. Yet something is different today, as the strange humming in Zoe's head grows stronger as she drew closer to the southern corner, where unknown forces await beneath the California sun.

A perplexed Joe crouched down, examining the disturbed earth between the rows of grapevines. He expected the telltale signs of gopher damage, but something was profoundly off. After twenty years of battling these pests, he knew their handiwork like the back of his hand. Yet these holes were different—more circular, the soil displaced in oddly uniform patterns, forming perfect concentric rings around each opening. The precision was unsettling, almost mechanical.

While examining the strange holes, Joe rolled the blue-gray stone between his fingers, a habit that always surfaced when something seemed off about his land. The white quartz band caught the morning sun, reminding him of how his father used to do the same thing when facing vineyard troubles.

"Dammit," he said, running his calloused fingers through the loose dirt. The sweet, earthy scent of the vineyard couldn't mask his growing concern. He couldn't afford another disease, not after last season's battle with powdery mildew that had cost him nearly half his crop. The memory of those white, powdery spots spreading across his leaves still kept him up at night. He'd spent thousands on organic fungicides and countless hours adjusting his canopy management, only to watch helplessly as the infection had crept through his grapevines like a ghost.

Joe pulled a small trowel from his back pocket and started to dig, his brow furrowed with worry. He understood too well how delicate the vineyard's health was; perfect soil conditions were paramount. Too much of anything could tip the balance needed for his grapes to thrive. He'd witnessed firsthand how poor drainage could ruin a root system, how excess nitrogen could scorch young vines, and how mineral deficiencies could turn promising harvests into worthless fruit. Each possibility ran through his mind, each worse than the last.

The soil felt different too—lighter somehow, as if it had been aerated by unnatural means. The typical sandy loam that characterized his vineyard had taken on an unsettling, clay-like consistency immediately around the holes. In two decades of farming, he'd encountered nothing like it.

As he dug deeper, his trowel struck something solid. Clearing more dirt with his hands, he revealed a perfectly round object, an orb, about the size of a tennis ball. Joe lifted it carefully, turning it over in his hands, a subtle vibration traveling up his arms as his fingers made contact. As he cleaned it off, he noticed the surface was impossibly smooth, unmarred by even the smallest scratch. For a fleeting moment, he thought he saw a subtle shimmer—something that seemed to pulse in rhythm with the morning light filtering through the grapevine canopy—but when he looked closer, it appeared completely ordinary.

"Just another remnant of the valley's history," he said, though something in his gut told him otherwise. He placed the orb on a nearby rock, his fingers lingering on its surface a moment longer than necessary. His phone buzzed unexpectedly in his pocket, but when he checked it, the screen showed nothing. He had more pressing concerns than mysterious objects; he needed to figure out what was causing these strange disturbances in his soil. The pattern of holes stretched down the row for at least thirty feet, each one identical to the last, as if something had moved methodically through his vineyard during the night.

Behind him, unnoticed, Zoe stood frozen at the far side of the vineyard. Her eyes locked onto the area where the orb had been buried, and though she couldn't explain why, she wasn't able to look away. Something about it called to her, a whispered name just beyond hearing, a melody played too softly to distinguish. The morning breeze seemed to still around her, and her skin prickled with goosebumps despite the warming air. The humming in her chest grew stronger, resonating with each heartbeat as she noticed the strange object her father had set aside. Her body tingled with an inexplicable urge to go to it, to touch it, to claim it as her own and understand the secrets it seemed to hold.

Joe continued examining the soil, consumed by his work. He took samples from various depths, comparing textures, searching for any sign of the cause behind such unusual destruction. As his thoughts meandered, he couldn't shake the lingering impression that the holes appeared to be the same diameter as the orb. Pushing that thought aside, he pressed on, desperate for a rational explanation.

The orb sat innocently on its rocky perch, looking for all the world like nothing more than an odd curiosity. But there was something about it—something that promised change was coming to the Bailey Vineyard. The morning sun caught its surface, and for just a moment, a pattern of light danced across the ground like ripples in a pond, spreading outward toward the distant hills. In its wake, the dewdrops on nearby grape leaves trembled, catching the light in prismatic displays that seemed just a touch too vivid to be natural.

Joe's rational mind struggled to process what his eyes were telling him. He blinked hard, attributing the strange light show to fatigue from too many early mornings. Yet as he turned back to his soil samples, his phone buzzed again in his pocket, this time with a rapid series of notifications that faded as quickly as they had appeared.

In the distance, Cathy's voice carried across the vineyard as she celebrated catching another rare Pokémon, completely unaware of the discovery that would soon change their lives forever. The morning chorus of birds had gone suddenly quiet, as if they too sensed something extraordinary in their midst. The only sound was the gentle rustle of grape leaves in the breeze, a peaceful counterpoint to the mounting tension in the air.

Joe remained perplexed by the soil samples, his gaze kept returning to the orb. Each time he looked, it seemed to shimmer just at the edge of his vision, only to appear perfectly ordinary when he looked directly at it. It was like seeing a star at night in your peripheral vision, but when you try to look directly at it, it disappears.

Zoe watched, her breath shallow, heart hammering against her ribs. A restless energy crackled in the air, unsettling and electric. Something was coming—something she couldn't name but felt deep in her bones. The orb beckoned, drawing her in—was it a whispered promise or a warning she couldn't quite make out?

Zoe stood at the end of the row, watching her father work between the grapevines as the morning sun stretched across the ground. A light breeze carried the sweet scent of ripening grapes, but something else caught her attention—something beyond the ordinary.

One foot moved forward, then another, drawn by an invisible thread. She hadn't intended to come out to the vineyard; her summer reading assignment lay forgotten on her desk. Yet here she was, pulled from the house by an inexplicable urge that grew stronger with each step.

Her heart fluttered in her chest—not the rapid beating of anxiety or excitement, but something different. It was as if it were responding to a frequency only she could detect, like standing too close to a bass speaker at a concert, except instead of sound, pure energy thrummed through her body.

Zoe paused, wrapping her arms around herself. The sensation reminded her of other moments when her intuition had spoken to her: the day she'd found a spring under the vineyard, the countless times she'd guided her father to the most promising grapevines without understanding how she knew. This was different. Those had been whispers; this was a shout.

Three rows away, the small orb sat on its rocky perch, deceptively ordinary at first glance. The surrounding air shimmered—or perhaps it was the way her vision blurred as tears welled up in response to its presence. Her feet carried her closer, and the strange sensation in her chest intensified. The vineyard itself seemed to hold its breath, as the familiar ground beneath her feet became charged with potential.

The air grew thick and heavy around her, like walking through water. Her hairs on her arms stood on end as she approached the orb, and memories flickered through her mind: a lifetime of being out of sync with the world around her, of sensing things others couldn't see or feel. Her mother called it intuition, but Zoe had always known it was something more.

This was different. This was direct, intentional, like a message written just for her. The very soil beneath her feet pulsed with meaning, drawing her toward the spot where the orb had been discovered. She could sense the exact location, even with her eyes closed, as if someone had marked it on a map inside her mind.

Stopping a few feet from the orb, Zoe's hands trembled at her sides. The urge to reach out and touch it, to unlock whatever mystery it held, was almost overwhelming. Yet something held her back—not fear, but a sense that she wasn't quite ready, that there was more she needed to understand first.

Her father continued his investigation nearby, oblivious to the profound shift taking place within his daughter. Zoe stood transfixed, caught between the ordinary world of the vineyard—the one she'd known all her life—and something else, something vast and unknown that seemed to reach out through this simple spherical object.

The wind picked up, rustling through the grapevine leaves, carrying whispers in a language older than words. Every odd feeling she'd ever had, every inexplicable moment of connection with the natural world, had been leading to this. Standing there, with her heart beating in time with some unseen force, Zoe Bailey knew she had finally found what she'd been waiting for her entire life—even if she hadn't known she was waiting.

In the dimly lit wine cellar, Cathy sat on the edge of the old wine barrel Joe had turned in to a stool, her face bathed in the ethereal blue glow of her phone screen. The familiar bouquet of aged oak, fermented grape, and earthen stone wrapped around her like a comfort blanket, even as her fingers trembled with anticipation. Around her, bottles of Joe's finest vintages rested in their custom-built cedar cradles, silent witnesses to her growing obsession.

Wrought iron sconces cast dancing shadows across the terracotta tiles, their warm light competing with the artificial glow of Pokémon Go. The industrial dehumidifiers hummed their steady rhythm in the background, maintaining the perfect climate for both wine and secrets. She glanced guiltily at the vintage Petite Sirah rack across the room, knowing Joe would be shaking his head at her choosing this sanctuary for her frequent "research" sessions.

"Oh my," she said, her voice barely above a breath as she watched her phone's display. "This is different."

On her screen, all three Galarian Legendary Birds writhed in impossible patterns, their digital forms stretching and distorting like rubber bands. She'd seen glitches before, but this... this was something else entirely. Her leather-bound journal lay open on the reclaimed wine barrel table, its pages filled with meticulous observations of the increasing anomalies surrounding Zoe.

"Temporal displacement event #47," she said, her normally neat handwriting growing jagged with urgency. "Multiple Legendary Pokémon manifesting simultaneously. All three Galarian Legendary Birds appearing at the same time outside event parameters." She paused, swallowing hard. "Movement patterns match pre-solar flare signatures from 2023."

Through the cellar's narrow window, she could see Zoe walking near the vineyard. With each step her daughter took, the Pokémon on the screen twisted more violently, their code seeming to break down and reform in patterns that made Cathy's stomach lurch. They were drawn to Zoe like iron filings to a magnet, just as the strange lights in the night sky had been last week.

Guilt gnawed at her as she documented her own daughter like some science experiment. What choice did she have? Her online community had laughed when she'd warned them about the solar flares, right up until the grid failed. They'd dismissed her theories about the quantum research facility in Nevada, until the "accident" made headlines.

Her fingers brushed against the 1920 Petite Sirah bottle - their secret lever. The deep punt and unmarked label distinguished it from its neighbors. With practiced movement, she rotated it counterclockwise, triggering the soft click that opened their sanctuary.

The hidden six inch steel door swung open, revealing the narrow passage to the bunker below. The familiar hiss of the hydraulic door usually calmed her nerves, but today it only heightened her sense of urgency. As she descended the metal steps, the muted sound of their old household vanished, replaced by the slight echo of her footsteps against the concrete.

Entering the underground shelter, Cathy was immediately enveloped by the cool air, a stark contrast to the warmth of the sunlit world above. The eight hundred square feet of their bunker felt both claustrophobic and comforting, the reinforced concrete walls standing as a silent guardian against the unknown. The military-grade bunks aligned against one wall were neatly made, each bearing a distinct personal touch from the family. Above them, practical shelving stored essential supplies—flashlights, blankets, and emergency kits—all meticulously organized.

In the center, the hum of specialized monitoring equipment filled the air, the blinking lights reflecting the current pulse of their situation. Cathy's heart raced as she approached the Faraday cage she'd insisted on installing, its mesh-like walls glistening under the fluorescent lights. Joe had grumbled about the added expense.

They had made the bunker a home of sorts, with a basic kitchen tucked in the far corner, its modest appliances ready for emergencies. It wasn't just a shelter; it was a sanctuary—calm and resolute amidst the chaos brewing above. The small bathroom boasted only the essentials, but its presence offered comfort and a reminder of life's mundane normalcy.

Here, within the depths of their home, they were prepared for anything. Drawing comfort from the bunker, she headed upstairs to the cellar.

Back at her observation post, another notification pinged. The Pokémon Go screen displayed impossible data - negative distances, physics-defying speed calculations, and creature signatures that seemed to exist in multiple locations simultaneously. Her throat tightened as she recognized the pattern. It matched the data spikes she'd recorded before the Boston electronic failures.

"I'm sorry, baby," she whispered, watching Zoe through the window. Her daughter paused near the old oak tree, and for a moment, every Pokémon on the screen froze, then shattered into fragments of broken code. "I wish I could tell you everything."

The weight of her secrets pressed down on her like the earth above the bunker. Joe thought she was overreacting with all the preparations, the monitoring equipment, the endless hours of documentation. Logan dismissed her Pokémon Go research as an excuse to play games, but they hadn't seen what she had. They hadn't noticed how the anomalies were escalating, forming patterns that kept her awake at night.

Her fingers traced the edges of her journal, brushing past pages of observations, theories, and fears. The latest entry stared back at her, a testament to how far down this rabbit hole she'd gone. Yet with each passing day, as Zoe's connection to these phenomena grew stronger, Cathy's certainty deepened. Something was coming - something that would make her previous predictions look trivial in comparison.

Cathy glanced out the window. Zoe stood there, her silhouette backlit by the rising sun. For a moment, Cathy saw her daughter's form shimmer, as if reality itself was bending around her. On the phone screen, Pokémon Go went completely dark, then rebooted itself.

Cathy's hand shook as she made her last note for the day: "The frequency of anomalies is increasing. Time between events now less than 24 hours. Whatever's coming... it's speeding up."

She closed her journal and slipped it into its hiding place behind a rack of Petite Sirah. As she climbed the cellar stairs, the burden of knowledge weighed heavily on her. The bunker was ready. The supplies were stocked. The monitoring equipment was in place.

As she emerged into the morning daylight, watching Zoe walk back toward the house, one question haunted her: Would any amount of preparation be enough for what was coming?

Steam rose from the roast chicken at the center of the Baileys' oak dining table, blending with the scent of fresh herbs from their garden and the earthy aroma of the vineyard drifting through the open window. Joe sat at the head of the table, his hands wrapped around a glass of their vineyard's Petite Sirah. The deep red wine caught the evening light as he took a slow sip. Cathy barely touched her food, sneaking glances at her phone under the table. Her fingers absently toyed with the basement door key hanging from her neck—a habit that had only worsened since the Pokémon Go anomalies started appearing. Across from her, Zoe pushed her potatoes around her plate, keenly aware of the orb resting in her father's workshop. Its energy seemed to pulse through the walls, making her skin tingle with each beat. Logan, her older brother, slouched in his chair. His college textbooks—physics and calculus—sat in a messy stack beside him, sticky notes poking out from the pages. His laptop was closed and shoved aside, as if he wanted to distance himself from any digital traces of the day's discovery.

"Found something weird in the vineyard today," Joe said, breaking the silence. His fingers traced the rim of his wine glass, a nervous gesture he'd developed over years of mediating family tensions. "Some kind of orb, perfectly smooth. Never seen anything like it." His voice carried the careful neutrality of a man walking a tightrope between his wife's mounting theories and his son's rigid skepticism. "It's probably nothing," Joe said, though his fingers told a different story as they traced the worn depression in his grandfather's worry stone. The familiar motion helped steady his thoughts as he tried to make sense of the day's events.

Logan's fingers drummed out complex equations on the table's edge—a habit born from countless nights of study. "Probably just some old relic. Remember those weird stakes we found last spring?" He barely looked up, but his shoulders tensed. "Everything's got a logical explanation if you actually look for it." The words carried the impact of countless arguments, particularly the recent heated debate about his mother's Pokémon Go obsession.

"This is different," Zoe interjected, her voice sharp with certainty. The pull toward her father's workshop intensified, like an invisible thread drawing taut. It reminded her of the day she'd known—just known—that something was about to happen to her grandmother, hours before the phone call came. "Dad, please... can I keep it in my room?"

"Keep it?" Joe's forehead creased with familiar worry lines, the same ones that appeared when discussing the vineyard's struggling sales. His eyes flickered to Cathy, remembering her increasingly detailed charts of local anomalies. "We don't even know what it is, Zoe."

Cathy's phone buzzed, its screen illuminating another distorted Pokémon. Her hand trembled slightly as she studied the image, then glanced toward the basement door. Behind it, shelves of emergency supplies and monitoring equipment waited in the darkness. "Maybe we should store it somewhere more... secure." Her voice dropped to a whisper. "The readings I've been getting lately match the patterns from last month's solar activity. Now this..."

"Mom, stop." Logan's textbooks wobbled as he straightened, his voice filled with frustration and worry. "It's just a rock. Why's everyone being weird about this?" He shot a pointed look at her phone. "You're sounding like those preppers on your forums again."

"It's not just a rock." Zoe gripped her fork until her knuckles whitened, the metal warming unnaturally in her hand. The connection resonated deeply inside her, making the air feel thick with possibility. "It's important. I know it is. Like I knew about the frost coming early last season, or where to find those underground springs for the irrigation system." Memories of other unexplained knowledge she had before events flickered through her mind—moments she'd learned to keep quiet about.

Joe studied his daughter's face, recognizing the same expression she'd worn during those inexplicable incidents he'd tried so hard to rationalize. "Zoe, honey—"

"This isn't about rocks," she interrupted, the words tumbling out. "I just... I need to keep it safe." The orb's presence pulsed stronger, like a heartbeat syncing with her own. "It needs me to keep it safe."

Logan slammed his pencil down, but his hand shook slightly. "Great, another one of Zoe's premonitions." He gestured toward the basement door. "Moms got you believing in all this too, hasn't she? First it was the solar flares, then the quantum anomalies, and now this?"

"Don't start, Logan," Cathy said, her tone sharp as she stared at the impossibly warped Pokémon on her screen. She pulled up her documented patterns—weeks of careful observation and data collection. "There are things happening that your physics books can't explain. The patterns are there if you'd just—"

"That what? Your Pokémon told you?" Logan pushed back his chair, the legs scraping against the floor. "I've got finals to study for. Let me know when everyone stops being crazy about a rock." He gathered his books, careful to keep his laptop screen hidden. "Some of us are trying to live in the real world."

As Logan's footsteps thundered upstairs, silence settled over the table like a heavy blanket. Joe looked between his wife and daughter, seeing the fear behind Cathy's theories, the genuine confusion in Zoe's connection to the unexplainable, and feeling the pressure of Logan's frustration with it all.

Finally, he sighed. "We'll keep it in the house," he said carefully, trying to bridge the widening gaps in his family. "Zoe, you can be its keeper, but if anything unusual happens—anything at all—you tell us immediately." His gaze drifted to the basement door, acknowledging Cathy's concerns without fully validating her fears.

Zoe could sense the orb's energy pulse from the workshop, patient, waiting. Something in her responded to that patience, as if they'd been meant to find each other all along.

Cathy's hand tightened around her phone as another notification lit up the screen. Her carefully documented patterns were accelerating, matching the growing tension in their home. The bunker below held supplies for any disaster, but she wondered if they were prepared for whatever was really coming.

The remainder of dinner passed in uncomfortable silence, broken only by the scrape of utensils and Cathy's occasional glances at her phone. Above them, Logan's footsteps paced across his room as he threw himself into the comforting certainty of physics equations. And somewhere in the workshop, the orb waited, its presence a growing pressure against the fragile balance of the Bailey family's world.

# CHAPTER 2

# THE ORB

Joe waited until the kids had gone upstairs before turning to Cathy in the dimly lit kitchen. The house had settled into its nighttime quiet, punctuated by the soft hum of the dishwasher and the distant creaks of footsteps above. Outside, the vineyard's shadow stretched across their property like a dark blanket, the grapevines swaying gently in the evening breeze. He leaned against the granite counter, arms crossed, his expression troubled.

"I don't like it, Cath," he said, keeping his voice low. "The way Zoe's fixated on that thing—it's not normal. You saw how she barely touched her dinner, just kept stealing glances toward the workshop."

Cathy dried the last of the wine glasses, her phone buzzing with another Pokémon Go notification. She silenced it, but not before noticing another strange glitch—Pokémon spawning and de-spawning rapidly near Zoe's room. "She's always been drawn to unusual things, Joe. Remember her rock collection phase? Or the time she convinced herself the basement was a portal to another dimension?"

"This feels different." Joe ran a hand through his graying hair, glancing toward the window where his beloved grapevines stood sentinel. "Those were kid things. This... I can't shake the feeling there's something off about that orb. What if it affects the vineyard somehow? You saw the dirt. We're already struggling with production costs, and if something happens to the crops—"

"I know what you mean about feeling something's off," Cathy interrupted, pulling up her Pokémon Go app. "Look at this. Every time Zoe's near, the app goes haywire. It's like... time itself gets confused." She showed Joe the screen, where the usually stable game world warped and twisted. "I've been experiencing these moments where everything feels out of sync, like we're living in two times at once."

Joe's brow furrowed as he studied the glitching screen. "Tomorrow, I'll examine the orb more closely in the bunker. Maybe there's something in my old military manuals about unexplained objects."

Upstairs, Logan sat bathed in the blue light of multiple monitors. On one screen, he ran an analysis of similar archaeological findings; on another, he'd mapped the geological anomalies reported in Fallbrook over the past decade. His custom-built rig hummed as it processed the data, but something about the electromagnetic readings from his DIY sensor array troubled him. The numbers made little sense—they suggested patterns that defied known physics.

Through his wall, he could hear Zoe moving around in her room. The ambient temperature in the hallway dropped several degrees whenever she passed near his sensors. He added another data point to his growing spreadsheet, trying to maintain scientific objectivity even as his rational mind rebelled against the implications.

Back in the kitchen, Joe and Cathy finished their nighttime routine in thoughtful silence. As they turned off the lights, the house seemed to hold its breath. Joe paused at Zoe's door, listening. The air crackled with energy, a silent prelude to a storm. As his hand grazed the doorknob, he briefly sensed a surge of energy akin to a heartbeat.

Cathy touched his arm gently, her phone screen flickering with impossible Pokémon spawns. She leaned in closer. "Come on," she said. "We'll deal with it tomorrow."

As they retired to their bedroom, the house settled into an uneasy quiet. In the vineyard, the grapevines swayed without wind, and somewhere in the distance, a coyote started to howl. Each family member lay awake, their minds turning over the day's events: Joe planning his investigation while worrying about his vineyard's future, Cathy documenting the growing anomalies in her game, Logan analyzing his disturbing data, and Zoe—unknown to them—about to witness something that would prove all their instincts right.

Darkness fell, and with it, the sense that they stood on the brink of profound change. In the bunker below, Cathy's equipment hummed to life unbidden, recording readings that wouldn't be discovered until morning. The walls seemed to pulse with an energy that matched the orb's rhythm, a synchronized heartbeat that only Zoe could feel.

Before going to bed, Zoe snuck downstairs and retrieved the mysterious orb. Sitting cross-legged on her bed, she cradled it. Its surface caught the moonlight streaming through her window, throwing iridescent patterns across her walls that seemed to form and reform into almost-recognizable shapes. Later that night, she could have sworn she heard whispers—not with her ears. Something deeper, more primal. The orb grew warm in her hands, its subtle glow intensifying with each passing second.

Through the walls, Logan's sensors registered an electromagnetic spike, setting off silent alarms on his monitors. In their bedroom, Cathy's phone lit up with impossible Pokémon spawns, while Joe daydreamed of his vineyard transforming into something new and productive.

Joe stood at his bedroom window, watching the rising moon paint the vineyard, his fingers absently tracing the window frame as he contemplated the day's strange discovery. Behind him, Cathy sat cross-legged on their bed, her face illuminated by her phone's screen, its glow creating shadows under her eyes.

"That's the third time in the last hour," Cathy said, her fingers trembling slightly as she refreshed the app again. "No, fourth. I'm losing count."

Joe turned from the window, noting the worry lines creasing his wife's forehead. "The game acting up again?"

"It's more than that, Joe." Cathy looked up, her blue eyes reflecting a deeper concern than mere gaming frustration. "Every Pokémon within fifty feet of Zoe's room just... disappeared. Not fainted, not glitched—disappeared. In all my years playing, documenting spawns, tracking patterns... I've never seen anything like this."

Joe rubbed his face, his wedding ring catching the lamplight. "Could be anything, honey. Bad signal, server issues—"

"Perhaps it's connected to that thing you found." Cathy set her phone aside, though her fingers itched to check it again. "You've seen how she's been acting since you dug it up. The way she looks at it, like it's... calling to her."

Down the hall, in her bedroom, Zoe sat in her window seat, the orb cradled in her palms. Its surface shimmered with an inner light that seemed to pulse in rhythm with her heartbeat, sending tiny waves of warmth through her fingers. Her algebra textbook lay forgotten beside her, numbers and equations blurring into meaningless symbols as the orb commanded her attention. Tiny goosebumps raised along her arms as the air around her vibrated with an energy she could feel but couldn't explain.

"Hey, Butt Nugget," Logan's voice cut through her reverie. He stood in her doorway, trying to maintain his usual casual demeanor, but she noticed how his eyes fixed on the orb. "Dad's looking for his paperweight."

Zoe clutched the orb closer, feeling its pulse quicken with her own. "It's not a paperweight."

"Right. It's totally an alien egg." Logan stepped into the room, his computer science textbook tucked under one arm. His attempt at humor couldn't quite mask the concern in his voice. "Just don't come crying to me when it hatches and eats your face. Though that might be an improvement."

Back in their bedroom, Joe pulled out his phone. "I've been researching similar objects online. Nothing matches exactly, but there are stories—"

"Stories?" Cathy stood, moving to join him at the window. Outside, the vineyard had taken on an otherworldly quality in the gathering dark. "What kind of stories?"

"Nothing concrete. Just forum posts about strange orbs, unusual occurrences." He lowered his voice, glancing toward the hallway. "Some mentions of government involvement in something called a Chronosphere, but it's all speculation. Nobody has ever seen one, at least nobody willing to talk about it." His chuckle, meant to be reassuring, missed the mark.

"Joe Bailey," Cathy's voice took on that familiar determined tone he knew so well, "if you're about to tell me I need to prove another conspiracy theory true, then so be it. But I'm more worried about men in black suits showing up at our door."

"No, no." He wrapped an arm around her shoulders, drawing her close. "But maybe we should be thankful you had me put in that damn bunker." His smile was genuine this time, though tinged with worry. "Your paranoia might actually pay off."

The night settled around the farmhouse like a heavy blanket. In her pastel blue room, surrounded by her beloved astronomy posters and the constellations she'd carefully painted on her ceiling, Zoe opened her journal. The pages were filled with dozens of sketches, each attempting to capture the orb's ever-changing essence. Just a moment ago, it seemed more blue than purple, with swirling patterns that reminded her of distant galaxies.

A floorboard creaked in the hallway, and she quickly slipped the orb under her pillow, feeling a pang of loss at breaking contact. Her mother appeared in the doorway, phone still clutched like a lifeline.

"Everything okay in here, ZoeJoe?" Cathy's phone screen flickered and died, as if on cue.

"Fine, Mom." Zoe smiled at the sound of her mom using her nickname, though her heart raced in time with the orb's hidden pulse. "Just finishing homework."

Cathy frowned at her dead phone, then at her daughter. Something in the air felt charged, like the moment before a storm. "You know you can talk to us if anything feels... different, right?"

"I know." Zoe's hand unconsciously moved toward her pillow, drawn to the warmth she could feel even through the fabric. "Everything's fine."

But as Cathy walked back to her bedroom, the house settling into its nighttime rhythm, nothing felt normal at all. The crickets outside had fallen silent, the usual owl calls absent, and the coyotes' howls seemed to carry new meaning. In the vineyard where the orb was recently discovered, the soil itself seemed to hum with residual energy.

Joe waited until Cathy returned before he said, "I saw her snatch the orb before going to bed. Should we take it away from her?"

"I don't think we can." Cathy sank onto their bed, her phone dark and silent beside her. "Whatever that thing is, I think it chose her. It's already part of her."

In her room, Zoe pulled the orb back into her lap, its gentle glow reflecting in her eyes and casting dancing shadows on the star charts above. She couldn't explain it, not even to herself, but she knew one thing with absolute certainty. This was just the beginning of something much bigger than their quiet life in Fallbrook.

Moonlight filtered through the lavender curtains of Zoe's bedroom window, moonlight shining across her collection of stuffed animals and the corkboard filled with photos of her family working in the vineyard. Mixed among the family photos were sketches of dreams she'd had - strange symbols and patterns she'd never understood but felt compelled to draw. The house entered its familiar nighttime routine, punctuated by the distant sound of Logan's music bleeding through the walls.

Zoe lay in bed, her purple comforter pulled up to her chin, fighting against the electric buzz of anticipation that kept sleep at bay. The events of the day tumbled through her mind: her father's discovery, the magnetic pulling sensation she'd felt in the vineyard, and now this peculiar object on her nightstand.

Just as her thoughts began to drift, a faint luminescence caught her attention. The orb, previously dormant, had begun to pulse with a gentle radiance that reminded her of fireflies on a summer evening.

"No way," she said, pushing herself up onto her elbows. Her heart hammered against her chest as she watched the subtle rhythm of light, like a heartbeat made visible. Was she dreaming? The soft glow reflected off her bedroom walls, creating dancing patterns that seemed almost alive. The light mingled with the glow-in-the-dark constellations on her ceiling, transforming her room into what felt like a portal to another world.

With trembling fingers, Zoe reached out toward the orb. The moment her skin contacted its surface, the glow intensified, as if recognizing her touch. The orb felt unexpectedly warm, like holding a cup of fresh tea, and beneath her fingertips, she could feel subtle vibrations that sent tingles up her arm - tingles that reminded her of the strange sensations she'd sometimes get before something significant happened.

She lifted the orb carefully, cradling it in both hands. Its surface came alive with shifting colors—deep sapphire blues swirling into rich purples and brilliant golds, creating patterns that reminded her of the pictures of galaxies she'd seen in her science textbooks. Through the translucent exterior, an intricate network of impossibly small mechanisms caught the light - tiny gears that shouldn't exist, crystalline structures that seemed to shift and change even as she watched, all moving in a dance that felt both ancient and futuristic.

"What are you?" she asked, turning the orb slowly in her hands. The pulsing lights seemed to respond to her voice, quickening their rhythm slightly. The question lingered as flashes of past unexplained memories surfaced—like when she told her dad they'd get a flat tire on a road trip, and not fifteen minutes later they did, or how she always sensed Logan's anger, no matter how well he hid it. This felt different though, bigger somehow, as if all those other moments had been preparing her for this.

A sudden thump from the hallway made her jump. The orb's glow dimmed immediately, though it continued to hum warmly in her palms. She heard her father's footsteps pass by her door—one solid step, then a soft scuff, the telltale rhythm of the limp he'd earned flying stunt kites at the Russian River in Northern California.

Zoe lay back against her pillows, still holding the orb close. Excitement and fear twisted together in her stomach like the gnarled grapevines in the vineyard. This was more than just some old artifact or forgotten piece of equipment—she could feel it in her bones, the same way she'd always felt things that others couldn't explain. But what exactly had her father unearthed in their vineyard? And why did she feel so deeply connected to it?

The orb pulsed once more in her hands, as if trying to answer her unspoken questions. Outside her window, the familiar silhouettes of grapevines stretched toward the star-filled sky, but somehow, everything felt different now. Something extraordinary had begun, and Zoe Bailey felt like she was at the center of it all - just as she'd always secretly hoped and feared she might be.

The soft glow of moonlight filtered through Zoe's bedroom window as she drifted off to sleep, the orb pulsing gently on her nightstand. She'd always felt different—the girl who didn't quite fit in at school, who felt things too deeply, who sometimes knew things she shouldn't. Now, staring at the mysterious sphere, she wondered if this was why.

The familiar world of her bedroom melted away, replaced by an endless expanse of stars and swirling galaxies painted in deep indigos and violets. Her stomach lurched with equal parts terror and exhilaration, the same feeling she'd gotten years ago when she'd somehow known about her grandmother's fall before the phone had rung.

Weightless, she floated through the cosmic void, her nightgown billowing around her like a nebula. The orb materialized before her, its glow intensifying with each passing moment. The stars seemed to dance to the rhythm of the orb's energy, each one twinkling in perfect synchronization with its pulse.

"*Come...*" The whisper echoed through the vastness, barely audible yet somehow clear in her mind. "*Time flows...*" Another whisper, this one fading before she could grasp its meaning. Part of her wanted to retreat, to wake up and shove the orb deep into her closet, where it couldn't turn her world upside down. But a stronger part knew it was already too late for that.

The orb's light grew stronger, its colors shifting from deep blues to brilliant golds. Zoe reached out, her fingers trembling as they neared the surface. Time seemed to bend around her—memories of yesterday's breakfast blending with tomorrow's homework, creating a dizzying whirlpool of memories. But some memories felt wrong, like photographs from a vacation she hadn't taken yet.

Images flashed before her: Mom's red hair catching the sunlight as she caught yet another Pokémon on her phone, Dad's eyes crinkling with laughter, and Logan—watching her with that mix of skepticism and concern she'd grown so used to lately. She wished she could be more like him, so certain about everything, so grounded in logic and reason. But she'd never been that way, had she?

"*Family... connected...*" The whispers grew more urgent, but their meaning remained just out of reach, like trying to catch smoke with her bare hands. A new fear gripped her—not for herself, but for them. Whatever was happening, whatever the orb wanted, it involved her whole family.

The orb pulsed one final time, and Zoe's eyes snapped open. She sat bolt upright in bed, her heart racing, her skin tingling with residual energy. Her pajamas were damp with sweat, and her hands trembled as she pushed her hair back from her face. The orb sat innocently on her nightstand, its surface shimmering in the pre-dawn light. The dream clung to her consciousness, refusing to fade like normal dreams.

Frustrated, she asked the orb, "What are you trying to say?" knowing somehow that this was more than just a dream. This was a message. If only she could understand what it meant. Her fingers traced the smooth surface, and for a moment, she thought she felt it respond to her touch, like a cat purring beneath her hand.

She glanced at her phone—3:33 AM. In a few hours, she'd have to face her family at breakfast, pretend everything was normal while carrying this weight of knowing-but-not-knowing. Logan would probably make another joke about her being weird, and for once, she couldn't argue with him. She was weird. Maybe she always had been.

But as she lay back down, one hand still resting protectively near the orb, Zoe realized something: she wasn't afraid anymore. Whatever this was, whatever she was becoming—it felt right. Like finding the missing piece to a puzzle she hadn't even known she was solving.

Leaning closer to the orb so nobody could hear, she said, "Okay," a small smile playing at her lips. "Show me what's next."

Zoe awoke to the soft light of dawn filtering through her curtains, painting the room in a gentle, golden hue. As she blinked away the remnants of sleep, her gaze instinctively fell upon the orb resting on her nightstand. Its colors shimmered in the early sunlight—blues, purples, and the faintest glimmer of gold over its surface.

She sat up, feeling a strange warmth radiating from it, a silent invitation that made her heart race with anticipation. Unlike any other morning, today felt different. Zoe reached out, her fingertips grazing the cool surface. A pulse of energy responded to her touch, as if the orb recognized her presence, a secret shared only between them.

Zoe leaned closer, captivated by the sight of the intricate inner mechanism visible through the translucent exterior. Tiny gears and crystals shifted in a cosmic ballet, and in that moment, an understanding unfurled within her. This was not merely an object; it was alive, vibrant with purpose, and it was calling her, urging her to awaken to something profound. She felt a kinship with it, an almost instinctual connection. The sensation was exhilarating, yet intimidating.

Fragments of understanding flickered through her mind. The orb wasn't just some discarded artifact or forgotten piece of technology. It was alive in its own way, conscious perhaps, and it had chosen her. The realization should have seemed absurd, but in that morning stillness, it settled into her bones with the weight of absolute certainty.

Zoe slid out of bed and walked to her window, drawn to the view she'd seen countless times before. The vineyard stretched out below, rows of vines catching the early light. Morning mist still clung to the lower slopes, creating an ethereal landscape that seemed to exist somewhere between reality and dreams.

She pressed her palm against the cool glass, taking in the familiar sight with new eyes. How many mornings had she looked out at these same vines, never suspecting that the ordinary world held such extraordinary possibilities? The land seemed different now - more alive, more purposeful. The neat rows of grapevines no longer represented just her family's livelihood; they were lines of energy, patterns that hinted at deeper mysteries.

A sparrow landed on a nearby branch, tilting its head as if sharing in her contemplation. Zoe smiled, feeling a surge of something like joy, but deeper and more complex. The dream had washed away the fear and uncertainty of yesterday building within her a steady resolve. Whatever this journey was, whatever the orb was leading her toward, she was ready.

She turned back to look at the orb, now catching the morning sun. She could have sworn she saw colors shifting beneath its surface, but they were subtler now, more like the suggestion of movement than the dramatic display of the night before. It was waiting, she realized, waiting for her to take the next step.

The world outside her window continued its morning routine - distant tractors rumbling to life, birds calling across the vineyard, the first hints of movement from elsewhere in the house. But Zoe stood still, absorbing the magnitude of what she knew lay ahead. The quiet beauty of the morning felt like a pause, a deep breath before a plunge into unknown waters.

She straightened her shoulders, feeling stronger and more certain than she had in her entire sixteen years. The orb had awakened something in her—a sense of purpose, a destiny she couldn't yet fully grasp but could feel it with all her heart. And somehow, she knew this was only the beginning.

# CHAPTER 3

# CONNECTION

Sunlight streamed through the kitchen window as the family gathered around the worn oak table. The aroma of coffee, sizzling bacon, and Cathy's signature cinnamon toast filled the air—a Bailey family breakfast tradition. Zoe slipped into her seat while her father worked on a crossword puzzle, Mom juggled Pokémon Go and breakfast, and Logan stayed glued to his phone.

The familiar warmth of the moment surrounded them, but for Zoe, everything felt different. The normal chatter seemed to come from far away, her mind consumed by the precious cargo in her backpack. Her hands trembled slightly as she unzipped it, just enough to brush against the cool surface of the orb. The contact sent a jolt through her fingers—a gentle vibration that only she could feel, like a secret whispered just for her.

"Earth to Zoe," Cathy called out, waving a piece of cinnamon toast in front of her daughter's face. "You're a million miles away this morning, sweetie."

Zoe flinched when the plate of cinnamon toast appeared in her line of vision, her backpack sliding awkwardly against her shoulder as she tried to cover her jumpiness. The smile she offered her mother was paper thin. "Just tired," she said, but the words felt hollow in her mouth. Something nagged at the edges of her consciousness. Her hand drifted to her collarbone, seeking the familiar weight of the locket, and found only empty air. A cold knot formed in her stomach as she met her mother's eyes. "Hey, have you seen my locket? I've looked everywhere."

The silver locket had been her grandmother's gift on her thirteenth birthday, a delicate family heirloom that had belonged to three generations of Bailey women. Inside, a tiny photograph of her younger self nestled against one of her grandmother smiling, both caught in a moment of shared laughter during their last summer together at the lake house. The familiar weight against her collarbone had become a comfort over the years, a tangible connection to the woman who'd taught her to trust her instincts, to look beyond the obvious. Its absence now felt like losing a piece of herself, especially with everything else feeling so... off.

The orb pulsed gently against her leg, causing her to forget about the locket for now, its energy seeped through the fabric of her backpack. Without thinking, she pulled it partially out, mesmerized by the way it shifted colors in the morning light—purple bleeding into green, blue swirling with gold. The breakfast chatter continued around her, but Zoe barely registered it, lost in the hypnotic display.

"Hey, that's weird," Logan commented suddenly, his eyes narrowed as he looked up from his phone. "I was just looking up 'ChronoSphere' online this morning. There's actually some fascinating theoretical physics behind the concept of Chronospheres and temporal manipulation."

Zoe's heart skipped a beat. Her instincts were to protect the orb, and she certainly didn't appreciate her brother doing research on it. She wanted to tell him he can't do anymore research, but forced herself to appear casual, though her fingers tightened instinctively around the orb in her lap. "Oh yeah?" she managed, trying to keep her voice steady. "What made you look that up?"

Logan shrugged, still scrolling. "Just went down a rabbit hole. You know how it goes."

"Speaking of rabbits," Joe interjected with a grin, "those aren't the only things making holes in our vineyard lately. How about helping your old man with some gopher patrol after school, Zoe?"

The orb pulsed warmly in response to Joe's mention of the vineyard, and Zoe had to resist the urge to gasp. She was struck by an overwhelming urge to call it something less scientific than 'ChronoSphere.' The name 'Sir-Swirls-a-lot' pops into her head, followed by 'Swirly'. She had to bite back a smile. Swirly is the perfect name, she decided.

"Sorry, Dad," she said as she carefully slid the orb back into her bag. "I've got... homework to catch up on."

Cathy looked up from her phone, her Pokémon Go screen momentarily forgotten. "Everything okay, honey? You seem distracted lately."

"I'm fine, Mom," Zoe assured her. "Just thinking about school stuff."

As breakfast winds down and the family begins to disperse, Zoe lingered at the table, her hand resting protectively on her backpack. The morning sun caught the edge of the orb through the slight opening in the zipper, sending a prismatic display across the kitchen wall. For a brief moment, time seems to slow, and Zoe feels the infinite possibility contained within her bag.

Later, she promised herself. Later, she'll unlock the mysteries of Swirly, but for now, she needed to maintain the illusion of normalcy, even as her world teeters on the edge of extraordinary change.

The kitchen fell into silence as Cathy and Joe finished loading the dishwasher, both lost in their own thoughts. Cathy's hands trembled slightly as she wiped down the granite countertop, leaving streaks on the surface that she absently wiped away. The morning sun shining through the window highlights the worry lines on her face.

"Joe," she said, setting down her dishcloth with deliberate care, "I think we need to call Becky." She hesitated, then said, "If anyone would notice strange patterns like what's happening with Pokémon Go around that orb, it would be her. She's always talking about quantum mechanics during our raid meetups."

Joe closed the refrigerator door with more force than necessary. "Your friend from the meetup group? The quantum physicist?" He crossed his arms, leaning against the counter. "Cathy, are you sure we want to involve outsiders in this? Especially with how Zoe's been acting?"

"I know it's a risk," Cathy admitted, running her fingers through her red hair. "But you've seen how that orb affects her. We're out of our depth here, and Becky's not just any outsider. She does advanced particle physics research at the lab. Plus," pulling her phone from her back pocket, she said, "she's been noticing something odd in the area already."

Joe's expression softened as he saw the fear behind his wife's determination. "Okay," he conceded, moving to stand beside her. "But careful is the watch word."

The call connected after two rings. "Cathy! Thank goodness you called," Becky's excited voice came through the speaker. "I was just about to message you about the anomalous spawn patterns near your coordinates."

"That's actually why I'm calling," Cathy responded, putting the phone on speaker. "How soon can you come over? There's something... unusual happening here."

"The data patterns are fascinating," Becky said, with her voice taking on a more professional tone. "I'm seeing quantum fluctuations in the GPS coordinates—technically impossible, according to standard physics models, but the numbers don't lie. The space-time signatures suggest localized temporal displacement."

Joe and Cathy exchanged alarmed looks. "In English, please?" Joe asked, his hand tightening on Cathy's shoulder.

"Time irregularities," Becky clarified. "Look, I know this sounds like science fiction, but the data suggests small distortions in the fabric of time itself. Pokémon Go is just sensitive enough to pick it up because it uses precise GPS tracking. I've been monitoring similar patterns across Fallbrook, but your location..." She paused. "The energy readings are exponentially higher than anything I've seen before."

Cathy took a deep breath, her voice dropped to nearly a whisper. "Becky, how fast can you get here? There's something you need to see. But this stays between us—no lab, no papers, nothing official."

"Twenty minutes. And Cathy? Whatever's generating these readings... be careful. The energy signatures are unlike anything in our current scientific understanding."

After hanging up, Joe pulled Cathy into a tight embrace. Snuggling up to her ear, he said, "I hope we didn't just make a huge mistake."

"Should we tell Zoe that Becky's coming?" Cathy asked, as she glanced toward the stairs where their daughter's room lay quiet.

"Not yet," Joe decided. "First, we'll get Becky's take. If anyone can help us understand what that orb might be—and what it's doing to our daughter—it's her."

Through the kitchen window, the morning sun caught the neat rows of grapevines, displaying alternating patterns of light and shadow across the vineyard. Somewhere upstairs, their daughter sat alone with an object that might be changing everything they thought they knew about reality itself.

The morning sunlight filtered through the kitchen windows, creating a warm glow on the granite countertops as Cathy and Joe finished cleaning up. A slight buzz of anxious energy filled the air, making even mundane tasks feel weighted with significance. The quiet hum of the dishwasher provided a steady backdrop to their racing thoughts.

Frustrated and concerned, Joe said, "I still can't believe we're doing this." Wiping down the counter with more force than necessary.

Before Cathy could respond, they heard the distinctive crunch of tires on gravel, followed by a car door slamming and quick, determined footsteps approaching the front door. Cathy's heart quickened—Becky had arrived.

The door swung open, and Becky Martinez stepped inside, her dark curls escaping from a messy bun. Her "Periodic Table of Elements" t-shirt caught the morning light, a fitting look for someone always buzzing with scientific curiosity. A close family friend and a quantum physicist at the local university, Becky was their go-to expert for anything unexplainable. Her sharp mind and unconventional theories earned both admiration and doubt in academic circles.

"Cathy! Joe!" Becky burst in, clutching a leather messenger bag and what looked like a hybrid between a smartphone and a Geiger counter. "I came as soon as I could process those readings I told you about. They're unlike anything I've ever seen!"

Cathy gestured toward the kitchen table, their unofficial command center for family crises. "Come sit. There's fresh coffee, and we have so much to tell you."

Becky set her device on the table, its screen displaying a cascade of multicolored wavelengths that pulsed in an oddly hypnotic pattern. "Start from the beginning," she said, pulling out a well-worn notebook covered in equations and diagrams.

Joe leaned against the counter, arms crossed, his hands betraying his tension. "It started with an orb I found in the vineyard. Initially, we thought it was an unusual artifact, but then..."

"Then everything started changing," Cathy continued, glancing at her phone. "Pokémon Go began showing impossible coordinates, registering phantom energy signatures. And Zoe—" her voice caught slightly, "Zoe seems drawn to it in ways we can't explain. Logan also mentioned finding references to a 'ChronoSphere' online this morning?"

Joe straightened. "He's been researching it, though he's trying to stay skeptical. Classic Logan."

The monitoring device suddenly emitted a series of sharp beeps, drawing their attention. Becky leaned forward, her dark eyes widening. "These energy signatures... they're not random. There's a pattern here, something almost... intentional."

"What exactly are we dealing with?" Joe's voice carried an edge of concern, barely masked by determination.

Becky took a deep breath, choosing her words carefully. "Based on these readings and what you've described, we could be looking at localized temporal anomalies. In simpler terms, the orb might be affecting time and space around it. Your Pokémon Go glitches? They're likely just the tip of the iceberg—digital systems detecting distortions we can't naturally perceive."

Cathy sank into a chair, her legs suddenly weak. "And Zoe's connection to all this?"

"That's what we need to understand," Becky said, pulling out additional equipment from her bag. "If she's somehow attuned to the orb's energy, she could be the key to understanding its purpose. But we need to be careful—this kind of power could be dangerous if not properly understood."

Joe's hands clenched involuntarily. "If anything happens to her..."

"That's why we need a controlled environment," Becky interjected softly. "The basement, or wine cellar, we could set up monitoring equipment, establish safety protocols. We study this methodically, prioritizing Zoe's wellbeing above all else."

The sound of footsteps on the stairs interrupted their planning. Zoe appeared in the doorway, her eyes immediately drawn to Becky's equipment. The morning light caught her face, highlighting a maturity that seemed to have appeared overnight.

"Is this about the orb?" she asked, her voice steady despite the weight of the question.

Cathy exchanged glances with Joe before nodding. "Yes, sweetie. Becky's here to help us understand what's happening. With the orb—with everything."

"You can call it Swirly," Zoe said, settling into a chair beside Becky. "That's what it likes to be called."

Becky's eyebrows rose slightly, but she simply opened to a fresh page in her notebook. "Tell me about that, Zoe. How do you know what it likes?"

As Zoe began to speak, Cathy reached for Joe's hand under the table, drawing strength from his solid presence.

"It started with colors," Zoe began, her voice taking on a distant quality. "Colors that shouldn't exist, but somehow do…"

The kitchen fell silent except for the scratch of Becky's pen and the steady pulse of the monitoring device, recording the first chapter of their new reality.

The moment Zoe left for school, Becky pulled her temporal anomaly detector from her messenger bag. The device, a hybrid of professional equipment and her own modifications, hummed to life with a soft electronic whine.

"We need to check the vineyard now," she said, her eyes gleaming with the same enthusiasm she usually reserved for rare Pokémon spawns. "These readings are getting stronger by the minute."

Cathy exchanged a concerned look with Joe. "Do you think it's connected to Zoe's behavior this morning?"

"Only one way to find out," Joe replied, already reaching for his work boots.

They made their way through the vineyard, the dew still clinging to the grape leaves. Becky led the way, dividing her attention between her detector and Pokémon Go. "These readings are stronger than any glitch I've ever tracked," she said, comparing the screens. "And trust me, I've mapped every anomaly in Fallbrook."

Joe noticed how the morning light caught the device's screen, reflecting mysterious patterns across Becky's face. "Over here," he called out, pointing to the spot where he'd found the orb. "This is where it all started."

As they neared the spot where Joe initially discovered the orb, Joe kneeled down, tracing the earth with his hands. He sensed more remained hidden. Becky stayed near him, her device beeping softly as the colors flickered on the screen.

The detector's quiet hum suddenly rose to an urgent chirp. Becky's eyes widened. "Whatever's here, it's powerful. The energy signature matches what I've been tracking through Pokémon Go's GPS glitches, but amplified."

Underneath his fingers, Joe could have sworn he felt a shift in the soil. Grabbing his shovel, he started to dig. After a few feet, he struck something hard. As he cleared the ground, an unexpected shape began to emerge—something that looked ancient and beautifully crafted.

"What is that?" Cathy asked as she leaned closer, watching what Joe was uncovering.

"I'm not sure," Joe said, brushing dirt away to reveal a smooth, stone-like structure. "It looks like it could be some kind of old relic—possibly left by the Luiseno tribe who once inhabited this land."

Becky squatted beside Joe, her eyes wide with wonder. "It could be a ceremonial artifact or even a marker. The carvings—look how intricate they are! They must have some meaning."

Joe worked diligently to uncover more, continuing to wipe away soil. As the shape became clearer, it revealed itself to be a circular stone structure approximately five feet in circumference, adorned with detailed carvings around the outer edges that hinted at a once-great significance.

"Whatever this is, it feels important," Cathy said, gazing at the artistry etched into the stone.

With a warning look, Becky said, "Agreed. But we should take extra care. We don't want to disturb anything or damage it."

After clearing away more dirt, they examined the structure as sunlight shined on its surface. The artifact added to the mystery surrounding the orb and its possible connection.

As they marveled at the stone structure, a sense of reverence washed over them. The intricate carvings appeared to tell a story, mythical creatures entwined with vines, the sun and moon intertwined in a dance, as if they had been frozen in time.

"What do you think this represents?" Cathy asked, leaning in closer to examine the carvings.

"I've seen similar motifs in Native American art," Becky said, brushing her fingers over the markings. "They often depict the connection between humanity and nature, the cycles of life. This might have served as a sacred site or a meeting place.

Joe stepped back, a mix of awe and curiosity. "It's hard to believe something like this is hidden right here beneath our vineyard. Who knows how long it's been here?"

Cathy looked up from the stone, her expression thoughtful. "Maybe it's been waiting for someone to discover it. We should record everything and try to find out more about its history, especially since it's connected to our land. There could be more to uncover."

"Definitely." Becky said, already pulling out her smartphone to take pictures of the site from various angles. "We need to record everything for further study."

As she captured images, Joe kneeled beside the stone structure, running his fingers along the edges. He could feel an odd warmth emanating from it, almost as if it were alive in some way, sending a shiver of excitement through him. He looked up at Cathy and Becky, who were both engrossed in their examinations. "I can't shake the feeling that whatever this is, it holds more significance than we realize," he remarked.

"I feel it too," Cathy agreed, her gaze wandered over the carvings. "There's something about it that feels... potent, like it's still connected to something beyond our understanding."

Becky paused, her phone still in hand, and looked between them. "Let's proceed with caution. This could be historical, an artifact we need to preserve and study. We should report this discovery to a local historian or archaeologist."

"Good idea," Joe replied, brushing more soil away from the stone. "First, let's check if there's something underneath. This pattern could be part of something larger."

With renewed determination, Joe began to dig more carefully at the base of the structure. As he worked, Cathy and Becky examined the carvings closely, piecing together what they might represent. The imagery seemed to weave a story of creation, depicting elements of the earth and sky entwined, figures that hinted at rituals or gatherings held by ancient peoples.

"Look at this one!" Becky pointed to a carving that depicted a figure raising its arms toward a celestial body. "It seems like a celebration or reverence toward something greater—perhaps a harvest or an astronomical event."

"Yes! It speaks to a connection with nature, and the energies of the land," Cathy mused, her excitement growing. "They likely revered the cycles of the seasons, the way we all should."

Just then, Joe's shovel struck something solid. He paused, heart racing at the thought of uncovering more secrets. With carefully applied pressure, he nudged the shovel beneath the object and began to lift—dirt spilling away to reveal a hidden groove along the perimeter of the structure.

"What's that?" Cathy leaned closer, her eyes wide with curiosity.

"It looks like... a channel," Joe said, brushing the dirt away. "It's as if there's a design continuing around the edge. It's almost as if it used to be a part of something larger."

Thinking out loud, Becky said, "Maybe it was designed to interact with an object.," Her mind racing with possibilities. "Like a ceremonial piece that complements what we've found."

As the last of the dirt fell away, Joe noticed a small indentation at the center—similar in size to the orb. The realization struck him like lightning, but he hesitated, unsure.

"Could it be...?" he trailed off, looking at Cathy and Becky.

"What is it, Joe?" Cathy asked, sensing his sudden shift in demeanor.

"Maybe this structure is somehow connected to the orb? It looks like the orb could fit into this indentation," he ventured, the enormity of the thought hanging in the air.

Becky blinked, her expression a mix of excitement and caution. "We don't know what this is yet! We need to be careful. If it is some sort of ceremonial structure, we shouldn't interfere without understanding its significance."

"I feel like we've already uncovered something incredible here, but part of me wants to see if the orb can connect with it," Joe confessed, weighing the implications.

Stepping in, Cathy said, "We should think this through. Zoe shouldn't be involved in this without fully understanding what it could mean. We need more information."

Becky nodded, her expression serious. "Let's document everything we've found. If this is significant, we should take our time to understand it and treat it with the respect it deserves."

Taking a deep breath, Joe set the shovel down and stepped back from the stone structure. "You're right. But I can't deny it feels like more than just a relic. It's infused with energy, and I can feel it calling out. We'll investigate further, but for now, we need to protect it and ourselves."

Cathy looked at them both, warmth in her eyes. "I'm so glad we're in this together. We'll bring Zoe in when the time is right."

They spent the next hour carefully recording their findings with notes and photographs, preserving every detail so they could study it later. As they worked, the sun, rising from the east, shined bright across the vineyard—a stark contrast to the depth of mystery they had uncovered.

Finally, after documenting everything, they stood back to look at what lay before them—a blend of history, potential, and an unknown future.

"Let's head back for now," Becky suggested, breaking the silence. "We'll regroup and discuss what to do next."

Across town at Fallbrook High School, sitting in her history class, Zoe felt a sudden, inexplicable shiver run down her spine.

# CHAPTER 4

# FIELD TRIP

The midday sun scorched Fallbrook High's concrete courtyard, but Zoe barely noticed. Her turkey sandwich sat untouched, wilting in its wrapper as her mind lingered on last night's dream. The usual lunch period chaos—bouncing basketballs, bursts of laughter, the steady hum of cafeteria fans—blurred into background noise.

"Earth to Zoe?" Carmel waved her hand in front of Zoe's face, her silver bangles catching the sunlight. Her usual playful smile carried an edge of worry. "You've been in another universe all lunch. What's going on with you?"

Zoe leaned closer to her best friend since seventh grade, lowering her voice. "I had this dream last night, Carmel. But it wasn't just any dream. It felt... real."

"Real how?" Carmel set aside her own lunch, dark eyes focused intently on Zoe's face. They'd shared hundreds of secrets under their favorite oak tree, but something in Zoe's tone made this different.

"It's like..." Zoe's hands moved through the air, painting invisible patterns. "I was floating in space, but not just floating. There were these lights, like auroras, but they were inside me somehow. And when I touched Swirly—"

"Swirly?" Carmel's eyebrows arched, a familiar gesture that usually preceded gentle teasing.

"The orb my dad found," Zoe said, feeling heat rise in her cheeks. Her hand unconsciously drifted toward her backpack, where the object in question lay hidden between her history textbook and math notebook. She could feel its presence, a subtle vibration that made her fingertips tingle. "I started calling it Swirly. When I touched it, this energy just... flowed through me. Like liquid starlight in my veins."

Carmel's expression shifted from curiosity to concern. She reached out and placed a warm hand on Zoe's arm. "You're actually serious about this, aren't you?"

The orb seemed to grow heavier in Zoe's backpack, its gentle pulse continuing to match her heartbeat as if they were one. She'd almost shown it to Carmel twice already, her fingers brushing the zipper before pulling back. How could she explain something she hardly understood herself?

"It's weird," Zoe said, her voice just above a whisper. "I feel like I've known about Swirly forever, even though we just found it. Like it's been waiting for me, calling me."

As if on cue, the orb's energy surged, sending a shiver down her spine. Zoe straightened, trying to appear normal as a group of freshmen walked past their spot.

"That's... intense," Carmel said carefully, studying her friend's face. In eight years of friendship, she'd seen Zoe passionate about countless things—astronomy projects, mystery novels, even their failed attempt at starting a school band. But this was different. There was an almost fevered light in Zoe's eyes that made Carmel uneasy.

The bell's harsh ring cut through their conversation, sending students scrambling for backpacks and half-eaten lunches. Zoe gathered her things carefully, conscious of the precious cargo in her bag.

"Just... be careful, okay?" Carmel stood, brushing grass from her jeans. "Whatever this is, whatever you're feeling—don't lose yourself in it completely. Remember who you are."

"I know what I'm doing," Zoe assured her, but the words felt hollow. The orb's presence hummed stronger now, like a song just beyond hearing range, beautiful and dangerous all at once.

Carmel shouldered her own backpack, her expression softening. "That's exactly what worries me," she said. "Just remember I'm here, whatever happens with your mysterious Swirly. You don't have to face it alone."

"Thanks, bestie," Zoe said, grateful for Carmel's unwavering support, even when she couldn't fully understand. As they joined the stream of students heading inside, Zoe felt the orb's energy pulse again, stronger this time. It was a reminder that while she might not be alone, she was definitely different—and that difference was growing stronger by the day.

Zoe meandered home from school along her usual route through Los Jilgueros Preserve, the orb a reassuring weight in her backpack. The late afternoon sun filtered through the towering pepper and pecan trees. She'd walked this path hundreds of times before, but today it felt different somehow.

Unable to resist, she pulled Swirly from her bag. As she walked, she tossed it gently between her hands, mesmerized by the way sunlight danced across its surface. Each time it touched her palm, a subtle vibration hummed through her fingers, as if the orb were trying to communicate.

The air suddenly thickened, shimmering like heat waves rising from summer asphalt. Colors blurred and reformed around her, and for a brief, dizzying moment, Zoe felt as if she were walking through thick syrup. The familiar sounds of cars passing on nearby Mission Road faded, replaced by a deeper silence broken only by birdsong and the rustle of leaves.

When her vision cleared, Zoe froze. The preserve's wildflower meadow and walking trails had vanished. Instead, neat rows of old avocado trees stretched toward the horizon, their glossy leaves catching the sunlight. A well-worn 1955 Chevy pickup truck sat parked near a tool shed, and somewhere in the distance, a radio played Elvis Presley's "It's Now or Never."

"This can't be real," Zoe said, clutching the orb tighter. Her heart raced as she tried to make sense of her surroundings.

Movement caught her eye. An older man worked among the trees, pruning branches with practiced efficiency. He wore canvas work pants held up by suspenders, and a faded cotton shirt with the sleeves rolled to his elbows. A red bandana stuck out of his back pocket, and a weathered Stetson hat shaded his face from the California sun.

He looked up as she approached, his expression curious but friendly. "Hey there," he said, wiping his hands on his pants. "I'm Donny. You seem a bit lost." His eyes flickered briefly to her modern clothing—her jeans and graphic t-shirt must have seemed as strange to him as his attire did to her.

"I think I am," Zoe managed, trying to keep her voice steady. "This... this was supposed to be the preserve. With wildflowers and walking trails."

Donny chuckled, leaning against a nearby tree. "Preserve? No, miss, this is Anthony Ranch. Been in my family since my father Arthur started it in 1922. You must be thinking of somewhere else." He gestured proudly at the orderly rows of trees. "We've got the finest avocado orchard in Fallbrook, thanks to my father's innovation."

Curiosity temporarily overcame her disorientation. "Innovation?"

"The earthen dams," Donny said, enthusiasm lighting up his face. "My father used a Fresno Scraper and horse team to build them. Created a whole series of check dams, one below the other. Stores about a hundred-acre feet of water now. Helps recharge our wells, especially during the dry spells." He pointed toward the northern edge of the property. "The agriculture department at UC Davis sends students here sometimes to study his methods. Even in 1960, these dams are considered groundbreaking.

1960? Zoe listened in shock, remembering mentions of Anthony Ranch in her father's stories about Fallbrook's history.

Looking at Donny with admiration, Zoe said, "That's incredible. You must be proud of what your father built here."

"That I am," Donny smiled. "Say, you're really not from around here, are you? Town's that way if you're looking to get back to the main road." He pointed northwest. "Just follow the dirt track past the loading shed."

"Thank you," Zoe said, already feeling the air beginning to shimmer again. "This place... it's special. More than you know."

As she hurried toward the direction he'd indicated, the world blurred once more. The feeling of moving through syrup returned, and when it cleared, she was back on the preserve's familiar trail. The late afternoon sun hadn't moved—as if no time had passed at all.

Zoe pulled the orb from her pocket, staring at it with newfound wonder and trepidation. "What are you?" she said. The orb pulsed warmly in response, its swirling colors seeming to dance beneath its surface.

She needed to research Anthony Ranch, to understand what had just happened. Did she really just visit 1960?

As she walked home, Zoe's mind raced with possibilities. One thing was certain: her connection to the orb was growing stronger, and this was only the beginning of what it had to show her.

The soft glow of Zoe's laptop cast an eerie light across her bedroom walls, illuminating the collage of printed articles about Fallbrook's mysterious past. Her fingers hovered over the keyboard, trembling slightly as each new search brought her closer to answers she both craved and feared. Swirly sat beside her keyboard, its iridescent surface catching the screen's light and throwing prismatic patterns across her scattered notes, the pulses seeming to intensify with her growing excitement.

"Okay, Los Jilgueros Preserve," she said, her mouth dry with anticipation. The light from her screen reflected in her eyes as she typed, each keystroke deliberate and careful. "Show me your secrets."

A black-and-white photograph caught her eye—a distinguished-looking man standing proudly beside a half-constructed reservoir. The caption read: "Arthur Anthony oversees final stages of reservoir construction, 1931." Her heart skipped a beat as the connection formed.

"Arthur Anthony?" Zoe leaned closer, her chair creaking beneath her. Another click revealed a family portrait: Arthur, his wife, and a young man labeled as Donald Anthony. "Donny," she whispered, her fingers brushing the screen as if she could reach through time to touch the familiar face of the man she'd met in what she now knew was the past.

Swirly pulsed against her palm as she grabbed her notebook, its glow intensifying as if responding to her discovery. "If Donny was just a young man in the 40s, then Swirly must have..." Her voice trailed off as she glanced at the orb, its inner mechanism swirling with deeper blues and purples than she'd ever seen before.

Time seemed to blur as she dove deeper into her research. Each new search revealed stranger and stranger results: forums discussing vanishing hikers, conspiracy theories about government cover-ups, and dubious accounts of time slips across the country. Most led nowhere, debunked by skeptical investigators or dismissed as hoaxes—just like Logan had dismissed her theories at breakfast last week, his mind refusing to consider the impossible.

Exhausted, Zoe said, "This is useless," Swirly hummed softly, almost encouragingly, and she found herself drawn back to the screen. Then she saw it—a pattern in the articles. Repeated mentions of military involvement, all centered around one location.

Her breath caught in her throat. "Camp Pendleton," she said, remembering how close the base was. Her hands trembled as she clicked through to a heavily redacted document, its header reading "Operation Chrono: Phase One Testing."

The timestamp made her stomach lurch: 1973. Words jumped out from the black-marked page like accusations: "temporal displacement," "unexplained phenomena," "test subjects." Each phrase sent a new chill down her spine.

The next page made her blood run cold. "During Trial Seven, subjects A through G experienced complete molecular dissolution. Recovery attempts unsuccessful. Current whereabouts unknown."

"They disappeared," Zoe said, her voice barely audible in the suddenly too-quiet room. She glanced nervously at Swirly, remembering how it felt when she'd first held it—that strange pulling sensation, like being tugged by an invisible thread through time. What if the military was still looking for it? What if they somehow tracked it to the vineyard?

Her racing thoughts scattered as a new link appeared: "Operation Chrono - Classification Level: Ultra Secret." The familiar term made her pulse quicken, and Swirly seemed to respond, its surface rippling with intense bursts of color. Zoe clicked through, her breath catching as a grainy image loaded—a spherical object, photographed in what looked like a military lab, its familiar shape making her stomach drop.

"Oh my," she said, unconsciously pulling Swirly closer. "Mom needs to see this." But she stopped short, remembering the strange glitches in her mom's Pokémon Go app, how the virtual creatures seemed to react whenever Swirly was nearby. What if it wasn't just coincidence? What if Swirly was affecting more than just her perception of time?

A soft knock at her door made her jump so hard she nearly knocked over her water bottle. "ZoeJoe?" Cathy's voice carried that mix of concern and curiosity that always meant she'd noticed something was off. "Everything okay in there? You've been awful quiet."

"Yeah, Mom!" Zoe quickly minimized her browser windows. "Just doing some research for... uh, a history project." The lie tasted bitter in her mouth—she'd never been good at keeping secrets from her mother.

"Well, dinner's ready." A pause. "And Logan's home—he's asking about the orb your dad found."

Zoe glanced at Swirly, its surface now swimming with lighter blues and sapphires, almost as if it was responding to her anxiety. The warmth from its surface spread through her trembling hands, oddly comforting despite everything she'd just learned.

"Be right there!" She carefully slipped the orb into her pocket, where it settled against her leg.

"Just need to save some stuff," Zoe called out, her fingers racing across the keyboard with renewed urgency. Logan's familiar heavy footsteps echoed in the hallway—the distinct sound of her brother returning from another long day of college classes, probably loaded down with his laptop and engineering textbooks. If anyone would question her research, it would be him with his relentlessly logical mind.

Her cursor hovered over the document title for a moment before she renamed it from "Fallbrook Weird Stuff" to "Pokémon Research"—mundane enough that even Logan's curiosity wouldn't be piqued if he borrowed her laptop. She could almost hear his voice: "Time travel? Really, Butt Nugget? There's got to be a scientific explanation."

Swirly pulsed as she typed her last notes, each bullet point feeling more significant than the last:

Donald Anthony = Donny (1960s) - CONFIRMED TEMPORAL SHIFT?

Camp Pendleton: Operation Chrono - MILITARY INVOLVEMENT

People vanishing - MOLECULAR DISSOLUTION??

ChronoSphere = Swirly - ACTIVE PROJECT??

"Zoe!" Cathy's voice carried a hint of impatience now. "Your father's waiting, and you know how he gets about family dinner!"

"Coming!" Zoe's hand trembled slightly as she closed her laptop. The impact of her discoveries pressed down on her shoulders like a physical burden. Her mom was already tracking anomalies through Pokémon Go, even if she didn't realize it. And Dad... was the most grounded person she knew. How could she tell him that his simple vineyard discovery might be connected to classified military experiments?

She paused at her bedroom door, her finger hovering over the light switch. The wall of articles seemed to watch her accusingly, each one a piece of a puzzle she was only beginning to understand. Her eyes caught on a yellowed newspaper clipping: "Strange Lights Reported Near Camp Pendleton, 1973." The same year as Operation Chrono. Not a coincidence—she was sure of it now.

"Yo, Butt Nugget!" Logan's voice boomed from downstairs, cutting through her thoughts. "The garlic bread's getting cold, and I'm not saving you any!"

Zoe switched off the light, but her mind blazed with possibilities and fears. Whatever Swirly truly was—whatever Operation Chrono had been attempting to achieve—she knew one thing with absolute certainty: her family needed to know. But how could she explain it without sounding completely unhinged? How could she convince Logan of what she'd seen? How could she convince her father that his vineyard might be at the center of something much bigger and potentially dangerous?

As she descended the stairs, Swirly hummed against her leg with an almost sentient rhythm, like it was trying to communicate. Was it encouragement? A warning? The smell of pasta sauce and garlic grew stronger with each step, mixing with the familiar sounds of her family's dinner routine: Dad's terrible puns, Mom's Pokémon Go notifications chiming softly, Logan's animated voice describing his latest engineering project.

Normal life. Regular family dinner. Except nothing felt normal anymore. Not with a piece of classified military history sitting in her pocket, and the weight of impossible knowledge pressing against her mind.

"There you are!" Joe's warm smile greeted her as she entered the kitchen. His eyes crinkled at the corners as he grinned. "We were starting to think you'd jumped to another time just to avoid kitchen duty."

Zoe nearly choked on her own breath, her hand pressing against the pocket where Swirly rested. If only he knew how close to the truth he was. The orb pulsed once, strongly, against her leg—and somewhere in the living room, her mom's phone chirped with another Pokémon Go notification.

She really needs to tell them, but where would she even begin?

Logan sprawled across his bed, surrounded by an avalanche of books and notes, the weight of his discoveries pressing down on him like the volumes scattered around him. A small desk lamp provided a warm glow over his space, illuminating his laptop and the spread of papers littered with sketches and hastily scribbled notes. The familiar scent of old books mingled with the metallic tang of his energy drink cans as he transformed his room into a makeshift research library.

His fingers traced the intricate hieroglyphs he'd been researching. The designs twisted and turned like ancient serpents, matching the odd symbols that had captured his attention. Something about the hieroglyphs spoke to him on a deeper level.

"This is ridiculous," he said, typing another search query: "Ancient artifacts and temporal displacement." The screen flickered with results, each more fantastic than the last. His eyes caught on a passage about the Luiseño peoples and their connections to celestial events. Another tab showed theoretical physics papers about time dilation and quantum entanglement.

Logan ran his hands through his disheveled hair, frustration evident in every movement. "There has to be a logical explanation," he said to himself, but the evidence before him suggested otherwise. His notebook filled with phrases that challenged his worldview: "quantum tunneling," "temporal anomalies," "chosen vessels."

Zoe's laughter from downstairs pulled him out of his research spiral. His sister's voice carried an additional weight now, knowing what he'd discovered. The thought of her facing these mysteries alone made his chest tighten. Despite his skepticism, he couldn't ignore the protective instinct that had guided their relationship since childhood.

With determined resolve, Logan began organizing his notes. Whatever this phenomenon was—scientific anomaly or something more mystical—he would face it alongside his sister. Together, they would unravel the truth behind the orb, the hieroglyphs, and the strange events transforming their lives.

As he closed his laptop, Logan caught his reflection in the darkened screen. The face looking back at him seemed different somehow—older, more serious. He realized some questions might never have satisfactory answers, and for the first time in his life, he was beginning to accept that possibility.

# CHAPTER 5

# HIDDEN DISCOVERY

The sun's last rays painted the vineyard in amber hues as Zoe slipped away from the dinner table, her heart racing with anticipation. Cradling the orb—which she'd taken to calling Swirly, though 'ChronoSphere' kept echoing in her mind—she headed to the ancient oak tree that had stood sentinel over their property for generations. Its gnarled branches reached toward the darkening sky like protective arms, creating a natural sanctuary for her exploration.

The well-worn bench beneath the oak welcomed her like an old friend. Settling onto its worn surface, Zoe held Swirly up to catch the last fragments of daylight. The orb's surface shimmered with an inner life, reminding her of the strange visions she'd experienced at Los Jilgueros Preserve. Her encounter with Donny and those mysterious avocado trees from another time still felt surreal, yet somehow connected to the object in her hands.

"What are you trying to say?" she said to the orb, her fingers tracing patterns across its smooth surface. Something deep within her consciousness seemed to stir. Following an instinct she couldn't explain, she pressed her thumb against a slightly visible seam in the orb's surface.

*Click.*

A hidden panel slid open with the precision of fine machinery, releasing a cascade of holographic light that took her breath away. Ethereal blue projections danced before her eyes—intricate symbols hovering in the air like fragments of a forgotten language. Some resembled the ancient petroglyphs she'd seen in her history books, while others appeared almost mechanical, pulsing with an inner rhythm that matched her heartbeat.

One symbol caught her attention: a spiral pattern that looked familiar to her. As she reached out to touch it, the projection responded, expanding into a three-dimensional map of what appeared to be Fallbrook—but not the Fallbrook she knew. This version showed structures and landmarks that seemed to span different time periods, all layered upon each other like transparent sheets.

"Zoe?" Logan's voice cut through her wonder. She turned to find him approaching, an EMF meter clutched in his hands—typical Logan, always trying to find a logical explanation. Behind him, their parents exchanged worried glances, but their expressions shifted to amazement as they caught sight of the holographic display.

"Is that... coming from the orb?" Cathy asked, reaching for her phone before stopping herself. Pokémon Go glowed on her screen, showing unusual activity in the area.

Joe stepped forward, his hands reaching tentatively toward the light show. "This has to be connected to that stone we found," he said with concern. "The one with the strange markings."

"The readings are off the charts," Logan said, waving his EMF meter around the area. "Whatever this is, it's generating some serious electromagnetic activity." Despite his usual doubts, there was a note of excitement in his voice.

Anxious, Cathy said, "Show them," her eyes darting between the orb and her phone's screen, where Pokémon were behaving erratically.

Together, they walked to the stone structure partially hidden by vineyard growth. The ancient carvings seemed to respond to their presence, taking on an almost metallic sheen in the fading light. At its center, a circular indentation caught the last rays of sunset.

"These markings..." Logan crouched down, brushing aside a tendril of vine with uncharacteristic gentleness. "They're not like anything I've seen in any archaeological database." His fingers traced the edge of a symbol that seemed to shift under his touch, taking on a metallic sheen in the dying light.

Zoe stood transfixed, her hand unconsciously reaching for the pocket where she kept Swirly. The markings look similar to the ones she had just seen. "It's like they're... waiting for something."

Logan glanced up sharply. "Don't start with that intuition stuff again, Zoe. We need facts, data, something I can actually analyze." But even as he spoke, his tablet screen flickered, its display distorting near the stone.

"Your precious tech seems to disagree," Zoe said, stepping closer to the structure's center. There, perfectly carved into the stone, sat a circular indentation that made her pocket feel suddenly heavy. "Logan, look at this."

He moved beside her, their shoulders touching as they both stared at the depression. Logan's disbelief was written all over his face as the marking around the indentation started to emit a faint glow.

"The size..." Joe said, looking between the orb and the indentation. "It's a perfect match."

Zoe's heart thundered in her chest. "Should we try it?"

After a moment's hesitation, Joe nodded. With careful movements, he took the orb and aligned it with the indentation. As it settled into place, a brilliant flash of light erupted from the connection point, briefly illuminating the vineyard in a supernatural glow.

The orb's light pulsed once, twice, then dimmed to a soft shimmer before fading entirely. An anticlimactic silence fell over the family.

"The EMF readings just spiked," Logan announced, frowning at his equipment. "But now they're... different. Like they're stabilizing into a new pattern."

"Look at this," Cathy said, showing them her phone screen. Pokémon Go displayed a swirling vortex of glitches centered exactly where they stood.

Zoe felt it—a subtle shift in the air, a sense of potential energy waiting to be unleashed. The connection she'd felt with the orb had intensified during those brief moments of activation.

"Maybe it needs time," she said, retrieving Swirly from the indentation. "Or maybe we're missing something." The holographic interface had vanished.

As darkness settled over the vineyard, they made their way back to the house, each lost in their own thoughts. Zoe clutched the orb close, her mind racing with possibilities. Whatever secrets Swirly held, whatever connection it had to the stone and the strange events at Los Jilgueros Preserve, she was determined to understand it all.

Behind them, unseen in the growing darkness, the ancient stone seemed to pulse once more, a brief flicker of energy that whispered of mysteries yet to be unveiled.

The morning sun shined on Main Avenue as Zoe clutched Swirly through her jacket pocket, her heart racing with possibility. She'd been planning this experiment since yesterday's revelation at Los Jilgueros Preserve, and now, standing before Ace Hardware, she couldn't quiet the trembling in her hands.

"Thirty years ago," she whispered. "Just show me thirty years ago." Swirly pulsed against her hip, like a gentle heartbeat responding to her plea.

Frustration crept in as she watched the automatic doors whoosh open and closed, spilling out weekend warriors with their DIY supplies. This wasn't working. Zoe pulled Swirly from her pocket, careful to shield it from curious eyes. The orb's surface shined with its characteristic blues and purples, but the hidden panel she'd discovered days ago remained stubbornly closed.

"Come on," she said, her thumb searching for the elusive edge. "You showed me the preserve. Why not this?" A passing couple's sideways glance forced her to tuck the orb away quickly, her cheeks burning.

Dad's stories about Hank's Hardware flooded back—tales of his first job, of the old-timer who'd taught him everything about tools and customer service.

The memory stirred something deep within her. Swirly's warmth intensified, spreading from her pocket through her entire body. Zoe closed her eyes, focusing on the connection she felt growing between them. She thought of Logan's teasing grin, Mom's late-night Pokémon hunts, Dad's hands teaching her about the vineyard—all the threads that wove her family together.

When she opened her eyes, the world rippled like disturbed water. The modern Ace Hardware sign flickered and dissolved, replaced by a hand-painted wooden board reading "Hank's Hardware". Through the windows, she glimpsed wooden floors worn smooth by decades of footsteps, brass bin labels gleaming in the morning light, and the unmistakable silhouette of a much younger version of her father learning the trade that would shape his future.

The vision lasted mere seconds before reality snapped back into focus, but it left Zoe breathless. She steadied herself against a lamppost, her mind reeling from the implications. This wasn't just some parlor trick—Swirly had actually shown her a slice of Fallbrook's past, a moment she'd only known through stories.

A fresh wave of anxiety mixed with her excitement. What if someone had noticed? What if the orb's power drew unwanted attention? The mighty oak tree at home called to her like a sanctuary, its ancient branches promising safety and wisdom.

As Zoe hurried toward home, Swirly's warmth spread through her with newfound purpose. Each step brought clarity—the orb wasn't just showing her random moments in time. It was revealing connections, the invisible threads that bound her family to this place, to each other, to time itself.

The oak tree's familiar silhouette appeared ahead, its leaves dancing in the late morning breeze. Mom always said the tree had special energy, that it was why Pokémon Go acted the strangest there. Now Zoe understood—some places held more than memories. They held doorways to the past, and somehow, she'd been chosen to see through them.

Under those sheltering branches, Zoe would begin to unravel the mystery of her connection to Swirly. But first, she needed to catch her breath and process what she'd just experienced. After all, it's not every day you discover you can peek through time's curtain—even if only for a moment.

Zoe settled onto the bench beneath the mighty oak tree, her body heavy with exhaustion from recent events. The familiar grooves of the wooden seat welcomed her as she closed her eyes, drawing in a deep breath. The soft grass tickled her ankles, while the sweet scent of ripening grapes through the vineyard, mingled with the earthy aroma of recent irrigation.

Swirly rested in her palm, its warmth syncing with her heartbeat. The orb's surface danced with shifting colors—deep purples melting into midnight blues, then bursting into brilliant gold, each transition sending tiny vibrations through her fingers. Focusing her energy, Zoe tried to tap into the strange artifact's pulse. The response was immediate and overwhelming.

The vineyard transformed around her. Leaves rustled without wind, birds fell silent mid-song, and the land itself seemed to hum with an otherworldly energy. It was as if every grape vine, every blade of grass recognized Swirly's presence and held its breath in anticipation.

"Okay," Zoe said, her heart hammering against her ribs. "Let's try this again."

With trembling fingers, she located the secret panel on the orb's surface. It slid open with surprising ease, and brilliant light erupted from within. Instead of the expected holographic interface, a projection burst forth—crystal clear images of Ace Hardware, exactly as she'd seen it earlier that day. Customers milled about, employees restocked shelves, all frozen in a perfect moment of time.

The progression continued relentlessly, each transition accompanied by a subtle pulse from Swirly that seemed to match Zoe's quickening heartbeat. Joe's Hardware materialized, its familiar sign weathered but proud. Then came Hank's Hardware, the storefront growing increasingly vintage with each transition.

"What are you showing me?" Zoe asked, transfixed as Good Guys Home Center appeared, its dated architecture a window into the past. Mayfair Supermarket emerged, its once-bright colors fading like watercolors in rain. The Buy and Save grocery store followed, its hand-painted signage speaking of simpler times. Finally, the projection settled on an empty lot—pristine earth waiting for the future to unfold.

Zoe leaned back against the oak's rough bark, her mind whirling with possibilities. Was Swirly responding to her recent trip to Ace Hardware? Or was it revealing something deeper, something woven into the very fabric of time itself? The weight of these questions pressed against her chest, making it hard to breathe.

The orb vibrated in her hand, its colors now subdued to gentle pastels. Around her, the vineyard's natural rhythm gradually resumed—birds tentatively returned to their songs, leaves danced in the breeze. But Zoe remained still, overwhelmed by the weight of what she'd witnessed and the countless questions it raised.

"Mom and Dad will never believe this," she said, running her thumb across Swirly's smooth surface. "They hardly believe in the power of prayer, let alone time travel."

Gravel crunched under approaching footsteps, startling Zoe from her contemplation. She looked up to see Logan practically jogging down the path, his laptop clutched tight against his chest, wearing that familiar intense expression she'd seen countless times before—the one that meant he'd disappeared down some rabbit hole and emerged with treasure.

"Zoe!" Logan called out, his voice carrying a mix of excitement and disbelief. "You're not going to believe what I found."

Zoe shifted on the bench, carefully tucking Swirly into her pocket. "What happened to 'this is all nonsense?'" she teased.

Logan dropped onto the bench beside her, balancing his laptop on his knees. "Yeah, well, that was before I spent six hours diving into some seriously weird archaeological forums." He opened his computer, revealing dozens of browser tabs. "The Ancient Artifacts Network, TimeWatch Archives, even some classified documents I probably shouldn't have access to. Remember the stone formation mom and dad found? There are similar stones documented across different continents, all with nearly identical markings. And every single one has legends about a 'Chosen One' associated with them."

Zoe's hand pressed against her pocket, feeling Swirly's responsive warmth. "What kind of legends?"

"According to these sources, the stones were meant to be anchor points." Logan turned the screen toward her, showing ancient drawings of figures holding orb-like objects. "They believed certain individuals could use special artifacts, which look suspiciously like your little friend there—to navigate through time. The Mayans called them 'portals of the gods,' while ancient Persian texts referred to them as 'windows between worlds.'"

Leaning in closer to examine the drawings, Zoe said, "Through time?" The figures in the ancient artwork held orbs that could have been Swirly's twins. "Logan, I have to tell you something. Just now, Swirly showed me—"

"Hold that thought," Logan said. "First, look at this inscription they found in Peru." He pointed to a series of intricate symbols that looked remarkably similar to the markings on their stone. "It talks about a 'vessel of time' that would 'answer only to the one whose heart beats in rhythm with the eternal pulse.' The same pattern appears in excavation sites across South America, Asia, and even parts of Europe."

Zoe pulled Swirly from her pocket, watching its colors swirl and pulse in response to her touch. The orb seemed to glow brighter as she held it up to compare with the images on Logan's screen. "You think that's me? The Chosen One?"

"I don't know, but I think we need to test it," Logan said, his voice dropping to a conspiratorial whisper. The afternoon sun highlighted the same determined expression he wore during his most ambitious science projects.

"Test it how?" Zoe asked, eyeing her brother suspiciously. The last time Logan had suggested testing something, it had involved their dad's drone and ended with a furious neighbor, a broken window, and a grounding that lasted three weeks.

Logan closed his laptop with a decisive click and set it aside. "The stone formation has that circular indentation, right? And based on these accounts, it's meant to be some kind of activation point." He leaned forward, his eyes darting around the vineyard despite their isolation. "What if we take Swirly back there and try to..."

"Dad already tried placing Swirly in the center," Zoe interrupted, absently rolling the orb between her palms. "If you recall, nothing happened. But listen, I need to tell you about what just happened with Swirly." She described the progression of images she'd witnessed, the way time had seemed to peel back layer by layer through the history of the hardware store.

Logan's skeptical expression softened into genuine fascination, his mind visibly processing this new information. "Wait, so it showed you actual historical changes? That's... that's incredible." He pulled out his phone and started taking notes. "And this happened right after you opened the panel? What were you thinking about when it started?"

"I was just thinking about my experience at Ace Hardware today, but it wasn't like before. Instead of the interface, it was like watching a movie in reverse." Zoe held up Swirly, its surface now pulsing with a gentle golden light that seemed to reach out toward Logan. "I think it's trying to tell us something."

"Or show us something," Logan said, his eyes reflecting the orb's glow. "Listen, the stone formation we found—It's a perfect circle, right? And if you look at it directly from above, we see a pattern similar to what's inside the orb. The ancient texts refer to it as a 'temporal compass.'"

Zoe leaned forward, intrigued despite her reservations. "So, you think there's a connection?"

"I think it's worth investigating." Logan stood up, brushing off his jeans with one hand while gesturing excitedly with the other. "The forums mentioned something about 'temporal resonance' between the stones and the artifacts. If we position Swirly in the center of the formation, or should I say, if YOU position it in the center..."

"We might trigger something, because it's me putting it in place," Zoe finished, already getting to her feet. The possibility sent equal waves of excitement and apprehension through her. "But what if it's dangerous? Mom and Dad would freak if they knew we were experimenting with this. Remember what happened when they caught you trying to build that Tesla coil in the garage?"

Logan grinned, the same mischievous smile he'd worn during countless childhood adventures. "That's why we're not going to tell them yet. Come on, aren't you curious? This could be huge! And unlike the Tesla coil, I've actually done my research this time."

Zoe hesitated, feeling Swirly's warmth intensify in her hand. The orb's colors swirled faster, almost urgently, as if responding to their conversation. She thought about her parents, about the responsibility of wielding something so powerful. But the pull of discovery was stronger.

"Okay," she finally agreed, squaring her shoulders. "But we need ground rules. If anything feels wrong—"

"We bail immediately," Logan said, already gathering his laptop. "Trust me, I've thought this through. The equipment I borrowed from the lab should help us monitor any unusual energy signatures."

As they headed down the path toward the stone formation, Zoe couldn't shake the feeling that they were about to cross a threshold from which there would be no return. Swirly pulsed in her pocket like a second heartbeat, growing stronger with each step toward the ancient stones that waited silently in the vineyard's shadows. Guardians of secrets they were only beginning to understand.

Zoe stood at the edge of the ancient stone circle, her heart pounding against her ribs. Swirly felt unusually warm in her trembling hands, its surface reflecting the golden light in ways that made the mysterious indentations seem alive with possibility. The familiar scent of grape vines carried on the breeze, grounding her in the present even as she prepared to step into the unknown.

"You sure about this?" Logan asked with an edge of worry. He stood a few feet back, unconsciously shifting his weight from foot to foot as he watched his sister.

Taking a deep breath that tasted of dust and anticipation, Zoe stepped onto the stone. The effect was immediate and overwhelming. Energy coursed through her body, making her skin tingle and her heart race. It was terrifying and exhilarating all at once - like standing on the edge of a cliff, knowing you had to jump but unsure if you'd fly or fall. Swirly's surface erupted in a dance of colors she'd never seen before, swirling and pulsating with an almost desperate intensity that matched her own racing thoughts.

"Logan," she said, her voice trembling as she glanced at her brother. "Something's happening. Something big."

"Be careful," Logan said, his usual sarcasm replaced with genuine concern. He shifted uncomfortably, torn between his instinct to protect his sister and his growing realization that everything he'd dismissed as impossible was happening right before his eyes.

Zoe looked down at the orb, its surface now rippling with deep purples and golds she'd never seen before. "What are you trying to tell me, Swirly? What do you want me to do?" The colors shifted in response, seeming to pull her toward the center of the stone like an invisible tide.

With small deliberate steps, she made her way to the central indentation. The air around her felt thick, charged with possibility, like the moment before a summer storm breaks. Each step sent vibrations through her body, as if the stone itself was humming with ancient power. Kneeling down, she gently placed Swirly into the perfectly sized depression.

Light exploded from the orb, enveloping Zoe in a brilliant cocoon of shifting colors. She felt weightless, connected to something vast and ancient. Energy coursed through her veins like liquid starlight, and for a brief moment, she could sense everything - every blade of grass, every grape on the vine, every heartbeat for miles around. Time itself seemed to flow through her like a river, showing her glimpses of what was, what is, and what could be.

"Zoe!" Logan's panicked voice seemed to come from far away, as if he was calling to her through water. "Maybe we should stop—"

The sudden thunderous roar of rotors cut through the air, shattering the mystical atmosphere. A military helicopter from Camp Pendleton appeared overhead, its dark silhouette a stark contrast against the evening sky. The downdraft whipped through the vineyard, sending leaves swirling around the stone circle as its shadow swept across them like a warning. In an instant, Swirly's light vanished. The colors drained away, leaving the orb looking dull and lifeless.

Zoe collapsed onto the stone, her legs too weak to hold her. "No, no, no," she said, snatching up the now-colorless orb with shaking hands. "Swirly, are you okay? What happened?" The orb appeared dead, but she could still feel its familiar warmth beating in sync with her heartbeat, like a frightened animal playing dead until danger passed. As the helicopter's sound faded into the distance, faint colors began to return to Swirly's surface, like a sunrise after a long night.

"Are you okay?" Logan rushed to her side, helping her sit up. His hands were steady, but his voice shook slightly. "What happened? What did you see?"

"I... I don't know," Zoe said, still trembling. She leaned against her brother, grateful for his solid presence. "It was like being connected to everything at once. Like I could feel time itself flowing through me." She clutched Swirly closer, its surface now shimmering with subdued but steady colors. "But Logan, something's coming. Something big. I could feel it. We need to protect Mom and Dad, protect everyone."

Logan said. "We need to tell them. All of it. No more secrets."

"They're going to be so mad at us for doing this without telling them," Zoe said, slowly getting to her feet. Her legs felt like jelly, and she swayed slightly before finding her balance.

"Maybe," Logan said, steadying her with a gentle hand on her elbow. "But after what I just saw..." He glanced at Swirly, then toward Camp Pendleton, where the helicopter had disappeared. "I don't think we have a choice anymore. That wasn't a coincidence, Zo. They know something."

As they walked back through the vineyard, the familiar rows of grapevines felt different somehow. Zoe couldn't shake the lingering sensation of that brief connection - how she'd felt the life flowing through every plant, sensed the deep history buried in the soil beneath their feet. Whatever Swirly was, whatever it was trying to show her, it was part of something much bigger than their family, or even Fallbrook itself.

"Remember when we were kids," Logan said suddenly, breaking the tense silence, "and you used to tell Mom and Dad there were 'time ripples' in your bedroom?"

Zoe nearly stumbled. "I'd forgotten about that. They thought I was just having nightmares."

"Maybe you weren't." Logan's voice was quiet. "Maybe you've always been connected to... whatever this is."

The orb pulsed in Zoe's hands, as if agreeing. Its colors had deepened now, richer than before the incident, like something had been awakened in its core.

"Hey, Yogi Bear." she said, using the childhood nickname she knew he pretended to hate.

"Yeah?"

"Thanks for believing me. Even when it probably sounds crazy."

Logan wrapped an arm around his sister's shoulders, pulling her close as they walked. "Someone's got to keep you out of trouble, Butt Nugget. Even if that trouble involves magical time orbs and ancient stones." He paused, then said more seriously, "Besides, you're not crazy. Not about this. And whatever's coming... we'll face it together."

They walked in comfortable silence, both lost in thought. As they approached the house, warm light spilling from the kitchen windows promised the comfort of home and family. But now that comfort felt fragile, something precious they needed to protect.

# CHAPTER 6

# FAMILY TIME

Zoe and Logan trudged back to the house in stunned silence, their footsteps heavy on the well-worn path through the vineyard. Swirly pulsed against Zoe's chest like a second heartbeat, its warmth both comforting and unsettling. The late afternoon sun created a slightly surreal atmosphere after what they'd witnessed at the ancient stone artifact.

"Mom's going to connect this to her Pokémon Go theories," Logan said as they reached the porch, his mind still struggling to rationalize what he'd seen.

Zoe managed a weak smile. "Maybe she's been right all along about those glitches." Her fingers traced the smooth surface of Swirly, drawing strength from its familiar presence. The orb had shown her something incredible, terrifying, and wonderful all at once.

At the back door, Zoe hesitated. The familiar squeak of the screen door hinge seemed unnaturally loud in the heavy silence. "What are we going to tell them?" she said, glancing at her brother. "They're going to think we're crazy."

Logan pushed his glasses up his nose, a habit that surfaced whenever he was processing complex problems. "We tell them exactly what happened. No embellishments, no theories. Just facts." He paused. "They deserve to know."

The kitchen enveloped them in warmth and the comforting aroma of garlic and herbs—Mom's famous spaghetti sauce simmering on the stove. The normality of it all felt jarring against the extraordinary events they'd just experienced. Joe stood at the counter chopping vegetables while Cathy stirred the sauce, her phone propped nearby, probably tracking Pokémon spawns.

Both parents looked up as the screen door clattered shut. Cathy's spoon froze mid-stir, her maternal instinct instantly picking up on their distress. "What happened?" She set the spoon down, wiping her hands on her apron. "You both look like you've seen a ghost."

Joe's knife stilled on the cutting board. "Everything okay?" His eyes zeroed in on how tightly Zoe clutched Swirly to her chest.

Zoe and Logan exchanged glances. Swirly's pulse seemed to quicken against Zoe's palm, almost encouraging her. She took a deep breath and stepped forward.

"Mom, Dad... there's something we need to tell you about Swirly—the orb," she began, her voice steadier than she felt. "And about that stone circle Dad found in the vineyard."

"Swirly?" Cathy's eyebrows rose, but she caught herself. "Never mind that now. What about the stone?"

Logan moved closer to his sister, unconsciously protective. "We discovered something... unprecedented," he said, choosing his words carefully. "Something that challenges everything I thought I understood about physics."

Joe set his knife down completely, turning to face them. "Go on."

Zoe's words tumbled out, describing the brilliant light, the strange sensations, the feeling of almost disappearing. As she spoke, Swirly's glow pulsed softly, visible even through her fingers, as if confirming her story.

Cathy's hand found Joe's arm, gripping it tightly. "Just like the anomalies in my game," she said. "The way the Pokémon act when..."

"When Zoe's nearby," Joe finished, his face grave. He ran a hand through his hair, a gesture Logan had inherited. "This is bigger than we thought, isn't it?"

Zoe nodded, relieved they weren't dismissing her story outright. "I think Swirly's trying to tell us something important. Something about protecting our family." She loosened her grip slightly, letting them see the orb's gentle glow. "I think we need to figure out what that is."

"Together," Logan said. "As a family."

Joe and Cathy shared a long look, years of partnership allowing them to communicate silently. Finally, Joe nodded.

"Alright," he said, his voice gruff with emotion. "But we do this smart. No more solo experiments. We keep records of everything. And at the first sign of real danger..." He let the sentence hang.

"We'll be careful," Zoe said, feeling Swirly's warmth surge in agreement.

The orb's glow brightened momentarily, ethereal light across their faces, uniting them in its otherworldly radiance. Cathy reached for her phone, but stopped herself, choosing instead to fully experience the moment.

"First things first," Joe said. "We need to secure that stone circle. If what you're saying is true, we can't risk anyone else stumbling onto it." He glanced at his half-chopped vegetables, domestic concerns suddenly seeming trivial.

Logan cleared his throat. "I've been thinking about that, Dad. The bunker you've been working on—if we could somehow move the stone there..."

"The bunker?" Cathy said, her eyes widening. She turned to her husband, a knowing look crossing her face. "Maybe my 'paranoia' wasn't so unfounded after all."

Zoe watched the exchange, still cradling Swirly. The orb's pulsating had settled into a steady rhythm that matched her heartbeat. "The bunker would be perfect," she said. "It's hidden, secure, and..." She hesitated, feeling a sudden certainty that she couldn't explain. "I think that's where Swirly wants to be."

"You can feel what it wants now?" Logan asked.

"Not exactly." Zoe struggled to find the right words. "It's more like... suggestions. Feelings. Like when you know something's right but can't explain why."

Joe ran his fingers through his hair again, leaving it standing slightly on end. "Moving that stone won't be easy. It's massive, and we'll need to be discrete. The last thing we need is neighbors asking questions."

"Or the military getting curious," Logan said, his face darkening. "That helicopter earlier... the timing seemed too convenient."

Cathy moved to the stove, turning down the heat under the now-bubbling sauce. "You think they know something about this?" The worry in her voice was evident.

"I don't know," Logan admitted. "But my research has turned up some interesting connections between Camp Pendleton and various classified projects. Nothing concrete, but..." He trailed off, looking uncomfortable.

Zoe felt Swirly pulse more intensely at the mention of the military. "We need to be careful," she said, her voice firm. "Really careful. I think... I think there's more at stake here than just our family."

The kitchen fell silent except for the gentle bubbling of the sauce and the soft hum of the refrigerator. Each family member was lost in their own thoughts, processing the magnitude of what they were facing.

Finally, Joe straightened his shoulders, decision made. "Alright, here's what we're going to do. Tonight, we eat dinner and try to act normal. Tomorrow, Logan and I will work on a plan to move the stone. Cathy, keep documenting any unusual activity on your Pokémon Go—it might be more relevant than we thought. And Zoe..." He paused, looking at his daughter with a mixture of concern and pride. "Keep working with Swirly. But be careful. No more experiments without at least one of us present."

"What about Carmel?" Zoe asked, thinking of her best friend. "She already knows something's going on with me."

"For now, the fewer people who know, the better," Cathy said. "Even Carmel. We need to understand what we're dealing with first."

Logan nodded in agreement. "The more people who know, the greater the risk of exposure. We need to protect this secret—and each other."

As if in response to Logan's words, Swirly's glow dimmed slightly, settling into a slight shimmer. Zoe could still feel its warmth, its steady pulse a constant reminder of the responsibility they all now shared. She glanced around at her family—Dad's worried frown as he returned to chopping vegetables with practice precision, Mom's distracted stirring of the sauce while sneaking glances at her phone, and Logan's furrowed brow as he likely ran calculations in his head.

"I should get my laptop," Logan said. "Start mapping out the logistics for moving that stone. We'll need to consider weight distribution, angles, equipment..." He trailed off, already heading for the stairs.

"After dinner," Joe called after him firmly. "Right now, we eat as a family. Try to maintain some normalcy."

Cathy let out a small laugh that bordered on hysteria. "Normalcy? Joe, our daughter just told us she almost disappeared into thin air, and that orb—" She gestured at Swirly "—is literally glowing in our kitchen. I think normalcy left the building a while ago."

"All the more reason to hold on to what we can," Joe said, reaching out to squeeze her hand. "We're still us. Still family. That hasn't changed."

Zoe watched her parents' interaction, feeling a surge of gratitude for how they were handling this. She'd half-expected them to confiscate Swirly or forbid her from going near the stone again. Instead, they were adapting, accepting, trying to understand.

"Mom," she said, "remember all those times you said Pokémon Go acted weird around me? Could you tell me more about that?"

Cathy's eyes lit up. "Well, it started about three months ago. Pokémon would spawn in impossible numbers whenever you walked past, and sometimes they'd glitch into these strange forms I'd never seen before. At first, I thought it was just server issues, but..." She paused, glancing at Swirly. "It only happened around you."

Logan, who had paused on the stairs, turned back. "Three months ago? Isn't that when Dad first noticed..."

"And when I started having those weird dreams," Zoe said, pieces starting to fall into place. Swirly pulsed in her hands, as if encouraging these connections.

Joe set down his knife again. "I think we need to start a timeline. Keep track of everything strange that's happened, no matter how small it seemed at the time. Logan, get your laptop now. Dinner can wait."

"Already on it," Logan called, thundering up the stairs.

Cathy moved to the kitchen table, clearing away the mail and random papers. "I've got screenshots of all the Pokémon Go glitches. I knew they'd be important somehow."

Zoe sat down at the table, carefully placing Swirly in front of her. The orb's glow seemed to brighten slightly. "I should write down my dreams too. They're getting clearer now," Zoe continued, watching the patterns Swirly cast on the table. "Like they're not just dreams anymore, but memories. Or maybe... warnings."

Logan returned with his laptop, setting it on the table. "I'm creating a shared document. We can all contribute to it, but it'll be encrypted and stored locally. No cloud storage." He glanced meaningfully at his father. "Just in case."

Joe nodded approvingly at his son's caution. "Good thinking. Cathy, those screen-shots—"

"Already transferring them to a secure folder," she said. "I've been marking locations too, mapping where the strongest anomalies appear." She paused, looking up. "They form a pattern, centered on our vineyard."

Swirly pulsed brighter for a moment, drawing everyone's attention. Zoe placed her hand on the orb, feeling its familiar warmth. "It's like... it's confirming what Mom's saying." She closed her eyes, concentrating on the sensation. "There's something about the land itself. Something important."

"The stone circle," Logan said, typing rapidly. "It can't be a coincidence that it was buried here, on our property." He looked up at his father. "Dad, what do you know about the history of this land? Before your generation?"

Joe straightened in his chair, his face etched with concern. "I should have paid more attention to those stories. Dad tried to tell me so many times, but I just..." He shook his head. "I was too focused on modernizing the vineyard, making it profitable. I thought all that history was just... ghost stories."

"It wasn't your fault, Joe," Cathy said. "None of us could have known." She glanced at her phone, still displaying the strange patterns of Pokémon spawns. "Though maybe we should have noticed the signs sooner. The way this land has always felt different."

Logan was already pulling up more documents on his laptop. "Look at this - there's a pattern of unusual incidents reported around our property dating back to the 1950s. The military's interest peaked during something called 'Operation Chrono' but then everything just... stops. Like the records were wiped clean."

"Operation Chrono?" Zoe repeated, feeling Swirly pulse stronger at the words. The orb's surface swirled with deeper colors, almost as if responding to the name. "I read about that earlier. That's when seven people went missing."

"That's about it," Logan frowned, scrolling through his documents. "There's not a lot about it. Just something about 'complete molecular dissolution.' Whatever they were testing, it went wrong. Really wrong."

Zoe held Swirly closer, feeling its warmth pulse in time with her racing heart. "The dreams I've been having - I keep seeing seven figures. They're always just out of reach, like shadows at the edge of my vision. What if they're the ones who disappeared?"

"And what if they're trying to tell us something?" Logan said. "Through Swirly, through these temporal anomalies - what if they're trying to prevent something from happening again?"

The kitchen fell silent except for the soft bubbling of the forgotten sauce on the stove. Joe stood and walked to the window, looking out over the vineyard that had been in his family for generations.

"The bunker," he said finally, turning back to his family. "We need to focus on moving the stone into the bunker, but it looks to be pretty heavy."

Logan closed his laptop with a decisive click. "We can use the old tractor and that chain winch system from the wine cellar."

"I'll monitor the Pokémon Go frequencies," Cathy said. "They've always spiked before anything... unusual happens. It might give us some warning."

Zoe stood, still cradling Swirly. "And I need to try to understand these dreams better.

"Be careful," Joe warned, moving to put a hand on her shoulder. "Whatever happened with Operation Chrono, it was powerful enough to make the military bury every trace of it. We need to be aware, smart, and prepared."

As the family stood together in the kitchen, united in their concern and determination to unravel the mystery before them, Swirly pulsed against Zoe's chest - a reminder of the strange, possibly dangerous, but undeniably important journey they had all embarked upon.

The soft clinking of dishes filled the kitchen as Cathy carefully placed the last dish in the drying rack. The evening light filtered through the window, providing a golden hue in the kitchen. She wiped her hands on a dishtowel and turned around just in time to see Joe pouring himself a glass of their own vineyard's wine. A weariness lingered in the corners of his eyes, but his offbeat smile always managed to reappear, a constant anchor amidst the whirlwind of recent events.

"Think Zoe's doing okay?" Joe asked, swirling the deep red liquid in his glass. "She seemed pretty wound up after dinner."

"I hope so," Cathy said, watching the last rays of sunlight paint the kitchen walls in amber hues. "Though with that orb..." she trailed off as the phone rang, slicing through the calm of the evening. She exchanged a glance with Joe, who lifted an eyebrow in curiosity, before crossing to the wall phone Joe refused to get rid of.

"Hello, Cathy here," she answered, her voice as steady as she could manage.

"Hey Cathy, it's Becky," came a familiar voice on the other end, tinged with an edge of excitement.

"Hi Becky! What's up?" Cathy said, instantly alert.

Becky's voice softened slightly, mixing urgency with a sense of anticipation. "I've been doing some more digging about that stone you found buried near where you found that orb. You won't believe this, but I managed to get in touch with an archaeologist who specializes in ancient relics—Dr. Jonathan Cleary. He's incredibly fascinated by the stone and is eager to take a closer look."

Cathy's eyes widened as she glanced at Joe, her mind racing. "An archaeologist? Becky, you know how cautious we've been. What do we really know about this guy?"

"I understand, Cathy. But listen, Dr. Cleary is highly reputable. He's published numerous papers and is recognized globally for his work on ancient civilizations and their technologies. I checked his credentials. He's the real deal," Becky said, her voice resolute but understanding of Cathy's hesitation.

Joe, noticing the gravity in Cathy's expression, drew closer, his wine glass suspended in mid-air. "What's going on?" he mouthed.

Cathy held up a finger, asking him to wait. She walked over to the kitchen window and glanced out. "Becky, given everything that's happened—Zoe, the orb. I'm not sure we should involve someone outside the family."

"I get it, Cathy, I do," Becky said. "But think about what this could mean—this stone might hold the key to understanding everything that's happened. Dr. Cleary isn't just any outsider; his expertise could be invaluable. Plus, think about the security. You'll have more protection if someone like him validates what we're dealing with."

A moment of silence stretched between them. Cathy could hear the faint sound of Joe's soft breath beside her.

"We can't ignore this forever," Cathy said finally, her voice soft but firm. "I think... I think we should at least consider it."

"Exactly. I'm not saying we hand over the stone immediately. We can arrange for him to come and observe under controlled circumstances. We'll be careful, Cathy," Becky said, her tone laced with cautious optimism.

Taking a deep breath, Cathy turned back to Joe. "Becky's found an archaeologist—Dr. Jonathan Cleary. He wants to examine the stone. She says he's highly reputable and has experience with relics like ours," she said.

Joe's brow furrowed as he considered the implications. "It's a risk, but it could also provide answers. If he's legitimate..."

Cathy nodded, the weight of his agreement bolstering her decision. "Becky, all right. We'll do it. But we need to be present, and we need to control the situation. I don't want any surprises."

"Of course," Becky said, relief evident in her voice. "I'll arrange everything. It's going to be okay, Cathy. We're in this together."

As Cathy hung up, she felt a mixture of anxiety and hope. The kitchen seemed smaller, the air heavier, knowing that their secrets were on the brink of exposure. She turned to Joe, her eyes reflecting both their trepidation and their resolve.

"What about Zoe?" Joe asked quietly after Cathy hung up. "She's already so connected to all this. Bringing in an outsider..."

"I know," Cathy said, leaning against the counter. "But maybe understanding the stone will help us understand what's happening to her too."

Upstairs, a soft thud. Joe and Cathy shared a knowing look - Zoe was supposed to be asleep, but clearly, she was still experimenting with the orb.

"We should tell her tomorrow," Cathy said, her voice just a whisper. "About Dr. Cleary."

Joe nodded, taking another sip of wine. "Logan too. He might actually be excited about having an expert involved. You know how he's been researching everything he can find about ancient artifacts."

"That's what worries me," Cathy admitted, crossing her arms. "Logan's curiosity combined with Zoe's... connection to all this. What if bringing in an expert makes things more complicated?"

The wall phone suddenly crackled with static, making them both jump. Through the interference, they could hear what sounded like distant voices, speaking in words they couldn't quite make out. Just as quickly as it started, the interference stopped.

Joe set his wine glass down with a decisive clink. "We need answers, Cathy. Whatever's happening here - the orb, the stone, these... occurrences - it's bigger than us. Dr. Cleary might be a risk, but keeping everything secret could be even riskier."

Cathy walked to the window, looking out at their vineyard bathed in moonlight. The ancient stone was out there, slightly visible in the darkness, yet somehow she could feel its presence. Just like she could feel the orb's energy radiating through the ceiling above.

"You're right," she said finally, turning back to Joe. "But we need to be smart about this. Set some ground rules."

The sound of footsteps on the stairs made them both turn. Logan appeared in the doorway, his laptop tucked under his arm, his face illuminated by an unusual mix of moonlight and the purple glow that seemed to follow him down.

"Mom, Dad," he said, his voice carrying an urgency that immediately caught their attention. "I think you need to see this."

He placed his laptop on the kitchen table, the screen displaying what appeared to be an academic paper. The title read: "Temporal Displacement and Ancient Artifacts: A Study of Energy Signatures in Archaeological Finds" by Dr. Jonathan Cleary.

"I've been doing some digging," Logan said, his fingers drumming nervously on the table's edge. "And this Dr. Cleary? He's been researching something very specific. Something that sounds a lot like what's happening here."

Cathy and Joe exchanged glances, their earlier conversation taking on new weight. "How did you know about Dr. Cleary?" Cathy asked, though she already suspected the answer.

"I wasn't eavesdropping," Logan said, raising his hands. "But when you mentioned an archaeologist to Dad, I started searching. The thing is..." He scrolled down the page, pointing to a paragraph. "He's been tracking similar phenomena across different sites. Energy signatures, unexplained temporal anomalies, and..." He paused, looking up at his parents. "Artifacts that seem to respond to certain individuals."

The purple glow from upstairs intensified momentarily, as if responding to Logan's words. The kitchen lights flickered, and somewhere in the distance, a dog started to bark.

Joe moved closer to read the screen, his earlier weariness replaced by focused attention. "What exactly are you suggesting, Logan?"

"I'm suggesting," Logan said, lowering his voice, "that maybe Dr. Cleary isn't just coming to study our stone. Maybe he's been looking for something exactly like this. Like what Zoe can do."

Cathy felt a chill run down her spine despite the warm evening air. She thought about Becky's enthusiasm, about Dr. Cleary's reputation, about all the strange events that had been occurring since they found the orb. "We need to be careful," she said finally. "Very careful."

"There's more," Logan said, clicking on another tab. "Look at where his funding comes from." He turned the screen toward them, revealing a familiar name that made both parents freeze: Camp Pendleton's division of Defense Advanced Research Projects Agency (DARPA).

The kitchen fell silent except for the distant sound of crickets and the soft hum of the laptop. The decision they'd just made about Dr. Cleary's visit suddenly felt much more complicated, and potentially much more dangerous.

Above them, in Zoe's room, the orb pulsed one final time before going dark, as if sensing the gravity of what was to come.

Later that evening, Zoe perched on the edge of her bed, cradling the shimmering orb in her hands. The connection with Swirly had grown stronger each day, like a friendship blossoming into something deeper. *It's trying to tell me something*, she thought, *but why me? Why our family?*

The swirling colors within pulsated in perfect synchronization with her heartbeat, and she could swear she felt emotions emanating from it—curiosity, urgency, and something else... was it fear?

"Show me," she said, her fingers tracing the intricate patterns. "Show me what you are."

The surge came without warning. Raw energy coursed through her body like lightning, different from before—stronger, more insistent. Her spine straightened as Swirly erupted with light. *This is it*, she thought. *This is what we've been building toward.*

Above the orb, holographic symbols materialized. Zoe's hands moved instinctively across the interface, each motion feeling more natural than the last. A small voice in her head whispered caution—*what if this power comes with a price?*—but she pushed it aside.

"Oh, my gosh!" The words escaped her lips, equal parts terror and wonder.

Footsteps thundered up the stairs. Her door flew open as her family burst in, their faces illuminated by Swirly's otherworldly glow.

"Zoe!" Cathy reached for her daughter, but stopped short. Zoe recognized her mother's expression—the same look she wore when checking Pokémon Go for anomalies. Not fear, but intense curiosity mixed with maternal concern.

Logan stepped into the room, his phone already out to record everything. "This is impossible," he said, struggling to process what he was seeing. "The energy output alone should be—"

"Put the phone down," Joe said. His eyes darted to the windows, checking if the light show was visible from outside. Prior to taking over the family property, Joe had spent several years in the military, which taught him to always think about security first.

The room filled with projected figures that defied explanation—beings that straddled the line between human and divine. Their wings stretched impossibly wide, composed of light and energy rather than flesh and feather.

*They're beautiful*, Zoe thought, *but something about them feels... wrong. Like they're not supposed to be here. Like we're seeing something forbidden.*

Logan took a halting step forward. His hands trembled as he lowered his phone. "Those aren't... they can't be..." For once, her tech-savvy brother seemed at a loss for logical explanations.

"Angels?" Joe's voice was barely audible. His military training evident in how he positioned himself between his family and the apparitions, even though they were just holograms. Zoe noticed his right hand reaching for a weapon that wasn't there.

Cathy moved closer to Zoe, her mind clearly racing. "The patterns in their movement... it's like what I've been seeing in the Pokémon Go glitches, but amplified." She pulled out her phone, but the screen went black the moment she tried to record.

*Swirly doesn't want to be documented,* Zoe realized. *It's choosing what to show and when.*

The figures shifted and morphed, responding to Zoe's unconscious commands. With each interaction, she felt a deepening connection, but also a growing unease. The power flowing through her was intoxicating, yet somehow dangerous—like standing too close to the edge of a cliff.

The celestial beings dissolved, replaced by the stark silhouette of Mount Palomar Observatory. But this time, Zoe noticed something different in the projection—dark shapes moving in the observatory's shadows, figures that seemed to be watching, waiting.

*They know we're coming,* she thought with sudden certainty. *And they're not all friendly.*

Cathy gripped Joe's arm. "The observatory? But why—" Her voice trailed off as she noticed the shadowy figures too. Her Pokémon Go experience had taught her to spot anomalies, and these definitely qualified. They also reminded her of Zekrom, one of the scarier Pokémon.

The light show ended abruptly, plunging the room into relative darkness. Swirly's glow dimmed to a subtle pulse, leaving them in stunned silence. Zoe felt drained, as if the orb had borrowed some of her energy for its display.

"Did everyone else see..." Zoe couldn't finish the sentence. Her hands trembled as she held Swirly closer, feeling suddenly protective of it.

Logan had recovered enough to shift into analytical mode, but Zoe noticed his voice wasn't quite steady. "The beings, the observatory—there has to be a connection. But why show us potential hostiles? Are we being warned or guided?"

"Or both," Joe said. "Those shadows weren't random. Someone's watching that observatory."

Cathy sat beside Zoe, wrapping an arm around her shoulders. "Honey, this is bigger than we thought. Maybe we should think carefully before—"

"No," Zoe interrupted, surprising herself with her conviction. "We need to go. Swirly's trying to warn us about something, but also showing us where to find answers." She looked down at the orb, its surface now showing ripples of red she'd never seen before. *Warning colors*, she realized. *Like a coral snake.*

The family exchanged loaded glances, each processing not just what they'd witnessed, but the implications of what might lie ahead. Their ordinary lives had just taken an extraordinary turn, and the path forward led to an observatory where both answers and dangers seemed to wait.

Joe squeezed Cathy's hand, then looked at Zoe with a mix of pride and concern. "If we do this, we do it smart. We do it as a family." He glanced at the windows again. "And we need to be careful who we tell. I've got a feeling we're not the only ones interested in what Swirly can do."

Logan nodded, already pulling out his laptop. "I'll start researching the observatory's security systems and staff. If someone's watching it, maybe they've left digital footprints."

Zoe hugged Swirly closer, feeling its warmth pulse in response. *We're in this together now*, she thought to the orb. *Whatever's coming, whatever those shadows mean, we'll face it together.*

But as her family began planning their next moves, she couldn't shake the feeling that they were stepping onto a path that would change them all forever—for better or worse, remained to be seen.

The morning sun set the Bailey vineyard aglow as Becky's car kicked up dust along the driveway. Her hands gripped the steering wheel tightly, knuckles white with tension as she rehearsed her apology for the hundredth time. The weight of her mistake pressed heavily on her shoulders as she approached the familiar house.

Inside, Cathy wound her vibrant red hair into a messy bun, the aroma of fresh coffee filling the kitchen as she poured two steaming mugs. The doorbell chime interrupted her morning routine, sending a jolt of apprehension through her. Something about the urgent tone made her pause before opening the door.

"Becky?" Cathy's voice carried both welcome and worry. "Come in. You look troubled."

Becky stepped inside, her usually composed demeanor cracking under stress. "Cathy, I need to explain something, and I owe you all an apology."

Joe appeared from the hallway, work gloves in hand, his usual warmth replaced by cautious concern. "What's this about, Becky?"

Becky's fingers twisted nervously around her bag strap as she explained about the archaeologist and his contact with Camp Pendleton, and, more importantly, about his interest in temporal anomalies in Fallbrook. The color drained from Joe's face as understanding dawned.

"You said he was an archaeologist, not some temporal scientist with ties to the military!" Joe's voice carried the sharp edge of betrayal. "This was supposed to be about examining the stone. Not all of this other nonsense!"

"I tried to fix it!" Becky's voice trembled. "I told him it was just a student prank, that the stone was fake—"

"But the damage is done," Joe cut in, pacing the floor like a caged lion. The wooden boards creaked under his agitated steps.

Cathy stepped between them, her presence a calming buffer. "What's done is done. We need to focus on protecting what we have now."

Joe's jaw clenched, but he nodded slowly, his anger gradually giving way to determination. "You're right. And the first step is moving that stone somewhere safe." He turned to Becky, his voice firm but measured. "I appreciate you coming to warn us, but I think it's best if you head home now. The less you know about what we're doing next, the better."

After Becky's departure, the family gathered in the kitchen. Joe pulled out a worn notebook and sketched a rough plan while Logan calculated the possible weight of the stone based on its visible dimensions. Cathy made fresh coffee, her hands steady despite her racing thoughts, and Zoe sat quietly, feeling Swirly's warmth pulse against her back through her backpack.

Within the hour, they were outside. The morning sun had burned away the coastal fog, and the earth was warming beneath their feet as Joe and Logan positioned themselves on opposite sides of the stone. They started the excavation methodically, their shovels breaking ground in a synchronized rhythm. The earth yielded reluctantly to their tools, releasing its ancient secret one careful scoop at a time, while Cathy and Zoe watched from nearby, ready to help if needed.

Zoe, comforted by Swirly's presence in her backpack, remained transfixed on the ancient stone, its markings seeming to shift and dance in the changing light.

"Look at this," Logan called out, brushing dirt from a newly exposed section. "The stone's pretty thick and looks heavy."

Cathy documented their progress, her phone capturing both the physical work and the strange glitches that seemed to follow Zoe. When the Galarian Zapdos appeared on her screen without the use of a daily incense, her excited cry drew brief attention before everyone returned to their tasks.

As the sun climbed higher, Joe called an end to the day's work. "That's enough for now. Tomorrow, we'll see about moving it somewhere safer." His eyes drifted toward the distant fence line, as if expecting uninvited visitors at any moment.

That evening, as darkness settled over the vineyard, the family retreated indoors, each carrying the weight of their discovery differently. In her room, Zoe held Swirly close, its gentle pulse having a calming effect. Whatever came next, they would face it together as a family.

# CHAPTER 7

# NEIGHBORLY ADVICE

The aroma of Cathy's lasagna mingled with the growing tension in the Bailey's dining room. Zoe could feel Swirly's energy building upstairs as she and her family huddled around the kitchen table, discussing the archaeologist's military contact.

Three sharp knocks echoed through the house, cutting Joe off mid-sentence about moving the stone.

"Who could that be at this hour?" Cathy whispered, moving to peer through the curtains. Her breath caught. "It's Mr. Peterson."

Through the gathering dusk, their elderly neighbor stood on the porch, his tall, lean frame slightly stooped with age. His hands clutched an old leather book, knuckles white with intensity.

Zoe felt Swirly's energy surged again from upstairs. *Something's different*, she thought. *Swirly's trying to tell me something.*

Joe opened the door, shoulders tense despite his casual tone. "Mr. Peterson, this is unexpected. Please, come in and have a seat."

The moment Mr. Peterson crossed the threshold, his pale blue eyes, sharp despite his age, fixed on the staircase. His cardigan, complete with a pocket protector stuffed with multicolored pens, spoke of old habits from an engineering career. Logan, reading the room, smoothly positioned himself between their visitor and the stairs, catching Zoe's worried glance.

"I've been observing," Mr. Peterson began, his voice carrying the slight tremor of age but firm with purpose. He settled into their living room armchair, the leather book creaking open to reveal old photographs. "The lights, the energy fluctuations. They're back after all these years."

Cathy's hand slipped to her phone, ready to record everything. The photographs, dated 1950, showed familiar light patterns that made Joe's jaw clench. The images were remarkably clear despite their age, showing the Bailey vineyard bathed in ethereal lights that matched what they'd been seeing.

"Your grandfather, Joseph," Mr. Peterson said, his finger tracing an image, trembling slightly. "He found something too, didn't he? Changed him completely." A knowing look crossed his lined face.

Upstairs, Swirly pulsed in perfect rhythm with Mr. Peterson's words. Zoe could feel it, like a heartbeat, echoing through the house, growing stronger with each passing moment.

Logan shifted in his chair, his initial defensive posture softening as Mr. Peterson pulled out a small notebook filled with hand-drawn graphs and calculations. The pages were worn at the edges, covered in precise handwriting and complex equations.

"You see," Mr. Peterson said, spreading the papers across the coffee table with methodical care, "I've been monitoring electromagnetic fluctuations around your property for decades." He adjusted his wire-rimmed glasses, revealing dark circles under his eyes that spoke of countless nights of observation. "Started back in '82 when my equipment went haywire one night." His finger traced along a dramatic spike on one of the graphs.

"Electromagnetic anomalies?" Logan leaned forward. "What kind of equipment are you using?"

Mr. Peterson's eyes lit up, years seeming to fall away as he engaged with Logan's interest. "Started with basic EMF meters, but these days..." He patted a battered leather satchel by his feet. "I've got a whole setup. Magnetometers, spectral analyzers, even built my own temporal displacement sensors based on some old theoretical physics papers."

"Temporal displacement?" Logan's eyebrows shot up. "You mean like—"

"Time distortions," Mr. Peterson finished, pulling out another chart with hands that shook with excitement rather than age. "Look here. See these patterns? They match perfectly with theoretical models of localized temporal anomalies. The same patterns your great-grandfather documented."

Joe and Cathy exchanged worried glances as Logan reached for the charts. The overhead light caught the metallic ink of the graphs, making them seem to shimmer like Swirly's surface.

"These readings…" Logan said, his fingers tracing the patterns. "They're similar to what I've been recording near the oak tree." He glanced up, suspicion warring with curiosity. "But how did you—"

"Know about them?" Mr. Peterson smiled, crow's feet deepening around his eyes. "Been watching you set up your equipment from my property. Through my workshop window." He pulled out a complex diagram from his satchel, the paper crinkling with age. "You've got good instincts, son, but you're missing something crucial in your measurements."

Logan's jaw tightened, pride briefly flickering across his face. "What am I missing?"

The elderly neighbor leaned forward, his voice dropping to a whisper. "The resonance frequencies." His fingers, stained with ink, traced complex waveforms. "They operate on a quantum level, creating what I call 'temporal echoes.' Your instruments are only catching half the story."

Upstairs, Swirly pulsed stronger, its energy reaching Zoe like waves of warmth. "Logan," she interrupted, unable to contain herself, "he's right. Remember those weird readings you couldn't explain last week?"

"The harmonic distortions…" His eyes widened. "They weren't equipment malfunctions at all, were they?"

"No," Mr. Peterson confirmed, his expression grave. Outside, the oak tree's branches cast moving shadows across the living room wall, like fingers reaching toward them. "They were signatures of something far more extraordinary. Something your family has been connected to for generations."

The scientific discussion transformed the room's atmosphere. Logan, usually the family skeptic, was now fully engaged, his notebook out, scribbling equations and questions. Even Joe seemed fascinated, watching the technical exchange between his son and their mysterious neighbor while absently rubbing the stone he always carried.

"I've got some equipment designs," Mr. Peterson said, carefully pulling out detailed technical drawings. "Modified to detect these specific temporal signatures. Might help with your research." The diagrams showed intricate modifications to standard measuring equipment, annotated with precise handwriting that had grown shakier over the years.

"But why help us?" Logan asked, sudden suspicion sharpening his tone. "Why now?"

Mr. Peterson's expression turned serious, the overhead light creating deep shadows across his face. "Because what's happening here…" He glanced meaningfully toward the stairs where Swirly's energy pulsed stronger. "It's bigger than all of us. And you're going to need better tools to understand it. To protect it."

The word 'it' hung in the air, heavy with implication. The room fell silent except for the gentle ticking of the grandfather clock in the corner.

As Mr. Peterson prepared to leave, he placed a final paper in Logan's hands, his fingers lingering on the document. "These are the frequency ranges you'll want to monitor." He paused at the door, silhouetted against the porch light. "And Logan? Sometimes the most incredible scientific discoveries are the ones that challenge everything we think we know."

The door clicked shut behind him, leaving the family in thoughtful silence. Through the window, they watched his tall figure disappear into the growing darkness, his shadow merging with the evening shadows of their vineyard.

Logan stared at the papers in his hands, his mind visibly racing. His eyes caught on a list of coordinates with corresponding dates scribbled in the margin, each notation precise despite the shaky handwriting.

While Logan and her parents crowded around his laptop at the dining room table, Zoe slipped upstairs to retrieve Swirly. The orb seemed to hum with anticipation in her hands, its surface alive with swirling patterns of deep red and violet.

"Look at this!" Logan's voice carried up the stairs, his excitement palpable. By the time Zoe made her way down, he'd spread Mr. Peterson's notes across the table, dinner dishes hastily pushed aside. His fingers flew across his laptop keyboard. "These temporal signatures perfectly match the data I collected last Tuesday when Zoe was..."

"Watching Ace Hardware transform to a dirt lot?" Zoe supplied, settling into a chair with Swirly now cradled in her lap. The orb hummed contentedly, its surface catching the warm light from the dining room chandelier.

"Exactly." Logan pulled up a series of charts, his earlier skepticism completely forgotten in his excitement. "But Mr. Peterson's calculations suggest something I hadn't considered. The energy isn't just radiating outward - it's creating some kind of localized temporal bubble."

Cathy, who had been documenting everything on her phone, looked up with a puzzled expression. "In English, please?"

Joe chuckled, the sound warm and reassuring in the tension-filled room. "Yeah, son. Some of us didn't major in quantum physics."

Logan's brow furrowed in concentration as he searched for simpler words. "According to these calculations, that wasn't just a vision you had, Zoe. You were actually creating a contained field of altered temporal flow." His voice grew more animated. "And get this - Mr. Peterson's readings show these fields have been appearing sporadically on our property for generations."

Joe leaned forward, his coffee forgotten. "Since my grandfather's time?"

"At least," Logan confirmed, pointing to a series of numbers in Mr. Peterson's notebook. The pages crinkled under his finger. "Major temporal events in 1952, 1978, 1993... each time, something significant happened with the Bailey family."

Cathy pulled out her phone again. "The coordinates he left. Could they be connected to some of these events?"

"That's exactly what I'm thinking," Logan said, excitement building in his voice. "And there's more. These frequency patterns Mr. Peterson recorded? They're almost identical to the energy signature Swirly gives off when Zoe uses it."

As if responding to its name, Swirly pulsed in Zoe's hands, its colors deepening. "It's like Mr. Peterson knew exactly what to look for," she said quietly, running her fingers over the orb's smooth surface. "Like he's seen something like Swirly before."

"But how?" a concerned Joe asked. "And why didn't he just come out and say it?"

Logan shook his head, studying another diagram. "Maybe he couldn't. Or maybe he was protecting something - or someone." His eyes flickered briefly to Zoe. "But his data is solid. These readings... they're going to help us understand what's really happening here."

"And the stone?" Cathy reminded them. "The one your dad found?"

"According to these calculations," Logan said, tracing a complex formula with his pen, "it could be acting as some kind of amplifier for whatever Swirly does. The temporal fields are strongest when Zoe's near the stone."

Zoe clutched Swirly closer, feeling its warmth intensify. "Is that why it feels stronger there? Like it's trying to show me something?"

"Probably." Logan began inputting more data into his laptop, the keyboard clicks mixing with the gentle hum of Swirly. "And with Mr. Peterson's modifications to my equipment, we might figure out exactly what it's trying to tell you."

The family fell into thoughtful silence, broken only by Logan's typing and Swirly's soft hum. Outside, the old oak tree stood sentinel in the darkness, its leaves rustling secrets to the night wind.

"One thing's for sure," Joe finally said, placing a protective hand on Zoe's shoulder. "Whatever this is, whatever Swirly's trying to tell us - it's been waiting for our family for a very long time."

"And now," Cathy added, gathering Mr. Peterson's notes with careful hands, "we have more help understanding it than we realized." She gestured to the papers spread across the table. "Even if that help comes from unexpected places."

Logan looked up from his laptop, a rare smile crossing his face. "You know what this means, Zoe? We've got some serious experimenting to do."

Cathy held up her hand, her expression firm but gentle. "First, we need to do some research. Tomorrow, let's split up to investigate the orb and the stone based on what Mr. Peterson has told us. Logan, you head to the local library in the morning. The rest of us will search the attic for old family records and photographs, anything that might help us understand what's happening."

They each nodded in agreement, the weight of discovery heavy in the air. As they retired to their rooms for the night, each family member's mind raced with possibilities of what tomorrow might bring.

# CHAPTER 8

# RESEARCH

The attic stairs protested with each step as Joe and Cathy climbed into the space above their home. Afternoon light filtered through the small dormer window as dust motes danced in the golden beams, and the musty scent of aged wood and forgotten memories filled their nostrils.

"I can't believe we've never really gone through all this stuff," Cathy said, pulling her red hair into a ponytail. Her hands trembled as she surveyed the overwhelming collection of family artifacts. She sneezed as Joe shifted an old trunk, sending a cloud of dust spiraling through the light.

"Dad always said great-great-grandpa Bailey was some kind of scientist," Joe mused, his hands running along the trunk's brass latches. His usual lighthearted demeanor gave way to something more contemplative. "But he never knew exactly what he did. I know the Baileys ran the old telephone exchange on Main at some point. Mr. Peterson's story about the orb and stone structure... there has to be something here."

Cathy used her phone as a flashlight to illuminate the darker corners. The beam caught something that made her breath catch. "Look at this," she called out, reaching for a leather-bound journal wedged between two boxes and an antique Victrola record player. The spine was cracked and faded, but the gold lettering still caught the light: *E.L. Bailey, 1893.*

Joe moved closer as Cathy carefully opened the journal. The pages crackled with age, filled with meticulous handwriting and detailed sketches. One drawing made them both freeze—a perfect rendering of the orb that now fascinated their daughter.

"Holy..." Joe said, touching the page with reverence. "That's impossible."

Cathy's hands shook as she turned the page, her voice dropping to a whisper. "Listen to this: '*The orb continues to defy all known laws of physics. Its connection to the stone remains unclear, though I suspect they are but parts of a greater mechanism. I fear what others might do should they discover its true purpose...*'"

As she continued to flip through the journal, a loose newspaper clipping fell from between the pages. The paper was dated 1973, with a headline partially visible: "Longtime Resident Reports Missing Family Heirloom."

"Joe, look at this," Cathy said, as she smoothed out the fragile paper. "It says your grandfather reported a break-in at the vineyard. The only thing taken was... 'a cherished family heirloom of significant importance.'"

Joe reached for another journal, this one newer, dated 1974. His hands stilled as he read the first page. '*After months of searching, the orb has returned to us, though I fear it carries new secrets. Military vehicles have been seen near the property, and strange lights appear in the sky above Mount Palomar. I've heard whispers of something called Operation Chrono...*'

"Operation Chrono?" Cathy's eyes widened, her hand automatically reaching for her phone. "Isn't that what Logan found in his research? The military experiments with those missing soldiers?"

Joe nodded grimly. "Seven of them. All vanished without a trace." He continued reading, his voice growing more concerned. "*The orb seems different now. The patterns inside have changed, become more complex. Whatever they did to it during those missing months has altered its nature. I pray they never discover its true location again.*"

"So the military had it," Cathy said. "They must have tried to use it in their experiments." She grabbed her phone and started typing quickly. "We should tell Logan about this. His research about Operation Chrono wasn't just coincidence—it's all connected."

"There's more," Joe said, pulling another box forward with renewed urgency. Inside, they found a collection of photographs, their edges worn soft with time. One depicted a stern-looking man standing in front of construction scaffolding in an area that had recently been excavated. His eyes seemed to pierce through time, holding secrets they were only beginning to uncover.

"Joe," Cathy's voice trembled, her usual Pokémon Go enthusiasm replaced by genuine fear, "I think we're in way over our heads here. Whatever you found and now Zoe is totally attached to... whatever this thing is... it's been in your family for generations. And now we know the military was involved..."

Joe sat back on his heels, scratching his chin thoughtfully. His usual quick humor was nowhere to be found as he studied the photograph, seeing his family legacy in a completely new light. "Yeah, but the real question is—why did it choose Zoe? And what exactly did my great-great-grandfather get our family mixed up in? What did the military do to it?"

The attic seemed to grow darker as clouds passed over the sun, casting the space in periods of dark that felt suddenly oppressive. From somewhere below, they heard Zoe's voice, engaged in what sounded like an animated conversation. They exchanged worried glances.

"Who's Zoe talking to?" Cathy asked.

Joe's face hardened with concern. "It must be the orb. Nobody else is here."

They scrambled toward the attic stairs, the journals and photographs clutched in their hands, their discoveries adding new urgency to their need to reach their daughter. The mystery of Operation Chrono and its connection to their family's past weighed heavily on their minds as they descended.

Zoe lingered in her room, pretending to search one last time for her grandmother's locket. Her fingers traced the familiar shelves and drawers, finding nothing but dust and disappointment. She held her breath, counting her family's footsteps as they faded down the hallway, each muffled thud marking the seconds until she could be alone. When silence finally blanketed the house, she reached for Swirly, her hands trembling as they closed around the orb. Familiar warmth steadying her nerves as she settled cross-legged on her bed, jaw set with determination.

"Okay, Swirly," she said. "Those coordinates Mr. Peterson gave us, let's start with —33.35641, -116.86499—what do you know about them?" She traced the numbers in the air as she spoke them, watching as the orb's iridescent surface pulsed with increasing intensity. The shimmering blues and purples swirled faster, almost eager to share their secrets.

With a soft click that made Zoe jump, the hidden panel slid open. The air before her shimmered and distorted as a holographic scene materialized. Her breath caught in her throat as the image of a young military officer took shape, his uniform crisp and precise despite the translucent quality of the projection. His face was contorted with rage, jaw clenched so tight she could see the muscles working beneath his skin as he jabbed his finger at something just out of view.

A chill ran down her spine despite the warmth radiating from Swirly. Though the hologram was silent, she could feel the fury radiating from him. Her fingers tightened around the orb, protective.

The officer turned sharply, revealing what he'd been pointing at—a photograph tacked to a stark white wall. Zoe leaned closer, her heart skipping several beats. It was Swirly, captured in a black-and-white photograph. Bold red letters spelled out "MISS-ING" across the top of the image. The scene expanded slightly, showing glimpses of what could only be a military facility, most likely nearby Camp Pendleton—military-grade filing cabinets, maps on the walls, a calendar dated 1973.

"They lost you," an emotional Zoe said to Swirly. "But how did you end up in our vineyard?" The orb pulsed in response, its colors shifting to lighter purples and blues.

Before she could process this revelation, the hologram shifted and blurred. The military office dissolved like smoke, replaced by the dusty expanse of a construction site. Heavy machinery dotted the landscape—bulldozers and excavators that looked ancient by today's standards. Their vintage appearance and the grainy quality of the scene suggested this was from the same era as the military office.

Something about the location nagged at Zoe's memory. She squinted, leaning forward until her nose nearly passed through the holographic image. The terrain looked familiar—rolling hills, a particular formation of rocks in the background. Was that... Mount Palomar in the distance? She'd seen those same bulldozers in old photographs at school, during their local history project about the observatory's construction.

"Is this connected to the coordinates?" she asked Swirly, her mind racing with possibilities. The orb's surface rippled with golden light, almost like a nod. "What connection does the observatory have with—"

The sound of rapid footsteps in the hallway cut her off. Zoe's heart leaped into her throat as she recognized her parents' urgent pace. She barely had time to lower Swirly to her lap before her bedroom door burst open, the hinges protesting with a sharp squeak.

Her parents stood in the doorway, silhouetted against the hallway light. Swirly's glow dimmed instantly, like a child caught doing something forbidden. The last wisps of the hologram dissipated into nothing, but the lingering scent of ozone hung in the air.

"Zoe?" Her mother's voice wavered. "We saw lights under your door. Was that—did the orb just show you something?"

Joe stepped into the room, his hands fidgeting with his worry stone. "Logan found something at the library. About Camp Pendleton. About an experiment called Operation Chrono."

Zoe's fingers tightened around Swirly. The orb felt warmer than usual, almost warning her. She glanced between her parents and the orb, weighing her options. The image of the enraged military officer flashed through her mind.

"I..." she started, then paused. How could she explain what she'd seen without putting her family at risk? "Swirly was just showing me some old pictures. Of Fallbrook, I think." The half-truth tasted bitter on her tongue.

Cathy moved to sit beside her daughter, the mattress dipping under her weight. "Honey, let's be honest with each other. Everything that's happening—it's bigger than just us now."

"Your mother's right," Joe said, leaning against her desk. "Logan discovered records of seven soldiers who disappeared during some kind of temporal experiment. In 1973."

Zoe felt Swirly pulse against her palms, matching her quickening heartbeat. The coordinates Mr. Peterson had given them, the construction site she'd seen, the missing poster—it all started to align in her mind like constellation points forming a pattern.

"Dad," she said, "what if those soldiers didn't just disappear? What if they were sent somewhere? Or..." she swallowed hard, "... some*when*?"

The orb grew warmer in her hands, encouraging her. Zoe took a deep breath and continued, "Swirly just showed me something about Camp Pendleton. From the 1970s. There was an officer, and he was angry about losing something." She lifted the orb. "About losing *this*."

Her parents exchanged worried looks. Outside, the distant thrum of helicopter blades cut through the afternoon air. Swirly's surface swirled with dark red and burnt orange, reflecting their mounting anxiety.

"We need to move the stone," Joe said. "Before anyone else starts asking questions."

"But what about the coordinates?" Zoe protested. "Mr. Peterson gave them to us for a reason. And I think—I think Swirly's trying to tell us they're important."

Cathy reached out and placed her hand over Zoe's, her fingers brushing against the orb's warm surface. "Then we need to figure out what they mean before someone else does."

The orb pulsed once, as if in agreement. In that moment, Zoe realized their family had crossed a threshold—there would be no going back to normal after this. The only way was forward, through whatever mystery Swirly was slowly unveiling.

Logan hunched over the microfiche reader at the Fallbrook Historical Society, his shoulders tense as fluorescent lights hummed overhead. The musty smell of old papers and wooden cabinets filled his nostrils as he scrolled through the pages of the Fallbrook Enterprise. Each new article made his heart beat faster.

"Strange Tunnels Discovered Beneath Downtown," the headline from 1935 blazed across the screen. His fingers trembled slightly as he adjusted the focus, the machine's soft whirring echoing in the empty research room. The article detailed how construction workers had accidentally broken through into an elaborate tunnel system while laying new water pipes. The reporter speculated about bootleggers, but the engineering suggested something far more sophisticated.

"This makes little sense," Logan said, leaning closer until his nose nearly touched the screen. A detailed map accompanied the article, showing suspected tunnel routes. One line traced directly through what was now the Bailey property, connecting to another entrance near the historic El Real Hotel.

The elderly historian, Mrs. Martin, approached his desk. "Finding anything interesting?" she asked, adjusting her wire-rimmed glasses.

"Actually, yes," Logan replied, trying to keep his voice steady. "These tunnel systems - were they ever fully explored?"

Mrs. Martinez's expression darkened. "Some say they were. Others say there are passages we still haven't found, but to be honest, nobody's been able to find them since. It's as if they never existed. Fallbrook keeps its secrets well."

Logan photographed the article with his phone, already forming connections. The bunker under their house, its precise construction - could it have been built to connect with these older passages? The engineering seemed too advanced for simple prohibition-era smuggling.

As he dug deeper into the archives, more unsettling stories emerged. A 1935 article described local ranchers reporting "peculiar lights" in the hills around Fallbrook, followed by unexplained livestock disappearances. His fingers clenched the edge of the desk as he read about electromagnetic disturbances that matched what he'd been measuring in the vineyard.

Another article from 1967 featured blurry photographs of what witnesses claimed was a "large, shadowy creature" prowling the avocado groves at night. Logan's throat tightened as he recognized the location - less than a mile from where they'd found the orb.

"We're closing for lunch in fifteen minutes," Mrs. Martin called from her desk.

Quickly, Logan photographed several more articles. A 1973 piece about the Fallbrook Five made him pause - five children vanished. The incident had occurred on Main at the Packing House, now Harry's Sports Bar & Grill. The missing children were: Brian Miramontez (15), Alex Montgomery (10), Avery Clarke (5), Blake Reeves (12), and Lainey Anderson (7).

His phone buzzed: "Come home ASAP. Zoe's having another episode with the orb."

Logan gathered his notes, his mind racing. The tunnels, the lights, the missing time - patterns were emerging that he couldn't ignore. Maybe Fallbrook's "Friendly Village" facade hid something far more extraordinary. And maybe their family hadn't stumbled onto something new, but something that had been there all along, waiting to be rediscovered.

As he headed for the door, Mrs. Martin called out, "Logan? Sometimes the truth is stranger than we're willing to accept."

He nodded, clutching his phone with its photographic evidence. It was time to stop being such a skeptic and start connecting the dots. His sister's life might depend on it.

The screen door didn't just open—it exploded inward as Logan burst into the kitchen, his face flushed with excitement. The sight that greeted him stopped him cold: his family huddled around the kitchen table, their faces bathed in Swirly's otherworldly glow.

"What's happening?" Logan asked, letting his backpack slide to the floor with a heavy thud. The late afternoon light streaming through the kitchen windows seemed dim compared to Swirly's ethereal radiance.

"Logan," Zoe said, her eyes bright with wonder. "You're not going to believe this. Swirly... it showed me something. Actually showed me."

Cathy's hands trembled as she reached for her phone. "And that's not all." She pulled up a photo, sliding the device across the worn kitchen table. "We found this today."

Zoe leaped up, her chair scraping against the tile floor. "That's it! That's exactly what I saw in the vision!" She jabbed her finger at the mysterious figure in the photograph. "The construction site, the equipment—everything!"

Logan leaned in, his frown slowly morphing into something else—recognition tinged with disbelief. "This feels familiar. Like..."

"You've been there before?" Joe finished, exchanging a meaningful look with his son. "Zoe said the same thing."

Logan's eyes narrowed as he examined the picture. "The elevation, the terrain..." He traced the outline of the hills with his finger. "Wait a minute. Remember that field trip in high school? To the observatory?" He looked up at Zoe. "This is Mount Palomar—before they built it."

Cathy retrieved her notebook, its pages filled with careful observations. "It makes sense," she said, flipping through her notes. "The anomalies in Pokémon Go—they all point toward either Mount Palomar or here." Her finger tapped their location on a hand-drawn map.

"Are we actually saying this thing is showing us the past?" Joe asked.

"Not just the past," Zoe said, her hand hovering over Swirly's shimmering surface. "It's showing us connections. Places where something important happened... or will happen."

Logan couldn't tear his eyes away from the orb. "The observatory's more than just a research facility, isn't it? What if they're studying something besides stars up there?"

"Time," Cathy said, Pokémon Go glowing faintly, as if in response to Swirly's radiant light. "They could be studying time itself."

A heavy silence fell over the kitchen, broken only by the gentle hum of their refrigerator and Swirly's soft vibrations. The weight of their discovery showing on their faces.

Joe cleared his throat, his hands clenched tight. "Whatever this is, we need to be careful. If Swirly can do what we think it can, there are probably people looking for it."

"Good thing it chose us," Zoe said with unexpected certainty, drawing everyone's attention. "Or maybe we chose it. Either way, I think we're meant to protect Swirly and figure this out together."

Logan pulled up a chair, his expression now one of genuine curiosity. "Alright, Butt Nugget," he said, "Tell me everything you saw in that vision. Don't leave out a single detail."

Swirly's pulsating light scattered highlights across the kitchen table as the Baileys gathered for what might be their most important family meeting yet. The setting sun painted long stripes of amber through the windows, illuminating dust motes that swirled like tiny galaxies above their heads. Zoe cradled the device close, its warmth spreading through her palms like a whispered secret.

Joe unconsciously reached for the worry stone in his pocket—a habit passed down through generations of Bailey men. "A time-traveling device right here in Fallbrook?" He glanced at the family photos lining the walls, generations of Baileys watching over them. "And our family's been connected to this all along? It's like something out of those sci-fi movies Logan used to make us watch."

Logan adjusted his laptop screen, the glow highlighting the dark circles under his eyes. "The quantum resonance patterns don't lie, Dad. Look at these temporal wavelength signatures." He turned the screen, revealing complex diagrams. "Swirly and the ancient stone are perfectly synchronized, like they're two parts of the same system. The energy output is unlike anything I've ever seen in my physics classes."

"Just like that time with your science fair project," Zoe teased, trying to lighten the mood. "Remember when you tried to prove Mom's Pokémon Go glitches were caused by solar flares?"

"Hey, that was a solid hypothesis," Logan defended, but a small smile cracked his serious expression.

Cathy looked at her phone, Pokémon Go glitching wildly on the screen. "By the way, the electromagnetic interference is intensifying. Yesterday, all my Pokémon turned into Missing No, just like in the original Pokémon Red and Blue video games." She placed a protective hand on Zoe's shoulder, her voice softening. "But why Zoe? Why is she the only one who can truly communicate with it?"

A tingling sensation ran through Zoe's fingers as she stroked Swirly's surface. "It's like... it's been waiting for someone who could understand it." The orb's internal mechanisms shifted, creating patterns that reminded her of constellations. "When I hold it, I can feel echoes of our family's history, like memories frozen in time, and an energy like I've never felt before. It makes me feel whole and alive, like a part of me that was missing has finally clicked into place."

Joe leaned forward. "That's what concerns me. If what Mr. Peterson said about my great-great-grandfather is true, if he really found something similar back in the '20s..." He trailed off, remembering the stories his father used to tell about the strange lights in the vineyard.

"The stone's definitely been there longer than that," Logan interjected, pulling up another file. "Based on the weathering patterns and mineral composition, we're looking at centuries, maybe more. And these markings..." He zoomed in on a photo. "They're like the artifacts found near the Santa Margarita River, but different somehow. More advanced."

"But what happens when others realize what we've found?" Joe asked. "Camp Pendleton's just down the road, and after what happened with that helicopter..."

As if responding to Joe's concern, Swirly's light suddenly dimmed in Zoe's hands. A cool wave passed through her hand, and she knew instinctively what to do. "Watch this," she said, concentrating on the orb. The glow faded to almost nothing, though she could still feel its warmth.

Cathy's phone stopped glitching. "The interference... it's gone!" She stared at Zoe in amazement. "How did you know to do that?"

"I didn't... exactly. It's like Swirly told me. There's so much more it wants to show us about the stone circle, about why it's here." Zoe looked up at her family, her eyes full of determination. "About what we're meant to do with it."

"Then we test it," Joe said, squeezing the stone one last time before setting it on the table. The moment the stone touched the wooden surface, Swirly pulsed with an unexpected brightness. A faint blue tendril of light seemed to bridge the space between the orb and the stone, lasting only a fraction of a second. The stone appeared to vibrate slightly before settling.

Joe pulled his hand back, startled. "Did anyone else see that?"

"The worry stone," Logan leaned forward, his curiosity piqued. "Dad, how long has that been in the family?"

Joe reached for the stone, his fingers finding the familiar depression. As he rubbed it, a surge of energy coursed through him, electrifying and vivid. In that moment, the world around him blurred, and the air thickened with possibilities. He felt as if he was peering through a veil into the future.

Faintly, amidst the rush of visions, he heard Logan's voice—a reassuring mantra resonating in the background: "We're Baileys." Images flickered in his mind, and he pictured Logan squeezing Zoe's hand, the warmth of brotherly connection shimmering in the air.

As if startled from a trance, Joe dropped the stone, the rush of thoughts fading yet leaving a profound impression. "I think I just saw the future," he blurted out, his heart racing with excitement and fear. His family turned to him, wide-eyed.

"Four generations," Joe answered, staring at the stone with fresh eyes. "Great-great-grandfather said his dad found it in the creek that used to run through our property. Said it appeared the same day he found something..." His voice trailed off as he made the connection. "The same day he found something strange, but he never said what that was."

Zoe felt a surge of energy course through her body, stronger than before. Her connection to Swirly intensified, and for a brief moment, she could have sworn she felt the same warm comfort from the stone that her father always described. "They're connected somehow," she said, her voice filled with wonder. "All of it—Swirly, the stone circle, even this worry stone. They're all part of something bigger."

"We'll need to document everything," Logan said, already typing furiously on his laptop. "Energy readings, temporal disturbances, physical changes. I can set up monitoring equipment tonight."

"And I'll keep tracking the Pokémon Go anomalies," Cathy added. "They might help us establish patterns we can't see otherwise."

"First thing tomorrow," Joe declared, a newfound resolve anchoring him. "Logan and I will work on moving that stone. The bunker should be secure enough to hide it from prying eyes." He shared a knowing look with Cathy, years of partnership communicating volumes in a single glance. "We've prepared for something like this, even if we didn't know it."

"Are we really doing this?" Zoe asked, holding Swirly up. Its internal mechanisms radiated ethereal patterns across her face, and for a moment, the family could have sworn they saw a flash of another time—perhaps past, perhaps future—reflected on its surface. "Because once we start..."

"We're Baileys," Logan said, reaching across the table to squeeze his sister's hand. "When have we ever backed down from a challenge? Besides, someone's got to keep you from accidentally erasing yourself from existence."

Joe watched Logan in stunned silence. The vision he just had manifested itself right in front of him.

"Very funny," Zoe shot back.

"We're in this together," Cathy affirmed, moving to stand behind her children. "All of us."

Joe nodded. "Tomorrow, we start unraveling this mystery. Tonight, we plan."

As the family continued their discussion into the evening, Swirly pulsed with warmth in Zoe's hands, its rhythm matching her heartbeat. Outside, the last rays of sun painted the vineyard in deep purples and golds, the ancient stone waiting patiently in the gathering dusk. Tomorrow would bring their first real test, their first step into a mystery generations in the making. None of them could know just how far that path would lead, or how it would change not just their family, but perhaps the very fabric of time itself.

In the growing darkness, a single Pokémon appeared on Cathy's phone—a Celebi, the time-traveling Pokémon. There's no way to encounter Celebi in the wild. It can only be acquired through timed/special research tasks. She took a screenshot, adding one more piece to their expanding puzzle.

Zoe lay in her bed, moonlight streaming through her window as the distant sound of coyotes echoed through the vineyard. Swirly rested on her nightstand, its iridescent surface pulsing with gentle waves of blue and purple light. The familiar warmth of the orb's presence wrapped around her like a comforting blanket, even from a few feet away.

Her bedroom walls, once covered with posters of her favorite bands, were now adorned with maps of Fallbrook, spanning different decades. Logan had helped her create a timeline of strange occurrences in the area, stretching back to their great-grandfather's time. Even her collection of crystals seemed different now, their surfaces occasionally catching Swirly's light in ways that defied explanation.

She turned onto her side, watching the mesmerizing dance of colors within the orb. The past few weeks had changed everything. The dreams had become more frequent and vivid—walking through Fallbrook's streets in the 1960s, watching Donny tend to his young avocado trees, or seeing Model T cars rattling down dirt roads where modern buildings now stood. Future visions were hazier but more urgent, like looking through frosted glass at events that hadn't yet come to pass.

"What are you trying to tell me?" she whispered to Swirly. The orb's glow intensified, and she felt a familiar tingling sensation in her fingertips—the same feeling she'd experienced when they'd discovered the stone artifact. "I know something's coming. I just wish I understood what."

A pang of worry knotted in her stomach as she thought about her family. Mom had taken to patrolling the vineyard at odd hours, Pokémon Go spinning wildly whenever she approached the old oak tree. Just yesterday, a Charizard had appeared on her screen in impossible places, its date stamp reading both 2:15 PM and 1962 simultaneously.

Dad tried to hide it, but she'd noticed how he'd started carrying his old military backpack everywhere, ready to grab Swirly and run if needed. He spent hours in the bunker, reinforcing walls and installing additional security measures, the stone constantly in hand. Even Logan—her skeptical, science-minded brother—had replaced his usual "Butt Nugget" teasing with concerned glances and late-night research sessions about temporal anomalies.

Sometimes, late at night like this, Zoe caught herself longing for the simplicity of life before Swirly. Before Mr. Peterson's revelations about their family history, before the weight of prophecies and possibilities. Before she started seeing echoes of other times in familiar places. She missed being able to walk through Fallbrook without wondering if each stranger knew something about the orb, if each shadow held a threat.

A soft knock at her door made her jump. "Zoe?" her mom's voice called quietly. "Everything okay? I saw your light was still on."

"Mom?" Zoe called out before Cathy could walk away. "Do you ever feel like... like something's coming? Something big?"

Cathy entered, silhouetted in the doorway. The glow of her phone screen illuminated her worried expression. "Honey, I've been feeling it too. Pokémon Go's been showing things that shouldn't be possible. Date stamps that don't make sense. Pokémon appearing in places they can't be." She sat on the edge of Zoe's bed. "But whatever's coming, we'll face it together."

"I'm scared, Mom," Zoe admitted, her voice small. "Not of Swirly, but of what others might do to get it. What if those military helicopters come back? What if they find out about the stone?"

"That's why we're being careful," Cathy assured her, squeezing her hand. "Your father and Logan are working on moving the stone tomorrow. We'll figure this out."

After her mom left, Zoe retrieved Swirly from the nightstand. The familiar warmth spread through her hand, up her arm, and settled in her chest. "I won't let anything happen to you," she promised, cradling the orb close. "And I won't let anything happen to them either."

She placed Swirly back on her nightstand, watching as its colors swirled more slowly now, almost soothingly. But tonight there was something different about its pulse—an urgency she hadn't felt before. As sleep claimed her, Zoe glimpsed something in the orb's swirling depths: Mount Palomar's stark silhouette against a star-filled sky, and tall, radiant figures moving in the shadows beneath it. Before she could make sense of the vision, exhaustion pulled her under, but even in her dreams, Swirly's warning continued to pulse: time was running out.

The last thing she heard before drifting off completely was the distant sound of helicopter rotors, and Swirly's glow flickered—just once—in response.

# CHAPTER 9

# UNDERGROUND

The late afternoon sun painted the rows of vines in amber and gold. A cool breeze carried the earthy scent of ripening grapes and freshly turned soil as Joe and Logan positioned themselves on opposite sides of the ancient stone. Sweat beaded on Logan's forehead as he dug his fingers beneath the edge, his college-honed muscles tensing with effort.

"Ready?" Joe called out, his hands finding purchase on the opposite side. His eyes betrayed a mixture of determination and uncertainty. "On three. One... two..."

Logan suddenly jerked back with a startled yelp, his arms tingling as if he'd stuck his fingers in an electrical socket. "Holy shit!" He stumbled backward, shaking his hands vigorously. "That was... that was like touching a live wire, but different." Logan's mind immediately began cataloging the sensation, trying to rationalize it against everything he'd learned in his physics courses. Static electricity? Electromagnetic fields? Nothing quite fit.

Joe straightened up, worry lines creasing his face. "What exactly do you mean? It shocked you?"

"Not exactly shocked," Logan said, flexing his fingers as he analyzed the lingering sensation. "It was more like... energy? Like when your foot falls asleep, but all at once and way more intense. Dad, this goes against every principle of electromagnetic theory I've studied."

Joe, ever the practical one, reached down to test it himself. The moment his fingers brushed the stone's surface, he yanked his hands back with a sharp intake of breath.

"Well, I'll be damned," he said, staring at his tingling fingers with a mixture of fascination and concern. "That's definitely not normal."

They stood in silence for a moment, the gentle rustling of grape leaves providing a stark contrast to the supernatural occurrence they'd just experienced. Logan ran through possible explanations in his head, each theory falling short of explaining what they'd just encountered.

"Maybe..." Joe ventured, his voice carrying a hint of determination that Logan recognized from countless challenges, "maybe if we try it together? A combined effort might tamp down the shock."

Logan shot his father a skeptical look, but nodded. Despite his reservations, there was something interesting about the stone that drew him back. They positioned themselves again, sharing a determined glance across the ancient artifact.

"One... two... three..." they counted in unison, their voices steady despite their apprehension.

As their hands gripped the stone simultaneously, something extraordinary happened. Instead of the shocking sensation, a warm, powerful energy coursed through their bodies, almost like liquid sunshine flowing through their veins. Logan felt suddenly weightless, powerful, as if gravity itself had decided to take a break.

"Dad, are you feeling this?" he asked, his voice filled with wonder. The stone, which should have weighed hundreds of pounds based on its size and density, felt no heavier than an empty cardboard box. "It's completely violating the conservation of mass principle!"

"Yeah, I'm feeling it," Joe responded, his eyes wide with amazement. "It's like... like I could lift a truck." He paused, then added with a nervous chuckle, "Your mother's going to think we've both lost our minds."

Together, they carefully raised the stone from its earthen bed, decades of accumulated soil falling away as they lifted. What should have required heavy machinery or a team of workers was accomplished by father and son with surprising ease. The stone moved as if it were floating on air, guided by their synchronized movements.

"The wine cellar," Joe said decisively. "Whatever this thing is, we need to keep it somewhere secure and out of sight. Between the military helicopter and that archaeologist Becky mentioned..."

Logan nodded, thinking of the hidden bunker behind the wine racks. As they approached the kitchen door, the stone humming faintly between them, he couldn't help but wonder what Zoe would make of all this. His sister's connection to the orb suddenly seemed less far-fetched.

"Dad," Logan said, his voice lowered as they reached the kitchen door, "maybe we should keep this between us."

Joe met his son's eyes over the stone between them, his expression grave. "Yesterday I would have agreed with you," he said, "but something tells me we're way past the point of keeping secrets in this family. Whatever's happening here, we'll face it together."

The kitchen door creaked open as they carefully maneuvered the stone toward the basement wine cellar, Joe and Logan acutely aware that with each step, they were leaving the familiar world of grape harvests and wine production behind, venturing into something far more extraordinary and potentially dangerous.

Joe wiped the sweat from his forehead, his shirt already damp from the effort of reorganizing the hidden chamber. The beam of his work light cut through the musty air, shining across the concrete floor as he shifted another storage container. A hollow *thunk* echoed through the room, bouncing off the bare walls when he set the container down.

"That's not right," he said, his instincts that had served him well for decades suddenly alert. He tapped his boot against the spot, the sound distinctly different from the rest of the floor. Getting down on his hands and knees, ignoring the protest of his aging joints, Joe knocked his knuckles methodically across the surface, mapping out the hollow area.

His hands trembling slightly, he grabbed his phone and called upstairs. "Logan! Bring down the concrete saw and some chisels. I found something." He paused. "And bring your measuring tape."

Twenty minutes later, Joe and Logan had carefully cut through the thin layer of concrete, the dust settling around them in the beam of their work lights. What they discovered beneath stopped them both cold. Ancient stonework, its surface etched with familiar patterns they'd seen in the vineyard, lay beneath the modern flooring. At its center was a perfectly circular depression, its dimensions hauntingly familiar.

"Dad," Logan exclaimed, as he pulled out his phone to record the find, "that looks exactly like—"

"The stone we found in the vineyard," Joe finished. He ran his fingers along the grooved edge of the depression, feeling the same precise craftsmanship. "The dimensions... they're identical. Almost as if..."

Logan's mind kicked into high gear. "We should measure it, see how closely it matches up before we—"

"Get the stone," Joe interrupted, surprising himself with the urgency in his voice. Something deep in his gut, the same instinct that had guided him through decades of farming, told him this was right. This was meant to be.

They retrieved the stone from the wine cellar, its surface seeming to pulse faintly in the work lights, almost responding to their presence. Together, they positioned it over the circular depression, father and son moving in perfect synchronization.

"Ready?" Joe asked, looking at his son, seeing the same mix of excitement and apprehension he felt reflected in Logan's eyes.

Logan nodded excitedly. "Let's do it."

They lowered the stone into place. The moment it made contact, a sharp *click* resonated through the chamber, like an ancient lock turning. The stone rotated slightly on its own, as if guided by unseen hands, before settling with a final *snap* that seemed to echo through time itself.

"What the—" Logan started, but his words were cut short as brilliant light erupted from the seam where stone met stone. The illumination filled the chamber, causing their shadows to look like ancient cave paintings, before fading away and leaving father and son blinking in the sudden dimness.

Joe stared at the now-sealed stone, his heart pounding against his ribs. Where moments ago there had been smooth stone, a handle had emerged, its surface bearing the same intricate patterns they'd found in the vineyard.

"Get your mother," he said quietly, his voice rough with emotion. "And Zoe. They need to see this. Whatever this is... it's meant for all of us."

Logan was already heading for the stairs, his footsteps echoing with urgency. Joe remained kneeling beside the stone, his hand hovering over its surface, feeling the warmth radiating from it. The pragmatic farmer in him struggled to process what he'd just witnessed, but he couldn't deny the truth before his eyes.

"What have we gotten ourselves into?" he whispered to the empty chamber, his words carrying both fear and wonder. "Will wonders never cease?"

The wine cellar's familiar must gave way to something older, stranger as the family descended into the bunker. Their footsteps echoed off the concrete walls, a chorus of excitement and apprehension mixing with the hum of fluorescent lights. They found Joe crouched beside the stone slab, now seamlessly merged with another stone beneath the floor—as if they'd always been one piece.

Zoe felt Swirly pulse in her pocket as she approached the merged stones. The symbols around the handle seemed to shimmer, calling to her the same way the orb did. "Dad, that stone's literally fused with the floor," she said, fighting the urge to reach out and touch it. "That's not physically possible."

Cathy circled the stone, her experienced eyes scanning for patterns like she would in her Pokémon Go hunts. "The markings around that handle—they're identical to the ones on the orb. Joe, honey, this can't be a coincidence."

Logan crouched. "The molecular bonding between these surfaces is simply amazing," he said, pulling his phone out to take a picture of the phenomenon. "The metal composition of the handle appears to be unlike anything I've seen before."

"QUIET!" Joe's voice reverberated through the underground space. His hands reached for the mysterious handle, years of yard work evident in every callus. "Let's just see what happens when we pull this thing."

A heavy silence fell over the family. Joe wrapped his fingers around the handle and pulled. A sharp hiss filled the air, followed by the grinding of stone against stone. The ancient surface shifted, revealing itself not as a mere archaeological curiosity, but as a hatch leading into the darkness below.

"Holy…" Logan whispered, peering down. Battery-powered lights flickered to life along the walls of a tunnel, illuminating a sturdy metal ladder descending into the earth. The air that wafted up carried the musty scent of decades past, tinged with something metallic and strange.

Joe, his expression a mix of wonder and concern, said, "You know, there've been stories for years about tunnels under Fallbrook. Prohibition-era stuff. Some old-timers even claimed they started here at our vineyard." He shook his head in disbelief. "My great-great-grandparents never breathed a word about it, though. We searched for years but found nothing."

"Let's go down there," Zoe said, her voice trembling with excitement as Swirly seemed to vibrate in response to her words.

Cathy placed a protective hand on her daughter's shoulder. "Let's be smart about this. Who knows how stable it is down there?"

After a brief family huddle, they came to a decision. Joe looked at his son. "Logan, you're with me. We'll do a quick reconnaissance." He turned to his wife and daughter. "Cathy, you and Zoe stay up here. Keep watch. We don't know, the hatch could close automatically."

"Be careful," Cathy said, her eyes reflecting worry as she watched her husband and son prepare to descend into the unknown depths beneath their bunker.

As Joe and Logan prepared for their descent, Zoe clutched the orb in her pocket, its warmth intensifying. The fluorescent lights flickered momentarily, creating a dramatic backdrop to the ancient stone hatch. Whatever secrets lay below, Zoe knew they were one step closer to understanding the true nature of their family's connection to these mysterious artifacts.

Joe and Logan descended the metal ladder, each rung solid beneath their feet despite its apparent age. The temperature dropped noticeably with each step down, and an unusual metallic scent tickled their nostrils. Joe couldn't shake the memory of his grandfather's stories about secret passages beneath the vineyard—tales he'd always dismissed as fancy until now.

"This is definitely not what I expected," Logan said, running his hand along the tunnel wall. Despite being carved from earth, the surface felt unnaturally smooth, almost glassy. "Feel this, Dad. Some kind of sealant, maybe?"

Joe nodded, his attention drawn to the electric lanterns that lined the passageway at regular intervals. Their soft, steady glow giving an otherworldly light to the tunnel. "These shouldn't be working," he said, his voice hushed with wonder. "No power source, no visible wiring, yet they're as bright as if they were recently installed."

The passage towered above them, easily twelve feet high, with enough width for them to walk shoulder to shoulder. Logan, at his full height of six feet, felt dwarfed by the space. Their footsteps created a symphony of echoes—soft thuds against the sealed floor, alternating with the crunch of scattered gravel. "Bit excessive for a bootlegging operation, don't you think? The engineering alone would have cost a fortune."

After about a hundred feet, the passage opened into a vast chamber that took their breath away. Ancient wooden barrels lay scattered across the floor, their staves rotted and collapsed, still bearing the faint smell of whiskey and wine. But it was the architecture that stopped them in their tracks.

"Look at these arches," Joe said, his voice resonating with perfect acoustics in the cavernous space. The ceiling curved gracefully overhead, the architectural style reminiscent of ancient Roman construction rather than 1920s California. Each arch bore intricate geometric patterns that reflected the lantern light. "This is way more sophisticated than some prohibition-era bootlegging tunnel," Joe finished, his flashlight beam tracing the elegant curves. "This is old. Really old."

A deep rumble from above sent a shiver down Logan's spine. He instinctively stepped closer to his father, though the tunnel remained solid. The sound seemed to resonate with the symbols carved into the walls, making them appear to shimmer momentarily.

"Just traffic on Main, probably," Joe said, though his tone suggested he wasn't entirely convinced. His mind wandered to Zoe and the orb—what connection did they have to all this? "These branches though…" He gestured to the many corridors splitting off from the main tunnel. "They seem to head in every direction, like a planned network."

They explored several more chambers, each as vast and empty as the first, their footsteps echoing off walls that clung to untold secrets. Each room bore the same impossible architecture—soaring arches that defied both time and engineering logic.

"Dad," Logan's voice was quiet, thoughtful. He pulled out a small notebook and began sketching the patterns. "These symbols carved into the archways—they're the same as the ones on the stone hatch. And on Swirly. The probability of that being coincidence is practically zero."

"I noticed that too," Joe replied, studying the ancient markings while fighting an internal battle between curiosity and parental concern. "Your sister might need to look at these, though I'm not sure how I feel about her coming down here."

After discovering yet another branching tunnel, they exchanged knowing looks. "We could get lost down here pretty easily," Logan said, checking his phone. "No signal, by the way. The walls must be lined with something that blocks transmission."

"Yeah, we should head back," Joe agreed, brushing dirt from his jeans. "We need to map this place out properly. Bring proper equipment, markers, maybe some of those survey tools from the vineyard."

As they turned back toward the entrance, Logan paused. "Dad? What do you think this really was? I mean, bootleggers didn't build this. This is… something else entirely. The engineering principles alone suggest technology we don't even have today."

Joe's flashlight beam played across the smooth walls one last time, illuminating symbols that appeared to pulse with their own inner light. "I don't know, son. But I've got a feeling Zoe's orb might have something to do with it. These tunnels, Swirly, the strange events lately—they're all connected somehow. Let's go tell the others what we found. Your mother's probably worried sick by now."

They retraced their steps through the towering passages, both lost in thought about what other secrets might lie waiting in the labyrinth beneath their feet, and what it might mean for their family's future.

# CHAPTER 10

# THE PACKING HOUSE

While their parents' voices drifted down from above, discussing mapping strategies and safety protocols, Logan gathered his research equipment in the bunker. The air felt heavy with anticipation, carrying the metallic tang of the ancient stone mixed with the sterile scent of modern electronics. Zoe perched on a folding chair, absently running her fingers across Swirly's surface while watching her brother meticulously arrange his instruments.

"So," Logan began, adjusting a frequency scanner that emitted a soft, rhythmic beeping, "I've been thinking about the theoretical physics behind all this." His hands trembled slightly as he calibrated the sensitive equipment. Every measurement had to be perfect—Zoe's safety might depend on it. "Everything we've seen goes against conventional physics, but there might be a logical explanation."

"Like what?" Zoe leaned forward, genuinely interested despite her brother's tendency to overcomplicate things. Swirly pulsed, almost like it was listening too.

"Well," Logan switched on his tablet, "quantum entanglement could explain the connection between you and Swirly. These energy readings we've been getting? They're consistent with theoretical models of temporal displacement."

Zoe rolled her eyes, but couldn't hide her affectionate smile. "You mean time travel, right? Why can't you just say time travel?"

"Because it's more complicated than—" Logan stopped mid-sentence, catching Zoe's exaggerated imitation of his serious expression. "Very funny, Butt Nugget."

A sharp beep from one of Logan's sensors cut through their banter. The frequency scanner's display flickered erratically, its needle jumping beyond the normal range.

"That's weird," Logan said, frowning at the readout. "These readings... they're like when we first found the stone, but stronger."

Zoe straightened, her expression serious. "I know what we need to do." She stood up, holding Swirly at eye level. "Those missing kids from 1973—the Fallbrook Five. We could see what happened to them."

Logan had his doubts. "Zoe, that was decades ago. We don't even know if—"

"But we have to try," Zoe interrupted, her voice soft but intense. "They were our age, Logan. They had families, friends, futures... and they just vanished. What if we could find out what happened? What if we could help?"

Logan studied his sister's determined expression, recognizing that familiar stubborn set of her jaw. "At least let me run some preliminary tests first—"

"The hatch!" Zoe exclaimed, already moving toward the ancient stone. "The indentation—it's the same size as Swirly. It's meant to work together!"

"Hold on," Logan called out, hurrying to close the hatch. Despite his reservations, his hands moved efficiently, securing the seal. "If we're really doing this, we need complete contact between the orb and the stone surface." He checked his monitoring equipment one last time, noting the increasingly erratic readings. "Just... be careful, okay? And if anything feels wrong—"

"I know, I know." Zoe took a deep breath, positioning herself over the hatch. Swirly's surface shimmered with intense colors that only she could see, its warmth spreading up her arms. "Trust me, Logan. This feels right."

Logan's instruments erupted in a cascade of beeps and alerts. "These readings are crazy," he said. "The quantum field is already starting to fluctuate, and we haven't even—"

"Here goes nothing," Zoe said, lowering Swirly toward the circular indentation. The orb seemed to hum with anticipation, its surface rippling like liquid starlight.

"Wait!" Logan called out, but it was too late. The moment Swirly touched the ancient stone, reality itself seemed to bend.

A brilliant white light erupted from the point of contact, so intense that Logan had to shield his eyes. The light didn't just illuminate the bunker—it seemed to bend around corners and through solid objects, defying the basic laws of physics. His equipment screamed with readings that should have been impossible, the displays flickering between numbers that made his head spin.

Then, as suddenly as it had appeared, the light vanished. The emergency lighting system sputtered to life, creating an eerie glow throughout the bunker. The sudden silence was deafening.

"Zoe?" Logan called out, his voice cracking. He blinked rapidly, trying to clear the afterimages from his vision. "Can you hear me?"

Nothing.

"ZOE!" He spun around, heart thundering in his chest. The bunker remained as it had been moments before—his equipment still humming, tablet still recording data, the ancient stone hatch still firmly in place.

But where his sister had stood, there was only empty air. Both Zoe and Swirly had vanished completely.

Logan rushed to the hatch, his resolve crumbling as panic set in. His hands trembled as they traced the now-empty indentation. The stone felt cool beneath his fingers, but the ancient symbols carved around its edge pulsed with a faint, rhythmic light.

"No, no, no," he said, pulling up the readings on his tablet. The data scrolling across the screen confirmed his worst fears—massive temporal displacement, quantum tunneling signatures, spatial distortion patterns that shouldn't have been possible. "This is bad. This is really, really bad."

The bunker door burst open as Joe and Cathy rushed in, responding to the commotion.

"What happened?" Cathy asked, as she franticly scanned the room. "Where's Zoe?"

Logan gestured helplessly at the stone hatch, his usual eloquence deserting him. "We... we were running an experiment. The Fallbrook Five—she wanted to see what happened to them. She put Swirly in the indentation and there was this light..." His voice broke. "She's gone. She just... disappeared."

"My baby," Cathy said, gripping the edge of a nearby table. Her phone buzzed in her pocket—probably another Pokémon Go notification—but for once, she didn't even reach for it. "Logan, where did your sister go?"

Logan pulled up the temporal signature data. "According to these readings... June 15, 1973. The exact day those kids disappeared." He looked up at his parents, face pale. "You don't think she's actually..."

"In 1973?" Joe finished, standing up with a determined set to his jaw. "After everything we've seen lately, I'm not ruling anything out." He placed a steady hand on his son's shoulder. "What else can you tell us from your readings?"

Logan forced himself to think like a scientist rather than a terrified brother. "The energy signature is still active, just barely. Like... like an echo." He pointed to a line on his tablet's display. "Whatever happened, I don't think it's permanent. There might be a way to bring her back."

"Then that's what we're going to do," Joe said. "Show us everything you've got. Every reading, every theory. We're getting your sister back."

As the family huddled around Logan's equipment, the symbols on the ancient hatch continued their rhythmic glow, like a heartbeat counting down the moments until Zoe's return—or marking the time since her disappearance into the past.

The question wasn't just whether they could bring her back—but what she might find in 1973, and whether solving one mystery might unravel something far bigger than they'd imagined.

Zoe blinked against the bright summer sun, her head spinning as the sudden time jump left her momentarily disoriented. Swirly pulsed in her hand—she didn't even remember grabbing him during the flash in the bunker. Her heart raced as she tried to process what had just happened, the familiar yet alien streets of 1973 Fallbrook stretching before her like a living photograph.

The El Real Hotel stood proudly before her, "The Packing House" sign looking new. A bell-bottomed teenager walked past, a transistor radio blaring "Dream On" by Aerosmith. Zoe pressed Swirly closer to her chest, drawing comfort from its steady warmth as she gathered her courage.

Taking a deep breath, she pushed open the heavy wooden door to the restaurant. The aroma of home-cooked meals and freshly baked bread mingled with cigarette smoke from the bar area. Exposed wooden beams crossed the ceiling, and antique chandeliers providing a warm glow in the dining room. Black and white photographs of old Fallbrook lined the walls—scenes of avocado groves, citrus orchards, and farmers standing beside their harvests. Everything looked so new, yet somehow ancient at the same time.

The restaurant buzzed with the dinner crowd, waitresses in burnt orange uniforms weaving between tables with plates of steaming food. Large, rustic tables made from reclaimed wood dominated the space, while intimate booths lined the walls. The clinking of silverware and murmur of conversations filled the air, creating a cozy atmosphere that would have been comforting under different circumstances. A jukebox in the corner switched to "Let's Get It On" by Marvin Gaye.

Movement in the corner caught her eye. A group of children huddled around a booth, their laughter rising above the restaurant chatter as they played some sort of game. Zoe counted five children—three boys and two girls. Their clothing marked them as kids from another era: bell-bottom jeans, brightly patterned shirts, and sneakers that looked like they belonged in a vintage photograph.

The smallest girl wore her dark hair in two long braids tied with yellow ribbons, while the oldest boy had a distinctive red baseball cap turned backward on his head. They seemed so alive, so real—not at all like the faded newspaper clippings she'd seen of the Fallbrook Five.

Her heart nearly stopped when the boy in the red cap, probably around twelve, casually slipped behind the corner booth and... vanished. There was no flash, no sound—he simply ceased to exist. Before she could process what she'd seen, the girl with braids followed, disappearing just as mysteriously. One by one, the remaining children ducked behind the booth, each vanishing without a trace.

None of the adults in the restaurant seemed to notice, as if the children were invisible to everyone but her. The jukebox continued playing, dishes clattered, and conversations carried on, oblivious to the tragedy unfolding in their midst.

With trembling legs, Zoe approached the booth. Behind it, partially concealed by dark wooden paneling, she discovered a narrow opening. So they didn't disappear after all. The passage beyond was dark, but not frightening—somehow familiar. Glancing back at the oblivious diners, she squeezed through the gap, Swirly's warmth giving her courage.

Stone steps led downward, worn smooth by countless footsteps. As she made her way down, a grinding sound behind her made her jump. The opening had sealed itself, leaving no trace of its existence. Panic fluttered in her chest, but Swirly's beating grew stronger, almost reassuring.

The children's voices echoed ahead, their laughter bouncing off the walls. The air grew cooler as she descended, carrying that same metallic tang she'd noticed in the tunnels back home—or rather, forward home. Her mind raced with the implications of what she was witnessing. Was she meant to be here? Had Swirly brought her to this specific moment for a reason?

The passage leveled out, and Zoe found herself in the same tunnel system Logan and her father had explored just hours ago—or would explore, fifty years from now. But here, in 1973, the walls seemed newer, their coating more pristine. The electric lanterns providing light as the children ran ahead.

"Wait!" she called out, her voice echoing off the walls. "Please, you don't understand!"

Following the sound of their footsteps, Zoe realized they were heading toward her family's vineyard. The tunnel twisted and turned, but where other passages branched off, the children kept going straight, seeming to know exactly where they were going. Their footsteps echoed with purpose, as if drawn by some unseen force.

"Wait!" she called out again.

At the sound of her voice, the children turned, stopping abruptly when they spotted Zoe. Their eyes widened with fear, and the boy in the red cap grabbed the hand of the smallest girl with braids.

"Who are you?" he demanded, backing away. "You're not supposed to be down here!" His voice carried authority beyond his years, protective of the younger children.

"Please," Zoe said, holding up her hands. "I'm trying to help. I know what's about to happen—"

"You can't stop it," the girl with braids interrupted, her voice eerily calm. "They're waiting for us."

"Who's waiting?" Zoe asked, taking a cautious step forward. "Please, let me help you."

The children backed away, their expressions a mix of fear and... was that anticipation? They moved as one toward the dead end, right where the ancient stone would one day be installed in her family's bunker. The electric lanterns shining on their faces made them look older, wiser somehow.

The boy in the red cap stepped forward, placing himself between Zoe and the others. "You need to leave," he said. "This isn't for you to see." His eyes flickered to Swirly, recognition flashing across his face. "Where did you get that?"

Before Zoe could process his words, a brilliant flash of white light engulfed the smallest girl—the one with braids. When it faded, she was gone. The others didn't scream or cry; they seemed to be waiting their turn. Zoe's chest tightened as she realized they knew exactly what was coming.

"No, please!" Zoe reached out, but another flash took the second child, a boy with wire-rimmed glasses who'd been quietly watching her the whole time.

"They promised to show us everything," the red-capped boy said, as another flash claimed the third child. "All of time and space. We're not disappearing—we're going on an adventure."

"Hurry up, Brian!" the fourth child yelled. Flash! He vanished, leaving only the boy in the red cap. He looked directly at Zoe, his expression of worry melting into a peaceful smile. "Maybe we'll see you again, time traveler."

The final flash of light took him before Zoe could respond, leaving her alone in the tunnel with far more questions than answers. She stood frozen, Swirly burning hot in her hand, as the weight of what she'd witnessed crashed over her.

These were the missing children—the Fallbrook Five. But they hadn't been taken against their will. They'd chosen this, somehow knowing what awaited them. And that boy... he'd recognized Swirly, or something like it.

The stone beneath her feet pulsed with energy, matching Swirly's increasingly frantic warmth. White light bloomed around her, so bright it erased the world. Her last thought before the light consumed her was of Logan, and how he'd never believe what she'd discovered—if she made it back home at all.

Then everything went white.

Logan rubbed his tired eyes. Joe paced behind him, his boots scuffing against the concrete floor, while Cathy frantically searched news archives from 1973, her fingers trembling on the keyboard. The sudden chirp of her phone pierced the tense silence, making them all jump.

"It's Becky," Cathy said. Her friend's concerned voice came through clearly on speaker.

"Cathy, something's happening over there. My instruments are showing unprecedented temporal fluctuations, and Pokémon Go is manifesting anomalies I've never encountered. All readings are centered on your property."

Cathy exchanged a meaningful look with Joe, who was nodding. "Actually, Becky... we need your expertise. It's... complicated, but—"

"Say no more. I'll be there in ten minutes."

While they waited, Cathy absently opened Pokémon Go, seeking any distraction from her mounting worry about Zoe. "Might as well check what Becky mentioned—" In augmented reality, or AR mode, she swept her phone around the room, expecting the usual Pidgeys or Rattatas. Instead, her screen glowed ominously, revealing something breathtakingly beautiful yet terrifying standing atop the stone hatch—a stunning, ethereal being with magnificent wings that shimmered with iridescent light, scattering a halo of colors around it.

The creature's eyes were large and luminous, filled with an ancient wisdom that felt both inviting and foreboding. It hovered above the ground, its presence permeating the air with a palpable energy that tingled against her skin. Despite its otherworldly grace, there was something unsettling about the way its form flickered between solid and translucent, as if it were simultaneously part of this world and another, more mysterious realm.

Cathy's breath caught in her throat, captivated yet fearful. The wings unfurled, revealing intricate patterns that seemed to ripple with the cosmos itself—stars, galaxies, and swirling nebulae danced within their folds. It opened its mouth, and a harmonious, celestial sound echoed forth, not quite a voice but a melody that resonated deep within her soul, stirring emotions long buried.

"Mom?" Logan's voice trembled, breaking her reverie as he moved closer, trying to comprehend the unfathomable being displayed on the screen. "What... is that?"

With every passing second, the being's gaze felt more penetrating, as if it could peer into the very essence of their existence. It leaned closer, and for a moment, Cathy felt an inexplicable warmth and light wash over her, as though she were being embraced by the creature's very aura. But beneath that beauty lurked a palpable intensity that sent chills down her spine.

Suddenly, images swirled around the being, fleeting visions of children playing and laughing in a sunlit meadow—joyous yet tinged with sorrow, reminding her of the disappearances that haunted Fallbrook. The air felt electric, alive with possibilities and dangers intertwined.

In a moment of awe and terror, Cathy reached out to touch the screen, but as her finger made contact, the being recoiled, its expression shifting into one of concern as ripples of energy pulsed through the screen. A sudden gust of wind inexplicably swept through the bunker, causing the lights to flicker, amplifying the creature's otherworldly presence.

"Get back!" Logan shouted, stepping protectively in front of Cathy, his heart racing as the glowing figure seemed to swell in intensity, becoming both more beautiful and more intimidating.

"Mom, don't!" he said, but Cathy was entranced, transfixed by the being that felt like a bridge between their world and an unknown cosmos. Just then, it emitted a hauntingly beautiful hum that filled the space, a sound that resonated with her very being—a call to both wonder and caution.

As quickly as it appeared, the angelic being shimmered and dissolved into glowing particles of light, swirling and twinkling in the air like stars, before vanishing completely. The silence that followed was deafening, leaving Cathy breathless and wide-eyed.

"What was that?" Cathy managed to say, the glowing remnants fading from her vision, as the lingering sensation of warmth enveloped her.

"I—I don't know," Joe replied, still staring at the screen, his expression a mix of awe and trepidation. "But whatever that was... it felt significant. And real."

Cathy's mind raced with the implications of their encounter. "It was beautiful, but... frightening too. It felt like it wanted something from us," she murmured, still recovering from the experience, her heart pounding in sync with the echoes of the being's melody.

Logan scrutinized the phone screen, replaying the moment in his mind, searching for details he might have missed. "What if it's connected to Zoe? Or the orb?" he suggested, glancing nervously at the stone hatch where the apparition had stood.

"Or the children," Cathy added, her voice rising. "It could be a sign—some sort of warning or a message tied to their disappearances. Maybe it knows what happened."

Joe rubbed his worry stone anxiously, glancing from the phone to the hatch. "We need to figure out how this all fits together," he said. The gravity of their discoveries felt heavier than ever. "If the military is interested, could they already know about these... beings?"

The family fell silent, the weight of unanswered questions hanging in the air. Cathy fought back tears, overwhelmed by concern for Zoe and the mystery that seemed to envelop them.

Before they could process this revelation any further, the bunker erupted in a brilliant white light that seemed to pulse with its own heartbeat. Static electricity crackled through the air as they shielded their eyes, hearts pounding in unison. The light collapsed in on itself, leaving behind a familiar figure standing on the stone hatch.

"Zoe!" Cathy's cry was raw with relief as she rushed forward, enveloping her daughter in a fierce embrace. The rest of the family quickly joined, forming a protective circle around her.

"Do you have any idea what you put us through?" Logan's voice cracked, his usual demeanor crumbling. "I thought we'd lost you to some temporal void!"

"Where were you, sweetheart?" Joe asked, keeping one protective arm around her shoulders. "What happened out there?"

Zoe's words tumbled out, her eyes bright with discovery. "The Packing House, 1973! Dad, I saw them—the Fallbrook Five! They were just kids, laughing and playing like nothing was wrong." She paused, clutching Swirly tighter. "I followed them through a hidden passage behind one of the booths, down into these same tunnels." Her voice softened. "They vanished right here, one by one, in the same kind of light that brought me back."

"But where did they go?" Logan was already documenting everything, his mind racing with possibilities. "The temporal displacement could have sent them anywhere—forward, sideways, to parallel dimensions…"

"I don't know," Zoe admitted, looking down at Swirly, which pulsed in response to her touch. "But these tunnels aren't just smuggler routes. They're part of something bigger—a network of temporal pathways. And this spot—" she tapped the stone hatch with her foot, causing a faint ripple of blue energy to spread outward, "—it's more than a doorway. It's a nexus point."

Logan's fingers sliding across his tablet. "That would explain the quantum readings I've been getting. The stone isn't just a portal; it's an anchor point in spacetime."

The basement door creaked open above them, and Becky's voice echoed down. "Hello? Cathy? My readings are nuts down there!"

The family exchanged loaded glances. Cathy clutched her phone, the screenshot of the ethereal being still glowing on the screen. "We need her help," she said. "These beings, the tunnels, the missing children—it's all connected, and we're in over our heads."

Joe ran his hand over the stone in his pocket, a habit that had intensified since they'd found Swirly. "Agreed. But we need to be careful about how much we reveal. If the military's already interested…" He left the threat unspoken.

"Bring her down," Zoe said with unexpected authority, Swirly brightening in her grip. "She's part of this somehow. I can feel it."

"Come down, Becky!" Cathy called up, her voice steadier than she felt. "But please… close the door behind you."

As Becky's footsteps approached the bunker, Joe turned to Zoe, placing both hands on her shoulders. "No more solo adventures through time, young lady. We do this together or not at all." His stern expression softened. "I can't lose you to whatever took those children."

Zoe nodded, but her eyes were drawn back to the stone hatch, its ancient symbols seeming to pulse with hidden meaning. Somewhere across time and space, five children from 1973 were waiting to be found. And somehow, she knew finding them was just the start.

The family stood together as Becky descended the stairs, her equipment beeping frantically. The orb glowed softly in Zoe's hands, a reminder that their quiet life in Fallbrook had transformed into something extraordinary—and potentially dangerous.

The mysteries were mounting: the ethereal beings, the missing children, the military's interest, and the true purpose of the tunnels beneath their feet. But at least now they wouldn't face them alone.

# CHAPTER 11

# NEED FOR PROTECTION

The bunker's dim, flickering light showed the electromagnetic shielding along the walls, while the musty scent of earth and aging concrete hung thick in the recycled air. The cramped space, barely large enough for the metal table and scattered equipment, amplified the unease that permeated the room. Becky leaned against the metal table, her lab coat wrinkled from hours of work, dark circles under her eyes betraying her exhaustion. She crossed her arms, her voice steady but tinged with urgency.

"I'm telling you, Cathy, this town is a powder keg. Lights in the sky, the weird power surges, and don't even get me started on the missing time reports. Something is happening here, and it's getting worse."

Cathy perched nervously on the edge of a military-surplus crate, her fingers drumming an anxious rhythm on its surface. Her hands trembled as she fumbled with her phone, the screen's glow illuminating her worried expression. Finally, she blurted, "You think that's weird? Wait till you see this." She thrust the screen toward Becky.

The image showed a hulking shadow, vaguely monstrous, with glowing eyes that had sent shivers down Cathy's spine when she'd snapped the picture. But when Becky leaned in, adjusting her glasses, she frowned and squinted.

"That's... a Snorlax."

"What?" Cathy snatched the phone back, her face flushing. "No, it's—" Her words caught in her throat as her eyes confirmed the truth. The terrifying creature she'd been so sure she'd captured was now unmistakably a Snorlax, cartoonishly dozing in front of what appeared to be the bunker door.

Cathy's face turned crimson. "No way. That's not what I saw! I swear, Becky. It had glowing red eyes, claws—like it came out of a nightmare!"

Becky tried to suppress a smirk, but the absurdity broke through. "Well, unless Snorlax has been hitting the gym and mastering holograms, I think something's messing with your phone."

Cathy slumped back against the crate, muttering, "Like a Snorlax would even fit in here…"

The levity was short-lived. Cathy reached into her bag, her expression growing serious as she pulled out a stack of photos. "Look, this isn't the only strange thing I've seen," she said, spreading them out on the table. "These were in our attic. They're old and weathered, but they show something… here." She pointed to one of the images, her finger tracing the outline of a familiar structure.

"That's… the observatory," Becky said, recognizing the massive dome in the grainy images. Mt. Palomar. "I know that place like the back of my hand. My mom used to take me there on clear nights. And I know the site manager, Hunter Thorne. He's George Hale's great-grandson—the guy who built the telescope. If there's anything suspicious going on up there, Hunter would know."

"Can we trust him?" Cathy asked, her eyes scanning the photos again.

Becky hesitated. "Hunter's solid. But if something's happening that involves… this," she gestured at the images and Cathy's phone, "we keep it vague. He doesn't need to know about missing time or scary Snorlaxes."

Cathy let out a nervous laugh. "Agreed. So, what's the plan?"

Becky grabbed her laptop, its cracked screen providing a faint glow. "We dig. Let's see if we can find more pictures of the observatory online. Schematics, site maps, anything. If something's being hidden up there, we'll need to know the layout."

The two fell into silence, save for the clatter of keys and the hum of the generator. As they searched, a creeping thought lingered in the back of Cathy's mind: whatever was out there, it would not wait for them to figure it out.

The morning sun shined through the windows as Cathy packed trail mix and sandwiches into a cooler. Zoe perched on a barstool, drumming her fingers against the granite countertop, her excitement obvious. Logan, trying to maintain his teenage cool, leaned against the doorframe, though his occasional glances at the backpack containing Swirly betrayed his interest. Becky had arrived early, her curiosity evident in her rapid-fire questions about recent events.

Joe watched them all, the stone warm in his pocket as he absently rubbed it. The vineyard needed attention. The new irrigation system wasn't quite dialed in, and real gophers had taken over where the ancient stone was found. "You guys go ahead," he said, kissing Cathy on the cheek, breathing in the familiar scent of her shampoo. "Take lots of pictures for me."

As their car disappeared down the winding driveway, kicking up dust that caught the morning light, Joe grabbed his pruning shears and headed out to work. The familiar weight of the tools in his hands usually brought comfort, a connection to the generations of Baileys who had worked this land before him. Today, though, something felt different.

The afternoon sun beat down on his shoulders as he methodically thinned another grapevine. Sweat trickled down his back, and the sweet-earth smell of the vineyard filled his nostrils. Then it hit him - that distinct, unsettling sensation of being watched. The hair on the back of his neck stood up, and his hands stilled mid-cut.

He straightened slowly, scanning the rows of vines stretching across the rolling hills of the Bailey Family Vineyard. Nothing seemed out of place, yet the feeling persisted. His mind wandered to Cathy's recent strange experience with Pokémon Go in the bunker, with that otherworldly creature staring through the screen.

The memory of Cathy installing the game on his phone surfaced - her excited babbling about "raid battles" and "helping her catch legendaries" had seemed so trivial then. Now, though... Joe pulled out his phone, fingers fumbling as he searched for the colorful icon she'd insisted he keep "just in case."

He headed toward the bunker, passing under the mighty oak tree. Its ancient branches seemed to reach for him like grasping fingers. The familiar comfort of the tree felt different now, charged with an energy he couldn't explain.

Inside the bunker, the air cooled his sun-warmed skin as he activated the app's AR feature. His heart thundered in his chest as he pointed the camera toward the hatch. For a moment, nothing happened. Then, through the phone's screen, a figure materialized - a military officer, his colonel's insignia gleaming under artificial light. The man's stern face was intent, his eyes scanning methodically over what appeared to be reports.

Joe's breath caught in his throat. Though the figure seemed unaware of his presence, icy dread settled in his stomach as he watched the colonel's movements. The military man's presence meant only one thing - someone knew about the orb, about Zoe's connection to it. His mind raced with possibilities, each worse than the last. If the military was involved, how long had they been watching? What did they know about his daughter's abilities?

"Over my dead body," he said, his jaw clenching as the colonel continued his methodical review. His hand instinctively reached for the stone in his pocket, its smooth surface offering little comfort now.

Joe killed the app with trembling fingers and hurried back outside, positioning himself where he could observe the street while appearing to work. His heart nearly stopped when he spotted the parked sedan across the way, its driver sitting motionless behind the wheel, clearly watching the property.

The afternoon crawled by as Joe divided his attention between his silent phone and the ominous vehicle. He thought about the bunker beneath his feet, about the ancient stone they'd moved there, about Swirly and all its mysteries. Most of all, he thought about Zoe - his little girl that was somehow in the center of it all.

The sun dipped behind the coastal mountains, as Joe stood among the vines his family had tended for generations, his phone clutched in one hand, his eyes never leaving the sedan. The weight of protecting not just his family but their legacy pressed down on him like a physical burden. Whatever forces were gathering - military, supernatural, or something else entirely - they'd have to go through him first.

He touched the rough bark of a grapevine, drawing strength from its deep roots in the earth. "Come on," he whispered, willing his family's safe return. "Come home."

As darkness settled over the vineyard, Joe's resolve hardened. He might not understand everything that was happening, but he understood this: nothing would harm his family while he drew breath.

The sedan's engine hummed to life and started to pull away. But Joe knew better than to feel relief. This wasn't an end - it was the beginning.

The morning sun painted Mt. Palomar's winding roads as the SUV climbed higher into the clouds. Cathy gripped the door handle at each hairpin turn, Pokémon Go forgotten in her lap. In the back seat, Logan pressed his face against the window, rattling off facts about the observatory's construction while Zoe sat quietly, one hand pressed against her pocket where Swirly's warmth intensified with each mile marker they passed.

"The altitude changes are affecting my readings," Logan said, frowning at his tablet. "There's something different about the electromagnetic field up here."

Zoe nodded absently, watching the vegetation thin and transform from dense chaparral to scattered pines. The air grew noticeably cooler and thinner as they ascended, making her slightly light-headed—or perhaps it was Swirly's increasingly urgent pulses against her leg.

The observatory materialized like a pearl against the mountain's dark crown, its massive dome catching the morning light. A testament to humanity's ambition to reach for the stars. Becky led them toward the entrance, her professional demeanor masking her excitement as she explained the facility's significance.

"The Hale Telescope was the world's largest effective telescope for nearly 45 years," she said as they approached the entrance. "Some say it's seen things that were never meant to be discovered."

Logan raised an eyebrow. "That sounds more like science fiction than astronomy."

"Sometimes the line between the two isn't as clear as we'd like to think," Becky responded with a knowing smile.

Inside, the observatory hummed with purpose. Banks of sophisticated equipment lined the walls. The air carried the sharp scent of electronics and filtered air, along with something else—an indefinable energy that called to Zoe.

Cathy pulled out her phone, frowning at the screen. "Pokémon Go is acting strange again. These aren't any Pokémon I've ever seen before."

The main observation room stretched before them, dominated by the legendary Hale Telescope. Its massive frame reached toward the dome above, the 200-inch mirror hidden behind protective covers. The structure's sleek, geometric lines represented both an engineering marvel and humanity's relentless quest to understand the cosmos.

Scientists worked quietly at their stations, faces illuminated by the glow of their monitors. Streams of data flickered across screens—star charts, spectral analysis, and strings of numbers that painted pictures of distant galaxies.

Hunter Thorne appeared, his footsteps echoing across the polished floor. He looked younger than they expected, with intelligent eyes that seemed to take in everything at once. "Welcome to Palomar," he said, extending his hand to Cathy. "Dr. Martinez said you were interested in our current research projects?"

As Hunter led them through the facility, explaining the telescope's capabilities and current studies, Zoe felt Swirly growing increasingly agitated. The orb's warmth had become almost uncomfortable, its pulsing matching some hidden rhythm in the building itself.

She found her attention drawn to the eastern wing, where the corridor disappeared behind key-carded doors. An invisible force pulled at her, growing stronger with each step. Without thinking, she interrupted Hunter's explanation about stellar photography.

"What's in that section?" she asked, pointing

Hunter's enthusiastic demeanor faltered, his smile freezing in place. "That's a restricted area," he said quickly, eyes darting to the security cameras mounted in the corners. "Sensitive equipment. We're actually conducting some classified research for—" He stopped abruptly, clearing his throat. "Speaking of which, I have another appointment I need to get to."

Hunter's footsteps could be heard down the corridor as he hurried away from the tour group, his heart pounding. Once around the corner, he pulled out his secure phone and dialed a number he wished he could forget.

Logan exchanged glances with Zoe. "Well, that wasn't suspicious at all."

Cathy stared at her phone, tilting it toward the restricted wing. "The readings are strongest in that direction. Look at this." She showed them her screen, where a strange, ethereal Pokémon-like creature seemed to hover near the locked doors. Unlike normal Pokémon, this one appeared almost translucent, its form shifting and wavering like heat waves off hot pavement.

"That's not a normal game glitch," Logan said, pulling out his tablet to take readings. "The electromagnetic disturbance I detected earlier is centered in that wing too."

Zoe took a step toward the forbidden corridor, drawn by an irresistible force. Swirly's pulsating had become almost frantic, matching her quickening heartbeat. But before she could get closer, a security guard materialized from a nearby alcove.

"This area is off-limits to visitors," he stated, his hand resting casually on his radio. His eyes lingered a fraction too long on Zoe's pocket, where Swirly's glow was just visible through the fabric.

Becky stepped forward smoothly. "Of course, we were just leaving. Thank you for the tour." She gestured for the others to follow her toward the exit.

As they made their way out, Zoe noticed two scientists at their workstations exchange meaningful glances. The first, a middle-aged man with thick glasses and a furrowed brow, was studying a monitor showing unusual energy patterns. The second, a woman whose face was illuminated by her screen's glow, gave an almost imperceptible nod.

As the observatory grew smaller in the rearview mirror, its white dome gleaming in the afternoon sun like a sentinel guarding ancient secrets, everyone in the SUV was silent, each of them contemplating what happened at the Observatory.

Zoe cradled Swirly, watching colors swirl beneath its surface. One thing was certain—Mount Palomar Observatory held secrets far beyond its astronomical research, secrets that somehow connected to their mysterious orb and its powers.

The tension was palpable as they descended the mountain. Cathy's phone buzzed, making everyone jump. She glanced at the screen, her face paling slightly.

"It's another one of those strange Pokémon," she said, turning the phone so the others could see. "But this one's different. It looks almost... military?"

Logan leaned forward to study the screen. The figure resembled a uniformed soldier, but its form was translucent, shifting between dimensions like a glitch in reality. "The readings are getting stronger," he said, checking his tablet. "Whatever's happening up there, it's affecting a much larger area than we thought."

"We need to tell Dad about this," Zoe said, still cradling Swirly. The orb had begun to pulse again, but differently now—more like a warning than the excited energy it had shown in the observatory. "About Hunter, the restricted wing, everything."

Becky navigated another switchback, her knuckles white on the steering wheel. "There's something else," she said, glancing in the rearview mirror. "I know Hunter wrote some research papers quite some time ago about temporal anomalies. Papers that disappeared from academic databases shortly after I found them."

"Disappeared?" Logan asked in disbelief. "Digital papers don't just disappear."

"They do when someone wants to hide something," Becky replied. "And based on what we saw today, I'd say there's a lot being hidden at that observatory."

Zoe felt Swirly grow warmer in her hands. The orb's surface swirled with deeper colors, and for a moment, she thought she saw a reflection of the observatory's restricted wing in its depths. "We have to go back," she said. "Whatever's in that east wing... it's important. I can feel it."

"It's also dangerous," Logan countered, but his voice lacked its usual dismissive tone. "Did you see how quickly that security guard appeared? And those scientists watching us... they knew something."

"My Pokémon readings matched some anomalies I've been tracking around Fallbrook," Cathy added, still staring at her phone. "It's all connected somehow—the orb, the observatory, these strange appearances in the game."

As they descended further into the valley, the observatory's dome disappeared behind the mountain's shoulder. But its presence lingered in their minds, along with the growing certainty that they'd stumbled onto something far bigger than they'd imagined.

"We need a plan," Logan said finally, his mind already working on the problem. "If we're going back—and it seems we have to—we need to be smarter about it. More prepared."

Zoe nodded, feeling Swirly pulse in agreement. "But we also need to be careful. I don't think we're the only ones interested in what's behind those doors."

Becky took a deep breath as they turned onto the main highway. "I have some old contacts in the astronomical community. Let me see what I can find out about Hunter Thorne and that restricted wing. There might be more to his family's connection to the observatory than he's letting on."

As if in response, Swirly emitted a soft glow, its light reflecting off the car windows like distant starlight. The same light they'd seen when they got close to the restricted wing, Zoe realized—a light that held secrets they were only beginning to understand.

The rest of the drive passed in thoughtful silence, each person lost in their own contemplation of what they'd discovered. But one thing was clear: Mount Palomar Observatory was more than just a window to the stars. It was a doorway to something else entirely, and somehow, Swirly was the key.

As they approached Fallbrook, Zoe caught a glimpse of a black SUV in the side mirror. It had been there for the last few miles, maintaining a careful distance. She clutched Swirly tighter, saying nothing, but the orb's warning pulses told her everything she needed to know.

They weren't just looking for answers anymore. They were part of something bigger, something that others—powerful others—wanted to keep hidden.

The setting sun cast a golden hue over the Bailey Family Vineyard as the family car pulled into the driveway. Cathy squinted at the unusual drone hovering over their property. Living near Camp Pendleton, the family had grown accustomed to the occasional military flyover, but this drone was different - larger and more ominous.

Logan spoke up. "Jeez, that thing is definitely not your average hobbyist drone."

"Maybe it's a realtor or a neighbor?" Zoe suggested, her voice filled with uncertainty.

Joe was still working among the grapevines as they pulled in. He wiped his brow with a bandana and jogged towards them, concern etched on his face.

"Weird day, huh?" he said, noticing their anxious expressions.

"You have no idea," Cathy replied as she stepped out of the car. "We were introduced to Hunter, and things got really strange when Zoe asked about a restricted area. Swirly was acting weird, too."

Joe's brows furrowed. "I had my own bizarre moment," he said. "I felt like someone was watching me, so I decided to pull up the Pokémon Go you installed on my phone and go check the bunker. A colonel from the marines popped up on my screen. It was pretty surreal and spooky. I felt like he was looking for something. When he disappeared, I went back outside and there was a car across the street..."

Cathy looked concerned. "We didn't see any car, just a utility truck by the power pole when driving in. It was unusual enough for us to slow down and almost stop."

Logan chimed in, "A drone, a mysterious car or truck. This is all starting to sound a little creepy. They could be spying on us, maybe looking for Swirly."

Joe nodded thoughtfully. "Well, maybe we should see if we can't secure Swirly in the bunker, so no signal gets out. Let's test Swirly with the door completely closed. We'll see if anyone's able to track what's going on."

Becky, ever the vigilant scientist, raised her hand. "Hold on a second," she said. "I have some equipment in the car that can measure for any signal changes. Give me a minute."

As Becky grabbed her gear, Zoe looked at her dad. "Logan thinks we need to be extra careful. I know we have to protect Swirly, but it's all getting so... intense. I'm starting to worry about the entire family."

Joe placed a reassuring hand on her shoulder. "Don't worry, we've got this. We're in this together."

Minutes later, with the equipment in hand, they made their way to the basement. Zoe went into the bunker while the others stayed behind. Cathy with Pokemon Go open, Logan with his equipment and Becky with hers, while Joe watched the 'team' do their thing.

Once inside, Zoe secured the door and leaned against the cool metal wall, her heart pounding. Swirly pulsed in her hands, its surface rippling with swirling colors that seemed to respond to her anxiety. The familiar warmth of the orb against her palms brought a measure of comfort in the enclosed space.

"Alright, Becky, let's get started," Cathy said, her voice steady despite her obvious concern. She held her phone ready, wondering if Pokemon Go had become more than just a game—perhaps a window into something far more mysterious.

Becky methodically set up her equipment outside the bunker door. Various monitors and sensors came to life. The primary unit featured a complex array of frequency analyzers and electromagnetic field detectors, each calibrated to detect the slightest energy fluctuation.

"The baseline readings are stable," Logan reported, his eyes scanning multiple displays. "We're looking for any anomalous signals that might penetrate the bunker's walls."

Joe stood watch. "How will we know if it's working?" he asked, unable to hide the worry in his voice.

Inside the bunker, Zoe held Swirly closer and said, "It's okay. We're going to figure this out." The orb's pulsing seemed to sync with her heartbeat, creating a calming rhythm in the oppressive silence.

Becky's equipment suddenly registered a slight change. "There!" she exclaimed, adjusting several dials. "We're getting minimal energy signatures, just above background radiation. They pulse every thirty seconds but..." she paused, analyzing the data, "they're far too weak to be detected beyond the house's foundation."

Logan nodded, cross-referencing the readings with his own equipment. "The bunker's working better than we hoped. Any signals Swirly's emitting are being contained effectively."

"That's a relief," Joe exhaled, his shoulders relaxing slightly. "But we need to stay vigilant. That drone wasn't here by accident."

Cathy glanced at her phone's screen, watching for any unusual Pokemon activity. "At least we know Swirly's safe down here. But what do we do about whoever's watching us?"

The family exchanged knowing looks. They had protected Swirly for now. The question of who was watching them—and why—still hung heavy in the air.

In the cool silence of the bunker, Zoe sat cross-legged on one of the military-style bunks, the rough canvas material crinkling beneath her. The air held that familiar mix of earth and metal, tinged with the sharp scent of her dad's wine barrels stored in the corner. Holding Swirly in her open palms, she watched as the orb's surface rippled with colors that seemed more responsive than usual.

"I know you can understand me," Zoe said softly. "You've been trying to tell us things, haven't you?"

The orb's internal mechanism shifted, its crystalline structures realigning as if in response. Then, something extraordinary happened. Swirly began to rise from her palms, floating inches above her hands. Zoe's breath was taken away as she watched the orb suspend itself in mid-air, spinning slowly while displaying spectacular patterns across the bunker walls—intricate mandalas of light that shifted from deep sapphire to burning gold, creating a lifelike feel to the walls.

"Oh my god," she said, her heart thundering in her chest. Hesitantly, she reached out to touch the floating orb. The moment her fingers made contact, a surge of energy coursed through her body like liquid lightning. It started at her fingertips, racing up her arms and spreading through her chest, down to her toes. Instead of pain, she experienced a rush of power that made her feel as if she could move mountains. Her senses heightened dramatically—she could feel every vibration in the bunker walls, hear the subtle hum of the emergency lights, even sense the weight of the earth above them.

*Is this what it feels like to be more than human?* She wondered, both thrilled and terrified by the sensation.

Trying to steady her racing heart, Zoe focused on the floating orb. "We need a better way to communicate." She paused, remembering the traffic lights on her way to school. "Do you understand colors? Like green and red?"

Swirly pulsed immediately with green, then red, repeating for several seconds. The display was so deliberate it made Zoe sit up straighter, the residual energy still tingling like carbonation in her veins.

"Wait... yes and no? Do you understand yes and no?" Her voice quivered with excitement as Swirly cycled through the colors again, its levitation becoming more stable as it hovered at eye level.

"This is like trying to teach Logan how to say gracias," she said, then brightened. "Okay, let's make this simple. When I ask you a question that needs a yes or no answer, can you show green for yes and red for no?"

The orb flashed a brilliant green, spinning faster in apparent excitement, sending cascading rainbows across the military-grade storage containers lining the walls.

Zoe could hardly contain herself. "Let's test this. Am I sixteen years old?" Green pulse. "Is Logan younger than me?" Red pulse. "Is my mom's hair red?" Green pulse, then red pulse, then green, and then, with a smile, she remembered her mom dyed her hair.

She leaned forward, the residual energy making her feel invincible. She was ready to ask about Mount Palomar, the question that had been nagging at her since their visit to the observatory. The orb seemed to sense her anticipation, its internal gears spinning faster, the levitation height increasing slightly.

Just then, the heavy bunker door swung open with a metallic groan. Startled, Zoe nearly tumbled off the bunk as Swirly dropped into her hands, sending one final powerful surge through her body before its glow diminished. Becky's silhouette appeared in the doorway, her testing equipment in hand.

"Good news," Becky announced, descending the stairs. "Whatever signals Swirly's putting out, they're not penetrating the bunker walls. You're completely masked down here."

Zoe quickly slipped Swirly into her pocket, her hands still trembling from the energy surge. Should she tell her family about what just happened? Would they understand, or would it only increase their worry? The orb's warmth against her leg felt like a secret between friends.

"That's... that's good," Zoe managed, trying to hide her shaking hands and the excitement in her voice. For the first time since finding the orb, she felt like they were on the verge of real answers. The residual energy from their connection lingered, a reminder of the power they had just discovered.

In her pocket, Swirly pulsed gently, as if reassuring her there would be time later for more questions. But Zoe knew something fundamental had changed between them. She wasn't just holding a mysterious artifact anymore—she was connecting with something far more powerful than she'd imagined.

As the morning sun was catching the last traces of dew in the vineyard, Joe and Logan surveyed their property, marking spots for security cameras. Recent events were making their usual easy conversation stilted and purposeful.

"If we put a camera here," Logan said, pointing to the old oak tree, "we'll have coverage of the entire western approach." His voice carried a hint of strain, betraying the fear he tried to mask. "Nobody could reach the bunker without being seen."

Joe nodded, appreciating his son's methodical approach while fighting his own rising anxiety. They spent the morning installing a network of high-resolution security cameras, each capable of night vision and motion detection. The cameras went up strategically around the property's boundaries, hidden among the vineyard rows and mounted at high vantage points.

"Your mother's been after me to do this for months," Joe said, managing a weak smile as he mounted another camera. "Guess sometimes it takes a crisis to get moving."

Logan paused as he watched his father. "Do you think we're overreacting? I mean, what if we're just seeing threats where there aren't any?"

"Better safe than sorry," Joe replied, though his eyes constantly scanned the horizon. "Especially with what Zoe's been experiencing."

They continued their work methodically, installing motion-activated LED flood-lights at key points along the perimeter. Inside the house, they upgraded the existing alarm system with sensors on every entry point. The basement received special attention, with pressure sensors and hidden motion detectors near the entrance.

The bunker, their primary concern, proved more challenging. Logan stood before the hatch, frowning at its simple design. "This is our weak point," he said, running his hand along the edge. "No matter what we do up here, the hatch itself has no actual security."

Joe joined him, sharing his son's concern. "Maybe that's by design," he mused. "Whatever this thing is, it's been here longer than we have."

They transformed the bunker's communications room into a security hub, installing monitors for camera feeds and backup power systems. As Logan programmed the final settings, Joe watched the screens come to life, showing multiple angles of their property.

"It's strange," Logan said. "how normal everything looks out there. You'd never know..." He trailed off, leaving unspoken the bizarre events that had led them to this point.

Joe squeezed his son's shoulder. "We'll figure this out. Together." But as they climbed back to the surface, both father and son couldn't shake the feeling that their security measures, however thorough, might not be enough against whatever was coming.

Above ground, the vineyard continued its peaceful existence, the vines swaying gently in the afternoon breeze, oblivious to the tension building beneath their roots. The new cameras blinked silently, watching, waiting, as the Bailey family prepared for whatever might come next.

Colonel Marc O'Reilly's boots clicked against the polished concrete floor of his underground command center at Camp Pendleton. The facility lay hidden beneath what appeared to be an abandoned textile factory - its brick walls old and crumbling, covered with patches of moss and ivy. To maintain the illusion of neglect, gaping holes exposed rotting wooden beams, while shattered windows sat behind rusted bars. A faded sign reading "Patterson Textiles Co." completed the deception, making the building virtually invisible to curious eyes.

The contrast between the dilapidated exterior and the state-of-the-art facility below was stark. Fifty feet underground, polished floors and gleaming equipment replaced the facade of decay. The colonel's command center occupied the heart of the complex, a windowless room that hummed with the sound of surveillance equipment. Its walls, lined with monitors displaying various feeds from the Bailey property. Banks of servers filled adjacent rooms, their cooling fans creating a constant white noise that masked conversations from potential eavesdroppers.

His face reflected on the dark screens as he paced, hands clasped behind his back. Operation Chrono's history weighed heavily on his shoulders. Seven faces haunted his dreams - Private Randy 'Buddyro' Briggs, Corporal Liam "Sledge" Hartman, Lieutenant Aidan "Scout" Vega, and the others - all vanished during that fateful experiment in '73. Their personnel files, worn from countless reviews, lay scattered across his desk alongside current surveillance reports.

The sharp ring of his secure line cut through the ambient noise. "O'Reilly," he answered, recognizing Hunter Thorne's number.

"Colonel, they were here today." Hunter's voice crackled through the encrypted connection. "The Bailey family, along with Dr. Martinez. The girl... she seemed drawn to the restricted area. Started asking questions about the temporal research wing."

O'Reilly's jaw tightened. "Did they see anything?"

"No, sir. I ended the tour before they got too close. But there's something about that girl - she kept reaching for her pocket, like she was checking something. And the readings in that section went haywire while she was here. Maybe we should consider bringing them in officially. The girl's connection to the artifact—"

"That's not your concern," O'Reilly cut him off. "Your job is to maintain the observatory's cover and keep the restricted wing secure. Nothing more." O'Reilly hung up.

"Sir," Lieutenant Sanders called from his monitoring station. "The temporal readings from the Bailey property are off the charts."

O'Reilly's jaw clenched. After years of waiting, the Chronosphere had resurfaced. His previous experiments with the device had revealed its selective nature - how it responded differently to each handler. But before he could fully understand its mechanics, the orb had vanished, leaving him with nothing but questions and a mandate to find it.

"Keep the drone in position," he ordered, studying the infrared imagery of the vineyard. "And make sure those new sensors are properly calibrated. We can't afford to lose the signal again."

The colonel wiped sweat from his brow, remembering how earlier that day they'd had to pull back their surveillance vehicle when Joe Bailey grew suspicious. They'd quickly shifted to more covert methods - hidden cameras, EMF detectors, and remote monitoring systems scattered throughout the property.

A sudden chill ran down his spine. The feeling of being watched crept over him, a prickling sensation made its way up his neck.. His eyes darted around the command center, scanning the shadows between the banks of equipment.

"Colonel!" Sanders' voice cracked with urgency. "We're losing the signal!"

O'Reilly rushed to the main display, watching as the steady pulse of the orb's energy signature flickered and died. His fists clenched at his sides, knuckles white. Not again. Not when they were so close.

"Run a diagnostic! Check all frequencies!" he barked, leaning over Sanders' shoulder to study the readings.

For three agonizing minutes, the screens showed nothing but static. Then, just as suddenly as it had vanished, the signal returned, stronger than before.

O'Reilly exhaled slowly, his eyes fixed on the erratic indicator. Whatever - or whoever - was interfering with their equipment, one thing was obvious: they weren't dealing with an ordinary family. The Baileys needed to be watched more closely.

"Pull up the historical records on the Bailey family," O'Reilly commanded, settling into his chair. The leather creaked beneath him as he leaned in to study the monitors.

As the files populated his screen, his mind drifted back to the last moments before the original team vanished. He could still hear Corporal Hartman's last transmission:

"Sir, something's wrong with the temporal field. It's... it's pulling us in—" Then nothing but static.

A soft beep drew his attention back to the present. The drone's thermal imaging showed movement in the Bailey's vineyard - a small figure moving near the old oak tree.

"Enhancement on sector four," he ordered.

The image zoomed and cleared, revealing who he believed was Zoe Bailey standing alone in the darkness. Even through the grainy footage, O'Reilly could see the familiar shimmer of the Chronosphere's energy signature around her. Something also looked familiar about her, but he couldn't quite grasp why.

Sanders, not wanting to upset O'Reilly, said, "Sir, these readings... they're identical to the ones from '73. Just before we lost contact with Colonel Briggs and his team."

O'Reilly's fingers drummed against his desk. "Keep all systems running. I want eyes on that girl 24/7. And get me everything you can find about her family line. There has to be a connection we're missing."

He pulled out an old, worn photograph from his desk drawer - the original Operation Chrono team, standing proud and unaware of their fate. His thumb traced over their faces, remembering how each of them had handled the orb differently. None of them had shown the kind of connection this young girl seemed to have with it.

"What makes you so special, Zoe Bailey?" he said to himself, watching as the girl's figure disappeared back into the darkness of the vineyard. "And what do you know about our missing team?"

The monitors flickered again, briefly this time, like a warning. O'Reilly couldn't shake the feeling that somehow, somewhere in time, the lost members of Operation Chrono were watching... waiting. And perhaps, through this girl, he can finally find some answers.

# Chapter 12

# MILITARY CONTACT

Colonel Marc O'Reilly hunched over his desk in the dimly lit office, surrounded by walls plastered with surveillance photos, temporal readings, and maps of Fallbrook. The faces of seven missing soldiers staring back at him from a worn photograph on his desk.

His fingers traced the latest monitoring reports, leaving sweat marks on the papers. The years of obsession had carved deep lines into his face and streaked his dark hair with gray. Every night, he still heard their screams—his men disappearing into the void when the Chronosphere malfunctioned. Or had it? Maybe they had simply found what he couldn't—the right person to control it.

The monitoring equipment provided background noise as he studied the recent data from the Bailey property. His jaw clenched at each gap in surveillance, each moment when the orb vanished from their instruments. The Baileys were clever, he had to give them that, but they were playing with forces they couldn't understand. The family thought they could hide the most powerful artifact ever discovered from the United States military. His fist clenched, knuckles white with determination.

A strange sensation crept up his spine—that familiar feeling of being watched. He whirled around, scanning the empty office. For a moment, he thought he saw a shimmer in the air, like heat waves rising from hot asphalt. The monitoring equipment squealed, then fell silent.

"Not again," he growled, slamming his fist on the desk. The photo of his missing men rattled in its frame.

He pulled up the classified file on the Baileys on his computer. Joe Bailey's stern face filled the screen—a man protecting his family. Next came Cathy, then Logan, and finally... Zoe. O'Reilly paused, that nagging feeling returning. Something about the girl's eyes seemed hauntingly familiar, like a memory just out of reach.

Standing, he walked to his wall of evidence. Red strings connected photos, documents, and newspaper clippings spanning decades. He traced the path from the original Operation Chrono to the present day. The Baileys weren't the first family to possess the orb, but they would be the last.

"Time to end this game," he said, reaching for his phone. A direct confrontation might be risky, but he was done watching from the shadows. He needed answers—needed to know why this teenage girl could control the orb when trained soldiers had failed.

As he dialed his superior's number to request authorization for contact, his hand trembled slightly. Was it excitement or fear? The last time they had the orb, seven good men had vanished without a trace.

The phone rang, and O'Reilly straightened his spine. This time would be different. This time, he would bring the Chronosphere home, whatever the cost. And maybe, just maybe, he'd finally learn what happened to his men.

Zoe slumped against the sun-warmed brick wall of the school building, her fingers absently tracing the rough texture of the concrete where she sat. The playground buzzed with the familiar chaos of recess—bouncing basketballs, and the constant chatter of her classmates enjoying their brief freedom. The familiar weight of Swirly in her pocket was missing, leaving an emptiness that seemed to spread through her entire being. She felt exposed, vulnerable—like part of herself had been left behind in the bunker at home.

"Zoe! Oh my gosh, you'll never believe what happened!"

Carmel's voice cut through her melancholy like a shaft of sunlight. Her best friend plopped down beside her, practically vibrating with excitement, her dark curls bouncing with every animated movement. The silver friendship bracelet they'd made together last summer caught the light as she gestured enthusiastically.

"So, you know Jason from Mrs. Peterson's class? Well, we're officially together now! He asked me yesterday after school, but honestly, it feels like we've been dating forever. Like, last week when we were working on the science project together…"

Zoe couldn't help but smile as Carmel launched into a detailed account of her day-old relationship as if recounting an epic romance spanning decades. Her friend's enthusiasm was infectious, momentarily pushing aside her worries about Swirly and the mysterious watchers her parents feared.

When Carmel finally paused for breath, her eyes softened with concern as they fell on Zoe's empty pocket. "Hey, what's up with Swirly? You always have it with you."

Zoe's smile faded. Looking around to ensure no one was within earshot, she leaned closer to her friend. "We think someone's watching us," she whispered. "Mom and Dad made me leave Swirly at home. We've got him hidden away."

The words tumbled out then—about the strange happenings at home, the trip to Mount Palomar Observatory, and the growing sense that something bigger than they understood was unfolding. With each detail shared, Zoe felt both lighter and more anxious, knowing she couldn't take the words back once they were spoken.

"The Observatory?" Carmel's eyes lit up with unexpected recognition. Zoe's stomach clenched, already sensing what was coming. "My Uncle Hunter works there! He's always talking about the weird stuff they—"

"Wait, what?" Zoe's heart skipped a beat. Cold dread washed over her as she grabbed Carmel's arm. "Your uncle works at Mount Palomar?"

"Yeah! He's been there for years. Should I ask him about—"

"No!" Zoe's voice came out sharper than intended, making Carmel flinch. She softened her tone but kept her grip firm on her friend's arm. "Carmel, you can't tell anyone about this. Not your uncle, not Jason, not anyone. Promise me."

Carmel's expression shifted from surprise to understanding. "Of course, bestie." She crossed her heart solemnly, then gave Zoe a reassuring hug—the same way she had since they were in kindergarten together. "Besides, what kind of best friend would I be if I couldn't keep a cosmic secret or two?"

The bell rang, its harsh buzz shattering their private moment. As they stood to head back to class, Zoe felt both relieved and worried. She trusted Carmel completely—they'd been through everything together since first grade—but now she couldn't help wondering just how many connections to the Observatory were out there, and who else might be watching?

The afternoon sun was starting its trek toward the horizon as Logan and Becky swept their detection equipment methodically across the property. Cathy and Joe followed close behind, their eyes scanning the surrounding area with newfound wariness. The late autumn breeze and the rustling of leaves masked the tension in the air.

The familiar rumble of the school bus drew their attention to the main road. Zoe burst from the doors, her backpack bouncing as she sprinted toward them, her face a mixture of excitement and concern.

"What's going on?" she called out between breaths, her eyes darting between the strange devices in their hands. "Did something happen while I was at school?"

"Looking for uninvited guests," Joe replied, his attempt at humor failing to mask the worry lines around his eyes. He unconsciously shifted his position to stand between Zoe and the vineyard's perimeter.

Becky suddenly froze, her brow furrowing as she studied the readouts on her device. The afternoon light caught the concern in her expression. "This is... interesting," she said, tapping the screen. "I'm getting energy signatures similar to the orb's, but that's impossible. It's secured in the bunker."

"What readings?" Cathy asked, leaning closer to study the display. Pokémon Go buzzed, but for once, she ignored it.

"The thing is," Becky continued, adjusting several dials, "when we tested it before, the orb was practically dormant. But these readings..." She looked at Zoe thoughtfully, recognition dawning in her eyes. "Maybe it's not just about the orb itself. Maybe we need to see what happens when it's actually active—when Zoe's working with it."

"You mean with the holograms?" Zoe asked, unconsciously touching her pocket where Swirly usually rested. The empty space felt wrong somehow.

Before anyone could respond, Logan's equipment erupted in a piercing electronic shriek. Everyone jumped, and Logan scrambled to silence the device. The sound echoed across the vineyard, sending a flock of startled birds into flight.

"Sorry," he said, sweeping the device in a careful arc. "But guys, this is definitely something. Military-grade surveillance equipment, from what I can tell." He pointed toward a cluster of vines, where late afternoon sunlight caught something distinctly unnatural among the leaves.

After some careful searching, they found it—a sleek, metallic object a little larger than a matchbox, its housing designed to blend seamlessly with the vineyard's natural elements. The device's lens caught the sunlight, winking at them like a mechanical eye.

Joe studied it, jaw clenched, before grabbing his well-used shovel from nearby. "Well," he said, voice tight with controlled anger, "there's only one thing to do with unwanted electronics in a vineyard." He dug a deep hole and unceremoniously buried the device, each shovelful of dirt landing with satisfying force.

Cathy glanced nervously at the freshly turned earth. "Are you sure that's wise? Won't they know we found it?"

"Better than leaving it where they want it," Logan offered, still scanning the area. "But there could be more. These things usually come in networks." His fingers flew over his tablet, mapping potential locations based on signal patterns.

"Tomorrow," Joe declared, wiping his hands on his jeans. He looked at his family, his expression softening as it settled on Zoe. "Right now, I think we need to understand what we're actually dealing with." He gestured toward the house. "Ready to show us what Swirly can really do?"

Zoe's face lit up, though anxiety flickered in her eyes. "In the bunker?"

"Safest place for it," Cathy agreed, already heading toward the house. Pokémon Go buzzed again, more insistently this time. "And Becky can get her readings while you work with it. Maybe we can figure out why these energy signatures keep appearing."

As they made their way to the wine cellar entrance, Logan hung back with his sister, his equipment still humming softly. "Just... be careful," he said, reaching out to squeeze her shoulder. "We don't know who's watching or what they want."

"Always am," Zoe replied with a forced grin, but her hand trembled slightly as she reached for the cellar door. The weight of unseen eyes pressed down on them all—the surveillance device a tangible reminder of the powers circling their family, hunting for Swirly.

The hidden door to the bunker swung open with a soft hydraulic hiss, the sound oddly comforting in its familiarity. One by one, they descended into their fortified sanctuary, leaving the watched vineyard behind. The temperature dropped noticeably as they entered the specially shielded chamber where Swirly waited, its presence a subtle warmth in the cool air.

Joe stood next to Zoe, his eyes drawn to the gentle shimmer of the orb. The comforting presence of the orb was suddenly overshadowed by a chilling vision that flashed before him as he rubbed the worry stone: a military vehicle, dark and imposing, rolling up the driveway. Three men stepped out, their silhouettes sharp against the dimming light, a sense of foreboding curling in his gut.

The warmth of the chamber faded to icy unease as he felt the weight of what he feared might be his future. Joe's heart raced, pounding against his ribcage like a desperate alarm. The pit in his stomach churned violently, a sickening mixture of anxiety and dread. He glanced at Zoe, her expression a mix of curiosity and uncertainty, and he felt a fierce urge to protect her bubble of innocence from the impending reality.

Joe's mind raced, torn between the fear of what may await them outside and the impulse to prepare for whatever confrontation was coming. He could see it in his mind's eye: the men, their intentions hidden behind stoic faces, drawing nearer to his family, drawn by the very thing that connected the worry stone to Zoe—Swirly.

He swallowed hard, wishing he could shake the vision from his mind, but it clawed at him, vivid and insistent. "I can't let this happen," he thought, gripping his family's heirloom tightly. It was a small piece of rock, yet it felt like a lifeline, reminding him that even in the darkest moments, he would do everything in his power to keep his family safe.

Meanwhile, Becky began setting up her equipment with efficiency, her hands moving surely despite the tension in her shoulders. Multiple screens flickered to life, each displaying different wavelength readings and energy patterns.

"Okay, Zoe," she said, adjusting several sensors and glancing at the teenager. "Show us what you and Swirly can do. But if anything feels wrong—anything at all—we stop immediately."

Zoe nodded, approaching the pedestal where Swirly rested. As her fingers brushed its surface, the orb's colors began to shift and swirl, responding to her presence like a loyal friend welcoming her home.

In the bunker's fluorescent glow, Zoe held Swirly, its surface shifting like oil on water. The familiar weight felt reassuring against her palms as the device's warmth pulsed in rhythm with her heartbeat. "I want to try something bigger than just testing if Logan and Becky can detect us," she announced, her voice steady despite her racing heart. "I want to go to The Packing House in the seventies."

"Honey, are you sure that's such a good idea?" Cathy asked, reaching out with maternal concern, her fingers hovering protectively near her daughter's shoulder. The worry lines around her eyes deepened as she studied Zoe's determined expression.

To both their surprise, Swirly pulsed with a bright, emerald green light at Cathy's question, indicating yes. The unexpected response made them both jump slightly.

"Did... did Swirly just respond to you?" Zoe asked, her eyes wide as she stared first at the orb, then at her mother. The implications of this recent development sent her mind racing.

"I thought only you could communicate with it," Cathy said, unconsciously leaning closer to examine Swirly's still-glowing surface. The air seemed to crackle with possibility.

Zoe shook her head, equally amazed, before squaring her shoulders and focusing back on the task at hand. Her fingers trembled slightly as she carefully opened the panel on top of Swirly, revealing the now-familiar holographic interface floating above it. The ethereal light patterns danced in the air, but despite her careful movements through them, nothing happened.

"Oh, right," she mumbled, remembering their previous discoveries. "Mom, shield your eyes. I need to put Swirly in the indentation."

As the orb settled into its ancient cradle, a brilliant white light filled the bunker, momentarily washing out all detail. When Zoe's vision cleared, she found herself standing in The Packing House, surrounded by the warm woods and vintage charm of 1975. The scent of coffee and fresh-baked bread hung in the air, and somewhere a radio played "Sweet Emotion" by Aerosmith. A discarded newspaper on the counter confirmed the date: July 15, 1975.

Her heart nearly stopped as her gaze fell on a familiar face at the counter. There, dressed in a crisp military uniform with captain's bars gleaming on his shoulders, sat the same man she'd seen in Swirly's holographic projection. He was younger, his dark hair without the gray at the temples, but those piercing eyes were unmistakable. He turned, noticing her with mild surprise, and Zoe felt a chill run down her spine.

"Hi, I didn't notice you come in," he said pleasantly, his voice carrying the same commanding tone she remembered from the hologram. With a look of curiosity, his eyes lingered over her modern clothing. "I'm Marc," he offered with a smile that didn't quite reach his calculating eyes.

"Nice to meet you," Zoe managed, her pulse thundering in her ears. Swirly grew warmer in her pocket, as if sensing her distress. "But I have to go." She turned and hurried out, feeling his gaze boring into her back as she fled.

The moment she stepped onto the sidewalk, she clutched Swirly through her pocket. "We need to get back to the bunker now!" The words had just left her lips when the white light enveloped her again, and she found herself back in the concrete room, her legs shaking beneath her.

Zoe's scream of panic echoed off the walls, bouncing back at her like a physical force. The bunker door flew open with a metallic shriek as Joe raced down the stairs, taking them two at a time, the stone clutched tightly in his hand.

"What happened? Are you hurt?" he demanded, reaching for his daughter with trembling hands. He looked for any sign of injury.

Zoe trembled against her father's steadying grip, her words tumbling out in a breathless rush. "The man... the one Swirly showed us in that hologram... he was there! At The Packing House in 1975. He said his name was Marc!" She clutched Swirly tighter, drawing comfort from its familiar warmth. "But he was younger, maybe in his twenties."

Joe's face drained of color as Cathy moved closer to Zoe. "Tell us everything, honey. Every detail." She pulled out her phone, then stopped, realizing she couldn't document this like one of her Pokémon anomalies.

Logan, who had been analyzing data on his laptop, looked up sharply. "Hold up. We need to approach this logically." He pushed his glasses up his nose. "If it's the same Marc, that would make him around seventy now. Are we sure about the identification? The implications of this connection are... significant."

"I know what I saw," Zoe insisted, still pressed against her dad's protective embrace. Swirly's surface now swirled with agitated patterns of deep red and electric blue, reflecting her emotional state. "He was younger, but those eyes... they were exactly the same. The way he looked at me, like he was trying to figure something out."

"The same man who's been searching for Swirly," Cathy whispered, her hand finding Joe's. "But how is that possible? What does it mean?"

Their simple test had just uncovered a connection that spanned decades, suggesting a mystery far deeper—and potentially more dangerous—than they'd imagined.

Swirly pulsed quietly in Zoe's hands, its colors gradually shifting to a deep, warning red.

As morning mist lifted from the vineyard, sunlight caught the remaining dew like scattered diamonds across the grape leaves. Logan studied his detector, its soft beeping barely audible above the gentle rustle of wind through the vines. "Got another hit," he called out, gesturing toward the western section of the property where the old oak tree stood.

The crunch of tires on gravel cut through the peaceful morning air. A dark green military Humvee wound its way up their driveway, dust billowing behind it like an ominous cloud. The Baileys exchanged worried glances as three uniformed men emerged from the vehicle, their boots hitting the ground, just as Joe had seen in his vision.

"That's him," Zoe said, her fingers wrapping protectively around Swirly. The orb pulsed against her palm, matching her quickening heartbeat.

"The man from The Packing House yesterday, but decades older," she continued. "And he's the same officer Swirly showed us in a hologram." Her stomach twisted as she watched his familiar features approach—the same sharp eyes that had looked at her curiously across The Packing House counter, now worn by time and obsession.

Joe recognized him instantly from his Pokémon Go encounter in the bunker. Colonel Marc O'Reilly moved with military precision, his silver-streaked hair and lined face telling the story of years spent in pursuit of something—or someone. Two younger officers flanked him, their expressions carefully neutral but their stance ready for action.

"Mr. Bailey, I'm Colonel Marc O'Reilly." Marc extended his hand, knuckles tightening as Joe reluctantly shook it. "Colonel O'Reilly." His eyes flickered briefly to Zoe, so quick it might have been missed by anyone not watching for it. The Colonel pointedly ignored introducing his companions, their presence more threat than courtesy.

"Could we step inside for a chat?" The words were polite, but the tone left no room for debate.

Joe planted his feet firmly, shoulders squared. "Outside is fine." He gestured to the wooden patio table beneath the ancient oak tree, its branches spreading above them like protective arms.

As they settled around the table, Swirly's warmth intensified in Zoe's pocket, its pulses growing more urgent. She could feel its warning, its need to stay hidden from this man who had spent half a lifetime searching for it.

"Mr. Bailey," Marc began, maintaining a facade of civility. "I'll be direct. Years ago, Camp Pendleton conducted a classified project—Operation Chrono. During this project, we lost something of extreme importance. A device." He paused, studying each face around the table. "Recently, we've detected its unique signature here in Fallbrook, specifically on your property."

Joe's face remained carefully neutral, though Zoe could see his jaw tighten. "Meaning?"

"The device is highly dangerous," Marc warned, his composure cracking slightly. "Radioactive. It poses extreme risk to anyone near it, especially in untrained hands." His gaze lingered on Zoe again, longer this time, confusion and recognition warring in his expression.

When the Baileys remained silent, something snapped in the Colonel. His fist crashed against the wooden table, making them all jump. "Good men died looking for this device!" he roared, years of frustration breaking through his professional veneer. "You're putting your entire family at risk, not to mention all of Fallbrook!"

The Colonel's attention suddenly fixed fully on Zoe, all pretense dropping away as recognition bloomed. A memory from forty-plus years ago crystallized in that moment—the strange girl in strange clothes who had appeared at The Packing House, unchanged after all these decades.

Joe, misinterpreting the Colonel's intense stare at his daughter, erupted. "You need to leave. Now. And don't come back."

"Mr. Bailey, you don't understand—" Colonel O'Reilly started, still staring at Zoe.

A cold wave of realization washed over Zoe as she met the Colonel's gaze. Her stomach twisted into knots as she realized that he recognized her, the way he was looking at her with the same curious look as he did at The Packing House counter just yesterday. It had been decades for him, yet here he was, filled with a desperate kind of recognition. Her hand trembled against Swirly, its pulsating increased rapidly in response to her growing panic. The impossible truth of what she'd done by traveling back to 1975 crashed over her: she hadn't just observed the past, she'd become part of it. And now that young officer she'd met stood before her, aged but unmistakable, putting together the pieces of a puzzle that spanned nearly fifty years.

"I understand perfectly," Joe cut him off, standing. "You're threatening my family. We're done here."

The Colonel rose slowly, his mind racing between the impossible memory of 1975 and the present moment. "This isn't over, Mr. Bailey," he said, his voice carrying a mix of threat and bewilderment. "That device... and now this." His eyes flickered back to Zoe. "There's more going on here than you realize."

"The only thing going on here is you trespassing on private property," Joe growled, stepping between Colonel O'Reilly and his daughter. "Leave. Now."

Logan moved closer to Zoe while maintaining a skeptical eye on the soldiers. "Dad's right. You have no warrant, no proof, just accusations."

The two officers looked to Colonel O'Reilly for direction, their hands hovering near their sidearms. The Colonel held up his hand, signaling them to stand down. "Very well, Mr. Bailey. But understand this—what you're dealing with is beyond your comprehension. People have vanished trying to understand its power."

"What power? What exactly are you referring to? This device that you so ineptly lost years ago?" Cathy stepped forward, her phone clearly recording the encounter.

Colonel O'Reilly's eyes narrowed at the phone, then swept across the family before settling once more on Zoe. "Not threatening, Mrs. Bailey. Warning." He straightened his uniform. "We'll be watching. When things go wrong—and they will—you'll wish you'd cooperated."

As the military men retreated to their vehicle, Joe maintained his stance. The moment their car disappeared down the driveway, he turned to his family.

"Inside. Now. All of you."

"Dad," Zoe's voice trembled slightly. "He recognized me. I could see it in his face."

"I know," Joe replied, ushering them toward the house. "And that makes him even more dangerous."

Logan glanced back at where his detector had registered the signal. "What about the other—"

"Not now," Joe cut him off. "We need to talk about what just happened. And what we're going to do next."

As they hurried inside, Swirly pulsed with an urgent purple glow, as if sensing the gravity of their situation. The Colonel's visit had confirmed their worst fears—they weren't just dealing with a curious military officer, but a man who had spent decades obsessing over the very thing they now possessed. And somehow, impossibly, Zoe's brief journey to the past had complicated everything even further.

The kitchen clock ticked relentlessly, each second marked by Swirly's glow. Steam spiraled from untouched coffee cups into the morning air, where dust motes danced in shafts of sunlight streaming through the vineyard-facing windows. Outside, a military helicopter's distant thrum set everyone on edge.

"Those files he carried." Cathy pushed her mug away, her phone already in hand. Her fingers instinctively opened Pokémon Go before she caught herself. "Not everything needs documenting," she said, switching to a news search instead. "But that date - 1973. Operation Chrono."

Joe's worry stone emerged from his pocket, its smooth surface warming quickly under his agitated touch. The white quartz band caught the light, seeming to pulse in rhythm with Swirly. "Seven soldiers, five decades of silence," he murmured, connecting invisible dots. The stone's familiar groove deepened under his thumb as he weighed family safety against the need for answers.

"Give me an hour with Camp Pendleton's network." Logan's fingers drummed against his laptop, his mind rebelling against what they'd witnessed, even as his hands itched to map the quantum anomalies. "Their security's good, but-"

"No." Joe's stone clacked against the table with finality. "We do this clean. Nothing that leads back to us. Not with O'Reilly watching."

Zoe cradled Swirly closer, its pulse quickening. Through their connection, fragments of memories flickered: test chambers, frightened voices, a blinding flash. "He knew what this was. The way he looked at it... like he'd seen it before."

"Public records first." Cathy fought the urge to document the moment, her phone heavy in her hand. "News archives, declassified reports. There has to be something."

"While you research," Zoe stood, "I need to understand why it reacts to him. The bunker's Faraday cage might help isolate the signal."

"I'll help set up the monitoring equipment." Logan closed his laptop, already mentally reviewing the quantum field algorithms he'd developed. "These readings lately... they're identical to the anomalies I detected near Mount Palomar."

"The cage needs reinforcing anyway." Joe pocketed his stone, though its warmth lingered against his leg. "The copper mesh still bears scorch marks from last week's temporal surge."

"Be careful down there." Cathy warned. "That Colonel... something in his eyes wasn't right. Like he was haunted."

"Or haunting," Zoe whispered, her connection with Swirly intensifying as she moved toward the bunker stairs. Each step brought new whispers of past experiments, failed tests, and lost souls seeking redemption.

The family split into their assigned tasks, footsteps echoing through the house. In the kitchen, the coffee grew cold, forgotten in the rush to unlock decades-old secrets. Through the vineyard's rows, each grapevine stood sentinel, while somewhere in the distance, that helicopter continued its ominous circle.

Down in the bunker, Logan's custom monitoring setup blinked with warning lights, each sensor tracking a different aspect of Swirly's energy signature. The Faraday cage hummed with potential, its reinforced walls containing whatever secrets were about to unfold. Zoe placed Swirly in the center of the cage, and for a moment, everything electronic in the bunker flickered in unison.

"Did anyone else feel that?" Cathy asked, descending the stairs with her phone recording despite her earlier restraint. The device's screen showed strange distortions, pixels shifting into impossible patterns.

Joe's worry stone grew inexplicably warm in his pocket, its quartz band glowing faintly in sync with Swirly's pulses.

The morning sun cast long shadows through the vineyard's rows above, but down here, in their fortified sanctuary, the Bailey family stood united, ready to face whatever truths emerged from the intersection of past and present, science and supernatural, fear and family.

# CHAPTER 13

# THEFT

Colonel Marc O'Reilly leaned over his desk in the dimly lit office at Camp Pendleton, surrounded by towering stacks of yellowed files. The wall behind him had become a sprawling web of photos, maps, and red string—all centered on a grainy surveillance photo of the Bailey family home. His fingers, stained with coffee and ink, traced the fading type on a classified document marked "Operation Chrono - 1973."

Three empty coffee cups testified to his sleepless determination. The ancient desk lamp shining harsh light across decades-old reports, each one documenting failure after failure. Time travel had remained stubbornly theoretical, despite the orb's mysterious properties. The device had yielded only fragments of data before its disappearance—temporal disturbances, electromagnetic anomalies, unexplained energy signatures.

The Colonel's face reflected in his computer screen as he cross-referenced locations. His military-trained mind assembled the puzzle pieces. Two locations in Fallbrook had shown unprecedented levels of temporal activity: the Bailey property and a seemingly unremarkable building on Main Avenue's 100 block.

"What's the connection?" he said, rubbing his temples. The answer came through property records dating back to the early 1900s. His hands trembled slightly as he pulled up the digital archive, not from caffeine, but from the thrill of discovery.

"Edwin L. Bailey," he said, a predatory smile crossing his face. The name jumped out from a century-old deed—Joe Bailey's great-great-grandfather, owner of Fallbrook's first telephone exchange. The same location that now housed a realty office and yogurt shop had once been a hub of communication, owned by the Bailey family.

Colonel O'Reilly stood, his chair scraping against the floor. He gathered his service weapon and badge, movements precise and practiced. The coincidence was too perfect—the Bailey connection, the temporal readings, the orb's disappearance. As he strode toward his vehicle, his phone buzzed with a message about another urgent matter requiring his attention. He ignored it.

"Time to see what secrets that yogurt shop is hiding," he said to himself, his voice carrying the edge of a man whose obsession had finally found its target. His black SUV pulled away from the base, heading toward Fallbrook's Main Avenue—and perhaps the answers he'd spent years pursuing.

The bunker's LED lights shined across the concrete walls as the Bailey family gathered around the steel table. The low hum of Logan's monitoring equipment filled the otherwise silent room.

Zoe's hands trembled slightly as she withdrew Swirly from her pocket. The orb seemed heavier tonight, more purposeful. As she placed it on the table's cool surface, iridescent patterns danced across the walls, creating an otherworldly atmosphere in their underground sanctuary.

"I think I've figured out a better way to communicate," Zoe said. She glanced at Logan, who was adjusting his instruments. "Swirly responds to direct questions. Maybe if we—"

"Just remember what happened last time," Joe interrupted, the stone moving faster between his fingers. "We need to be careful about what we ask."

Cathy lowered her phone. "Honey, maybe we should—"

But Zoe had already placed her hand on Swirly. The orb's surface rippled beneath her touch, its colors intensifying. "Show us what Colonel O'Reilly wants," she said. "Show us why he's hunting you."

The temperature in the bunker dropped several degrees. Logan's equipment erupted in a cacophony of beeps and whines as Swirly rose from the table, defying gravity. Joe instinctively stepped toward Zoe, while Cathy gasped, nearly dropping her phone.

"That's... new," Logan said.

A holographic image materialized above them, showing a detailed map of Fallbrook. The image zoomed in on the air park, highlighting a nondescript building. Text appeared: "Operation Chrono Research Facility." The scene shifted, revealing Colonel O'Reilly's face, contorted with obsessive determination as he addressed a group of armed personnel.

"Sweet Jesus," Joe said, his stone forgotten in his clenched fist.

Cathy's fingers flew across her phone's screen. "That building's been abandoned for years. It's out by the airport."

"Hiding in plain sight," Logan mused, his eyes darting between his readings and the projection. "Classic misdirection."

Zoe hadn't moved, her hand still hovering near Swirly. The orb's glow had become erratic, its colors shifting rapidly between deep purple and angry red. "Something's wrong," she said. "Swirly's afraid... no, not afraid... warning us."

As Joe, driven by instinct, rubs the smooth surface of the stone, a familiar yet unsettling vision unfurls from the depths of his mind. In this glimpse, he finds himself and his family cornered in a brightly lit room, the atmosphere thick with tension as a group of armed military men, their faces obscured by shadows, aim their weapons at them with steely determination. Each gun barrel glints ominously, reflecting the erratic flickers of light that illuminate the space, amplifying Joe's sense of dread. His gut wrenches with worry, twisting in knots as he contemplates the imminent danger that looms over them. Yet, amidst this turmoil, an unexpected wave of calm washes over him like a gentle tide, perplexing him further.

In the heart of this chaos, he questions the origins of this tranquility. Is this a prophetic warning of what lies ahead, or could this be a sign that somehow they will emerge unscathed from the looming confrontation? The cryptic nature of the vision both fascinates and terrifies him, prompting a torrent of thoughts that swirl in his head like leaves caught in a whirlwind. With every heartbeat, uncertainty grows, yet the underlying sense of reassurance lingers, compelling him to keep this vision close to his chest. After all, the potential future he glimpsed could be fraught with peril, and he wonders if sharing it would only sow seeds of fear in his family's hearts. So, he silently resolves to carry this burden alone, holding on to the hope that they can navigate whatever challenges tomorrow may bring.

"We need to check this out," Joe said, though his voice carried a hint of uncertainty. "But we do this smart. We do this together."

"I can hack into the local property records," Logan offered, already typing on his laptop. "Maybe there's a paper trail."

"Tomorrow," Cathy insisted, her maternal authority brooking no argument. "We plan tomorrow. Tonight, we process what we've learned."

Swirly's glow gradually steadied, but Zoe couldn't shake the feeling of urgency it had conveyed. As her family discussed logistics, she kept her hand near the orb, drawing comfort from its warm presence while wrestling with the weight of what they'd discovered.

In the bunker's artificial light, surrounded by her family, yet connected to something far beyond their understanding, Zoe realized their normal life was slipping away with each new revelation. The question was: were they ready for what would replace it?

The late August sun beat down on South Main Avenue as Colonel Marc O'Reilly adjusted his tactical vest, studying the adjacent buildings. Lieutenant James Colton stood nearby, his tablet displaying multiple overlapping heat signatures and EMF readings from both the realtor's office and ice cream parlor.

"Sir, these readings match the pattern we documented at the Bailey property," Colton reported, his voice low and precise. "But the energy signature is approximately thirty percent stronger."

O'Reilly nodded, trusting his second-in-command's meticulous analysis. "Team Two, secure the perimeter," he said into his comm. "Johnson, initiate civilian evacuation. Gas leak protocol."

Colton efficiently coordinated the evacuation, his calm demeanor helping to ease the civilians' concerns. The realtor—a middle-aged woman in a coral blazer—clutched her designer purse to her chest while the yogurt shop owner herded customers out, leaving behind half-eaten sundaes and melting milkshakes.

"Lieutenant, run a cross-analysis with the historical blueprints," O'Reilly ordered, moving toward the back wall where modern drywall met century-old brick.

Colton's fingers flew across his tablet. "Already processing, sir. The old telephone exchange blueprints show some inconsistencies with the current building layout. There's roughly three feet of unaccounted space behind this wall." He hesitated before he said, "Similar to other locations we've investigated."

O'Reilly ran his hands along the wall's surface, his EMF meter chirping erratically. Colton watched his superior's movements with growing concern, noting the familiar signs of obsession with O'Reilly's stance and breathing patterns. He discretely added these observations to his encrypted personal log.

"Thermal imaging, now," O'Reilly demanded. "And bring in the Phase four equipment from vehicle two."

"Sir," Colton interjected, "Protocol suggests we should wait for the full spectrum analysis before—"

"Bring it in," O'Reilly cut him off, his tone brooking no argument.

Outside, fire trucks and utility vehicles arrived, maintaining their cover story as Colton orchestrated the arrival of their specialized equipment. He noticed O'Reilly's hands trembling slightly as ultraviolet light revealed markings on the brick.

"Sir," Colton approached carefully, a tablet displaying multiple datasets. "Demolition team is standing by, but these density readings suggest—"

"No demolition," O'Reilly said, eyes fixed on the wall. "Look at these readings. There's something behind here. We need to check the exterior access point."

In the back alley, dumpsters and delivery entrances masked what most would assume was just another service door. But O'Reilly's trained eye caught the subtle differences in the brickwork—variations that wouldn't register to civilians but screamed of purpose to someone who knew what to look for.

"Clear this area," he ordered, watching as his team efficiently cordoned off the narrow space.

Colton held up his tablet, its screen displaying a complex overlay of the building's structure. "Sir, the thermal imaging shows a distinct pattern in the mortar lines. They're spaced differently than the surrounding brickwork—approximately 1.7 millimeters wider."

O'Reilly ran his hands along the brick surface, methodically searching. His fingers traced the irregular mortar lines until they formed a perfect square, roughly three feet on each side. At its center, he felt a slight depression—almost imperceptible unless you knew exactly what to look for.

"Here," he said, pressing his EMF meter against the spot. The device shrieked to life, its display flashing a warning red. "Johnson, log these readings. Colton, get me the UV light again."

Under the purple glow, ancient symbols emerged. More importantly, the UV light revealed what they'd missed before: a series of concentric circles etched into the mortar, each one slightly deeper than the last.

O'Reilly pressed the center circle.

A soft click echoed in the alley. O'Reilly rotated the depression clockwise, following the pattern of the circles until a second click sounded. His heart hammered against his ribs, though his exterior remained carefully composed. Years of military discipline couldn't quite mask the tremor in his hands as he pressed inward one final time.

The brick panel swung inward, revealing a dark passage and what appeared to be a hatch. Colton immediately began scanning the entrance, his concern growing as the readings matched almost exactly with those from the Bailey property.

"Sir?" Colton prompted, noting O'Reilly's unusually long pause. "Your orders?"

The Colonel stood transfixed by the discovery, his hand resting on the cold metal. Colton observed the subtle signs of his commander's internal struggle with growing unease.

The hatch itself was a marvel of engineering—a heavy circular door nearly four feet in diameter, crafted from an unfamiliar metallic alloy that seemed to absorb the light from their tactical lamps. Around its circumference, the same intricate symbols they'd found while working with the Chronosphere. O'Reilly grasped the handle and pulled, requiring surprising force. The mechanism released with a pneumatic hiss, suggesting an airtight seal. As the door swung outward, their lights revealed a perfectly cylindrical tunnel extending down into darkness. The walls of the tunnel appeared smooth, almost like a glassy surface. Most striking were the many lights that flickered on, lighting the tunnel as if it had been waiting for them.

"Get me satellite thermal mapping of the entire downtown grid," O'Reilly finally ordered. "I want to know exactly where this tunnel system leads."

"Sir," Colton spoke up, carefully choosing his words, "local authorities are asking about street access. The gas leak cover story has a limited window of effectiveness."

O'Reilly barely seemed to hear him, lost in studying the hatch. Colton exchanged worried glances with other team members, his hand unconsciously moving to the secure phone containing his encrypted reports about O'Reilly's increasingly erratic behavior.

"Secure this location," O'Reilly finally commanded. "No one enters without my direct authorization. Full surveillance package, Colton. Everything we've got."

"Yes, sir," Colton responded, already programming the automated systems. He paused, then said, "Should I include this in the official report to Command, or..."

O'Reilly's sharp look answered that question. Colton nodded, making a mental note to update his personal logs later. As he coordinated the team's efforts to secure the site, he couldn't shake the feeling that they were crossing a line—one that might not lead them back.

"And Colton," O'Reilly called out as he turned to leave, "get me everything we have on the Bailey girl's movements. Every detail."

"Yes, sir," Colton replied, watching his superior's retreating form. Once alone, he pulled out his secure phone and added a new entry to his encrypted file: "Colonel's fixation on civilian minor intensifying. Recommend immediate review of operational parameters."

The metal door sealed with a heavy clang, leaving Colton alone with his growing concerns and the weight of decisions yet to come.

Colton exchanged a quick glance with Martinez as they gathered around the hatch. He'd documented every sign of O'Reilly's escalating fixation, each decision that pushed ethical boundaries. This unauthorized pre-dawn raid was just the latest red flag.

The descent into the tunnels left Colonel O'Reilly visibly energized—his movements becoming more animated with each step. Their LED tactical lights revealed walls that defied explanation: smooth, almost glassy surfaces that couldn't possibly be from the Prohibition era. Ancient symbols, eerily similar to those from their research files, caught the light at regular intervals.

"Remarkable," Colton said. "The construction suggests technology far beyond—"

"Focus, Lieutenant," Colonel O'Reilly snapped, though his own eyes darted hungrily across every detail. "We're not here for a historical survey."

They methodically cleared each chamber, Colton marking their progress on his tablet while keeping one eye on his commanding officer. Colonel O'Reilly's breathing had become shallow, his movements increasingly urgent as they discovered a branch leading toward Harry's Bar and Grill. But it was another passage that made Marc freeze—one that seemed to angle directly toward the Bailey property.

"This is it," Colonel O'Reilly said, an unsettling smile playing across his face.

Colton stepped closer, keeping his voice low. "Sir, we should document this properly. Protocol dictates—"

"Protocol?" Colonel O'Reilly turned sharply. "This is beyond protocol, Lieutenant. This is destiny."

The passage narrowed as they approached what their calculations indicated should be the Bailey's location. Colton noticed the Colonel's hand repeatedly touching his sidearm—a nervous tic he'd developed recently. At the top of a set of rough-hewn steps, a hatch waited.

When the handle turned without resistance, Colton's unease deepened. This was too easy.

The bunker beyond was a testament to paranoid preparation. O'Reilly moved immediately to a crude Faraday cage where the object of his obsession pulsed with an otherworldly light.

A sharp beep cut through the silence. Security sensors.

"Sir," Colton warned, "this could be—"

But O'Reilly was already moving, pulling a lead-lined satchel from his pack. The Chronosphere seemed to respond to his presence, as he quickly sealed it away.

Colonel O'Reilly yelled, "Move out," as he remained behind to set up an EMP device.

They retraced their steps at double time, the Colonel clutching the satchel with white-knuckled intensity. Only when they were back at the realtor's office, the hatch secured behind them, did Colton allow himself to breathe normally.

In the vehicle, Colton watched his commanding officer in the rearview mirror. The Colonel kept one hand on the satchel, murmuring words too quiet to hear. The man's obsession had reached a new level.

"Sir," Colton ventured carefully, "what about the surveillance feeds?"

"The EMP burst from the device will have corrupted any digital recording systems in the bunker. Standard failsafe." O'Reilly's response was automatic, rehearsed, but his eyes never left the satchel.

As they passed through Camp Pendleton's gates, Colton made a mental note to check his secure channels. Someone higher up needed to know how far O'Reilly's obsession had progressed. But as he watched the Colonel hurry toward his private lab, satchel clutched possessively to his chest, Colton wondered if it might already be too late.

Cathy's morning ritual of checking her Pokémon Go account came to an abrupt halt when her phone buzzed with a different kind of notification. The bunker's security alert flashed across her screen, her heart skipping a beat as she read: "Motion Detection - Bunker Breach 06:47 AM."

"Joe!" she called out, her voice cracking. "Joe, get down here!"

The sound of hurried footsteps thundered down the stairs. Joe appeared, still in his sleep clothes, the stone already working between his fingers. "What's wrong?"

"The bunker. Someone's been in the bunker." Her fingers flew across her phone, pulling up the security feed, but the screens showed only static. "The cameras are down."

Logan emerged from behind his father, laptop already open. "The entire system's been scrambled," he said. "Some kind of electromagnetic pulse fried the circuits. This wasn't amateur hour, Dad. This was professional."

Joe was already moving toward the cellar and headed straight for the wine rack, rotating the special bottle that concealed their bunker entrance. The mechanism clicked, but something felt off. The usual smooth swing of the hidden door had a slight catch—someone had recently tampered with it.

"Zoe stays upstairs," Joe commanded as they heard their daughter's footsteps above. "Logan, keep her there."

"But Dad—" Logan started to protest.

"Now, Logan!"

Cathy followed Joe down into the bunker, her phone's flashlight beam cutting through the darkness. The emergency lights flickered weakly, another sign of the system disruption. The space looked mostly untouched at first glance, but Joe moved with purpose toward the hidden chamber.

"No, no, no," he said, the stone nearly slipping from his increasingly sweaty grip. The Faraday cage stood open, empty except for the faint residual glow that always lingered after the orb's presence.

"It's gone," Cathy said, her hand covering her mouth. "They took it."

Above them, they heard Zoe's voice rise in distress, followed by Logan's attempted reassurances. The connection between Zoe and the orb was so strong that she'd sensed its absence even before seeing the empty cage.

Joe's face hardened as he examined the cage. "Military precision," he said, pointing to the clean cuts on the security seal. "This has O'Reilly written all over it."

"Dad!" Logan's voice carried down from above. "You need to see this. I've got something on the thermal imaging backup. It wasn't affected by the EMP."

Cathy grabbed Joe's arm as they hurried back upstairs. "Joe, if they have the orb..."

"I know," he cut her off, his voice grim. "Everything changes now."

They emerged into the cellar to find Logan had set up his laptop on the wine-tasting table. Zoe stood behind him, her face pale, one hand pressed against her chest as if in physical pain.

"I can't feel it anymore," she said, her voice small. "It's like... like someone cut off a part of me."

Logan pulled up the thermal imaging footage. "Look here," he said, pointing to three heat signatures moving through their bunker. "They knew exactly where to go. They've been watching us, studying us. And this?" He zoomed in on one figure. "The way he moves, his posture—that's military training."

"O'Reilly," Joe confirmed.

"But how did they find the tunnel entrance?" Cathy asked, Pokemon Go forgotten in her hand.

"It's hard to say," Logan said, pulling up a map of Fallbrook. "They must have found one of the old access points. If I cross-reference the thermal readings with the town's original blueprints..."

"None of that matters right now," Joe said. "What matters is getting it back. That orb isn't just some military toy—it's connected to Zoe. To all of us."

Zoe stepped forward, her initial shock giving way to determination. "We have to get it back," she said. "It's not just about us anymore. They don't understand what they're dealing with."

The family fell silent, the weight of their new reality settling over them.

"So," Joe said finally, placing the worry stone on the table with deliberate care, "how do we break into Camp Pendleton?"

# CHAPTER 14

# RECOVERY

Dawn crept over the Bailey Family Vineyard, painting the sky in watercolor strokes of amber and rose. The morning fog clung to the grapevines like ghostly fingers, creating an ethereal backdrop for what might be their most dangerous undertaking yet.

In the farmhouse kitchen, Cathy moved with her usual efficiency, though her hands trembled slightly as she set down a plate of barely touched scrambled eggs. The scratch of forks against plates echoed unnaturally loud in the tense silence.

Zoe sat hunched at the table, her usually bright eyes dulled with exhaustion. Dark circles shadowed her face, and her skin held an almost translucent quality. She pushed her eggs around the plate, the loss of Swirly manifesting as a physical ache in her chest.

"Honey, you need to eat something," Cathy said, placing a gentle hand on Zoe's shoulder. "We need our strength today."

Logan, already on his second helping, glanced up from his phone where he'd been studying satellite images of the facility. "Mom's right, squirt. Can't save the world on an empty stomach."

Joe stood at the window. The sunlight caught the silver in his temples, evidence of the stress of recent weeks. "We stick to the plan," he said, turning to face his family. "Logan and I will recon the perimeter while you two—"

"Dad," Zoe interrupted, her voice hoarse but determined. "I need to be closer. I can... I can feel Swirly. Like an echo." She pressed a hand to her sternum, trying to explain the inexplicable pull.

Cathy and Joe exchanged worried glances. The connection between their daughter and the orb had grown stronger, but so had the toll it took on her.

"Two hours," Joe finally conceded, his jaw tight. "We scout for two hours, then regroup. No heroics, no separating." He looked pointedly at Logan, who had already started packing his laptop and what looked suspiciously like hacking equipment into his backpack.

The family moved with quiet purpose, gathering supplies: burner phones, water bottles, first aid kit. Through the kitchen window, the sun continued its ascent, burning away the morning mist and revealing a deceptively peaceful day in Fallbrook.

As they prepared to leave, Cathy caught Joe's hand, their fingers intertwining. "Whatever happens today," she said, "we face it together."

Zoe watched her parents, drawing strength from their unity. Despite her exhaustion, despite the hollow ache where Swirly's presence should be, she felt a surge of determination. They would find Swirly. They had to. The alternative was unthinkable.

Joe looked at each member of his family in turn. The sun highlighted Cathy's red hair, caused shadows under Zoe's eyes, and gleamed off Logan's laptop bag. His family. His responsibility. The earlier vision into the future from the stone worried him and calmed him all at the same time. What did it mean? Were they making the right choice? He gave them all a reassuring smile.

"Dad?" Logan's voice cut through Joe's thoughts. "You okay? You looked like you zoned out for a second there."

"Just thinking," he said, patting the pocket containing the stone. "Let's move out. Stay alert, stay together."

The Bailey family stepped out, leaving behind the safety of their home for the uncertainty that lay ahead. The vineyard's shadows stretched before them like nature's own countdown, marking the beginning of what could be their most crucial mission yet. Joe took up the rear, his hand never leaving the stone, its smooth surface both a comfort and a warning of what was to come.

Joe led his family along a trail that wound through dense California chaparral just behind the Fallbrook Air Park. Logan discovered a hole in the perimeter fence leading to Camp Pendleton. The sun was just creeping upward as they made their way onto the base, lighting up the abandoned structures beyond the perimeter fence.

"Not much further," Joe said, gesturing toward a cluster of deteriorating buildings ahead. "These old structures date back to the Korean War era. Most folks think they're just forgotten storage units."

The facility emerged from the undergrowth like a forgotten movie set. Old brick walls rose before them, partially concealed by stubborn vines that seemed to pull the structure back into the earth. Broken windows gaped like hollow eyes, their frames rusted and bent. A faded sign, barely legible through layers of grime, read "Patterson Textiles Co."

Logan pulled out his modified EMF detector. "These readings match Swirly's energy signature," he said, tapping the screen. "He's definitely here somewhere."

Zoe clutched her chest, her face lighting up despite her exhaustion. "I can feel him," she said excitedly. "He's scared... and angry. Colonel O'Reilly has him locked up somewhere below us." Her connection to the orb had grown stronger since its theft from their bunker, like an invisible tether pulling her forward.

"Remember what we discussed," Joe cautioned. "We get in, find Swirly, and get out. No confrontations if we can avoid them."

They approached a partially collapsed wall that seemed oddly intact despite its appearance. Cathy noticed fresh scuff marks in the dirt. "Someone's been through here recently," she observed.

The family squeezed through a narrow passage that led deeper into the structure. The transition from genuine decay to carefully crafted camouflage became apparent as they proceeded through a second passage, emerging into a corridor that bore telltale signs of regular use.

A metal door stood propped open at the end of the passage, a folding chair beside it, with an ashtray and a still-smoldering cigarette. The short hallway beyond was dimly lit by flickering LED lights poorly disguised as old fluorescent fixtures.

"He's closer," Zoe said, her hand pressed against her heart. "Down... we need to go down."

As they turn a corner in the hallway, the hollow sound of a door slamming echoed behind them, followed by approaching footsteps. Joe's eyes darted around frantically before spotting an open door marked "Storage." They slipped inside, finding themselves in a room cluttered with an odd mixture of genuine antiquities and modern equipment.

"Get down," Joe hissed urgently, guiding his family behind a stack of sleek black crates partially hidden by older wooden boxes. They huddled together in the darkness of the recessed corner, a leaning wooden board providing additional cover.

Zoe's eyes were wide, not with fear, but with certainty. "Swirly's right below us," she said. "There's some kind of lab…"

The footsteps grew louder, accompanied by the jingling of keys and the murmur of voices. Joe wrapped his arms protectively around his family as they pressed deeper into their hiding spot, the gap behind the crates just large enough to conceal them all. Through a small gap between crates, they could see the doorway.

Their mission to rescue Swirly had only just begun, and already they were trapped between discovery and their goal. In her heart, Zoe could feel Swirly responding to her presence, its energy pulsing like a beacon in the depths of the facility, calling her.

The family held their breath as Colonel O'Reilly's voice carried down the hallway, growing clearer as he approached.

"… wasn't just luck finding that tunnel entrance," O'Reilly was saying, his footsteps pausing near the propped door. "The old realtor's office renovation exposed it. Once we found those Prohibition-era blueprints, it was just a matter of following them to the Bailey property."

"And the orb, sir?" Another voice asked.

"Damned thing's gone inert," O'Reilly growled in frustration. "Sitting on the lab table like an expensive paperweight. No energy readings, no color, nothing. We've tried electrical stimulation, sonic waves, even radiation exposure. It's like it's… sleeping."

Zoe's heart ached with tears welling in her eyes. Joe squeezed her shoulder gently, while Cathy bit her lip to keep from making a sound.

"But you're certain the girl is the key?" The subordinate asked.

"I saw her with my own eyes, Jenkins. The Packing House, 1975. She walked right past me, clear as day, wearing modern clothes. Had to be her—same red hair, same face. She knows how to activate it, how to control it. We just need to—" He broke off suddenly. "Did you hear something?"

Logan's detector had slipped slightly in his sweaty hands, making the faintest scraping sound against the concrete floor. The family froze.

"Probably just the old building settling, sir," Jenkins offered. "We should go. Dr. Chen is waiting for you in the lab."

"Fifty feet of solid earth between us and any prying eyes," O'Reilly said, his voice moving past the storage room. "Perfect place to unlock the orb's secrets... once we figure out why it's shut down."

Their footsteps receded, followed by the distant sound of elevator doors opening and closing.

Joe waited several long moments before whispering, "Everyone okay?"

"Swirly's protecting himself," Zoe said, wiping her eyes. "He won't work for them. He can't."

"Did you hear what he said about seeing you in 1975?" Logan asked in disbelief. "I still can't believe it."

"We need to find that elevator," Cathy said matter-of-factly, though her voice shook slightly. "Fifty feet down—at least we know where they're keeping Swirly now."

Joe rubbed the stone, feeling an unusual warmth from it. "They don't know we're here yet. That gives us one advantage." He peered through the gap between crates. "Let's move, but quietly. Zoe, can you still sense which way?"

Zoe nodded, her face set with determination despite her pallor. "He's calling me. I'll find him."

After several tense minutes of silence, Joe carefully led his family out of the storage room. The hallway was empty now, their footsteps echoing softly against the hard floor despite their attempts at stealth.

"There," Logan said, pointing to a modern card reader partially concealed behind a rusted electrical panel. The elevator doors were camouflaged to match the aged walls, but now that they knew what to look for, the seams were visible.

Cathy examined the card reader with concern. "How are we going to—"

But Zoe was already moving forward, drawn by Swirly's pull. As she approached, the card reader emitted a soft beep and flashed green. The elevator doors slid open silently.

"He's helping us," Zoe said softly, managing a faint smile despite her exhaustion. "Swirly still has some power, even from down there."

They stepped into the elevator, its modern interior a stark contrast to the decaying facade outside. Joe pressed the single button marked "Research Lab," and the doors closed with a quiet whoosh.

"Fifty feet down," Logan said, watching the floor indicator light move. "That's a lot of dirt between us and the surface."

Cathy reached for Joe's hand, squeezing it tightly. "No turning back now."

The elevator hummed as it descended. Zoe stood straighter, her connection to Swirly growing stronger. "He knows we're coming," she said.

Joe gripped the stone, its warmth matching the determination in his heart. As the elevator slowed its descent, the Bailey family shared a look of unified purpose. Whatever waited for them behind those doors, they would face it together.

The floor indicator showed they had reached their destination. The elevator came to a smooth stop.

For a moment, they stood in tense silence, waiting for the doors to open and reveal whatever fate awaited them in the research lab beyond the doors.

The elevator doors slid open with a soft hiss, revealing the sterile expanse of the research facility. Joe pulled his family back into the shadows.

"There," Logan said, pointing to a bank of towering servers humming with quantum processors. The family crouched behind them, their breathing shallow in the cold, filtered air.

The laboratory sprawled before them like something out of a sci-fi movie. Holographic displays flickered with temporal equations. In the center of the room, a reinforced containment chamber pulsed with an otherworldly glow. Workstations arranged in concentric circles surrounded it, each hosting sophisticated equipment that seemed decades ahead of its time.

Zoe's gasp cut through the ambient hum. "Swirly," she choked out.

On a sterile examination table, Swirly lay motionless, its usually vibrant surface dull and lifeless. Colonel O'Reilly loomed over it, his face twisted with frustration as he addressed a team of anxious researchers.

"I don't care what it takes," Colonel O'Reilly snarled, slamming his fist on the table. "If we can't activate it, we'll take the family. The girl will cooperate when her parents' lives are at stake."

Cathy grabbed Zoe's arm, but it was too late.

"Hook up the electrodes," O'Reilly commanded. "Five thousand volts might wake up our little friend."

"NO!" Zoe burst from their hiding place, shrugging off Logan's desperate grab. "SWIRLY, TO ME!"

The laboratory erupted into chaos. Swirly exploded with light, its surface rippling through impossible colors—ultraviolet, infrared, colors that shouldn't exist. It shot upward, spinning like a miniature galaxy, before streaking toward Zoe with the force of a meteor.

The orb slammed into her outstretched palm, and Zoe transformed. The sickly pallor that had haunted her since Swirly's theft vanished. Raw energy surged through her, crackling beneath her skin. Her hair defied gravity, dancing in an unseen current, while her eyes burned with an ethereal glow.

"Weapons up!" Colonel O'Reilly barked. A dozen laser sights danced across the Bailey family. "Not the girl! Target the others!"

"Take aim!" O'Reilly commanded, his voice cracking with desperation. Red laser dots steadied on the Baileys.

Lieutenant Colton stepped forward, his face tight with concern. "Sir, this is madness. They're civilians—they're just kids!"

"Stand down, Lieutenant," O'Reilly said, but Colton moved between the soldiers and the family.

"Colonel, you're not thinking clearly. We're supposed to be protecting people, not—"

The sharp sound of the Colonel's pistol being drawn cut through the tension. The Colonel now aimed directly at Joe Bailey's chest, his hand trembling with rage.

"I said stand down!" O'Reilly's eyes had taken on a wild, unfocused quality that made Colton step back. "This is bigger than protocols, bigger than any of us! We need a working Chronosphere!"

Zoe straightened, her entire being changing. An ethereal light emanated from her skin, rippling like the aurora borealis. Her hair floated as if suspended in water, each strand shimmering with an inner light. Her eyes, normally hazel, now swirled with the same iridescent colors as Swirly, as if the orb's essence flowed through her very being.

The crack of O'Reilly's pistol shattered the air.

"NO!" Zoe screamed, thrusting Swirly skyward. Time crystallized around them.

The bullet hung suspended three feet from Joe's chest, a perfect ring of displaced air rippling around it. O'Reilly's face was frozen in a rictus of maniacal determination, gun smoke curling in motionless tendrils around the barrel. Colton's expression captured the exact moment horror transformed into disbelief.

Only the Baileys remained animated within their bubble of unfrozen time. Cathy reached out with a trembling hand to touch the suspended bullet, jerking back as if burned when her finger contacted the frozen projectile.

"That's... that's a .45 hollow point," Logan said, his face pale. "Dad, he was really going to..."

"We need to move," Joe said firmly, though his voice quavered slightly. "Now."

As they raced past the frozen tableau, Zoe paused briefly beside Colton. "Thank you for trying," she whispered to his static form.

The family fled through the emergency exit, leaving behind a laboratory that looked more like a macabre wax museum than a military installation. The frozen figures stood as testament to how far O'Reilly had fallen, and how close they'd come to tragedy.

In the silence of the frozen lab, as the family's footsteps faded, two things began to move: the bullet, which slowly dropped to the floor with a soft *tink*, and Colonel O'Reilly's trigger finger, twitching with unrelenting purpose.

# Chapter 15

# Edwin

A heavy fog clung to the Bailey Family Vineyard, transforming the neat rows of vines into ghostly sentinels standing guard over the land. The approach of a military vehicle cut through the mist, its tires crunching against the gravel driveway. Lieutenant James Colton sat motionless behind the wheel for a moment, his usually immaculate uniform showing subtle signs of strain—a slightly loosened collar, a visible coffee stain on his cuff.

Before he could knock, Cathy opened the door, her phone unconsciously gripped in her hand. "Lieutenant," she greeted, genuine warmth coloring her voice despite the tension of their last meeting. "Please, come in. Coffee?"

The contrast between the inviting interior and the tension visibly coiled in Colton's shoulders was stark. Family photos lined the walls, capturing laughter and love, while the old oak tree stood sentinel outside the window, its branches reaching and disappearing into the fog.

Emerging from his study, Joe met Colton's gaze with a mix of respect and caution. "Lieutenant."

"Mr. Bailey," Colton nodded, accepting a steaming mug from Cathy. "Beautiful morning. This fog and the vines remind me of my grandmother's place in Napa."

The small talk lingered awkwardly in the air, much like the fog outside—present yet insubstantial. Colton's eyes drifted to the stone in Joe's hand, its surface gleaming with the history of generations.

Leaning against the doorframe, Logan crossed his arms, having abandoned his textbooks on the coffee table. He narrowed his eyes at Colton, trying to gauge his true intentions.

Silence stretched until Cathy set aside her untouched coffee, a frown crossing her features. "Something's wrong, isn't it?"

Colton placed his mug carefully on a coaster, his expression shifting as he met her gaze. "There are... changes happening at the base." He drummed his fingers once on his knee before stilling them. "The kind of changes that concern me—concerns for friends."

Zoe appeared at the top of the stairs, drawn by some invisible thread to the unfolding moment. The energy of the orb pulsed faintly from her pocket, a rhythm known only to her.

Colton's eyes flickered briefly to Zoe's pocket, then back to his coffee mug. His voice dropped to a whisper. "You know, there's an old saying in quantum physics—observation changes the outcome. But sometimes..." he paused, choosing his words carefully, "sometimes the outcome is already set, and it's the observer that changes."

Joe's hand stilled on the worry stone, its surface suddenly warm against his palm.

"That Chronosphere," Colton continued with a sense of urgency. "it doesn't just respond to her. It's responding to all of you, in ways you haven't noticed yet. And we don't believe you're the first family it's chosen." He glanced at the stone in Joe's hand. "Though you might be the last."

"The artifact you found," Colton continued carefully, "it's not just ancient, it's primordial, dating back to the beginning of time. And your family name, Bailey—it appears in records that are classified, highly classified. Records from 1963 about something called Operation Chrono, which the Colonel was involved with in the 70s. There are even older records—far older."

Outside, the fog thickened, pressing against the windows like a living, breathing entity. Cathy's phone buzzed with a Pokémon Go notification, but she didn't bother to check it this time.

"I can't say more," Colton said, standing and straightening his jacket. "I've already revealed too much. The main reason I'm here is to inform you that the Colonel has been temporarily pulled from the project. For now, you won't have to worry about him... but he will return."

Zoe descended the final steps, standing defiantly tall despite her youth. "Thank you, Lieutenant Colton."

As the door closed behind him, the family remained frozen in place, weighing the significance of Colton's words and their possible involvement in Operation Chrono.

Through the window, Colton's vehicle gradually disappeared into the fog, much like a memory slipping silently into the recesses of time itself.

As fog gave way to the sun, the Baily family was processing Colton's warning. Joe's measured steps creaked against century-old floorboards. On the leather couch, Cathy kept one hand on Zoe's shoulder, the other unconsciously reaching for her phone.

"Artifacts dating back to the beginning of time," Cathy repeated. She glanced at her daughter, concern written all over her face.

Logan hunched over his laptop. "Found something," he announced, swiveling the screen. "Great-great-grandfather Edwin wasn't just any telephone operator. The exchange was a hub of unexplained phenomena." His fingers drummed nervously against the keyboard. "Reports of calls connecting to impossible times and places."

"The tunnels," Joe murmured, pausing his pacing. "Dad always said Edwin knew more about them than he let on." The stone pulsed warmly, and a vision flashed—Zoe, safe but changed, emerging from the bunker with newfound knowledge.

Zoe cradled Swirly, its iridescent surface shifting from deep purple to midnight blue. The orb's inner mechanism whirred softly, responding to her touch. "We have to go back," she said, determination hardening her voice. "Swirly's trying to show us something about Edwin."

"Absolutely not," Joe started, but the stone grew warmer, challenging his protest.

Cathy pulled up her phone, scrolling through documented anomalies. "The temporal disturbances have been increasing. Whatever this is, it's accelerating."

"The physics alone makes this insane," Logan interjected, running a hand through his disheveled hair. "Time paradoxes, butterfly effects—" He gestured at his screen full of equations.

Zoe stood. "But that's why it has to be me. I can feel it—Swirly knows how to navigate the timelines safely."

The room fell silent save for the soft hum of Logan's laptop and the distant whisper of wind through the vineyard. Joe felt the stone pulse once more, showing him the same vision of Zoe's successful return.

"If—" Joe's voice cracked. He cleared his throat and tried again. "If you go, we need rules. Safeguards."

Cathy straightened. "We'll create protocols." She squeezed Zoe's shoulder. "And you'll stay connected through Swirly at all times."

Logan closed his laptop with a sigh of resignation. "I'll monitor temporal disturbances from here. Any anomaly, any disruption—"

"I come straight back," Zoe finished.

"Here's what we know about February 1916," Logan said, spreading printouts across the kitchen table. "The exchange was already busy with the war in Europe. Perfect cover for any unusual activities." He handed Zoe a modified smartphone, its case covered in strange symbols. "I've configured this to record temporal anomalies. And yes, I installed Mom's Pokémon Go app—" he smiled at his mom "—since it seems oddly attuned to the disturbances."

Joe leaned forward. "Look for anything about the tunnels, but don't go exploring them alone. And if Edwin mentions any artifacts—"

"Record everything," Cathy finished, then gasped. "Oh Lord, you can't go dressed like that!" She eyed Zoe's ripped jeans and vintage band t-shirt. "Come with me."

In the attic, dust motes danced in the afternoon light as Cathy pulled out a large trunk. "Your great-great-aunt Ruth's clothes," she explained, lifting out a high-necked blouse in cream-colored cotton. "She'd be about your age in 1916."

The outfit they assembled felt like a costume: the blouse with its delicate pearl buttons, a navy wool skirt that brushed her ankles, and leather boots with tiny buttons up the sides. Cathy's eyes welled up as she pinned Zoe's hair into a simple Gibson girl style. "My baby," she whispered, hands trembling.

Back downstairs, Logan cleared his throat. "Let's face it, the phone won't work for calls, but it'll keep recording data." He pulled his sister into a tight hug. "Don't do anything I wouldn't do—which still leaves plenty of room for trouble."

"Remember," Joe said, his voice rough with emotion. "Edwin's wife Lily..." He paused, struggling with the weight of family secrets across time. "She might not know about any of this—the orb, the tunnels. If Edwin knows, that doesn't mean she does."

He pressed a worn envelope into Zoe's hand. Inside was a small photograph of their family, taken last Christmas at the vineyard. Joe's hands lingered over the envelope. "I've written a note on the back—things only Edwin would understand about our family, about the stone." His voice cracked slightly. "If he's anything like me, he'll recognize the truth of it. But Lily..." He met Zoe's eyes, his own glistening. "He might be carrying the burden of all of this to protect her."

Zoe nodded, understanding the layers of meaning in her father's words. She carefully tucked the envelope into her borrowed skirt's hidden pocket, feeling the weight of both the photograph and her father's unspoken fears. "I'll be careful, Dad. Promise." She reached up to touch the worry stone in his hand, and for a brief moment, both father and daughter felt a surge of connection—as if the stone itself was binding their promise across time.

"Just..." Joe pulled her into a fierce hug, "come back to us, ZoeJoe. Whatever you learn, whatever happens, just come back."

The childhood nickname, rarely used now that she was sixteen, brought tears to Zoe's eyes. In it, she heard all the bedtime stories, skinned knees, and daddy-daughter moments that had led to this impossible goodbye. She hugged him tighter, breathing in the familiar scent of his aftershave mixed with the vineyard's earth, committing it to memory.

Cathy fussed with Zoe's collar, fighting tears. "I packed you a small bag with essentials and some basic supplies." She touched Zoe's cheek. "My brave girl."

In the bunker, Zoe stood on the portal, heart pounding beneath the unfamiliar clothes. Swirly pulsed in her hand, its surface swirling with deeper, richer colors than she'd ever seen. The family gathered around her, their faces a mixture of fear and pride.

"I love you all," Zoe said, her voice catching. She looked at each of them one last time: Logan trying to hide his worry behind a confident smile, her mother barely holding back tears, her father gripping the stone like a lifeline.

Taking a deep breath, she inserted Swirly into the portal's center indent. The orb's light intensified, spreading in a spiral pattern across the stone surface. A warm breeze swept through the bunker, carrying the scent of old books and ozone.

The last thing Zoe saw was her family's faces, frozen in a moment of love and concern, before the world dissolved into a kaleidoscope of light and shadow. Then, with a sound like a distant bell, she vanished—leaving only the echo of her goodbye hanging in the air of the empty bunker.

Joe's worry stone grew warm, and in his mind's eye, he saw Zoe stepping into a crisp February morning in 1916, and the dirt streets of a Fallbrook he'd only seen in photographs. The vision brought both comfort and concern as the family stood in silence, already counting the moments until their daughter's return.

The blinding flash subsided, leaving Zoe shivering in the crisp February air of 1916. Her outfit offered little protection against the biting wind that whipped down Main Avenue, carrying the musty scent of wet earth and sodden wood. She wrapped her arms around herself, cursing her lack of foresight about appropriate time-travel attire.

Fallbrook of 1916 sprawled before her like a sepia photograph come to life. Mud-slicked streets bore deep wagon ruts, and horses stamped impatiently at hitching posts, their breath forming delicate clouds in the winter air. Shop owners in waistcoats and long skirts battled the aftermath of what must have been significant flooding, pushing brown water from their doorways with long-handled mops.

The telephone exchange building stood exactly where she expected, its red brick façade somehow younger, crisper. But across the street, where the El Real Hotel should have been, stood something altogether different. Zoe's breath caught in her throat as she took in the magnificent Hotel Ellis, its Victorian architecture soaring four stories into the gray sky. Ornate white trim decorated the deep burgundy exterior, and elegant bay windows reflected the weak winter sunlight.

*This can't be right*, she thought, her hand reaching for her phone. *Logan never mentioned this place in any of his research.*

With trembling fingers, she pulled out her phone, trying to shield it from curious eyes. The mere presence of the device felt like a dangerous anachronism. Yet somehow, impossibly, Pokémon Go was still running. Her heart thundered against her ribs as she activated the AR feature, pointing it toward the hotel's grand entrance.

The screen flickered, and her stomach lurched. There they were—the same ethereal creatures they'd encountered in the bunker, their translucent forms floating and weaving through the hotel's façade. Dozens of them, more than she'd ever seen in one place. They seemed to pulse with an inner light, their movements creating patterns that made her head spin.

"I knew you'd come today."

The voice, low and urgent, came just before a firm hand gripped her upper arm. Zoe tried to jerk away, but the stranger's grip was iron clad. He was dressed impeccably in a period-appropriate suit, but something about him seemed... off.

"Let go of me!" she hissed, very aware of the curious glances from passersby.

"Zoe Bailey," he said, her name rolling off his tongue with familiar ease, "you need to come with me. And for heaven's sake, put that phone away before you create a paradox that'll make our recent flood look like a garden sprinkler."

Her blood ran cold. The stranger's knowledge of her name, the phone, even the casual mention of time paradoxes—it all suggested something far more complex than a simple time jump. Her intuition, the same that had first drawn her to the orb, now hummed with warning and... recognition?

"Who are you?" she whispered, even as she slipped the phone into her pocket.

"Someone who's been waiting a very long time to meet you," he replied, steering her across Main Avenue. "And we have much to discuss."

As they crossed the street, Zoe instinctively stepped back as a horse-drawn carriage clattered past, muddy water splashing from its wooden wheels. The rich, earthy smell of horses mixed with the damp air, creating an atmosphere that felt completely alien to her modern sensibilities.

The stranger noticed her hesitation and smiled apologetically. "I imagine this is quite different from what you're used to," he said, guiding her around a particularly deep puddle. "No paved roads or concrete sidewalks yet, I'm afraid. The flood from two days ago didn't help matters either."

His tone brightened as they carefully picked their way across the muddy street. "But don't worry—this flood will change everything. When it washed out the tracks down at the Santa Margarita River, it actually did us a favor. They'll rebuild the railroad with a direct line into Fallbrook." He paused, his eyes twinkling with what seemed like foreknowledge. "And soon, San Diego Gas & Electric will bring power to our little town. Quite the exciting times ahead."

Zoe studied his face, trying to decode the strange mix of historical knowledge and futuristic awareness in his words. "You seem to know a lot about what's coming," she ventured carefully.

"I noticed you admiring the Hotel Ellis," he said, smoothly changing the subject. "It's quite something, isn't it? William Ellis—the owner—he's really created something special here. Did you know he employs local hunters to supply the kitchen with fresh venison, duck, and quail?" He gestured toward the impressive structure. "All the vegetables come straight from the Ellis Ranch too."

They paused at the hotel's entrance, and he continued, clearly enjoying sharing his knowledge. "The dining room is becoming quite famous, thanks to Ellis's wife Adelle, their daughters Nellie and Birdie, and their exceptional Chinese cook, Yong Sing."

His voice took on a hint of nostalgia, though the events he spoke of were supposedly happening in the present.

"Though I should warn you," he added with a knowing smirk, "the amenities aren't quite what you're used to in 2024. Only one bathroom per floor, and hot water?" He shook his head. "Let's just say it's a precious commodity."

Zoe's eyes widened at his casual mention of 2024, but before she could respond, he added softly, almost to himself, "It's a shame they'll tear it down in 1958. By then, it will be called Hotel Naples. Such a waste."

The casual way he moved between past, present, and future made Zoe's head spin. The orb in her pocket seemed to pulse warmly, as if responding to his words. She had so many questions, but one thing was becoming clear—this mysterious stranger was far more than just a well-informed historian.

"Who *are* you?" she asked again, more insistently this time. "How do you know about 2024? About me?"

He turned to her, his expression shifting to one of earnestness. "Why, I'm Edwin Bailey, of course. Zoe, you should have realized that. Logan specifically directed you to this moment and place to meet me." With a knowing look, he gestured, guiding her away from the hotel and across the street toward the telephone exchange, its sturdy brick facade inviting them closer.

The brass bell above the door chimed one final time as Edwin locked it behind them. Zoe's eyes adjusted to the dim interior, where afternoon sunlight filtered through tall, dust-moted windows. A watermark, brown and cruel, stretched across the lower portion of the wall—evidence of the recent flood's invasion.

The exchange room sprawled before her. Several switchboards lined one wall, their cables hanging like dark vines, while the opposite wall displayed Edwin's curious side business: a collection of phonographs in various states of repair. Some gleamed with polished brass horns, while others sat partially dismantled on his workbench, their internal mechanisms exposed like mechanical organs.

"Is that Thomas Edison's original model?" Zoe asked, pointing to a particularly ornate piece.

Edwin smiled, running his fingers along the phonograph's wooden base. "Good eye. But we have more pressing matters to discuss, don't we?" He turned to face her, his green eyes twinkling. "Like how I knew your brother Logan would calculate the exact moment you needed to arrive here."

Zoe's hand went to her pocket where Swirly rested. "How do you know about Logan? About any of this?"

"Because, my dear, I'm a time-traveler, much like yourself." Edwin reached into his vest pocket. "And I believe this belongs to you." In his palm lay her grandmother's silver locket, its chain pooled like liquid moonlight.

"My locket!" Zoe gasped, snatching it. "I thought I had lost it, but you took it. Why?" She stopped.

"I took it knowing you would come here at this time. I did it so you'd understand the importance of the necklace. Logan will require the use of it in due time. I was also there when Colonel O'Reilly stole the orb," Edwin said grimly. "I was there, hidden in the vineyard. The worry stone showed me what would happen, you see. I tried to prevent it, but some moments in time must play out as destined."

"You were there?" Zoe's voice quavered. "Then you saw how Swirly saved us? When it froze time just as Colonel O'Reilly was about to—" She couldn't finish the sentence.

Almost in response to her distress, the orb floated from her pocket of its own accord, flashing brilliant green light that filled the exchange with ethereal shadows. Edwin stepped back, awe painted across his features.

"Extraordinary," he whispered. "In all my years as its guardian, I've never seen it respond like this. It was dormant, almost sleeping, during my time with it." He moved closer, studying the lights. "But somehow, I always knew it was waiting. Waiting for you, Zoe."

"What do you mean?"

Edwin gestured to the orb. "The orb—Swirly, as you call it—contains powers beyond our comprehension. But it chooses its true wielder carefully. In your hands, it can not only freeze time, but fight off the enemy and bend reality itself. You can create temporal bridges, view alternate timelines, even—" He paused. "Even change the fabric of history, though that comes with grave responsibility."

Zoe watched as Swirly descended back into her waiting hands, its light dimming to a gentle pulse. "How did you find it? Where did it come from?"

Edwin pulled up two chairs, their wooden legs scraping against the floor. "That's quite a tale. It began at the Bailey homestead. Though I'm afraid even I don't have all the answers about its true origins. Some mysteries, it seems, are meant to unfold slowly—even for time travelers."

"It was an earthquake," Edwin continued, his eyes distant with memory. "Or at least, that's what we all thought at the time. I was in the basement, cataloging my collection of phonographs—I kept most of them there back then. The entire house started shaking, but it was... different. Not like any earthquake I'd felt before. The tremors had a rhythm to them, almost like a heartbeat."

Zoe clutched Swirly tighter as Edwin spoke, feeling its warmth pulse in sync with his story.

"That's when I heard it—that distinctive hum. It seemed to come from behind the old root cellar wall. The stone blocks had shifted, revealing a cavity that shouldn't have been there." He leaned forward, lowering his voice. "Inside was a small chamber, lined with what looked like metal I'd never seen before. And there, floating in the center, was the orb."

Thunder cracked outside, making Zoe jump. Edwin glanced nervously at the windows before continuing.

Edwin's expression shifted from concern to something darker as he moved towards the window. "There's something about Colonel O'Reilly you need to understand," he said. "What you're seeing—the man hunting you—it's not entirely him. At least, not anymore. He's being controlled."

Swirly's light pulsed anxiously in Zoe's hands.

Edwin moved swiftly from the window, his expression grave. "The Colonel isn't working alone," he said. "He's being controlled by beings far more ancient and dangerous than you can imagine—the Anunnaki."

Swirly pulsed, its light shifting to a deep purple as Edwin spoke the name.

"The Anunnaki," he continued, working to move the Victrola, "are beings who came from the stars thousands of years ago. They've been manipulating human history from the shadows, waiting for the right moment to reclaim what they believe is theirs." The hidden door creaked open, revealing the dark passage beyond. "The orb? It's one of their artifacts, but it wasn't meant for them. It was left here by a faction of their own kind—ones who wanted to help humanity protect itself against their eventual return."

A sound like crackling electricity filtered through the ceiling, followed by multiple sets of footsteps materializing above them.

"That's not just O'Reilly up there," Edwin whispered urgently. "Listen to that sound—it's their technology. They've given him a corrupted version of time travel, a temporal tether that lets him track you through time. But it comes with a price." He pulled out his worry stone, which vibrated in response to the energy above. "Each jump he takes affects him mentally and physically. It robs his soul."

Swirly flared red as boots thundered on the porch outside.

"The Anunnaki chose O'Reilly carefully," Edwin explained as they entered the tunnel. "His military background, his dedication to family and duty, his unwavering belief in authority—they twisted those qualities, using their technology to slowly bend him to their will. They started by threatening to harm his wife and daughter, and now each time he uses their version of time travel, their control over him grows even stronger."

The sound of splintering wood echoed from above—they'd breached the exchange.

"The orb chose you, Zoe, because you can do something they fear." Edwin led her deeper into the tunnels, Swirly's light illuminating ancient symbols carved into the walls. "You can travel through time naturally, without damaging the temporal fabric, and you can sense the difference between their corrupted technology and the orb's pure energy. More importantly, you combined with the orb, are no match for the Annunaki. You have much more power than you know Zoe."

A temporal crackle echoed through the tunnels—some from ahead, others behind.

"They're using their tethers to spread through the network," Edwin whispered. "Different agents from different times, all controlled by the Anunnaki, all converging here." He studied the stone, which now glowed faintly. "But they don't know what these tunnels really are."

"What are they?" Zoe asked, noticing how Swirly's light made the wall symbols shimmer.

"They're part of an ancient defense system, built by the same faction that created the orb. Somewhere in this maze is a chamber that holds the truth about everything—why the Anunnaki came to Earth, why some of them chose to help us, and how to stop those who would enslave humanity through temporal manipulation."

Swirly suddenly pulsed intensely, its light revealing more complex patterns of symbols stretching down one particular tunnel.

"The orb recognizes this place," Edwin said, eyes wide. "It's trying to show us the way to the chamber where the library is located, but we have to hurry. The longer O'Reilly uses their technology, the stronger their hold on him becomes. And if they capture you and the orb…" He glanced nervously at the shadows. "They'll have everything they need to rewrite human history in their image."

More temporal crackling echoed through the tunnels, closer now.

"Ready?" Edwin asked, gesturing toward the passage where the symbols glowed brightest.

Zoe nodded, holding Swirly tight as they descended deeper into the earth, away from their pursuers and toward truths that had waited millennia to be revealed.

The ancient doors creaked open, revealing a sight that made Zoe's breath catch in her throat. Before them stretched a vast chamber that defied the laws of space and time. The ceiling arched impossibly high, its apex lost in darkness despite the soft, amber glow emanating from floating orbs that drifted lazily through the air.

"This is impossible," Zoe whispered, her voice echoing off walls lined with towering bookshelves that seemed to stretch endlessly in both directions. The shelves themselves were a marvel—dark wood inlaid with swirling patterns of silver and gold that seemed to move when caught in her peripheral vision.

Edwin smiled. "Impossible is relative when you're dealing with the Annunaki, my dear Zoe."

The air hummed with an energy that made Zoe's skin tingle. Ancient texts and modern tablets sat side by side, while holographic displays flickered between the stacks, showing star charts and temporal maps that shifted and changed as she watched.

"Before we begin," Edwin said, his expression growing serious, "there's something you need to know about. In your time, there's a Victrola in your attic—your father inherited it. Inside the base, there's a hidden compartment. You'll find a letter there, explaining everything about the worry stone. Its power is... significant."

Zoe clutched Swirly tighter. "Is that why Dad can sometimes see what I see now?"

"Exactly." Edwin's eyes grew distant. "The stone and the orb are connected, just as our family is connected through time." His voice cracked slightly. "This... this will be our only meeting, Zoe. I've waited my entire life for this moment to help prepare you."

"Prepare me for what?"

"A civil war of sorts. You see, the Annunaki faction that created this library, they've been waiting for you. You're the key to saving both our worlds. And in order to do that, they believe you must defeat the ruling Annunaki."

"A war? An actual war?" she asked incredulously. "I can barely handle high school English, and now I'm supposed to fight in some kind of... what, an alien civil war?"

Edwin moved closer, his footsteps echoing through the vast chamber. "Not fight in it, Zoe. End it."

The enormity of it all hit her at once, and she dropped into a nearby chair—its dark wood etched with symbols that seemed to swim before her eyes. Her trembling fingers found their way to her hair, twisting the strands as her mind raced with implications.

As Edwin pulled a large tome from the shelf, ethereal text suddenly projected into the air above it. "Here," he said urgently. "This is what we've been waiting for." He traced his finger through the floating symbols. "It speaks of the convergence, and why you were chosen."

"What exactly happens during this convergence?" she asked, watching as Edwin traced his fingers over the glowing symbols.

"According to these texts," Edwin said, his face illuminated by the hovering glyphs, "it's when the barriers between dimensions grow thin. The opposing Annunaki faction plans to use this convergence to implement their ultimate solution for humanity." He glanced up at her, his expression grave. "They've been patient, waiting thousands of years for the right alignment."

"The Anunnaki are formidable figures," Edwin continued, "towering over humans with some as tall as twelve feet. Their skin shimmers with an iridescent quality, reflecting a spectrum of colors that shift with the light. Their eyes are large and expressive, and change color depending on their emotions. One moment, their gaze could sparkle with a piercing blue, the next, they could swirl into a molten amber.

From across the room, Edwin retrieved another book, its pages glowing with a blue light. "And I think I've found something to help with your Colonel O'Reilly problem. The time travel is affecting him, changing him. There's a way to stop it, and to block his ability to track you."

"The orb wasn't meant for him," Edwin explained. "Each time he forces a temporal jump, it corrupts him further. The Annunaki designed it to work with specific genetic markers—our family's markers. For others..." He shook his head. "It's like a poison."

They moved to a large oak table at the center of the library where Edwin spread out their findings. The floating orbs gathered closer, as if listening to their planning. "The facility under Mount Palomar—it's a decoy. The military only knows about that one. These tunnels, this library, they belong to us. To you."

"The Victrola note," Edwin said, sketching a diagram, "it explains how to properly attune the stone. Your father's natural connection to it is strong, but untrained. Once he learns to use it properly, he'll be able to help shield your family from detection."

The orb hummed louder, and Zoe felt a familiar tingling sensation. Their time was running short.

"Remember," Edwin said urgently, "the Victrola, the tunnels, and most importantly—trust yourself. The orb chose you for a reason."

Zoe squeezed his hand, fighting back tears. "I wish you could come with me."

"I'll be with you through time and blood." He smiled, though his eyes were wet. "Now go. Save both our worlds."

As the orb's energy began to build around her, Zoe took one last look at the library—at this impossible room full of knowledge and power, and at her ancestor, who had waited so long to help her find her way. The last thing she saw before the temporal shift took her was Edwin, standing among the floating lights, his proud smile fading into the streams of time.

"Wait!" Zoe called out, fighting against the orb's pull. "You never told me how to stop the opposing faction!"

Edwin's voice came through the growing temporal distortion, each word deliberately clear despite the growing distance between them. "The answer is in the Victrola, Zoe. Everything you need to know about the convergence is hidden there. But be careful—" His next words were lost in the rushing sound of time displacement.

The library blurred around her, its floating orbs of light stretching into streaming ribbons of color. Through the chaos of the transition, Zoe clutched the knowledge she'd gained like a lifeline: the truth about Colonel O'Reilly's condition, the hidden tunnels, the coming war between the Annunaki factions, and most importantly, the Victrola waiting in their attic.

As reality began to reform around her, one last whisper from Edwin reached her consciousness: "Trust the stone, trust the orb, but most of all, trust yourself. The fate of two worlds depends on it."

Reality snapped back into focus, and Zoe found herself in the familiar confines of the bunker. The temporal displacement faded, leaving her buzzing with excitement and purpose. Swirly pulsed rapidly in her pocket, sharing her enthusiasm.

"Oh my god, oh my god, oh my god!" She bounced on her toes, barely able to contain herself. Everything made sense now—the orb, the stone, even Colonel O'Reilly's strange behavior. And the Victrola! The answer was literally in their attic this whole time.

"DAD! MOM! LOGAN!" She took the bunker stairs two at a time, her feet thundering against the metal steps. "You guys are never going to believe this!"

She burst through the bunker door into the wine cellar, practically vibrating with energy. "GUYS! I know what we have to do!" Her voice echoed through the house, carrying the same excited tone Joe had seen in his vision just days before.

The orb pulsed once more in her pocket, almost like a chuckle, as if to say, *Well, what are you waiting for? Let's get started.*

Zoe grinned, taking the cellar stairs three at a time. Sure, she had to save humanity, stop an alien civil war, and somehow help Colonel O'Reilly—but right now, she just couldn't wait to tell her family everything she'd learned.

After all, how often does a sixteen-year-old girl get to announce she's the key to saving two worlds?

The kitchen fell silent as Zoe finished recounting her journey through time. Sunlight streamed through the window, providing a warm glow across the worn wooden table where her family sat transfixed. Her mother's phone lay forgotten beside her coffee cup, Pokémon Go still glowing on the screen.

"And you're certain about the library?" Logan leaned forward. "A hidden repository of alien knowledge just sitting under Fallbrook this whole time?"

Zoe clutched Swirly closer. "I know how it sounds, but I was there. The tunnels, the books, everything Edwin showed me—it was real."

Joe stood abruptly, his hand finding the stone in his pocket. "The victrola. If what Edwin told you is true..." He headed for the attic stairs, taking them two at a time.

Minutes later, the antique phonograph sat centered on the kitchen table, its brass horn reflecting patterns of light from the orb. Joe's fingers traced the wooden base, searching for any sign of a compartment.

"Dad, seriously?" Logan rolled his eyes, reaching over. His tech-savvy fingers found the hidden catch almost immediately. "It's a simple pressure-release mechanism. See?" The false bottom popped open with a soft click.

"Show-off," Joe said, but his voice caught as he pulled out two yellowed envelopes—one marked "Joe" in careful period handwriting, the other "Zoe."

Cathy moved closer as Joe unfolded his letter with trembling fingers as he read:

"Dear Joe, Your daughter is remarkable. Though our meeting was brief, I saw in her the same light that drew me to the orb so many years ago. The worry stone you carry is more than a family heirloom—it's a key. When properly attuned, it will allow you to pierce the veil of time itself, to see what was and what may be. More importantly, it will shield you and yours from those who would do you harm, both earthly and otherwise.

To activate it, hold it to your heart while touching the orb. The rest will come naturally.

Take care of them, Joe. The path ahead is difficult, but you won't walk it alone. -Your great-great-grandfather Edwin Bailey."

Zoe's letter was longer, the pages covered in detailed instructions about the orb's capabilities and warnings about the coming convergence. Her eyes widened as she read about dimensional travel and the mysterious Enki, a strange creature who is part of the faction working to stop the convergence.

Joe stood in the center of the kitchen, Edwin's instructions echoing in his mind. He held the stone against his heart, its familiar smooth surface warming against his chest. With his other hand, he reached for Swirly, meeting Zoe's encouraging nod.

The moment his fingers touched the orb, a surge of energy coursed through him. The stone pulsed with a deep blue light that synchronized with Swirly's iridescent glow. Joe gasped as the kitchen seemed to blur around him, reality splitting into layers of time—past, present, and future overlapping like transparent sheets.

"Dad?" Zoe's voice seemed to come from both now and then, echoing across temporal planes.

Joe's vision shifted, colors intensifying. The stone's quartz vein emitted a soft humming vibration that resonated through his chest. He could suddenly see traces of temporal energy flowing through the room like ribbons of light—gold threads connecting his family members, echoing its shared history and possible futures.

Around Zoe, the threads were particularly bright, spiraling outward from Swirly in complex patterns. But now he could actually see them, understand them. The stone was teaching him, downloading generations of knowledge directly into his consciousness.

"I can see..." he whispered, his voice carrying an otherworldly resonance. "I can see everything. The timelines, the possibilities..." His free hand reached out, fingers tracing the invisible currents of time. "There's so much more than just past and future. It's like... like a web, all interconnected."

As the power settled into him, Cathy moved closer, her phone's Pokémon Go screen suddenly bursting with new information. "Joe, look at this," she said, stepping beside him. The closer she got, the clearer her screen became.

"Wait a second," Logan said, reaching for his mom's phone. "If these creatures in Pokémon Go are actually Annunaki in disguise, there has to be a pattern." His fingers tapping the screen as he scrolled through Cathy's recent captures.

Cathy grabbed the phone back and shifted even closer to Joe, their shoulders touching. "The shinies I've been encountering—they're not following normal spawn rates. And they only appear clearly when I'm near you." She pulled up a particularly rare specimen, its coloring a striking gold and amber.

"Those colors..." Zoe gasped, "they match Edwin's description of Enki's eyes! He's part of the faction that is trying to stop this nonsense."

Logan grabbed his laptop from the counter. "The regular Pokémon appears for everyone, but these special ones—the potential Annunaki—they only show up on Mom's screen when she's within a few feet of Dad."

To test the theory, Cathy walked to the other side of the kitchen. The mysterious Pokémon on her screen became fuzzy, almost transparent. As she returned to Joe's side, they snapped back into focus, their auras now distinct and clear.

"Look at the aura effects," Zoe pointed out. "The ones with a blue glow could be friendly, like Enki, but these red ones..." She indicated several particularly menacing specimens.

"Hostile Annunaki," Logan finished. "And look at the spawn locations of the red ones. They're all clustered around—"

"Camp Pendleton," they said in unison.

Zoe touched the orb to her mother's phone, causing both to pulse with a soft light. The Pokémon Go screen flickered, and suddenly new symbols appeared around certain creatures—ancient markings that only she could read.

"Well, that's new," she said, studying the glowing symbols. "I think Swirly just gave us a translation key. These marks... they're like Annunaki name tags!"

"Great," Logan smirked. "all we have to do is catch powerful interdimensional beings like they're digital monsters. No pressure."

"Actually," Cathy said, a familiar gleam in her eye as she grabbed her spare battery pack, "that's exactly what we're going to do." She tucked her arm through Joe's. "Ready for a hunting expedition, honey?"

Joe looked at his reflection in the window, startled by his transformed appearance. His normally brown eyes now held traces of the worry stone's blue light, tiny flecks of quartz-like luminescence sparkling in his irises.

"The stone didn't just give you powers," Zoe said softly, Swirly pulsating in harmony with the stone. "It changed you. Like the orb changed me. We're connected to them now, really connected."

As if in response, Cathy's phone buzzed. A new raid had appeared at the old hotel site, featuring a creature none of them had ever seen before.

"Well," Joe said, the worry stone's power flowing through him like a constant current, "I guess we're ready for that raid now." He wrapped an arm around Cathy's shoulders, his newfound abilities humming with protective energy. "Let's go find ourselves an Annunaki."

The family headed for the door, Joe and Zoe leading the way, their newfound powers humming in synchronization. Behind them, reality rippled slightly, adjusting to the presence of two humans who were now something more—guardians of time itself.

# CHAPTER 16

# BRIAN

The Bailey kitchen buzzed with nervous energy that morning as Joe laid out the plan over breakfast. Logan hunched over his laptop, already working on encrypting their phones, while Cathy organized her notes from recent Pokémon Go anomalies around the observatory.

"You'll monitor any unusual activity?" Joe confirmed with Logan, who nodded without looking up from his screen.

"And I'll keep documenting the frequency spikes through the app," Cathy said. "Just... be careful up there. Hunter was acting strange during our last visit."

"Define strange," Joe said.

"Like he was watching us," Logan interjected, finally looking up. "Not just regular security stuff."

Zoe jangled the car keys. "We should get going, Dad. The observatory opens in an hour."

The drive to Mount Palomar started quietly, with Zoe behind the wheel of their SUV. Joe watched her handle the winding mountain roads with a mixture of pride and apprehension, remembering teaching her to drive just months ago. Now here they were, investigating supernatural phenomena together. The forest pressed in around them.

Joe's hand kept returning to the worry stone in his pocket. Something felt different about it today—heavier, almost alive. The smooth surface seemed to pulse against his palm, as if the weight of time itself were compressed into its unassuming form.

Glancing out the window, Joe studied the thickening forest. The trees seemed to lean inward, their branches reaching like gnarled fingers over the road. A sense of unease prickled at the back of his neck. Hunter's odd behavior during Cathy's visit wasn't just suspicious—it was threatening.

"I think I need to try something," he said, breaking the silence.

Zoe turned to him, eyebrows raised. "What kind of 'something'?"

Joe pulled out the stone, its blue-gray surface catching the morning light. "This. I've... never really used it before. Not intentionally. But if we're walking into something dangerous, I think we need to know what we're up against."

"Dad..." Zoe's voice wavered between concern and curiosity. She pulled the car onto a scenic overlook, killing the engine. "Are you sure? We don't even know what it might do to you."

"That's exactly why I need to try it," Joe said, studying the stone's familiar groove where generations of Bailey thumbs had worn their mark. "If this thing can actually show me glimpses of what's coming, we need that advantage now."

Taking a deep breath, Joe closed his eyes. He gripped the stone tightly, its warmth spreading up his arm like liquid sunshine. The world around him faded, replaced by a crystal-clear vision.

He stood inside the observatory, near the massive telescope. A young technician was calling someone on an intercom. "Hunter here," came the response. The technician's face was pale, panicked. Hunter burst through a doorway, making straight for a bank of monitors.

Joe moved closer, realizing no one could see him. On the screen was a security feed showing himself and Zoe in a restricted area, approaching an elevator with only two buttons—main floor and storage area.

Hunter snatched up a phone. After one ring: "Colonel O'Reilly, we have a problem."

The scene shifted. Joe found himself in a vast underground chamber, all stone and dimly lit. He spotted himself and Zoe crouched in a corner, hiding. Waiting. But for what?

Joe's eyes snapped open with a gasp. The stone burned hot in his palm, and his heart hammered against his ribs. Zoe gripped his arm, her face pale.

"What did you see?" she asked.

Joe swallowed hard, his mouth desert-dry. "Hunter's involved in something big. There's... there's something under the observatory. I saw us hiding there, and Hunter was calling the Colonel about us."

Joe nodded grimly. "We need to be careful. They're watching for us already."

Ahead, the observatory's dome rose against the morning sky like a sentinel. Joe slipped the stone back into his pocket, its warmth lingering like a warning. Whatever secrets lay beneath Mount Palomar, they were about to find out—ready or not.

Zoe shifted the car into drive, her jaw set with determination. "Well," she said, "at least we know where we need to go now."

"Yeah," Joe agreed. "Right into the heart of it."

The Bailey's SUV rolled to a stop in the Mount Palomar facility's parking lot. Zoe killed the engine. Through the windshield, the research building loomed before them, its modern glass facade reflecting the morning sun.

"Ready?" Joe asked, glancing at Zoe in the driver's seat.

Zoe nodded, pulling Swirly from her jacket pocket. "Remember, we'll only have a few minutes once I freeze time. The closer we get to the lab, the harder it'll be to maintain."

She closed her eyes, focusing on Swirly's energy. A familiar tingling sensation spread through her body as reality shifted around them. The world outside became still - a bird hung motionless mid-flight, leaves paused in their dance with the wind.

They moved swiftly through the frozen tableau, passing motionless security guards and researchers caught in mid-stride. Their footsteps echoed in the unnaturally silent hallway as they made their way to a restricted elevator at the far end of the building.

Inside the elevator, time resumed its normal flow. Zoe sagged against the wall, exhausted from the effort. Joe punched in the code Logan had discovered - 3317. The elevator descended deeper than seemed possible, the digital floor indicator continuing well past the building's apparent basement levels.

The elevator doors parted silently, revealing a vast chamber that defied the expected scale of Mount Palomar's underground. Zoe and Joe crouched behind a row of storage containers, taking in the scene before them.

The laboratory sprawled across multiple levels, carved directly into the mountain's heart. Massive support columns of polished granite rose thirty feet to a ceiling threaded with cables that emitted an ethereal glow. The air itself seemed charged, carrying an electric taste and a low frequency hum that made their teeth ache.

Three distinct testing areas dominated the space. In the first, scientists clustered around what appeared to be temporal containment cells - shimmering bubbles of energy where objects and small animals existed in varying time states. Some moved at hyper speed, others frozen in perfect stasis. In one cell, a flower continuously bloomed and withered in an endless loop.

The second area housed what could only be described as consciousness transfer equipment. Pairs of reclined chairs faced each other, connected by arcing energy fields that sparkled with rainbow colors. Annunaki researchers moved between the stations, their golden skin reflecting the electronic displays that surrounded each setup. Human scientists worked alongside them, though they seemed to defer to the aliens' authority.

The third section, partially hidden behind frosted glass walls, contained rows of stasis pods. Through the translucent barriers, Zoe could make out human forms - children, suspended in a shimmering liquid that seemed to preserve them in a perfect state of unchanging equilibrium.

Military personnel patrolled designated paths between the sections, their weapons a strange hybrid of human and alien technology. Some wore devices that appeared to protect them from temporal effects, creating subtle distortions in the surrounding air.

A central control station rose on a platform in the middle of the chamber, where the lead Annunaki coordinated the facility's activities through holographic interfaces that responded to his mere thoughts. Data streams floated in the air, incomprehensible symbols flowing like digital rivers between stations.

"Look," Joe said, pointing to the commanding figure across the lab.

As Zoe looked at the central control station, her heart stopped when she spotted a familiar face. Brian - the boy in the red cap from the tunnels - was being led from one of the testing chambers. He looked exactly as she remembered him, as if he had been frozen in time. At five foot three, with dirty blond shoulder length hair, he was still wearing a red baseball cap. His face was ashen, his brown eyes hollow with fear. As if sensing her presence, he turned, their eyes meeting across the chamber. His silent plea for help hit her like a physical blow.

The elevator chimed behind them.

Colonel Marc O'Reilly strode out, flanked by armed soldiers. His face was set in grim determination as he approached the lead Annunaki. "Sir, we have a situation. Zoe Bailey and her father were spotted entering the facility. They're here, somewhere."

The lead Annunaki's eyes narrowed, scanning the laboratory. "Find them," he commanded, his voice resonating through the chamber. "The girl must not interfere with the convergence. Too much depends on these experiments."

Zoe gripped her father's arm, her mind racing. They had seen enough - the missing children, the experiments, the collaboration between the military and the Annunaki. But now they needed to find a way out before they were discovered.

Swirly quickly pulsed in her pocket, as if offering a solution. But could she muster the strength for another time freeze so soon? And what about Brian?

Joe squeezed her hand, the worry stone pressed between their palms. In that moment of contact, they both knew - they couldn't leave without trying to help him. Whatever was happening in this hidden lab, it had to be stopped.

Brian's eyes met Zoe's across the chamber, and in that moment of connection, something passed between them - an understanding, a plan. His hands, previously trembling, steadied as he approached one of the temporal containment cells housing a small potted plant.

The guards flanking him had become complacent, having escorted him through this routine countless times before. They didn't notice when his fingers brushed against the cell's control panel, didn't see the subtle changes he made to its temporal frequency settings.

The effect was instantaneous and catastrophic. The containment field collapsed, releasing a wave of temporal energy that rippled outward. Inside, the plant exploded through its entire life cycle in seconds - sprouting, growing, dying, and decomposing in a violent burst that overloaded nearby systems.

Chain reactions spread through the facility. Other containment cells flickered and failed. Alarms blared as emergency protocols activated, sending guards rushing to contain the temporal anomalies now spreading through the lab. The air filled with the scent of ozone and the sound of crackling energy.

"Temporal containment breach in Sector Seven!" a voice boomed over the facility's speakers. "All non-essential personnel evacuate immediately. Temporal protection protocols engaged."

Scientists scrambled to save their data while military personnel rushed to contain the spreading temporal anomalies. The lead Annunaki's voice cut through the chaos, commanding in multiple languages simultaneously.

Brian used the confusion to trigger a second failure. His fingers danced across another control panel, this time targeting the facility's primary power distribution hub. Sparks erupted from junction boxes as power surged through the system. The lighting flickered and dimmed, replaced by the harsh red glow of emergency systems.

In the consciousness transfer area, the energy fields between the chairs pulsed erratically. One of the Annunaki researchers shouted in their strange language as equipment started to overload. The rainbow-colored arcs of energy broke free of their containment, whipping through the air like temporal lightning.

"Containment fields are collapsing!" A human scientist yelled, backing away from his station. "We're losing stability in all test chambers!"

The stasis pods pulsed with an unsettling rhythm, their preservation fluid bubbling and swirling. Warning lights flashed across their monitoring panels, drawing more guards and researchers away from their posts.

Through the chaos, Brian caught Zoe's eye again and gave an almost imperceptible nod. The path between them had cleared as personnel continued to try to contain the damage. This was their chance.

The laboratory erupted into chaos as Brian's distraction took effect. Emergency lights strobed crimson across steel and glass surfaces while steam hissed from ruptured pipes, creating a concealing fog through which Zoe and Joe crept closer to their target.

"There!" Joe said, pointing to where Brian was huddled behind a bank of monitors.

Two Annunaki materialized through the steam, their forms towering over Zoe. The first raised a hand, energy crackling between its elongated fingers. The second spoke, its voice bypassing her ears and resonating directly in her mind: "The vessel must remain."

Zoe felt Swirly pulse with unprecedented energy. Acting on instinct, she raised the orb. Time distorted around the first Annunaki, aging the air itself until it crystallized, trapping the being in a temporal prison. The second lunged forward, but Zoe twisted Swirly counterclockwise, creating a bubble of accelerated time that made the alien move in slow motion.

"Stop right there, Zoe." Colonel O'Reilly emerged from the steam, his weapon trained on them. But something was different - his usual stern confidence wavered.

"They're lying to you, Colonel," Zoe called out, maintaining her focus on the trapped Annunaki. "They don't want to save humanity. They want to replace us. The children aren't vessels for power - they're vessels for consciousness transfer. The Annunaki are dying, and they want new bodies."

"That's impossible," O'Reilly said, but doubt crept into his voice. "They showed us their plans, their technology..."

"Look at Brian," Zoe pressed. "Really look at him. Do you really want to be a part of this? Even if it were true, they are stealing and torturing children for their own benefit, not yours."

The lead Annunaki appeared behind O'Reilly. "The girl speaks false truths. We offer ascension, evolution."

"Then why keep it secret?" Joe asked, gripping his worry stone. "Why experiment on children?"

O'Reilly's weapon wavered. Zoe saw the conflict in his eyes as pieces began falling into place - the missing records, the contradicting orders, the children's strange presence.

"The Convergence," O'Reilly said. "It's not about merging our species, is it? It's about replacing us."

"Colonel O'Reilly," the lead Annunaki's voice hardened. "Remember your oath."

But that moment of doubt was all Zoe needed. Swirly blazed in her hands, responding to her desperate need to escape. The orb's surface swirled with patterns she'd never seen before.

"Dad, Brian - hold on to me!"

The world shifted, reality bending around them. Zoe felt a sensation like being pulled through water, then snapped back. Suddenly, they were in the parking lot next to their SUV. The journey that should have taken minutes had happened in an instant.

"How did you—" Joe started, steadying himself against the vehicle.

"Get in!" Zoe shouted, helping Brian into the back seat. Through the facility's windows above, she could see Colonel O'Reilly looking down at them, his expression unreadable. For a moment, their eyes met across the distance. Then he turned away, facing the approaching Annunaki.

As Joe sped them away from Mount Palomar, Zoe held Swirly close, feeling its warmth pulse in sync with her racing heart. Brian sat silently in the back, but his eyes were clearer now, more present.

"Did you see that?" he finally said. "When you used the orb? For a second, I saw... everything. All the timelines, all the possibilities."

Zoe nodded, understanding flowing between them. "We'll save the others," she promised. "Now that we know the truth, we can fight back."

The SUV wound down the mountain road as sunset painted the sky in fierce oranges and reds. Behind them, Mount Palomar stood silent, its secrets no longer completely hidden. Zoe knew their revelation would have consequences - O'Reilly's moment of doubt would cost him, and the Annunaki would be coming for them with even greater determination.

But for now, they had won. They had Brian, they had the truth, and most importantly, they had discovered that Swirly's powers were still evolving. The real question was: what else was the orb capable of?

Joe glanced at Zoe. "Your mother's going to kill me when she hears about this."

Despite everything, Zoe managed a small smile. "Maybe we shouldn't mention the time-slip part just yet."

# CHAPTER 17

# HIDDEN MESSAGES

"There! That's definitely not a normal Pokémon." Cathy zoomed in on her phone screen, hands trembling slightly. The creature looked almost translucent, its form shifting between dimensions. But it was the eyes that caught Logan's attention - they changed from gold to amber, seeming to stare directly through the screen.

"Hold on," Logan said, connecting his laptop. "These color patterns... they're not random glitches." His fingers frantically tapping the keyboard as he pulled data from Cathy's Pokémon Go account.

He enhanced one particular image - a figure just visible behind a Charizard near the old oak tree. Those distinctive eyes seemed to pierce through time itself.

"That's him. That's Enki," Cathy whispered. "I remember those eyes. But look at the background."

Logan zoomed in further, applying various filters. "There's something embedded in the pixel patterns... some kind of code." He started running decryption algorithms. "It's like... it's like the images are layered. Each one contains different fragments of information."

Cathy scrolled through her screenshots. "They always appear at sunrise or sunset. And only in places with historical significance." She pointed to timestamps. "See? The El Real Hotel shows 1904, but that's..."

"Impossible?" Logan finished, then paused as his computer beeped. "Maybe not. Look at this."

Text began appearing on his screen, decoded from the images:

*Beneath time's veil lies truth*
*Where forbidden knowledge sleeps*
*Seek the guardian's golden gaze*
*When past and present meet*

"There's more," Logan said. He loaded another image - this one showing a strange distortion near the library. Hidden in its code was another message:

*Five points of power converge*
*Where history's shadows dwell*
*The key lies in the seventh hour*
*When time's barriers fell*

His voice trailed off as he noticed something else. "Mom, when exactly did you capture each of these?"

Cathy checked her Pokémon Go journal. "The first one was at 7:05 AM, then 7:05 PM the next day. Actually..." she scrolled through the data, "they were all at 7:05."

"The seventh hour," Logan said, turning back to the decoded text. He pulled up another picture - this one showing a strange aurora-like effect behind a Gyarados. Running it through his filters revealed new text, but this time in an unfamiliar script.

"That's not any language I recognize," Cathy leaned closer.

"No, but look at the pattern." Logan pointed to repeating symbols. "It's similar to the markings Swirly has shown us. If we cross-reference..." He loaded images they'd taken of the orb, comparing the patterns.

His computer chimed as another layer of code revealed itself. A sequence of numbers appeared:

41.3874° N, 74.2179° W appeared on screen, followed by more encoded text:

*When celestial bodies align*
*Seek the depths where knowledge dwells*
*Through the veil of mortal time*
*Where ancient wisdom tells*

"These coordinates," Logan said, typing rapidly. "They don't point to anywhere in Fallbrook." He accessed a mapping program, then frowned. "That's weird. The location keeps shifting, like it's..."

"Moving through time," Cathy finished, watching the marker bounce between different historical maps. "Look at the dates it's showing: 1904, 1847, 2023, 1973..."

Logan opened another screenshot - this one showing what appeared to be a Mewtwo, but its form was distorted, overlaid with geometric patterns matching those on Swirly. Within its coding, he found another message:

*Seven lost to time's embrace*

*Operation Chrono's price*

*Seek the truth in hidden space*

*Where soldiers paid the price*

"Operation Chrono," Cathy said. "The military project from 1973. Logan, pull up that list of missing soldiers you found."

The computer suddenly beeped rapidly as new code emerged from the combined images. A complex temporal equation filled the screen, numbers and symbols shifting like living things.

"That's not just code," Logan said, eyes widening. "That's a temporal mapping formula. Look at how it correlates to the moon phases and ley line intersections under Fallbrook."

Cathy checked her phone again, pulling up one last image. This one showed what appeared to be a doorway behind an Alakazam, but the doorway seemed to lead into infinite darkness. Within its pixels, they found coordinates for somewhere beneath Fallbrook, along with a time: tomorrow, 7:05 PM.

"The Library of Forbidden Knowledge," Logan whispered, recognizing the description from their research. "Enki's been leaving us a trail of breadcrumbs, leading us right to it."

"But why use Pokémon Go?" Cathy wondered, studying the shifting patterns.

"Because it's brilliant," Logan said, his excitement building. "Think about it - the game already uses AR and GPS. The Annunaki would never think to monitor it. And with millions of players worldwide, any energy signatures from their messages would be masked by normal game activity."

He pulled up one final image - a peculiar Pokéstop that had appeared briefly near their vineyard. Instead of the usual photo, it showed what looked like ancient text overlaid with modern binary code.

"Watch this," Logan said, running the image through multiple filters simultaneously. The screen flickered, and suddenly a holographic message appeared above his laptop, projected through his phone's camera:

*The Convergence approaches*

*Time's guardians have fallen*

*Only the Chosen remains*

*When the seventh bell calls*

*Seek the depths where knowledge hides*

*Before the vessels fill*

As they watched, the text transformed, revealing a complex series of interlocking circles and symbols - a temporal map.

"Mom," Logan's voice grew serious, "these aren't just random coordinates. They're waypoints in time. Look." He highlighted specific points on the map. "The El Real Hotel, Operation Chrono, the day Zoe found Swirly - they're all connected. And tomorrow night..."

"All the points converge," Cathy finished, seeing the pattern. She grabbed her phone, dialing quickly. "We need to reach Zoe. Now."

Logan was already sending the decoded data to his sister's phone. "The Library of Forbidden Knowledge isn't just a place," he explained as they waited for Zoe to answer. "It's a nexus point where multiple timelines intersect. And according to these readings..." He pointed to fluctuating energy signatures in the data, "it's becoming unstable."

Cathy's phone crackled with strange static as Zoe answered. Through the interference, they could hear Swirly's distinctive hum.

"Zoe," Logan said urgently, "we found something. Enki's been leaving messages in Mom's Pokémon Go. We know where you need to go next, but..." He glanced at the temporal map, where countdown numbers had appeared in the corners. "You've got less than 24 hours before the convergence points align."

As if in response, every electronic device in the room flickered. Through Logan's phone camera, a new figure appeared in AR - a full manifestation of Enki, his golden eyes flaring with urgency.

"The veil between realities grows thin," his voice came through their devices, distorting the signals. "The Annunaki have accelerated their plans. They know we've made contact."

Logan's screens filled with cascading data - temporal coordinates, energy signatures, and fragments of ancient text. "These power signatures," he said, "they're identical to the ones Zoe described from Mount Palomar."

"The vessels," Cathy gasped, recognizing patterns from her previous encounters. She pulled up another Pokémon Go image, this one showing something strange, a distortion around the oak tree. "Logan, enhance this."

Enki continued. "The Convergence was never meant to be a single event. They've been preparing humanity gradually, selecting vessels throughout time. But now—"

His image flickered as interference cut across their screens. Through the static, they glimpsed another figure - golden and tall, its presence causing their devices to malfunction.

"They're tracing the signal," Logan warned. "Mom, get those last coordinates!"

Cathy quickly captured screenshots as Enki's last message came through in fragments:

*"Library... seventh hour... temporal nexus... find the Chronolith... before they—"*

The connection cut out completely. Their screens went dark, then rebooted. When they came back online, all traces of the strange Pokémon and messages had vanished from Cathy's game.

But Logan was smiling. "Got it. Everything downloaded before they cut us off." He turned his laptop to show a complete temporal map, each point marked with precise coordinates and timestamps. "Look at this - the Library isn't just hidden in space, it's hidden in time. These coordinates aren't just telling us where to go..."

"They're telling us when," Cathy finished, understanding dawning. She grabbed her phone, pulling up Zoe's contact. "Honey, are you still there? We know what Enki was trying to tell us. The Library, the El Real Hotel, the missing soldiers - they're all connected. But we need to hurry. According to these calculations..."

"We have until sunset tomorrow," Logan interjected, watching the countdown numbers on his screen. "After that, the temporal confluence ends, and the Library's entrance will be sealed for another seven years."

Through the phone, they heard Swirly's hum intensify. "Send me everything," Zoe's voice came through clearly now. "Dad, Brian and I will head to the first set of coordinates."

"Brian? Who's Brian... oh never mind, just be careful," Cathy told Zoe. "The Annunaki know we've broken their code. They'll be watching."

"Don't worry, Mom," Zoe replied, confidence in her voice. "They're not the only ones who can manipulate time anymore."

The call ended, leaving Logan and Cathy wondering who Brian was.

As soon as the call ended, a new notification popped up on Cathy's Pokémon Go - a raid battle at the oak tree. But the raid boss wasn't any known Pokémon; instead, it showed a swirling vortex of temporal energy.

"That's not part of the game," Logan said, analyzing the code. "Look at the countdown timer - 7:05. It's another message."

Cathy opened the raid screen, and hidden in the battle animation, they saw new coordinates flashing in sequence. Logan quickly recorded them, plotting each point on his map.

"Mom, these points..." He traced the pattern. "They form a perfect match to the ley lines under Fallbrook. And look at this." He overlaid the map with historical data. "Each intersection marks where a temporal anomaly was reported."

His computer chirped, decoding more hidden text within the raid animation:

*Seven points of power aligned*

*Seven souls through time displaced*

*Seven keys in vessels confined*

*Seven gates must be faced*

"The Operation Chrono soldiers," Cathy realized. "They weren't lost - they were sent somewhere. Or... somewhen."

Logan pulled up the dossiers they'd found. "Private Briggs, PFC Bragg, Corporal Hartman..." He matched each name to a coordinate. "They're not just coordinates in space - they're anchors in time. The soldiers are keeping temporal gateways stable."

A new image appeared in the raid battle - a complex series of interconnected circles and lines, resembling a clock face but with multiple layers of rotating rings.

"It's a temporal combination lock," Logan said, watching the patterns shift. "The Library isn't just hidden physically. It's locked in a specific moment in time. These coordinates, the soldiers, the Hotel Ellis... they're all tumblers in the lock."

Cathy's phone suddenly displayed a new notification: "Special Research Task Available." Opening it revealed a series of riddles, each corresponding to a historical event in Fallbrook:

*Where flame met fate in twilight's hour*
*Where soldiers seven stepped through time*
*Where ancient oak holds temporal power*
*Where knowledge sleeps in depths sublime*

"Each event," Logan explained, mapping the data, "creates a temporal resonance. Together, they form a key that will unlock the convergence."

He sent another urgent text to Zoe: "The coordinates we sent - they need to be combined with the coordinates in time and activated in sequence. Maybe the coordinates are at the library. Each soldier's last known location contains a temporal anchor. You'll need to use Swirly at each point to create a resonance cascade. But be careful - disturbing the anchors might alert the Annunaki."

Cathy studied the raid animation one last time before it vanished from her game. "There's something else... something about the oak tree. The way its shadow moves..." She pulled up her screenshots from different times of day. "Logan, look at this."

As they watched the shadow's progression, a pattern emerged - the tree's shadow was marking out the same geometric shapes they'd seen in Enki's messages.

"It's a sundial," Logan realized. "A temporal sundial. Tomorrow at sunset, the shadow will complete the pattern, creating the final key we need to unlock everything."

"But the Annunaki will be watching," Cathy said, concern evident in her voice.

Logan nodded grimly. "That's why we need to create a diversion. Mom, how many active Pokémon Go players are in Fallbrook?"

A slow smile spread across Cathy's face as she understood his plan. "Enough to create quite a distraction. I'll contact my meet up groups."

As they began planning, neither noticed the brief flicker in Logan's webcam, nor the figure that watched them through it, its golden eyes narrowing as it witnessed their discoveries.

The race to find the key to unlocking the convergence was about to begin, and time itself hung in the balance.

# CHAPTER 18

# THE CHRONOLITH

Joe swerved the car to the roadside, gravel crunching under the tires as Cathy's and Logan's frantic call lingered in his mind. The line went dead, and Zoe's steady, determined gaze met his, a quiet strength shining through her sixteen-year-old eyes despite the chaos swirling around them.

"Hold my hand, both of you," she said, her voice calm yet insistent. She reached into her pocket and pulled out Swirly, the orb glimmering faintly in her palm.

Before Joe or Brian could fully react, Zoe's fingers tightened around theirs, and Swirly pulsed. The world shimmered and faded, giving way to the cool, shadowed tunnels beneath Fallbrook. The scent of damp earth and stone wrapped around them, grounding them as their arrival echoed through the underground maze.

Zoe raised Swirly high, her voice clear. "Take us to the Library of Forbidden Knowledge." The orb responded, its iridescent glow intensifying as it lifted from her hand, hovering with a gentle hum. Colors danced across its surface like a living prism, and it glided forward, lighting the twisting passages.

Joe and Brian exchanged quick, awed glances, pulses racing as they followed. The tunnel walls shimmered faintly, resonating with Swirly's energy, guiding them deeper. The air grew crisp, thick with an ancient stillness, until they reached a towering archway carved with cryptic symbols. Swirly paused, bathing the entrance in light. Zoe took a deep breath and stepped forward.

The wall dissolved, revealing a vast chamber that took Joe's breath away. Shelves stretched into the shadows above, glowing orbs drifting between them, illuminating scrolls that pulsed with a soft inner light. "It's real," he said. "The Library of Forbidden Knowledge."

Holograms flickered to life—star maps, timelines, strange devices. A three-dimensional map of time glowed at the chamber's heart, its paths branching endlessly. A warm, resonant voice filled the space. "Welcome Chosen One."

Enki stepped from behind the stacks of books, his eight-foot frame radiant with quiet power. His bronze skin caught Swirly's glow, and his dark, silver-streaked hair framed a face softened by compassion. His blue robe rippled gently, and his deep eyes met Zoe's with a tender warmth.

"It is good to see you again. I see you decoded my messages," he said, his voice resonating deeply, causing a slight vibration in the nearby crystals.

"See me again?" Zoe asked.

"In time, you will meet me for the first time." Enki cautions, "When you do, you must not acknowledge that we have met at anytime now or in the past."

"Why all the secrecy and who are you exactly?" Zoe asked, keeping Swirly ready. "Why hide clues in a phone game?"

He smiled gently, stepping closer without menace. "Let me start by introducing myself again. I'm an Annunaki. My name is Enki first son of Anu. I've been watching you, Zoe Bailey. In this timeline and others. That orb—Swirly, you call it—is my gift to you, crafted for traveling through time and, as you will soon discover, for protection. It chose you to carry its light, and I'm here to guide you."

"Guide her?" Joe asked, eyeing the towering figure.

Enki's gaze flickered with a sudden fire, but it wasn't aimed at them. "Yes—to protect you from *him*. Enlil, my brother." His voice hardened, laced with a raw, simmering rage.

Zoe swallowed, clutching Swirly. "Why do you fight? Why's he after us? And Swirly—how's it part of this?"

"It began with the clay," he said, crouching to scoop a handful of wet earth. He molded it absently, fingers deft and sure. "This world was chaos once—formless, wild. My father, Anu, tasked us to tame it. Enlil, with his winds, swept the heavens apart from the earth. I, with my waters, filled the hollows and gave life to the dust. Together, we built order. But order is a fragile thing."

"How?" Brian asked, stepping closer.

Enki stood, letting the clay fall back to the ground, now shaped into a tiny human figure. "The Igigi, our lesser kin, toiled for us—digging rivers, mining gold. They grew weary, rebellious. I saw a solution: craft a new race to bear the burden. Humanity. I shaped your kind from this very clay, breathed life into you with the goddess of the mountains, Ninhursag's blessing. Enlil..." Enki's voice cracked with fury — "he despised you. Your voices, your lives—he called it noise. I cherished you; he sought to crush you and still does."

"The flood," Joe said.

Enki nodded. "He raged in the city of Nippur, convinced Anu to drown you. I defied him, saved Ziusudra, who then built a large ship in preparation for the great flood. Now Enlil's worse—plotting a *Convergence of souls*. He'd tear your minds apart, fuse every will into one wretched thing he can rule. No freedom, no light—just his tyranny. I'll never let him."

"A Convergence?" Joe's worry stone pulsed in his pocket. "Merge us all?"

"Yes," Enki growled, rising, his anger a storm held back for Zoe's sake. "He's twisted, rabid. The orb's my answer—a tool for you to slip through time, to fight him. He'll hunt it, Zoe, but I'll guide you."

Enki turned to the temporal map, tracing its lines with a gentle hand. "The Chronolith—an artifact to wield the Convergence globally. The Annunaki, led by Enlil watch all, which is why your mother's obsession with Pokémon Go has helped me hide messages to you. They'd never have thought to monitor human entertainment."

Enki waved his hand, and a section of the map expanded, focusing on a specific point in time. "What you saw at Mount Palomar is only the beginning. Enlil seeks an artifact - the Chronolith. With it, they can complete the Convergence on a global scale, transforming all of humanity into vessels and then fusing them into one."

He waved, focusing the map on 1904. "It's in Fallbrook's past—Hotel Ellis, October 12. Enlil's agents seek it too, bending time."

Zoe gripped Swirly, its warmth steadying her. "What do I do?"

A tome floated down, its pages alive with shifting images. "The Chronolith's first," Enki said. "A pendant worn by Courtney Chase, Room 217. Retrieve it before midnight, or the timeline breaks."

"Why then?" Joe asked.

"The Great Fire," Enki replied, his tone grave but kind. "A fixed point. The hotel survives, but the block burns. The Chronolith shields it—and draws Enlil's hounds. You'll face others there."

Brian pulled up a holographic-display. "I've seen soldiers in dreams—scattered through time."

Enki's eyes brightened. "The Seven—guardians from the First Convergence. Their essence was split to stop Enlil. Each holds a key piece. Brian, stay with me—we'll map them. You two,"—he faced Joe and Zoe — "secure the Chronolith."

He offered Zoe a crystal etched with patterns. "This sharpens Swirly's gifts—time-travel, slips. You're young, Zoe, but strong. It chose you for a reason." A portal opened in the shelves. "To Hotel Ellis, pre-sunset. The fire must happen, but the Chronolith stays safe."

Joe eyed a trunk that appeared. "Clothes?"

"Period attire," Enki said with a faint smile. "Hurry. Brian and I will track the Seven. Fail, and Enlil's Convergence swallows humanity's soul. I won't let him win, Zoe—not while I can help you."

Zoe studied the pendant's image, Swirly humming in her hand. Enki's compassion was a lifeline, but Enlil's shadow loomed vast and dark.

The portal's energy dissipated, leaving Zoe and Joe in a narrow alley behind Hotel Ellis. The setting sun cast golden light across Main Avenue, and the October air carried the scent of wood smoke and horses. Zoe adjusted her long skirt, grateful for the practical boots Enki had included with their period clothing.

"Remember," Joe said, checking his pocket watch - another of Enki's provisions, "we need to find Room 217 and Courtney Chase."

The hotel's back entrance led them into a busy kitchen area. Staff hurried past with trays and linens, paying no attention to them. The crystal Enki had given them hummed softly in Zoe's reticule, next to Swirly.

They made their way to the main lobby, where gas lamps provided a golden glow over the polished wooden desk and ornate furnishings. A group of well-dressed guests lounged in leather chairs, discussing the day's business at the Fallis Brothers' General Store.

"There," Joe nodded subtly toward the grand staircase. A young woman in a white dress descended, a familiar pendant glinting at her throat. Courtney Chase.

Before they could approach her, Zoe felt Swirly pulse urgently. Through the hotel's front windows, she glimpsed a tall figure across the street, its human appearance flickering slightly to reveal white, pale skin beneath and crimson red eyes.

"We're not alone. It looks like Enlil is already here," she said.

The Annunaki moved toward the hotel entrance, its eerie eyes scanning the lobby. Courtney continued down the stairs, unaware of the danger.

Suddenly, the pendant at her throat glowed faintly. Enlil's head snapped toward it, all pretense of normalcy dropping away.

"Now!" Zoe pulled Swirly from her reticule as chaos erupted.

Enlil moved like liquid mercury, his iridescent form blurring as it carved through the crowd toward Courtney. Screams erupted as hotel guests scattered. Zoe's heart thundered as she raised Swirly, feeling the orb's warmth pulse against her palm in sync with Enki's crystal.

Time seemed to slow as energy erupted from the orb, catching Enlil mid-stride. The blast lifted him off his feet, hurling him through the hotel's picture window. Glass exploded outward in a deadly shower, raining down onto Main Avenue as he crashed onto the pavement.

"Get Courtney upstairs!" Zoe shouted to her father, hiking up her dress as she raced down the hotel's front steps.

Enlil rose from the glittering debris, his angular crystalline markings across his face pulsed with red energy. Chaos erupted outside as pedestrians fled the scene. Enlil's eyes fixed on Zoe, rippling with ancient fury.

Swirly hummed in her grip as she channeled another burst of temporal energy. Enlil twisted aside with impossible speed, and the blue beam sliced through the air, striking the barbershop across the street. The blast slammed into the walls of the barbershop, igniting an oil lamp and sending flames everywhere. Smoke instantly began billowing from beneath the striped awning as the fire spread quickly.

Through the growing chaos, Enlil gathered energy between his elongated fingers, casting strange lights across his distorted form. Zoe raised Swirly again, knowing her next shot had to count—before all of Main Avenue went up in flames.

"The Chronolith belongs with its creators, not with some human," he spoke directly into Zoe's mind.

"It belongs to humanity's future," Zoe countered, raising Swirly again.

Their energies clashed in a spectacular burst of power, shattering what windows were left at the barbershop.

The church bell tolled frantically - the fire alarm that would summon Fallbrook's volunteer brigade. But Zoe couldn't focus on that now. Enlil pressed his attack, forcing her to dodge blasts of energy.

She could hear shouts as people noticed the growing blaze. The fire was spreading to neighboring buildings - the shoe shop next door was already catching fire.

"You cannot change what must be." Enlil's voice resonated in her head as they grappled. "The Convergence is inevitable."

Swirly pulsed in sync with Enki's crystal. Understanding flooded through her - this was more than just a fight for the pendant. This moment, this fire, was a nexus point in time.

The fire brigade's shouts filled the street as men rushed to form bucket lines. Through the barbershop's broken windows, Zoe saw the flames reaching the Fallis Brothers' General Store. The heat was intense now, and smoke filled the air.

Enlil lunged again, sending a powerful blast. "You understand nothing of what's at stake."

Zoe combined Swirly's power with the crystal, creating a temporal shield as Enlil's energy blast struck. "I understand enough. I've seen your vessels, your experiments. This ends here."

A tremendous crash echoed - the shoe shop's roof had collapsed. The fire brigade was losing the battle as the flames spread unchecked down the block. History was playing out exactly as Enki had shown them, but for very different reasons.

"Dad?" Zoe called out mentally, hoping he'd gotten Courtney to safety.

"We're secure," his voice came back, a new trick they'd discovered in the Library. "Courtney's pendant is safe. But Zoe - there's another Annunaki in the hotel!"

Enlil smiled coldly. "Did you think I came alone?"

Swirly pulsed with unprecedented power. The crystal in her other hand started to glow brightly, its geometric patterns matching those on the orb. Time itself seemed to bend around them as she realized what she had to do.

She let the temporal energies flow through her, remembering what she'd seen in the Library's time map. The fire wasn't just covering their tracks - it was protecting the timeline itself.

"You're right," she told Enlil. "I don't understand everything. But I understand this moment." She raised Swirly high, the crystal amplifying its power. "And I choose how it ends."

The temporal wave she released was unlike anything she'd created before. It caught Enlil in mid-attack, trapping him in a pocket of time. Enlil screamed with rage as he fought to escape.

The church bell tolled on as Zoe ran back to the hotel. Inside, she found her father standing over what was left of the other Annunaki. Courtney huddled nearby, clutching the pendant.

"My pendant," Courtney said, touching the jewelry at her throat. "I always knew it was special, but I never knew why until tonight."

Outside, the fire had consumed most of the block. The Fallis Brothers' store collapsed in a shower of sparks as the fire brigade fought desperately to save neighboring buildings. The Hotel Ellis stood untouched, protected by the Chronolith's power just as history recorded.

"We need to go," Joe said urgently. "The timeline is secure, but we can't be found here."

Courtney pressed the pendant into Zoe's hand. "I don't know who you are or where you're from," she said, "but I know this belongs with you now."

Zoe took one last look at the burning street through the hotel window. Modern Fallbrook would remember this as the Great Fire of 1904, never knowing its true significance. The shoe shop, the barbershop, and the Fallis Brothers' store, their destruction marking the end of one era and the beginning of another.

As they slipped away through the chaos, Zoe felt the combined weight of Swirly, the crystal, and now the Chronolith. Each thrummed with power, connecting the past, present, and future. They had won this battle, but the war for humanity's future was far from over.

The church bell's toll faded behind them as they made their way to the alley where they'd arrived. Zoe raised Swirly one last time, opening their path home. As they stepped through, she couldn't help but wonder - how many other moments in history held similar secrets? And what would Enlil try next?

The answers would have to wait. For now, they had the Chronolith, and with it, hope for humanity's future.

The ancient doors of the Library of Forbidden Knowledge groaned open, releasing a whisper of stale air that carried the weight of millennia. Zoe clutched the chronolith to her chest, its surface glowing a soft amber.

"You have returned," Enki's resonant voice caused the nearby crystals to hum in harmony. The Temporal Guardian's azure eyes fixed upon the chronolith, shifting slightly toward silver as he observed its altered state. "And you've awakened it."

Zoe stepped forward, her shoes silent against the ancient floor. "It... speaks to me now. Shows me things." She glanced at her father, seeking reassurance. "Things that haven't happened yet. Or maybe they have? It's confusing."

Joe placed a protective hand on his daughter's shoulder. "We need answers, Enki. Real ones this time. What's happening to my daughter?"

The eight-foot-tall guardian moved with fluid grace toward the central table, his six-fingered hand gesturing for them to follow. Ancient texts and crystalline displays materialized from the shadows, arranging themselves in a precise pattern.

"The chronolith," Enki began, his bio-luminescent markings glowing more intensely, "has chosen Zoe as its anchor in this timeline. It's unprecedented - never in twelve thousand years has it bonded with a human." He paused, studying Zoe with an expression that mixed concern with wonder. "Especially not one so young."

"But why me?" Zoe's voice quavered slightly, though her grip on the chronolith remained steady. "I'm nobody special."

Enki's expression softened, his azure eyes meeting hers. "That, young one, is where you are mistaken. Your timeline signature... it resonates at a frequency I've only seen once before, during the First Human Awakening."

Joe asked. "What exactly does that mean for her? For our family?"

The guardian waved his hand over one of the crystal displays, causing it to project a complex matrix of intersecting timelines. "It means, Joe Bailey, that your daughter may be the key to preventing what my people have set in motion. The Anunnaki believe they can control Earth's destiny, but they failed to account for one crucial variable." His eyes returned to Zoe. "You."

The chronolith pulsed brighter in response to his words. Zoe gasped as images flooded her mind - glimpses of possible futures, fragments of forgotten pasts.

"Dad," she said, her free hand reaching for his, "I'm scared."

Joe pulled her close. "We're in this together, kiddo. Whatever it takes." He looked up at Enki, his jaw set with determination. "But she's not facing this alone. Whatever your people have planned, they'll have to go through me first."

Enki's markings flickered with what might have been approval. "The chronolith chose wisely," he said, reaching for an ancient scroll. "Now, we must prepare. The temporal shields won't hold forever, and when they fail..." He let the sentence hang in the dusty air.

Zoe straightened her shoulders, drawing strength from her father's presence and the warm pulse of the chronolith. "Then teach us. Teach me. I need to understand what this thing is showing me."

The guardian nodded, his eyes gleaming in the ethereal light. "We begin now. The future - all possible futures - depends on what happens in this room today."

The chronolith's glow intensified as Enki began to share secrets that had remained hidden for twelve thousand years. In the Library of Forbidden Knowledge, surrounded by the accumulated wisdom of ages, a sixteen-year-old girl from Fallbrook prepared to learn how to save the world - whether or not she was ready.

Enki spread an ancient star chart across the central table. The crystalline display above it shimmered, overlaying modern constellations atop archaic symbols that seemed to shift and change as they watched.

"The chronolith," Enki said, his towering form seemed to grow in size, "was never meant to be a weapon. It was designed as a key." His elongated fingers traced patterns in the air, causing the star chart to ripple. "A key to understanding the fabric of time itself."

Zoe leaned forward, the orb in her hands pulsing in sync with the guardian's movements. "But why does it show me different versions of the same moment? Sometimes I see multiple things happening at once, like... like..."

"Like watching dozens of TV channels simultaneously," Joe finished, remembering her attempts to describe the visions. He absently rubbed the worry stone, and for a brief moment, he saw what she meant - fragmentary glimpses of countless possibilities, each as real as the next.

"Precisely." Enki's markings flared briefly. "What you're seeing, young one, are temporal nodes - points where multiple timelines intersect. The chronolith allows you to perceive them, but more importantly," he paused, his azure eyes intensifying, "it gives you the power to influence which path becomes reality."

Joe stepped forward. "Hold on. You're saying my sixteen-year-old daughter has the power to change reality? To alter time itself?"

"Dad," Zoe interrupted, her voice stronger than before. "I think I already have." The chronolith glowed brighter as she spoke. "Remember last week, when I told you not to take Live Oak Road? The accident that should have happened…"

"But didn't," Joe finished, realization dawning. He'd dismissed her warning as teenage anxiety at the time, but now…

Enki nodded solemnly. "She's beginning to understand her gift. But with it comes great responsibility - and danger." He waved his hand, and a new image appeared above the table: a familiar underground facility beneath Mount Palomar.

"The Anunnaki have noticed these changes. Minor alterations in the timeline create ripples they can detect. They believe they can control these ripples, bend them to their will. But they don't understand the true nature of time." The guardian's voice took on an urgent tone. "It's not a river to be dammed or diverted. It's more like…"

"A living thing," Zoe said, her eyes fixed on the chronolith. "It breathes. It adapts. It… it wants to be free."

Joe watched as his daughter spoke, seeing her not as his little girl but as something more - someone standing at the intersection of past and future, possibility and certainty.

"The question," Enki said, his voice resonating through the ancient chamber, "is whether you're ready to accept what comes next. Enlil, and his ilk, will not stop searching. They believe their destiny is to rule humanity's timeline. And now they know someone is interfering with their plans."

"We have to tell Mom and Logan," Zoe said, looking up at her father. "We need everyone if we're going to face this."

Joe nodded. "Family stays together. That's non-negotiable."

"Then let us begin the real training," Enki said. "Time is both our ally and our enemy, and there is much you both must learn."

The guardian raised his staff, and the Library of Forbidden Knowledge seemed to shift around them, ancient knowledge awakening at his command. In that moment, as father and daughter stood before the temporal guardian, the chronolith's glow bathed them in its otherworldly light, marking the beginning of a journey that would challenge everything they thought they knew about time, family, and the power of choice.

"First," Enki intoned, "you must learn about Operation Chrono, and the seven who vanished in 1973. Their story... is now your story."

Enki waved his hand, and seven distinct temporal signatures appeared above the central table, each pulsing with a different rhythm. "The Seven didn't vanish, as the military records claim. They were scattered - across time, across space, across dimensions."

Zoe's grip on the chronolith tightened as each signature sparked a different vision. "I... I can see them. Private Briggs is trapped in 2550 BC, during the building of the great pyramids. And Sergeant Bianca Winchester... she's in 2157?" Her voice wavered with uncertainty.

"Yes," Enki confirmed. "Each member of Operation Chrono was displaced to a different temporal node. The military assumed they were lost, but they became anchors - unintentional guardians of critical moments in time."

Joe asked. "But what does this have to do with the five children? With Brian?"

Before Enki could answer, Brian stepped out from behind one of the towering bookshelves. He had an ethereal quality to his movements. The chronolith in Zoe's hands pulsed with recognition.

"Brian," Zoe said.

The boy nodded.. "The others are still trapped. Under Mount Palomar, they're using us... using our connection to time to power their portal." His voice echoed as if coming from multiple moments at once. "They don't understand what they're doing. The damage they're causing."

"The five children," Enki said, his azure eyes dimming with concern, "were born with natural temporal sensitivity - like you, Zoe. My brother discovered them and..." He paused.

"They're using us as batteries," Brian finished as he moved closer to the table. "My four friends are still there. They think they're studying time travel, but they're ripping holes in reality itself."

Joe asked. "How do we get them out?"

The chronolith suddenly blazed with intense light as a series of images flooded her mind. "The Seven... they're connected to this. Each of them... they're protecting something. Knowledge, artifacts..." Her eyes widened with realization. "Parts of a key."

Enki nodded solemnly. "Now you begin to understand. The Seven weren't just scattered randomly. They were positioned by forces even the Anunnaki don't comprehend. Each guards a piece of knowledge," Enki continued, his elongated fingers tracing patterns in the air that formed a complex temporal map. "Knowledge that, when combined, could either seal or shatter the barriers between timelines."

Brian moved to stand beside Zoe, his presence causing the chronolith to pulse with a steady rhythm. "The other four children - Avery, Blake, Lainey, and Alex - are being held in different chambers under Mount Palomar. Each connected to a different temporal frequency." His voice sounded like someone far older than his apparent years.

"The military thinks they're just studying temporal phenomena," Brian continued, "but Colonel O'Reilly is working with a faction of the Anunnaki. They're trying to force open permanent temporal gates."

Joe's stone grew almost hot in his palm. "Sergeant Major Judy 'The Judester' Braggs," he said, the name coming to him through the stone's connection. "She's trying to send us a message through time."

Zoe nodded excitedly. "Yes," Zoe said. "Corporal Liam Hartman... he's in 1942, and he's been leaving clues. Those strange markings we found in the bunker - they're coordinates. Not just in space, but in time!"

Enki's markings flickered with approval. "The Seven scattered themselves strategically, each choosing a temporal anchor point where they could safeguard their piece of the puzzle. But they also left a trail - one that only someone with the chronolith could follow."

Brian informed them, "Avery can sense the patterns, like I can. That's why they keep her at the lowest level. She's the strongest of us still trapped there." His voice cracked slightly. "Alex tried to escape last week. The temporal backlash... it nearly killed him."

Joe stepped closer to the central table, where the temporal map glowed with interconnected lines of force. "So we need to gather the information the Seven are protecting before we can safely rescue the children?" The stone hummed in response, showing him fleeting images of underground chambers and humming machinery.

"Not exactly," Enki corrected, his azure eyes shifting to silver. "The knowledge the Seven protects isn't just information - it's power. Each piece reveals how to safely navigate specific temporal frequencies. Without that knowledge, any rescue attempt could collapse the children's temporal anchors, trapping them between moments forever."

Zoe's eyes widened as Swirly showed her a vision of the facility under Mount Palomar. "The Anunnaki - they're using Pokémon Go somehow, aren't they? All those players, their movements... they're creating patterns. Energy."

"Indeed," Enki confirmed. "They're manipulating the game's geographic data to create temporal resonance patterns. Every player becomes an unknowing participant in their attempts to stabilize the gates. I have been using it to communicate with you and your mother. I thought it was secure due to all the other Pokémon players. I thought it would confuse the Annunaki, but I was wrong."

"That's why Cathy's been seeing such strange glitches in the game," Joe realized, remembering her increasingly worried reports about bizarre Pokémon behavior around Fallbrook.

Brian stepped forward as he approached the chronolith. "We don't have much time left. The barriers between moments are getting thinner. If they break..." He shuddered. "The Anunnaki think they can control it, but they can't. No one can."

"Then we need a plan," Zoe said, the chronolith glowing brighter at her resolution. "We need to find at least some of the Seven first, learn what they know. Then we can rescue the others without risking their temporal anchors."

Enki raised his staff, causing the temporal map to shift and focus on specific points in time. "Private Briggs is the farthest in temporal proximity to your natural timeline. His knowledge concerns the safe extraction of temporally sensitive individuals. Finding him must be your first priority."

"But how do we even begin to—" Joe asked, but the worry stone suddenly grew hot, showing him a clear image: the Great Pyramids of Giza standing majestically against the backdrop of the desert, their ancient stones whispering secrets of time. In his vision, Private Briggs stood beside a cloaked figure, likely a priest of the pyramid, near a hidden chamber adorned with intricate hieroglyphs—hieroglyphs that matched the strange markings they'd found in their own family bunker. The worry stone had once been part of this sacred site, its temporal properties recognized and safeguarded by the ancients long before Briggs arrived there.

"Of course," Zoe said, the chronolith pulsating in harmony with her father's worry stone. "The builders of the pyramids understood the temporal energy of this land. That's why they embedded such powerful artifacts within."

"Precisely," Enki confirmed.

"They're increasing the power at Mount Palomar," Brian warned, his voice strained. "Avery's trying to dampen the effects, but she can't hold out much longer. Alex is getting weaker..."

Zoe stepped forward. "Then we split up. Dad and I can use the chronolith and the stone to find Briggs, while Mom and Logan..." She paused, looking at Enki. "They need to know everything. They need to start monitoring the facility."

"Your mother's connection to the Pokémon Go network could prove invaluable," Enki said. "The Anunnaki's use of the game has created unexpected vulnerabilities in their temporal shielding."

"But we have to be careful," Brian warned, his youthful face serious. "Colonel O'Reilly has stationed observers throughout Fallbrook. They're watching for temporal disturbances."

Joe asked. "How long do we have?"

Enki's eyes dimmed slightly. "The temporal barriers at Mount Palomar are degrading faster than expected. Without Briggs' knowledge of safe extraction protocols..." He left the implications hanging in the dusty air.

"Five days," Brian stated. "Maybe seven. Avery says... says the calculations are becoming unstable. The Anunnaki are pushing too hard."

Zoe held the chronolith close to her chest, its light beating like a heartbeat. "We need to go home first. Get Mom and Logan up to speed. Then..." She looked at her father. "Then we find Private Briggs."

"The Pyramids," Joe said. "That's going to be... interesting."

"Time is not linear," Enki reminded them, raising his staff. "Focus on the connections, not the distance. The stone will guide you to Briggs, just as the chronolith will ensure your safe return, but be warned - others may sense your temporal transitions. Enlil has agents scattered throughout history."

"And Colonel O'Reilly?" Joe asked, thinking of the military officer's growing obsession with their family.

"He is but a pawn," Enki's voice carried a note of sadness. "Though a dangerous one. His desire to control time has made him susceptible to Anunnaki influence. He believes he serves his country, but he follows a much darker purpose."

The ancient library seemed to pulse around them, its countless secrets waiting to be unveiled. But time - linear or not - was running out. Somewhere beneath Mount Palomar, four children struggled to maintain temporal stability while the Anunnaki pushed the boundaries of reality itself.

Zoe squared her shoulders, looking every bit the temporal guardian she was becoming. "Let's go home, Dad. We have a soldier to find."

The transition from Enki's library back to their living room left Zoe and Joe momentarily disoriented. The familiar scents of home helped ground them after their otherworldly experience.

Logan sat cross-legged on the floor, his laptop balanced precariously on his knees, while Cathy paced near the kitchen doorway. Both froze at Joe and Zoe's sudden appearance.

"Thank god," Cathy rushed forward to give both a hug. "The temporal readings went crazy, and then you were just... gone."

"Mom," Zoe's voice cracked slightly. "We found out what happened to Operation Chrono. The seven soldiers - they're alive. Scattered through time."

Joe sank into his armchair. "And we need to find Private Briggs first. Enki said he will be at the great pyramids in 2580 BC. He has crucial knowledge about safely extracting temporally sensitive individuals."

Logan's fingers flew across his keyboard. "The Operation Chrono files mentioned Briggs was their project overseer. But where exactly is he?"

"When is he, you mean," Zoe corrected. "And we have five days to find him before the temporal barriers at Mount Palomar completely break down."

"What happens in five days?" Cathy asked, settling onto the couch beside Zoe.

"The children at Mount Palomar," Zoe said, clutching the chronolith tighter. "When Dad and I went to investigate the facility, we found Brian there. He was being held in some kind of temporal containment chamber. We managed to get him out after he helped create a diversion."

"That's when we took him to Enki's library," Joe said. "Brian told us everything - about the other four children still trapped there: Avery, Blake, Lainey, and Alex. The Anunnaki are using their natural temporal sensitivity to power their experiments."

Zoe's voice cracked slightly. "Brian said Alex tried to escape last week. The temporal backlash nearly killed him. Avery's the strongest - she's trying to protect the others, but she can't hold out much longer. The barriers between moments are breaking down."

"The Anunnaki think they can control it," Joe said. "But according to Brian, they're wrong. If those barriers collapse completely..."

"That's where Briggs comes in," Zoe interjected. "He was part of Operation Chrono - he and six other soldiers. They didn't just vanish in 1973 like the military records claim. They scattered themselves through time, each protecting a piece of knowledge we need. Briggs has the extraction protocols - without them, we can't safely remove the children from the temporal containment chambers."

Logan closed his laptop. "So we have five days to find Briggs, learn his extraction protocols, and save four kids being used as living batteries by ancient aliens? No pressure."

"The worry stone." Joe held it up, watching it shimmer in the living room light. "It's showing me fragments - glimpses of where... when he ended up. The pyramids 2580 BC."

"And both the chronolith and Swirly can get us there," Zoe added. "But we have to be careful. Colonel O'Reilly has people watching for temporal disturbances."

Cathy moved to her computer. "I've been mapping the military surveillance points around town. They're focusing on areas with high temporal energy readings."

"We'll need to create a diversion," Logan said. "Something to mask your temporal jump signature when you go after Briggs."

Cathy's eyes lit up. "My meet up group. If we coordinate multiple raids around Fallbrook..." She grabbed her phone, already typing. "Becky and I have over a hundred active players in our Discord. The amount of movement and app activity should create enough interference."

"Mom's onto something," Logan said, pulling up his monitoring software. "Look at these readings from last week's raid hour. All those players moving around town, their phones accessing the game servers - it creates a kind of temporal static. The military's sensors would have trouble distinguishing your jump signature from all that background noise."

"Becky and I have been tracking temporal anomalies through Pokémon Go for months," Cathy said, scrolling through her messages. "We know exactly which raid locations generate the strongest readings. If we coordinate the groups..."

Joe nodded. "How quickly can you organize it?"

"When do you need them?" Cathy replied, already dialing Becky. "We'll set up a series of five-star raids across town, concentrated near the areas with the highest military surveillance. Our most active players love early dawn raids - they do them before work."

Zoe said. "The Pokémon trainers of Fallbrook, helping us save the world without even knowing it."

"Becky will understand," Logan noted. "She's been helping us monitor the temporal disturbances. She can position the strongest meet up groups where we need the most coverage."

"And we're sure these protocols will help us save the children?" Cathy asked.

Zoe nodded. "Brian confirmed it. Briggs specifically chose when and where to go. He knew someday someone would need this knowledge."

Logan pulled up a temporal mapping program he'd been developing. "If we overlay the historical energy readings with current surveillance blind spots..." He typed rapidly. "There. Three potential jump points where you might avoid detection."

"What about the Anunnaki?" Cathy asked. "Won't they sense the chronolith's activation?"

"Enki showed us how to mask its energy signature," Zoe explained. "But we can only maintain the cloak for about twenty minutes. We have to be quick, but I think with Mom's meet up groups we should be able to buy ourselves more time."

"I'll monitor the surveillance feeds," Logan offered. "Create a temporal static burst to help cover your jump signature."

Cathy moved to the kitchen. "Just promise me you'll be careful. Both of you."

Joe pulled his wife close. "We will. Our family is strong... we're the Baileys."

They spent the next hour preparing - gathering supplies, reviewing Logan's temporal maps, and synchronizing their watches. The chronolith pulsed steadily, while the stone grew warmer, both artifacts seeming to sense the approaching mission.

Tomorrow at dawn, they would attempt to rescue a soldier lost in 2580 BC. But tonight, they prepared - their ordinary living room transformed into a temporal mission control center, and the Bailey family once again standing together against extraordinary odds.

Outside, the night grew deeper, while somewhere beneath Mount Palomar, temporal barriers continued to weaken. The countdown to dawn had begun.

# CHAPTER 19

# BRIGGS

The gentle glow of smartphone screens illuminated Cathy's kitchen in the pre-dawn darkness. She and Becky huddled over steaming mugs of coffee while tapping away on their phones. The kitchen island had become their command center, scattered with hastily scrawled raid schedules and multiple devices showing Pokémon Go.

"That's forty confirmed for the Preserve," Becky said, her reading glasses perched precariously on her nose. "How many have you got for the Oak?"

Cathy's red hair fell forward as she leaned closer to her screen. "Just hit sixty-five. Never seen anything like it. These glitches are drawing trainers from as far as Oceanside." She absently rubbed her thumb across a crack in her phone's screen protector—a nervous habit she'd developed since the anomalies began.

Through the kitchen window, headlights cut through the pre-dawn mist as a steady stream of cars wound their way up the dirt road toward the mighty oak tree. The impromptu parking lot they'd created in the vineyard was filling rapidly, and the soft murmur of excited voices drifted across the property. Raid-ready players huddled in small groups, their faces illuminated by phone screens, sharing strategies and theories about the unusual spawn rates that had been occurring near the Bailey property. Some clutched travel mugs of coffee, others had breakfast burritos from El Torro Market and Robertito's Taco Shop, all of them eager for what they believed would be an epic raid.

From the living room came the sound of Logan's voice, tense with concentration. "The quantum fluctuation meter needs to be activated the moment you arrive, Dad.

Don't wait." He was surrounded by an array of cobbled-together devices, looking more like a mad scientist's workshop than their usual family space.

Joe stood nearby as he watched Logan demonstrate the equipment. "Run it by me one more time, son. What exactly am I looking for?"

Zoe sat cross-legged on the floor, her red hair tied back in a messy bun, examining what looked like a modified smartphone. Her fingers trembled slightly as she handled the device, betraying her nervousness about the impending journey. "Logan, are you sure these will work in... you know, ancient Egypt?"

"They better," Logan replied, though his voice carried a hint of uncertainty. "I've modified them to run on solar power and—"

"Wow, over eighty confirmed for our Mighty Oak!" Cathy's excited voice cut through their conversation. She looked up, catching Joe's eye, her expression shifting from excitement to concern. "Are you sure about this timing? With so many people coming..."

"It's perfect," Zoe interjected, standing up with sudden determination. "All those raiders will keep anyone from noticing when we..." She made a whooshing gesture with her hands.

Joe slipped his worry stone into his pocket and moved to embrace his wife. "We'll be careful, Cath. Promise."

Cathy set down her phone, her screen still buzzing with incoming messages from eager raiders looking for parking. "Just... come back to me, okay?" She pressed her face into his chest, inhaling his familiar scent.

"Seven minutes to raid time," Becky announced, her voice strictly professional, though her eyes betrayed her concern.

Logan stepped forward, adjusting his glasses with an air of seriousness. Holding out a sleek black box, he met his father's gaze. "Dad, listen carefully. This quantum fluctuation meter is crucial. If it hits 7.3, we need to abort immediately."

Joe raised an eyebrow, concern creeping into his expression. "Why 7.3? What's the problem?"

Logan took a deep breath. "If the readings cross that threshold, we risk tearing the fabric of time itself. I've read reports of experiments where fluctuations like this led to temporal anomalies, trapping people in loops or worse—locking them out of time altogether. It could mean you and Zoe get stuck between moments, unable to return."

He placed the device firmly in his dad's hands, emphasizing the gravity of his words. "I can't stress enough how dangerous this could be," Logan said, his voice steady. "If we hit that threshold, it won't just be a setback—we could lose you both in a temporal anomaly, forever caught in a place where time doesn't flow like it should. We can't let that happen."

Joe nodded, the weight of Logan's warning pressing heavily on him. He glanced at Zoe, whose own determination shone through her nerves, before looking back at his son. "Understood, Logan. We'll keep a watchful eye on the meter and come back if we get to that reading."

Zoe moved to stand beside her father, her hand instinctively reaching for the orb in her pocket. Through her thin jacket, its familiar warmth pulsed like a heartbeat, growing stronger as the moment approached.

"Meet up groups are assembling," Cathy said, checking her phone one last time. "The Preserve team is already reporting unusual readings on their games."

The kitchen fell silent, heavy with the weight of what was to come. Outside, the first hints of dawn painted the sky in shades of purple and gold. In less than five minutes, over a hundred Pokémon Go players would be gathered at two locations in Fallbrook, providing the perfect cover for what was about to happen beneath the ancient oak tree.

"Time to go, kiddo," Joe said, checking his watch.

Zoe stood, feeling Swirly's familiar warmth against her hip. The connection had grown so strong over the past few weeks that the orb felt like an extension of herself rather than a separate entity. Gone were the days when they needed the ancient portal in the bunker; her bond with Swirly had deepened into something far more profound. She could feel the temporal energies flowing through her now, like invisible currents in the air that only she could sense.

"Ready, Dad," she said, her voice steady despite the flutter of anticipation in her chest. She didn't need to explain anymore—her father understood. He had watched her progression from a nervous teenager who once needed the portal's structure to channel Swirly's power to someone who could now bend time and space through will and connection alone.

Zoe pulled Swirly from her pocket, its surface swirled with colors only she could see. The pre-dawn air hummed with energy—both from the gathering raiders and the building temporal power. She reached for her father's hand, feeling the rough calluses of vineyard work against her palm.

Outside, under the ancient oak, raid coordinators shouted instructions to the gathered crowd. "Thirty seconds to raid start!" someone called out. Phones raised in anticipation, the massive branches of the oak tree creaked softly in the morning breeze, as if the old sentinel knew what was about to happen beneath its canopy.

Through the window, Cathy watched as her husband and daughter stood together, their silhouettes merging in the dim light of dawn. Her phone buzzed with raid notifications, but for once, she hardly noticed.

"Now, Zoe," Joe said.

Zoe closed her eyes, feeling Swirly's power surge through her body. The connection flowed naturally now, like breathing. In her mind's eye, she saw their destination: the great pyramids, rising golden in the ancient Egyptian sun.

A brilliant flash of white light filled the kitchen, so intense it left afterimages in Cathy's and Logan's vision. In the space of a heartbeat, Joe and Zoe vanished—there one moment, gone the next.

Outside, the meetup group erupted in cheers as their battle began, their excitement drowning out the lingering hum of temporal energy. "Raid's live! Let's go!" someone shouted. The trainers, focusing intently on their phones, remained completely oblivious to the real magic that had just occurred.

Becky squeezed Cathy's hand. "They'll be okay," she said, but Cathy kept staring at the empty space where her husband and daughter had stood, wondering what ancient wonders they were seeing at that very moment, over four thousand years in the past.

Under the oak tree, the raid continued, unknowing participants in a cover story for something far more extraordinary than any mobile game could offer.

The morning sun crested the hills as waves of excitement rippled through the crowd gathered beneath the mighty oak tree. Shouts of triumph and gasps of disbelief mingled with the tap-tap of fingers on screens, creating a symphony of modern-day treasure hunting.

"Shiny Mewtwo! Perfect stats!" someone screamed from the back of the crowd. A cheer went up, followed by a chorus of phones chiming capture successes. The air was electric with anticipation as raid after raid spawned, each bringing rarer Pokémon than the last.

"This is insane," a tall trainer in a well-worn Pikachu hat exclaimed, his eyes wide behind thick-rimmed glasses. "I've got a hundred percent Rayquaza AND a shiny Groudon. This never happens!"

Becky moved through the crowd, clipboard in hand, coordinating the meetup groups. "Group C, you're up at the oak! Group D, position yourselves by the vineyard entrance. We've got a Shiny Dialga spawning in three minutes!"

The raiders had organized themselves into efficient teams, sharing portable chargers and snacks. Someone had set up a coffee station from the back of their SUV, the scent of fresh brew mixing with the morning mist. Local food trucks, hearing about the gathering through social media, had arrived, setting up an impromptu festival atmosphere.

"Has anyone else's game been doing that weird glitch thing?" a young trainer asked, holding up her phone. The screen showed swirling patterns of color around the raid locations, unlike anything in the normal game mechanics. Several others nodded, comparing their screens.

"It's been happening for weeks around here," a local player said. "But who's complaining? The spawns are incredible!"

Near the oak tree's massive trunk, a group of seasoned raiders huddled together, their expressions a mixture of joy and bewilderment. "Five perfect legendaries in one morning," one said, shaking her head. "This has to be some kind of record."

The celebration reached a fever pitch as a rare regional Pokémon appeared—Sigilyph, a Pokémon that should only be available in Egypt. Phones raised in unison as the crowd surged forward, their excited chatter drowning out the morning birdsong.

"Best raid day ever!" someone shouted, and the cry was taken up by others until it became a chant.

Cathy watched from the porch, her own phone forgotten in her hand. She smiled at the joy radiating from the crowd, even as her thoughts drifted to Joe and Zoe. If only these enthusiastic trainers knew that the "glitches" they were so excited about were ripples in time itself, echoes of something far more extraordinary than their game.

A young girl sprinted past, pigtails flying. "Mom! Mom! I got a Shundo Mewtwo! Look!" Her mother's proud smile reminded Cathy so much of Zoe that her heart ached.

By mid-morning, social media was ablaze with screenshots and stories from the Fallbrook raids. Pokémon Go forums lit up with theories about the unusual spawn rates and mysterious glitches. The hashtag #FallbrookRareSpawns was trending, drawing even more trainers to the area.

Logan appeared beside his mother, a knowing smirk on his face. "The temporal distortions must be affecting the game's random number generators," he said. "Creating some kind of super-spawn effect."

"As long as it keeps everyone looking at their phones instead of..." Cathy gestured vaguely at the area where her husband and daughter had been only moments ago.

A new round of cheers erupted as another legendary raid began. The oak tree stood silent over it all, its ancient branches stretching above the celebrating crowd, keeping its secrets safe as the morning wore on and the raids continued, one miraculous spawn after another.

In the distance, the first of many news vans could be seen approaching. The Fallbrook Phenomenon was about to go viral, providing the perfect smokescreen for the real magic happening beneath the surface of this seemingly ordinary California town.

The Egyptian sun blazed mercilessly overhead as Zoe and Joe materialized amid a landscape that defied everything they thought they knew about history. The Great Pyramid of Giza—or rather, its foundation—stretched before them, a massive construction site that would one day become one of the world's most enduring mysteries. Two smaller pyramids stood nearly complete in the background, their limestone facades gleaming white against the blue sky.

Joe fumbled with Logan's device, his fingers trembling slightly as he read the display. "6.9," he said, relieved it hadn't crossed Logan's warning threshold of 7.3.

"Dad," Zoe said, her hand clutching his arm. "Look."

Joe followed her gaze and felt his world tilt sideways. Moving across the construction site were Anunnaki, many towering twelve feet tall, their muscular frames gleamed a metallic gold under the Egyptian sun. They worked with an efficiency that made human construction look primitive.

Four Anunnaki moved in perfect synchronization, overseeing a group of Igigi laborers who carried massive limestone blocks that should have required hundreds of men. The Anunnaki wielded what appeared to be anti-gravity devices—sleek, silver instruments that emitted a strange glow, enabling the Igigi to make the multi-ton stones float as if they were mere pebbles. Above them, crystalline platforms hovered silently, transporting more blocks while what looked like holographic scaffolding guided the Igigi for the precise placement of the stones under the Anunnaki's command.

"The history books," Joe said, watching as a geometric beam of light cut through solid stone with surgical precision. "They got it all wrong."

Zoe's eyes darted between the various pieces of alien technology: pyramidal devices at each corner of the construction site generating some kind of force field, robotic assistants that seemed to measure and calculate alignments, and what appeared to be a central control platform floating above the entire operation.

They made their way cautiously toward the nearest completed pyramid, their footsteps muffled by the soft sand, as they approached an entrance cut into the smooth limestone face.

"If Briggs is here somewhere," Zoe said, "we need to—"

A sharp, metallic screech cut through the air. Several Anunnaki workers had stopped their tasks, their iridescent eyes fixed directly on the pair. One of them raised a crystalline device, emitting a series of pulsating tones that echoed across the construction site.

"That would be the alarm," Joe said, instinctively stepping in front of his daughter. His hand clutched the worry stone, and immediately, a vision flashed through his mind: Briggs, standing in a chamber marked with glowing hieroglyphs, three levels below the pyramid's entrance.

The vision dissolved as quickly as it had come. Joe blinked, finding himself surrounded by a circle of advancing Anunnaki, their towering forms growing larger in the harsh desert sun. Their anti-gravity devices now pointed at the intruders, humming with ominous energy.

"Dad?" Zoe's voice quavered slightly, but Joe could hear the determination beneath her fear—the same determination that had gotten them through impossible situations before.

"I know where Briggs is," Joe said. "But we've got a slight problem getting there." He counted eight Anunnaki warriors now, their metallic skin reflecting the sunlight like burnished bronze, their expressions unreadable.

The circle tightened. Behind them, the entrance to the pyramid—and Briggs—beckoned tantalizingly. But between the Baileys and their goal stood beings whose technology had built the very wonders they'd been taught were made by human hands.

Zoe's hand slipped into her father's, and he could feel her trembling. Yet when she spoke, her voice was steady. "Dad, Swirly... he's reacting to something."

Joe felt it too—a subtle vibration from Zoe's backpack where they'd stored the orb. The Anunnaki nearest to them tilted their heads in unison, as if sensing the energy emanating from their unexpected visitors.

They were trapped, surrounded by beings whose intentions were unknown, their only advantage the strange connection between the orb and this ancient place. As the sun beat down from above, father and daughter stood back-to-back, waiting for someone—or something—to make the first move.

Zoe stood at the pyramid's entrance, her father close behind her, as understanding flooded her consciousness. The knowledge felt ancient, as if it had always been there, waiting to be awakened.

Energy coursed through her body, her hair floating as if charged with static electricity, her eyes blazing with an inner light. The surrounding air crackled with temporal energy as she raised Swirly above her head. A low hum emanated from the orb, growing in intensity until it resonated through the stone structure itself.

"Sweet Jesus," Joe said, watching as translucent figures began materializing from Swirly's pulsing light. They emerged in concentric circles, each ring expanding outward like ripples in a pond. The phantom Annunaki warriors, their forms flickering, appeared by the dozens, then hundreds.

Joe gripped his worry stone, its familiar smoothness keeping him grounded as he watched his daughter command an army of temporal ghosts. The stone began showing him fleeting glimpses of their next moves. "Now, while they're distracted," he said, placing a protective hand on Zoe's shoulder.

The real Annunaki guards rushed to meet the phantom threat, their confusion evident as they passed through the incorporeal forms. Chaos erupted across the pyramid's courtyard, creating the perfect cover for their infiltration.

Inside the pyramid, crystalline lights pulsed along the corridors in familiar patterns. The same symbols they'd studied in their bunker lined the walls. Joe led them forward, his hand trailing along the hieroglyphs that seemed to shimmer under his touch.

As they descended deeper into the pyramid's heart, the air grew thicker. The temperature dropped, and their footsteps echoed despite their attempts at stealth. The walls themselves seemed to hum with the same energy that Swirly emitted, creating a resonance that made Zoe's skin tingle. Joe quickly checked Logan's device and saw that the reading had jumped to 7.2. Logan had warned they needed to abort if it reached 7.3.

"Dad," Zoe said, grabbing his arm. "Swirly... he's pulling me this way." The orb pulsed brighter, its swirling colors reflecting off the polished stone walls.

They rounded the last corner into a vast chamber that took their breath away. Suspended crystals cast a soft, ambient light across the room, illuminating towering shelves filled with ancient texts and artifacts. At the chamber's center, a figure stood waiting.

Sergeant Randy 'Buddyro' Briggs.

He stood before a curved altar, his six foot six solid frame casting a long shadow on the ground. His sharp, angular features were weathered by years of stress, and though his posture appeared relaxed, a military discipline underpinned every movement—an alertness that suggested their arrival was merely another appointment in his day. Close-cropped dark hair, now streaked with premature gray at the temples, framed his alert brown eyes. Beside him, a cloaked Annunaki stood motionless, its face hidden in the shadows of its hood. The being's presence felt different from the others they'd encountered—older, more powerful.

"The Baileys," Briggs said, his voice echoing in the chamber. "Right on schedule." He smiled, but it didn't reach his eyes. "Though I must say, that was quite a show upstairs, Zoe. Creating temporal duplicates? Impressive. You're learning to use the orb faster than we anticipated."

Zoe clutched Swirly tighter. The orb's surface swirled with deeper shades of purple, reflecting her growing unease. Joe stepped forward, positioning himself slightly in front of his daughter.

The cloaked Annunaki raised its head slightly, and though they couldn't see its face, they both felt its gaze move across them, lingering longest on Zoe and the orb in her hands. The air in the chamber grew heavy with anticipation, charged with the weight of secrets about to be revealed.

"I believe," Briggs said, gesturing to the ancient texts surrounding them, "it's time we discussed why you're really here—and what role your family has always played in this game of time."

The cloaked figure's movements carried an otherworldly grace as hands reached for the hood. The chamber's crystals started to pulse erratically, their light intensifying as if sensing the gravity of the moment. Joe's worry stone burned white-hot against his leg, and young Zoe's grip on Swirly tightened as the orb thrummed with an almost desperate energy.

Time seemed to slow as the hood fell back. The crystalline light caught the movement in strobing flashes, revealing the figure's face in dramatic bursts: a glimpse of a savage scar running from temple to jaw, silver hair woven through with threads of temporal energy that seemed to dance like living lightning, and finally—eyes that matched Zoe's own but held the weight of centuries. These eyes glowed with an inner fire, reflecting countless timelines lived, lost, and fought through.

Young Zoe gasped. The older version of herself was both beautiful and terrible—a temporal warrior whose very presence seemed to make reality shiver. Her face bore the subtle marks of impossible battles, yet beneath the scars lay an unmistakable echo of the young girl who now stood before her. When she smiled, the expression carried both infinite wisdom and infinite sadness.

The chamber's crystals flared brilliantly, scattering colorful lights behind the older Zoe—each one showing her at different ages, in different timelines, like a visual echo through time itself. Her voice, when she spoke, seemed to come from everywhere at once, layered with the weight of countless versions of herself.

"Hello, me," the older Zoe said, her words rippling through the chamber. "And hello, Dad. Again. Always. Through every timeline, through every version of this moment, you've stood by my side," the older Zoe's voice echoed, each word carrying waves of temporal energy that made Swirly pulse in response. The shadows behind her continued to shift, showing glimpses of battles, triumphs, and losses—a kaleidoscope of possible destinies.

Young Zoe stepped forward, drawn by an inexplicable pull. Her reflection in Swirly's surface began to merge with the image of her older self, creating a dizzying overlay of who she was and who she might become. "The scars..." she said, "How did—"

"Time leaves marks on all of us," her older self interrupted, touching the jagged line that ran down her face. The scar briefly glowed with the same energy that danced through her silver-streaked hair. "Some are more visible than others. This one? Protecting Dad in 1943. Worth every timeline."

Joe's stone suddenly blazed with heat, forcing him to pull it from his pocket. In his palm, it glowed with the same intensity as Swirly, and for a brief moment, he saw flashes of that future battle—his daughter, throwing herself between him and a temporal blast that would have erased him from existence.

"The stone remembers," older Zoe said, her eyes fixed on the glowing rock. "Just as Swirly remembers. Just as we all remember, even when we think we don't."

Briggs moved to the altar, his movements careful as reality rippled around the two Zoes. "The temporal convergence is accelerating," he warned. "They can feel it. They're coming."

The older Zoe raised her hands, and the chamber transformed. The walls became transparent, showing layers of time stacked upon each other like sheets of glass. Through each layer, they could see different versions of Fallbrook, of the military base, of moments yet to come and moments long past.

"In forty-eight hours," she explained, her voice gaining urgency, "Colonel O'Reilly will—"

A massive explosion rocked the chamber, far closer than natural physics should allow. The temporal layers shuddered, showing multiple versions of the blast occurring across different timelines. Crystalline shards rained down as the ceiling cracked.

"They're already here," Briggs shouted, drawing what appeared to be a weapon made of pure temporal energy. "The timeline's shifting faster than before!"

The older Zoe's eyes blazed brighter, temporal energy crackling around her like lightning. "We don't have time for the gentle approach anymore." She reached for young Zoe's hands, still clasped around Swirly. "Are you ready to become what we, you and me, need to be? To learn everything, all at once, no matter how much it hurts?"

Young Zoe looked at her father, seeing in his eyes both fear and absolute trust. The stone in his hand pulsed in sync with Swirly, creating a triangle of energy between the three of them.

"Show me," young Zoe demanded, her voice stronger than she felt. "Show me who we become."

The older Zoe's answering smile was fierce and proud. "Then brace yourself, little me. This is going to hurt."

She clasped her hands over Swirly, and the world exploded into light.

The moment their hands connected through Swirly, young Zoe's world shattered into a thousand pieces. Every nerve ending screamed as temporal energy coursed through her body. Her consciousness expanded violently, filled with centuries of memories that weren't hers yet—battles fought, lives lived, deaths died, all cascading through her mind in a torrent of experience.

"Dad!" she screamed, her voice echoing across multiple timelines. Joe lunged forward, but Briggs held him back.

"Don't break the connection," Briggs warned, struggling against Joe's paternal instinct. "She has to see it all!"

The chamber's crystals pulsed frantically, their light creating a dizzying storm of shadows and reflections. Young Zoe's hair began to float, charged with temporal energy, dark strands occasionally flickering silver like her older self's. Swirly's surface had become a maelstrom of color and light, its usual swirling patterns now a chaos of temporal information.

Through the pain, images burned themselves into her mind:

*A devastating explosion at Camp Pendleton, reality fracturing like broken glass...*

*Her father, older and battle-worn, teaching others to use worry stones as temporal anchors...*

*Area 51's true purpose, its underground levels filled with failed attempts at temporal evolution...*

*The Annunaki, revealed as humanity's future selves, manipulating time to prevent their own creation...*

"Too much," young Zoe gasped, her knees buckling. "It's too much!"

"Focus!" her older self commanded, gripping tighter. "Find the thread that matters. The one constant through every timeline."

Joe's stone suddenly blazed white-hot, its energy reaching out to envelop both versions of his daughter. Through their shared pain, he felt everything they felt, saw everything they saw. His voice cut through the chaos.

"I'm here, kiddo. Both of you. Always here."

Something clicked into place. The pain didn't lessen, but it became manageable as young Zoe grasped what her older self was showing her. Through every timeline, every variation, every possible future or past, one thing remained constant—family. The Baileys, standing together against the chaos of time itself.

The chamber shuddered with another explosion, this one close enough to send cracks spider-webbing across the walls. Through the temporal layers still visible around them, they could see multiple versions of human soldiers advancing, their weapons glowing with stolen time energy.

"Now you understand," the older Zoe said, her voice strained. "Why it has to be us. Why it has to be family."

Young Zoe nodded, tears streaming down her face as the last of the memories settled. "The Annunaki... they forgot what it means to be human. They forgot about family."

"And that's why they'll fail," Briggs said, checking his weapon. "But right now, we need to move. They're almost here."

The older Zoe released her grip, and young Zoe sagged into her father's arms. Swirly continued to pulse between them, but now its light seemed more focused, more controlled. The temporal energy that had been chaos moments before now flowed through young Zoe like a familiar current.

"Can you stand?" Joe asked, supporting his daughter.

Young Zoe straightened, her eyes now holding a hint of the same ancient fire that burned in her older self's gaze. "I can do more than stand," she said, raising Swirly. The orb's surface swirled with newfound purpose. "I know what we have to do next."

The older Zoe smiled proudly as another explosion rocked the chamber. "Then let's show them why you don't mess with the Baileys."

Joe checked Logan's device one last time and watched as it clicked over from 7.3 to 7.4. The device blared with an alarm, drowning out any coherent thoughts. Every surface seemed to pulsate as the very fabric of reality began to unravel around them.

As the alarm blared and the air crackled with dangerous energy, the younger Zoe stepped forward, her presence commanding and focused. "Dad, give me the Worry Stone!" she urged, her voice slicing through the chaos. With a mix of fear and trust, Joe pulled the smooth stone from his pocket and handed it to her. Cradling Swirly in one hand and the Worry Stone in the other, she closed her eyes, drawing on their combined powers. The stones pulsed together in resonance, creating a luminous barrier around them. Zoe felt the energies intertwine—the Worry Stone amplifying her connection to

Swirly. As she concentrated, she directed the collective energy towards Logan's device, forcing it back down to a stable level.

The alarm went silent, and the energy levels began to subside around them. They could see military soldiers through the temporal layers converging from different timelines with weapons raised. But now, young Zoe stood ready, Swirly humming with power in her hands. Beside her, Joe gripped his worry stone, its glow matching his daughter's determination. The real fight was about to begin.

The first temporal blast shattered the chamber's entrance, sending crystalline shards exploding inward through multiple timelines simultaneously. Young Zoe reacted instinctively, raising Swirly in a fluid motion she'd never made but had somehow performed a thousand times before. The orb pulsed, creating a barrier that caught the fragments in mid-air, suspended between moments.

"Channel it!" her older self commanded, moving to flank their position. "Remember what you just learned—time isn't linear, it's fluid!"

Military forces poured in through the breach, their tactical gear overlapping with strange temporal technology. Colonel O'Reilly led them, wearing a device that seemed to shift him between microseconds, making him nearly impossible to track.

Joe's stone blazed as he stepped between the soldiers and his daughter. "Zoe, whatever you're going to do—"

"Already doing it, Dad," both Zoes answered in unison. The younger one spun Swirly in her hands, transforming the suspended crystal shards into a whirlwind of temporal energy. Her older self moved in perfect synchronization, creating a complex pattern of overlapping time fields.

O'Reilly's voice cut through the chaos: "Secure the artifacts! Don't let them—" His words fragmented as he phased between moments, trying to outmaneuver their defenses.

Briggs engaged the first wave of soldiers, his temporal weapon creating pockets of slowed time that trapped them mid-stride. "We need an exit strategy!" he shouted. "They've got the main tunnels covered in every timeline!"

Young Zoe felt the knowledge surface from her recent temporal download. "Dad! The stone—it's not just a focus object. It's a key!"

Joe understood instantly, generations of Bailey intuition flooding through him. He raised the stone, its glow intensifying. Where its light touched the chamber walls, reality rippled, revealing glimpses of other times, other places.

"Cover me!" Young Zoe called out, combining Swirly's energy with her father's stone. The air crackled with temporal electricity as she began weaving moments together, creating something new.

O'Reilly appeared suddenly beside young Zoe, his temporal shifting device humming dangerously. "You don't understand what you're dealing with," he snarled, reaching for Swirly.

But Zoe had seen this moment—had lived it through her older self's memories. She pivoted smoothly, letting O'Reilly's grasp pass through empty air as she slipped between seconds. Swirly pulsed, and the Colonel found himself frozen in a pocket of compressed time.

"Actually," Zoe said, her voice carrying echoes of her future self, "I understand perfectly."

Across the chamber, her older self was weaving complex patterns of temporal energy, herding soldiers into pockets of slowed time. Briggs maintained a defensive position at the breach, his weapon creating a cascade of temporal barriers.

"The door, Dad!" both Zoes called out. "Third stone from the left, two minutes into the past!"

Joe pressed his stone against the indicated point, and reality split open. Through the tear, they could see the vineyard's bunker, but not as it was—as it would be, equipped with temporal technology and safety measures they hadn't installed yet.

"That's our exit," the older Zoe announced, backing toward the temporal rift. "But they'll follow us through any 'when' we go to."

Young Zoe felt the solution crystalize in her mind. She raised Swirly, its surface now a maelstrom of temporal energy. "Not if we go to every when at once."

Her older self smiled fiercely. "Now you're thinking like a time warrior."

Together, they began weaving time itself, creating a complex web of moments. Joe watched in awe as his daughter—both versions of her—manipulated reality with increasing confidence. The chamber filled with overlapping images: the vineyard across decades, the bunker through multiple timelines, paths branching and reconnecting.

"Briggs!" the older Zoe called out. "Get ready to move!"

O'Reilly's temporal device sparked as he fought against his temporal prison. "You can't just—"

"Watch us," young Zoe interrupted, feeling power surge through her. With a final burst of energy from Swirly, she and her older self pulled their selected moments together.

Reality shattered.

When it reformed, they stood in the bunker—but not just one version of it. They existed in multiple iterations simultaneously, each one separated from the others by mere moments, making it impossible for anyone to follow their exact path.

"That," Briggs said, looking around at the overlapping timelines, "was either brilliant or insane."

"Probably both," Joe added, steadying himself against a wall that existed in three different decades at once.

The older Zoe turned to her younger self. "And that was just the beginning. Ready to learn what comes next?"

Young Zoe looked down at Swirly, its surface now calm but glowing with newfound purpose. Through the overlapping timelines, she could see the challenges ahead—Area 51, the Annunaki, the true nature of time itself. But she also saw her family, standing together through every version of reality.

"Ready," she said.

The worry stone in Joe's pocket pulsed in agreement, and somewhere in the distance, temporal alarms began to sound.

Back in the Library of Forbidden Knowledge, Briggs slumped against one of the ancient shelves, his military composure cracking as timeline fragments crashed through his consciousness. His hands trembled as he pressed them against his temples, trying to sort through the cascade of competing memories.

"Sledge," he said. "The Judester... they were there, then they weren't. I remember them dissolving, but I also remember them surviving. Both happened. Neither happened." His eyes snapped open, wild with confusion. "Which one is real?"

"They all are," the older Zoe said, placing a steadying hand on his shoulder. "Every version happened somewhere, somewhen."

Joe watched the soldier struggle, his worry stone radiating warmth with newfound awareness. He could feel it now—not just the stone's warmth, but the threads of time woven into its very structure. Generations of Bailey hands had smoothed its surface, each touch leaving behind echoes of moments, memories, possibilities.

"Here," Joe said, moving toward Briggs. Following an instinct he didn't fully understand, he held out the stone. "This might help."

The older Zoe nodded encouragingly. "The stone can anchor him, Dad. You're starting to understand its true purpose," the older Zoe said, watching as Joe pressed the stone into Briggs' trembling hand.

The moment Briggs touched the stone, his breathing steadied. The wild look in his eyes faded as the stone's gentle pulse synchronized with his racing heartbeat. Joe kept his hand over Briggs', instinctively guiding the temporal energy.

"That's it," Joe said, memories of his own grandfather teaching him to use the stone surfacing with new clarity. "Let it sort through the timelines for you. The stone's been doing this for generations—helping Baileys make sense of things that shouldn't make sense."

Briggs closed his eyes, his military training finding purchase in this new reality. "I see them," Briggs said again, his voice steadier. "Judy's leading the advance team. Sledge is securing the perimeter. Little Tone... he's scared but trying not to show it." His free hand clenched. "They're not just memories anymore. They're happening right now, aren't they? All of it, always happening."

Joe nodded, feeling the stone guide him. "The stone shows you what you need to see. My grandfather used to say it was like a compass, but instead of pointing north—"

"It points to truth," young Zoe finished, watching Swirly's surface mirror the stone's glow. "All the truths, across all the timelines."

Enki moved closer. "The Bailey worry stone is unique among temporal artifacts. Unlike most objects that accumulate temporal energy by accident, it was deliberately created to serve as both anchor and guide."

"Created by who?" Joe asked, though something in him already knew the answer.

"By you," the older Zoe said. "Or rather, by a version of you. In a timeline where you understood more about what we were facing. You created it and sent it back, letting it gather power through generations of our family."

Briggs opened his eyes, more focused now. "The others—I can see where they ended up. Not just where they dissolved, but where they... scattered." He looked at the stone with new respect. "Different points in time. Different versions of reality."

"That's why they were never found," young Zoe realized, new memories clicking into place. "They didn't just disappear. They were dispersed across time itself."

Joe felt the stone pulse stronger, showing him possibilities. "We can use this, can't we? To find them? To bring them home?"

"Yes," Enki confirmed, "but it will require precision. Each soldier was scattered to a specific point in time for a reason. The temporal currents that caught them weren't entirely random."

"The Annunaki," Briggs said, the stone helping him grasp concepts that should have been beyond him. "They were watching even then. Manipulating the experiment."

The older Zoe nodded grimly. "Now you understand why we needed you to see the truth, Briggs. Why we had to save you first. Your connection to the others, combined with the stone's guidance—"

"Will help us track them down," young Zoe finished, watching Swirly's surface swirl with new patterns. "But we'll need more than just the stone and Swirly, won't we?"

"Indeed," Enki said, gesturing to the endless shelves around them. "Which is why we're here. The Library holds the knowledge we need—maps of temporal currents, records of anomalies, and most importantly, the true history of the Annunaki's involvement with humanity."

Joe looked down at the stone, feeling its potential in a way he never had before. It wasn't just a family heirloom anymore. It was a key, a weapon, a compass pointing toward a future they'd have to fight for.

"Then let's get started," he said, watching as Briggs steadied himself and stood straighter, military bearing returning now that he had a clear mission. "We have soldiers to save."

The ground beneath them suddenly trembled, sending ancient texts tumbling from their shelves. The Library's crystalline walls pulsed with an ominous red glow, and Enki's expression darkened.

"They're here," the older Zoe warned, her hand instinctively reaching for Swirly. "The Annunaki have breached the outer defenses."

The Library trembled as another blast hit. Enki's expression changed from concern to grim determination. "There's no more time," he said, his voice carrying ancient power. "Zoe, Joe, take Briggs and go. Now."

"But what about you?" Zoe clutched Swirly tighter, feeling its warmth pulse with anxiety.

The older Zoe stepped forward, her silver hair gleaming in the chaos. "We'll hold them back. Buy you time to find the others." She pressed a small crystal into young Zoe's hand. "When the time comes, you'll know what to do with this. Trust your instincts - they've never failed us."

Before Zoe could protest, reality itself seemed to tear apart. Through the breach stepped a figure that made even Enki step back - another version of Zoe, but this one was different. Her hair was dark as night, her eyes cold with power, and temporal energy crackled around her like dark lightning.

"I've been waiting for this moment," the dark Zoe said, her voice eerily familiar yet wrong. "When it all begins... or ends." Her gaze fixed on young Zoe with an unsettling smile. "Depending on which path you choose."

The older Zoe's face hardened. "Go!" she shouted, as Swirly's protective sphere enveloped young Zoe, Joe, and Briggs.

The last thing Zoe saw before time folded around them was her silver-haired self facing down her darker duplicate, while Enki began a chant that made the Library's very foundations shake. Through the chaos, she heard the dark Zoe's final words:

"You can't protect her forever. Eventually, she'll become me. Time always wins."

As they fell through the time-stream, Zoe clutched Swirly tighter, terrified not of what lay ahead, but of what she might become.

# Epilogue

Sixteen-year-old Zoe Bailey always believed her life was defined by her family's legacy in Fallbrook. But now, with Swirly pulsating in her hands, she stands on the precipice of a cosmic battle between destinies. The dark reflection of her future—a shadowy version of herself—haunts her every step. A warning that to save her loved ones, she might have to become the very monster she fears.

As Zoe navigates the winding paths of time alongside her family and the enigmatic Enki, she discovers that history is not just a collection of past events. It's a living tapestry, fragile and heavily influenced by the choices she makes now. The fate of the vanished soldiers and the infamous Fallbrook Five hangs in the balance, but with each revelation, the line between hero and villain blurs.

In a race against time, Zoe must confront her deepest fears: Can she protect her family without succumbing to the darkness within? As the clock ticks, history and destiny collide, and Zoe realizes that the battle for the future might require her to embrace powers she never knew she possessed.

This is only the beginning—a journey fraught with peril, where every decision could alter the very fabric of existence. The echoes of the past beckon, and the future waits in the shadows.

Stay tuned for book two—The Fallbrook Chronicles: Dancing with Time

Follow Elliot at ElliotStoneUnchained.com or on Facebook

# Author's Note

Writing this novel required a deep dive into Fallbrook's history. While I've done my best to honor historical accuracy, some creative liberties were necessary to serve the story.

For instance, the Hotel Ellis was indeed located on Main Avenue, but historically, it sat where the library stands today—about 50 yards from the street. However, I needed an epic fight scene with Enlil to spill onto Main, leading to the barber shop fire. The fire originated in a shop on the east side of Main Avenue and quickly spread to neighboring establishments, including a drug store, a barbershop, a shoe shop, and the Fallis Brothers' general store. The fire destroyed the entire block between Alvarado and Hawthorne Streets. The fire caused the community of Fallbrook to rethink its firefighting methods, which at the time consisted of a bucket brigade and church bells for the alarm.

The Bailey family name died with Edwin. Edwin and his wife, Lily, had one daughter, Angie, and he did run the town's telephone exchange and sold phonographs from the same location. In fact, the family lived in the same building.

The 1916 flood Zoe encounters was real. It resulted from Fallbrook Creek overflowing, leading to the Santa Fe Railroad abandoning the Santa Margarita Canyon route. The tracks were relocated to higher ground, running through what is now the Bank of America. In fact, the Coal Bunker's unusual shape was due to the railroad easement.

And then... there are the tunnels... Legends persist that secret tunnels existed beneath Fallbrook during Prohibition. However, no evidence has ever been found to confirm their existence. But hey, that's the fun of history, isn't it? Some things remain just on the edge of reality.

As for the Fallbrook Five... well, that's a story for another time.

# ACKNOWLEDGEMENTS

Writing a book is never a solo endeavor, and I owe a great deal of gratitude to those who have supported me along the way.

First and foremost, I want to thank my wife, Ruth, who has—like all author spouses—endured my grumpy disposition while I crafted this masterpiece. Though, if you ask her, she'll tell you I'm grumpy all the time. That's simply not true. I'm happy-go-lucky—happy I have Ruth, lucky I have Ruth, and yes, sometimes I just want to go—that was humor. I have to give credit where credit is due—she was the inspiration behind the Pokémon connection. At level 50, she has been mastering the world of those pesky (yet undeniably cute) creatures since the game's inception in 2016—dragging me along for the ride every step of the way. If there are any inaccuracies, that's all on Ruth.

A special thanks to my cousin Judy—The Judester—for being exactly who she is. She may prefer Ruth over me (a grievous offense), but in my endless quest to win her favor, I'm including this heartfelt acknowledgment: To my dear and precious cousin Judy, consider this my humble attempt at bribery. Thank you for being you.

My gratitude also goes to historian Tom Frew and the Fallbrook Historical Society for providing an incredible website for my research and for double-checking my facts. I did my best to stick with history, but I may have taken a few creative liberties—something Tom was quick to point out.

To the readers—thank you for embarking on this journey with me. Your time, imagination, and willingness to explore the unknown mean everything.

# About the Author

Elliot Stone's hour has struck. At last, he's unshackled from the mundane to pursue the obsession that's haunted him since his teenage years: weaving thrillers so electric they'll keep readers awake past midnight, second-guessing every shadow in every corner. As a kid, he'd conjure ghostly yarns in his head, the kind that'd make your pulse race and your spine tingle.

Living in the rolling hills of Southern California, Elliot revels in the stillness—until his two furry tyrants demand tribute. A German Shepherd with a warlord's glare, and an English Cream Golden Retriever whose cuddly moniker masks a velvet-pawed despot. When he's not scribbling, he's coaxing grapes from the earth, dueling over chess like a grandmaster wannabe, and just trying to enjoy the peace and quiet that alludes him at every turn.

www.ingramcontent.com/pod-product-compliance
Lightning Source LLC
Chambersburg PA
CBHW031030310726
48969CB00007B/1922